I0561990

THE QUIETUS HOUR

TALES OF THE NEPHILIM BROTHERHOOD

AUGUST ARREA

VII
PUBLISHING

First Edition 2024

ISBN: 978-1-7371661-8-4
Library of Congress Control Number: 2024908479

10 9 8 7 6 5 4 3 2 1

To request permissions, contact the publisher at:

VII Publishing
P. O. Box 1272
Clovis, CA 93613
www.viipublishing.com

Book Cover Design by: Diana Chituleska

To my grandparents,
August and Catherine Erro,
for beginning our family's story,
so that I might write mine.

And for being the light bearers of my life.

TABLE OF CONTENTS

CHAPTER ONE

THE TRIAL OF THE LIGHT BEARER

It went without saying that even the most unflinching of unfortunate souls who found themselves in the unenviable position of standing before the Iudicium Tribunal soon discovered their vertebrae to be deficient of the indomitability that once formed the steel to their spines. After all, to be summoned to appear before the jury comprised of nine of the most formidable angels ever to be given wings who were charged with meting out the ultimate punishment against those it tried was one step away from being brought before God himself. No one, however, would count Samael amongst such cowering defendants; something he most assuredly proved the day he stood before the tribunal as the indictment of his crimes was addressed by one of the leading members of the tribunal, the Archangel Sandel.

"You have seen the evidence; you have heard the irrefutable testimony. Both have proven without a shadow of doubt that one need not look any further than the accused standing before us as the flint from which was sparked the conflagration of insurrection that swept through our father's house in a brazen attempt to usurp his dominion," Sandel, a vision of cold, albino whiteness, stated pointedly, as he slowly paced the floor where Samael stood while eyeing him with a contemptuous look that rivaled the tone of his voice in its iciness.

"To kill a serpent, one must cut off its head; and make no mistake when I tell you this judicatory body is in the presence of a particularly baleful and slithering presence this day," continued Sandel as he came to pause before Samael and stare deeply into the pair of eyes reflecting an equal amount of disdain, if not more, in return.

"We have squashed beneath our heel this failed rebellion, and in doing so have lost a third of our traitorous brethren. Now theirs, rightly so, is eternal wallowing in the lake of fire. And while the insurgency was a futile exercise in rabid vanity and envy on the part of the Dragon to replace our beloved father on Heaven's throne, let it not be lost on this jury that it was a plot in which Samael served in the imperative role as both architect and fomenter. For that, his fate deserves nothing less than to share in the perdition of his Fallen collaborators."

It was a damning pronouncement, one which was punctuated with the far more damning verdict rendered by the tribunal immediately thereafter, beginning first with Sandel himself:

"Guilty!"

One by one, the other members of the tribunal made their concurring sentiments heard like the peal of bells from a clock tolling the midnight hour. Only when the eleventh "Guilty" verdict rang out did the chiming suddenly go silent.

Samael, who appeared more grave with the echo of each decree of judgment, cast his expectant gaze upward to the twelfth seat of a towering bench where Gotham sat looking equally as grim.

"The law clearly dictates any verdict handed down by the Tribunal must be unanimous, Gothamel," Samael voiced in a cool and almost amiably mindful manner.

Again, Gotham sat quietly staring ahead, as if possibly weighing a decision differing from that of the other members.

The corner of Samael's mouth curled slightly upwards to the sound of such silence. When again he spoke, his lips did not move; nor was his voice heard outside the confines of Gotham's skull.

"Your prudence serves you well, brother, in this moment of irresolution visited upon you," Gotham heard the voice very quietly coo. "You may not wear the shackles I do at this moment, but do not fool yourself into believing your wrists and ankles are unadorned by such manacles. See your way to absolving me and I, in return, will unyoke you of the servitude to the Light from which you've long been in need of emancipation."

Gotham's face grew visibly darker with every word purring seductively in an effort to entice him.

"Join us, Gothamel, and I will replace the footstool of a pedestal our father has positioned you atop with one of height worthy of your feet," Samael's seductive voice continued.

Only when Samael had finished with his invitation did Gotham lean forward with eyes alight in gold brilliance and break his silence with a firm and definitive "Guilty!"

Looking quite pleased with the casting of the final ballot, Sandel slowly retreated from the side of the now visibly enraged Samael whose eyes suddenly darted about the vast space surrounding him when an ominous rumbling met his ears.

"You will regret this; ALL OF YOU!" Samael cried out before settling his hate-filled gaze upon Gotham. "None more so than you. On that, you can mark my words!"

The floor beneath his feet suddenly began to disintegrate, and his wings, suddenly unfurled, began to beat in a desperate and furious attempt to keep him from succumbing to the long, precipitous fall leading to the fiery pit of damnation and all the hidden horrors within its flames now unfolded in view awaiting him.

"You will not cease the birth of my kingdom," Samael spit venomously to the tribunal, and to all ears within reach of his voice. "Whether it is built upon the crumbled foundation of my father's or rises up from the deepest depths of my banishment, MY KINGDOM WILL COME!"

The response that met his threat came not from any one member of the Tribunal but from overhead as a flash of lightning shot forth and struck Samael squarely on his temple, and with the branding of his sin seared into his skin he spiraled into free fall to the eternal fate waiting to welcome him.

~ ~ ~

Strangely, it was the memory of Samael's fall from Heaven Gotham found himself visiting while sitting quietly at one end of a great, crescent-shaped table made of blinding white quartz in the serene surroundings of a grand room. Ironically, he would come to know his own harrowing fall from grace and, unlike Samael, eventual redemption. It was a redemption through which Gotham found himself bequeathed a majestic pair of white wings to replace the gray pair from which he had been cruelly separated atop Broken Earth, and returned to the favored position he had once long held, including a seat on the Iudicium Tribunal. And it wasn't long after that fateful rebirth he and the other members of the Tribunal were hastily summoned to hear what was shaping up to be the most notable and consequential inquest to come before the body since the days of The Great War.

Exhaling deeply in his moment of rumination, Gotham leaned back in his seat and allowed his attention to roam upward to the exquisitely beautiful landscape of murals depicting life in Eden which decorated the vaulted ceilings. It had been quite some time since he last stepped foot inside Halcyon's walls, though he wrestled mightily to keep the memory from unfolding itself inside his head.

Halcyon, second only to Havenhid in terms of beauty and stature, resided on the eastern-most corner of Eden. Unlike Havenhid, its coming to be came not from the boughs and limbs of a mysterious grove of trees but by a no-less-than-mysterious mountain face of shimmering white rock. Nor was Halcyon's presence camouflaged from sight by its unseen architects; rather the structure–an exquisitely formidable relief depicting a cross between a citadel and a cathedral–was seemingly designed to be admired, and was the very first thing in all of Eden to be touched by the fingers of the awakening sun each and every morning.

The meditative, peaceful moment enjoyed by Gotham was abruptly ended when the other eleven members of the Tribunal entered the room from a side door. Gotham greeted each of the arriving angels with a cordial nod of his head, including Sandel who took his place at the end of the half-moon shaped table opposite Gotham and offered a return gesture that was barely amicable, at best.

The sound of the towering arched doors serving as the main entrance to the cavernous room suddenly were heard to open, and Gotham instantly straightened himself in his seat when he spied Jacob make his way inside. Accompanied by Anahel whose hand was placed with a measure of assurance upon his shoulder, the boy made his way slowly, if not cautiously, toward the front of the room where the Tribunal was assembled. There, Anahel gestured to Jacob to take seat in one of two chairs positioned behind a large ornate table.

Despite putting forth a brave face, the boy was visibly nervous; that much Gotham could plainly see as Jacob slowly eyed the imposing angels assembled before him, each seemingly more intimidating than the next. When Jacob's gaze finally came to where Gotham was seated, there was visible relief which the angel attempted to massage with a nod of reassurance.

"Chin up, Fledgling!" Jacob heard Gotham's voice resonate inside his head while the angel's mouth betrayed only the crook of a smile. "You've nothing to be nervous about!"

Next to arrive were the remaining members of the White Circle: Zuriel, Eksel, Haniel, Johiel, Rabacyel and Dalquiel, who not only served as overseer of the eastern lands of Eden, but Halcyon as well, in the same way Havenhid was placed in Anahel's care. Not surprisingly, the only one whose presence was noticeably missing was that of Damiel thanks in large part to a request made by Anahel at the bequest of Jacob who continued to feel the sting of betrayal at the hands of the angel with the freeing of his father Samael from the shackles of the Infernal Desert.

4

Once Dalquiel had taken his seat, the last of the spectators entered the room; and what an unexpected sight they proved to be, at least in Jacob's eyes. They emerged, seven creations of exquisite feminine loveliness, from the same side entrance the members of the Tribunal had earlier entered, and with the graceful movements of swans gliding across the surface of a tranquil lake, they made their way single-file along the outer perimeter of the room in fluid steps with wisps of the delicate chiffon-like material which gave shape to their Grecian-like gowns trailing behind. The collective beauty shared between the seven women was disarming, so much so that Jacob found himself somewhat unnerved by the passing vision. For it was a caliber of beauty Jacob himself had witnessed in the flesh only once before. It lived inside the Silent Forest, imprisoned within the dark waters of a pool concealing a now-destroyed Through who went by the name of Lilith. As he was quick to learn, however, such ravishing traits where Lilith was concerned were only skin deep and, instead, concealed a mask of monstrous horror far too grotesque to reminisce upon, even briefly. And as the seven beguiling, yet mysterious figures took their seats beside Dalquiel, Jacob found himself squinting hard as he focused his gaze on the women's long flowing manes of hair—each a unique shade of gold, mahogany, white, auburn, silver, amber and honey—for any sign of movement similar to the slithering live things discovered hidden within Litlith's long raven-colored tresses.

"Who are they?" Jacob, unable to quiet his intrigue any further, whispered to Anahel.

"In terms of these proceedings, they are meant to serve as witnesses," replied Anahel.

The proceedings, as Anahel deemed it, had been hanging over Jacob's head from the moment he answered the sound of tapping on his bedroom window back in Cain's Corner to discover a Gyrfalcon perched upon the sill who had been sent to serve him with a summons to appear before the body of the Iudicium Tribunal. Despite having run away, he had returned to Eden, in part to comply with the order and, to a larger extent, through the cajoling of Gotham, but he quickly came to second-guess his decision. Especially when he discovered shortly upon his much-heralded arrival back at Havenhid that the only topic of interest talked about more than the news of Samael's release from imprisonment in the Infernal Desert was, as luck would have it, the impending inquisition of Jacob Parrish. Or, as it became more commonly referred to amid the whispered rumors by the growing number of tongues set to wagging, "The Trial of Sam's Son."

Now, suddenly, the day had arrived where Jacob found himself in the glare of having to prove the one thing he never thought he'd have to: who he was. Little did he know it would be far more complicated than he could have ever imagined when the dreaded proceedings were finally called to order.

~ ~ ~

"The case against the defendant is one of exceptional uniqueness ever to be brought before this body for consideration," came the clarion voice of the angel seated at the center of the table occupied by the Tribunal by the name of Arafiel. "The fact that it involves a Nephilim child only adds to the unusual nature of the task before us. As such, we find ourselves forced to conduct these proceedings in a more, shall we say, adaptable environment for all involved parties."

Arafiel then extended a word of appreciation to Dalquiel for making available Halcyon and all its accommodations to the Tribunal for the duration of the proceedings, and Dalquiel replied with an obliging nod of his head.

"I, too, would like to thank Dalquiel for the hospitality and generosity he has shown thus far," Anahel was quick to rise to his feet and echo the sentiments before Arafiel could continue on with his remarks. "Halcyon has always existed as an especially radiant jewel in the treasure chest that is Eden, and I can't think of a more suitable place whose abundance of serenity, not to mention providence, will assist those of us gathered here this morn to bring to light answers to the many urgent questions which will undoubtedly be voiced in the coming days within the walls of this magnificent room.

"However, before we can take even one collective step toward the discovery of those answers, we must be sure the table at which we in this room are all seated, is set properly," Anahel continued with his remarks as he once more turned his attention back to the Tribunal, and more specifically, Arafiel. "With all due respect, Arafiel, I take umbrage with your choice of words in characterizing this Nephilim child, as you called him, as a defendant. The term 'defendant,' by its very definition, infers to an individual against whom a crime has been alleged."

"The day is still young," Sandel was heard to comment under his breath, though it escaped no one's ears.

"If by that remark, Sandel, you are insinuating you hold an indictment of some act of malfeasance concerning the boy unbeknownst to the rest of us present, then by all means serve it. Otherwise you would do yourself well in keeping such aspersions firmly behind your teeth."

The firm and pointed scolding came with a fire of rebuke from Anahel that, if directed at anyone else, would have made him sink, if only slightly, in his chair. Sandel, however, appeared to lean into the nose-slapping, and even offer a subtle coaxing grin in the face of such a reprimand.

"I find myself disheartened, though not entirely surprised, that I am tasked with having to remind this presiding body that this is not a trial. Nor, as Arafiel further implied, does there exist any semblance of a case against one Jacob Parrish," continued Anahel. "The boy has come here of his own free will to willingly answer those questions concerning an unexplainable circumstance which has proven itself mystifying, to say the least, to all of us; none more so than himself."

Arafiel, sitting back in his chair, with his long dark locks cascading over his shoulders and looking ahead with a flinty stare, appeared to take in Anahel's thoughtful if not pointed words.

"You are quite right, Anahel, in your chastisement," Arafiel conceded when at last he spoke. "This Iudicium Tribunal was christened with a most appropriate name: the tribunal of judgment. But we could easily have been given the equally apposite title of Veritas, or Truth Tribunal. I assure you when weighed together, neither tilts the scale in its favor when it comes to the duty of this governing body; neither will it in the course of these proceedings."

Anahel appeared relatively appeased by Arafiel's words of reassurance, but it was short-lived when Gotham took the brief respite that followed to lend voice to his own concerns.

"It is only recently that I've been returned to my position on this Tribunal. But, alas, I find myself wrestling with a quandary to which I see no appropriate resolution falling short of my seat being once more vacated, this time willingly," announced Gotham, to the collective puzzlement of everyone in the room.

"I'm not sure I follow, Gothamel," Ravenel, a member of the Tribunal whose long black mane of hair was secured in one thick decorative braid that ran across the very top center of his head and hung across his back like the tail of a show pony, commented. "Are you announcing a surrendering of your duty to this Tribunal?"

"I am suggesting that, in order to preserve the purity of the judgment and the truth in this particular inquest, it is incumbent on me to recuse myself."

The suggestion brought a murmur of confusion amongst the others seated at the table that was instantly silenced when Arafiel raised but a finger for quiet.

"I'm sure I speak for all of us assembled here, Gothamel, when I say it was with great elation to learn of your...deliverance; an elation we hoped had been properly extended to you when we welcomed you back to your rightful place amongst this body," the angel noted in a measured tone of sincerity and concern. "By what reasoning would have you sitting here at this moment pondering the act of recusal?"

"Need you ask?" Gotham posed the question and, when he saw from the blank looks on the faces of those seated around him except one that the answer was lost to them, he paused to take a thoughtful breath.

"I have watched over the boy seated before you since his first cries announced his arrival into the world. It is I who escorted him to Eden and into the halls of Havenhid. It is I who was present when the light of the seventh Grace which called for the convening of these proceedings revealed itself. And it is I who, for the better part of a year, have served as trainer to the one upon which I believe this suspected mantle has been placed. I have come to know this Fledgling inside and out, and dare I say have come to harbor a deep affection for him in the process, as though he were my own."

As Gotham spoke these unexpected words, Jacob found himself on the brink of being overcome with emotion, especially when the angel's gaze settled itself upon him with an undeniable look of endearment. He was almost grateful when Gotham, appearing suddenly conscious of his doting demeanor, steeled himself and looked away, or surely he would have shed a tear.

"I have come to an unwavering belief of who this boy Jacob Parrish is and the truth of what I witnessed that afternoon at Lions Bite," Gotham, his voice once more commanding, said. "How can I possibly remain seated here and allow the scales to which Arafiel referred fall where they may without knowingly placing my thumb upon it?"

Sandel, who was patiently if not tensely observing the reactions of his fellow Tribunal members with his darting eyes, was quick to respond before anyone else could grab the chance to speak.

"I must commend our brother's self-awareness coupled with a healthy dose of perspicuity to ensure the integrity of this Tribunal remains intact and untarnished," he said, though the sincerity of his sentiment was questionable at best. "If anything, he has gratefully unburdened me with the awkward position of having to voice these precise concerns this very morn, as I feared would be my duty to do so."

Arafiel barely gave Sandel an acknowledging glance choosing, instead, to keep his focus on Gotham.

"I must tell you I don't agree with this decision," he said, much to Sandel's chagrin.

"Yet it's a decision to which I must adhere," answered Gotham.

And with that, Gotham vacated the chair upon which he sat and, leaving his marked absence once more upon the Tribunal, he took himself a seat beside where Jacob and Anahel were sitting.

The Tribunal spent the next few minutes conferring with one another over how best to proceed. They then called upon Dalquiel to offer his counsel followed by Anahel, and after a short while of wrangling back and forth between all parties it was finally agreed one of the seven beautiful women Anahel had explained to Jacob were to serve as Witnesses to the proceedings–the one with the mane of mahogany-colored hair named Etirsa– would fill the vacancy left by Gotham.

"Are there any other issues you would care for us to contend with before we proceed?" a slightly annoyed Arafiel asked Sandel once the newest, impromptu member had taken her place at the table with the gracefulness of a butterfly landing on a fresh blossoming of honeysuckle.

"Now that you mention it," Sandel replied. "There remains a security matter that I would argue demands being addressed."

"Security matter? What possible security matter could exist here at Halcyon?" Dalquiel inquired with a subtle display of annoyance.

"It is not Halcyon of which I speak," said Sandel, "but the boy seated before us."

"What nonsense are you alluding to now, Sandel?" Anahel, his gaze narrowing itself with suspicion on the colorless angel, asked.

"I believe you know precisely that of which I speak," said Sandel. "The boy is in possession of the Spear of Destiny, or shall I say rather the Sword of Destiny as it's better known today after having been forged by Gothamel into the weapon as it currently exists. I wouldn't be surprised if the boy isn't armed with it at this very moment."

"What of it?" Gotham brusquely cut in. "It is no strange anomaly to find the scabbard within a Nephilim's wing to be occupied by the very thing for which it was created to hold. You will bear in mind the sword is one of the first tools the boys who come to Havenhid receive: gifts from the Watchers to aid in their training and their calling that comes after. The sword Jacob now carries is the one I personally gifted to him, as it was my right–nay, I say duty to do so."

Instead of responding to Gotham, Sandel looked to Arafiel to further make his case.

"The sword is far and beyond the most powerful weapon ever imagined. Are you comfortable sitting here knowing that this child–the offspring of our most sworn enemy, at that–stands mere feet from us armed with such a destructive instrument? I'm not so certain I could voice such confidence," said the white angel. "Why not too long ago, when I paid an unexpected visit to Havenhid upon hearing news that a non-sanctioned Blessing was being performed, the boy actually threatened me when I attempted to relieve him of the sword."

"Threatened you? In what manner?" inquired Arafiel.

"He invited me to take it from his grip, knowing that should I attempt such a thing it would end me right then and there," answered Sandel. "Who's to say such an attempt to end all of us on the spot should these proceedings not go his way won't be exercised, and who amongst us would have the power to stop it?"

"Come now, Sandel! Even you can't possibly be entertaining with any semblance of seriousness the ridiculous notion you're attempting to conjure," Anahel said with a chortle.

Clearly exacerbated with the topic at hand, Arafiel motioned to Anahel for silence with a subtle raising of his finger while keeping his attention on Sandel.

"What do you propose in settling this matter so that we can move forward?"

"I think it would be prudent and in the best interest of all parties that possession of the sword be relinquished into the custody of the Tribunal for the foreseeable future until it can be established in whose hands it truly belongs."

"That is a fact that has already been inscribed in stone like the Ten Commandments themselves," argued Anahel. "The sword belongs to the one who reveals himself to possess the seventh Grace, or as he will be better known as, the Light Bearer. That person sits beside me and before you this moment."

"No such thing has yet to be established by this Tribunal, and you are out of order in making such a declaration!" Sandel spat back vehemently.

The growing argument was suddenly stifled and all eyes shifted in unison to Jacob who was suddenly on his feet.

"What did I tell you?" Sandel whispered to the other members of the Tribunal as though an attack were imminent.

Ignoring Sandel, Arafiel acknowledged the boy asking, "You wish to say something on the matter?"

"The Sword of Destiny is something that was given to me by Gotham, and because of that it's come to mean a great deal to me," Jacob, trying his hardest not to reveal the nervousness he felt swelling inside him while addressing the intimidating body before him, said. "Where I come from, when you are given something, especially in the manner that this sword was given to me, it's to be cherished, and you hold onto it no matter what. But if it will put an end to the arguing and help move along the reason we are all here today, I'd be willing to hand over the sword to you—but only on the condition that you give your word it will be returned to me once these proceedings are finished."

Jacob instantly felt Gotham at his side and the angel's hand clasping his shoulder in a warm squeeze.

"The sword has been, until recently, in my care since the day I wrangled it away from the momentary grasp the Darkness had on it during the Great Civilian War more than three quarters of a century ago. I would argue, if such action is demanded, it's only fitting it be returned to my care for the duration of this inquest," suggested Gotham, before turning his gaze Sandel's way and adding snidely: "That is, if such an accommodation will adequately serve to calm the Archangel of the Plague's willies."

Sandel narrowed a contempt-filled stare first on Gotham and then Jacob when the boy couldn't help but let escape the snort of a chuckle incited by the caustic remark.

Before Sandel could unleash an appropriately scornful retort in return, Arafiel jumped in to comply with the middle-of-the-road suggestion, and in quick order Jacob stripped off his shirt in one swift movement to retrieve the contested sword that was secured within the plumes of his wings. Necks craned in order to catch a glimpse of the fabled sword, specifically the famous spearhead in all its aged beauty wedded between the hilt and blade. Once ownership of the weapon was placed in Gotham's hands, Arafiel called for the proceedings to begin.

~ ~ ~

"For those of us present today who have not been so privileged, let me introduce to you the son of Samael," Sandel announced in his opening argument as he slowly strode the stretch of floor between the massive table where the Tribunal was assembled and where Jacob, Anahel and Gotham were seated. "Unbelievably, we will be asked to adopt a creed of faith that will call upon each of us to actually acknowledge and embrace the idea that this Nephilim, this son of Samael is—I find myself gripped in the difficulty of even attempting to vocalize such an absurd notion—that he is the Light Bearer long foretold to us."

As Sandel struggled to make his tongue sound forth such an idea, he settled a most contemptible glare upon Jacob who did all he could not to wilt even slightly while captured in the icy stare.

"Now, we have all of us heard the extraordinary rumors in recent months surrounding the supposed divine ordainment we are made to believe has left its anointed mark on one Jacob Parrish. I trust I don't also have to remind everyone in this room of what it almost cost all of us when another reputed Light Bearer was heralded to have been revealed within the halls of Havenhid not so very long ago. Then, it was the spawn of a Fallen who nearly placed all of creation in peril by willfully handing over the most powerful weapon ever to have existed, called the Sword of Destiny, into Samael's hands."

It was all Gotham could do not to come at Sandel full force at the impudent mention of his son, especially now that the truth concerning that fateful day had been revealed and made known to anyone with a working pair of ears. Yet somehow, in that moment, he managed to leave Sandel untouched to continue on with his vile diatribe.

"What I fear to even contemplate," continued Sandel, "is what would Samael's own flesh and blood be willing to hand over to our common enemy?"

If he sought an answer to his speculative query, he did not wait for it, for he turned abruptly on his heel leaving Jacob to feel at least somewhat relieved to be free of the weight of the angel's burrowing gaze.

"We are all of us well versed in the wiles and ways of the Darkness; we have witnessed firsthand how it is capable of myriad deceptions. How many false prophets continue to walk the earth leaving their stain on the minds of gullible men? Have we not set ourselves well enough apart from those of mortal flesh who are easily deceived? And yet here we find ourselves frittering away the ticking off of minutes entertaining an absurd notion that we know in our hearts cannot be.

"It's said those who fail to learn from history are condemned to repeat it. Hear me when I tell you the sands of time, it would appear, have begun to move backwards through the hourglass," Sandel, focusing the whole of his attention on the Tribunal who, to his satisfaction, appeared to be marinating in the words coming from his mouth, said. "Whatever light this Nephilim comes bearing, I assure you it is not that which has been foretold."

Both Jacob and Anahel watched grim-faced as Sandel walked victoriously back to his seat, and it was clear from the expressions of the other members of the Tribunal that the opening argument was potent in its influence. Glancing over his shoulder, Jacob noticed the sway of Sandel's words extended far beyond the Tribunal when he glanced over at Johiel who offered a weak smile of confidence in return before quickly allowing his gaze to make leave of the boy's.

And for the first time since returning to Havenhid, Jacob found himself second-guessing whether he had made a giant mistake in deciding to come back to Eden instead of going home to Cain's Corner.

CHAPTER TWO

CRYPTS AND RUMBLINGS

The presence of the man dressed entirely in black standing motionless amongst the field of tombstones and grave markers would have proved an eery sight for anyone who happened upon it. There was, however, not a soul to be seen anywhere along the grounds of Calvary Cemetery, except for the man who, at first glance, could have easily been mistaken in passing for a minister awaiting mourners for a scheduled graveside service; albeit a minister who appeared to have been sucked through a time portal from the mid nineteenth century.

His face, while youthful and handsome, was as pale as that of several statues of angels carved from blocks of white marble positioned in nearby spots around him to keep watch over the cemetery's deceased residents. Yet despite such youthfulness there existed a deceit of age and history, particularly around the eyes, usually betrayed by the telltale markings of frown lines and crow's feet which were all but existent. Still, it was there, the age and long history, as visible as the dark, rust-colored corrosive stains marking the faces of the angel statues in a way which made them appear as if they were crying.

Except for the wisps of his long dark hair blowing about in the gentle autumn breeze, he remained as motionless as the statuary with whom he kept company, his gaze fixed raptly on a rather large crypt residing a short stroll away. The only movement that came from him was when he used his right hand to close the front of the long black overcoat he wore to help ward off the chill of the crisp wind; and then a few moments later when he suddenly became aware of movement at the spot where he stood causing his gaze to roll downward where it spied the presence of a rather large snake slithering its way between his feet.

He appeared neither startled nor surprised at the sight of the serpent as it brushed past his leg and over his shoes, even when its shape suddenly began to twist and morph itself to reveal, first, a pair of human legs followed by an equally human pair of hands. In an instant, the snake disappeared and in its place stood Lilith, wearing an elegant emerald and black-colored dress with a matching cape-like wrap.

"You look as if you are on your way to a celebrity-infested gala," the man remarked.

"And you, Miseri," Lilith, who was visibly flattered by the compliment, replied, "appeared from a distance as though you've just seen a ghost."

"Quite the opposite in fact," said Miseri. "There was a woman with her child paying respects to her beloved husband several rows over when I first arrived. As I stood watching, observing the strange ritual mortals embrace of leaving flowers and tears at the base of a grave marker, the young boy wandered away to explore the other burial plots. I couldn't help myself and delved into the images inside his mind until I found the one of his dad, then I took on that image myself. When eventually he looked my way and caught sight of his father standing where I am now he nearly jumped out of his skin; but never more so than when I immediately after morphed that image into something far too horrible for even the darkest regions of his own imagination to conjure."

There was blank emptiness in Miseri's eyes, and then the visible welling of tears; and for a moment it appeared as if the recollection of his deed brought with it a deep sense of remorse until, that is, there slowly came to surface a most demented of smiles.

"I don't think he'll ever be quite the same again," he remarked with a casual chuckle of perverted glee.

After closing his eyes as if to savor a moment longer the last vestiges of his sadistic prank with a grin of satisfaction pasted across his face, he then turned his renewed attention back to Lilith and said: "Since then I've been standing here wondering about the reason behind the cryptic message which summoned me here, to this place, in particular. Am I to surmise by your presence that the rumors are true?"

"Of what rumor do you speak?" Lilith inquired coyly.

"There's only one worthy of my mention," answered Miseri. "The last time any of us were called to this place was before–"

"If I didn't know better, I'd swear my ears could detect the warble of nervousness in your voice," Lilith interrupted Miseri.

"Nerv–? Obviously, the stretch of what's passed since we've last been in each other's company has rendered me unfamiliar in your eyes," said Miseri. "For what reason would I have to be nervous at this moment?"

"For what reason, indeed?" Lilith echoed with a cunning smile that left Miseri, and anyone who had ever come to witness such a look, feeling as though they were in the company of a particularly venomous species of spider in whose web they had yet to find themselves entangled.

~ ~ ~

If Miseri feared such a web might lurk somewhere in the immediate vicinity, he showed not the slightest hesitation of being led toward it when Lilith indicated it was time they be on their way. They walked together in the direction of the mausoleum Miseri had been earlier studying with a questioning eye when Lilith arrived unexpectedly in the shape of a snake.

The aged, stone structure built to look like a miniature, but no less impressive, manor with its six stately columns and decorative carvings served as a final resting place for one Randolph Boyd, an especially unscrupulous and vile newspaper publisher who found himself in the pathway of a well-aimed bullet fired off by one in a long line of revenge-filled individuals he had muckraked with malicious glee.

The harsh elements over the years had left its marks on the once pristine facade like rings staining a bathtub, and the overgrowth of bougainvillea winding its way around the pillars and up the sides of the building had already begun to wither in its annual retreat into dormancy with the approach of winter. A short flight of stone steps led the way to an arched doorway entrance where the family name "Boyd" was largely inscribed above a pair of ornate bronze doors whose beauty had long been eroded away and concealed beneath years of tarnish and neglect.

It took several strenuous attempts to turn the knob and push open one of the doors which at first felt as if it had been welded shut. When the door finally gave, it let out a strained, grinding creak signaling plainly and clearly how much time had passed since old Randolph Boyd had been gifted the company of a single visitor, much less one who mourned his passing; besides, of course, those of the arachnoid variety whose presence was made obvious by the telltale cobwebs dressing the corners and ceiling of the vestibule inside.

"Randolph Boyd...a most dastardly mortal ever to be given breath," Miseri remarked quietly while settling his gaze upon the large stone burial vault residing in the center of the vestibule. "How the Underneath and its diabolic residents eagerly awaited his descent."

Miseri gently ran his hand along the edge of the vault in what first appeared to be an affectional manner resembling a mourner reminiscing about a loved one's passing before he reached down and grabbed hold of a sculpted lion's head affixed to the side of the otherwise nondescript facade and gave it a firm twist. There came a loud rumbling and a noticeable tremor was felt deep within the concrete floor. The vault suddenly shifted and slowly started to roll on its own accord away from Miseri and Lilith, revealing the beginnings of a flight of stairs leading the way into a dark passage that had been hidden from sight underneath.

"Ladies first," Miseri, gesturing to the secret passage with a sweeping motion of his hand and gentlemanly bow, said to Lilith.

Never one to be timid of dark and forbidding things, whether in graveyards or elsewhere, Lilith hesitated not a second to take hold of her dress so as not to trip over the trailing hem and make her way down the stone steps into the awaiting blackness with Miseri following behind. The further they descended the colder and more dank the air became; just the sort of conditions one would expect inside a passageway leading deep into the bowels of a cemetery located beneath a burial chamber. At first, only the echo of their footsteps upon the stone slabs accompanied them, but soon there came the distant murmur of voices.

And then a light.

It was faint at first; its flickering presence illuminating what appeared to be an open doorway just a ways down at the bottom of the stairway. Lilith passed through it first followed by Miseri. His eyes instantaneously adjusted themselves to the dimly lit surroundings, and immediately they began to survey the small tomblike room and, more importantly, the faces of the small group seated around a rectangular table. And, at first glance, it looked to be as if a sort of macabre dinner party was taking place.

"Forgive my lateness, but one never knows quite how to dress for such occasions," Lilith announced while sidling up to the foot of the table where Thaniel was quietly sitting.

"Like a lizard, your reptilian traits benefit you quite well, I see," Thaniel commented as he took notice of the fact the Lilith had miraculously regrown the arm that had been severed clean just below the shoulder during an unfortunate encounter in the Silent Forest. "I can only imagine what Hydra-like apparition we'd now be witnessing if the blade that took your arm had instead amputated that pretty head of yours."

Lilith shifted an uncomfortably hateful glare onto the once distinguished angel and said to him in withering voice of contempt: "I believe you are sitting in my seat."

Knowing better than to draw forth the ire of the deceptively beautiful vision before him, especially in front of this particular gathering of guests, Thaniel simply responded with an apologetic nod and slid himself over as inconspicuously as possible one chair to the left

"You look as fetching as you always have," a voice instantly recognizable was heard to comment.

Lilith sank into her now vacated chair before allowing her wrap to fall away from her shoulders and replied to the compliment with an appreciative smile. Likewise, Miseri's gaze shot across the room like a pair of darts to the source of the familiar voice where much to his surprise—or, rather, debatable expectation—he found seated at the head of the table none other than Samael himself.

~ ~ ~

"Here, Miseriel," said Samael, gesturing to the empty chair to his immediate left. "I made sure to save you a seat close by my side."

The brief moment of hesitation Miseri exhibited before he slowly made his way to the other end of the table did not go unnoticed by Samael.

"It's Miseri," the latest arrival remarked quietly, yet surlily, as he sat himself in the chair reserved especially for him.

"What's misery?" questioned Samael.

"My name. You should be made aware I no longer go by my given epithet," answered Miseri.

Samael studied closely the visible flame of contempt and ire the mere utterance of the name alighted in Miseri's pupils and offered a simple nod of understanding in response.

"You don't seem all that surprised to find me...out and about," Samael said, changing the topic of conversation.

"I'd heard rumblings," said Miseri.

"Strange things, such rumblings are," said Samael. "I know of no other earthly place more deserving its named than the Infernal Desert. Gothamel more than extracted his pound of flesh when he left me interned there. It's a place of ungodly solitude and languishing, where the only sounds left to remind me of the existence of existence during my time of rot was the sizzling of my skin as it blistered in the scorching heat and the chattering of my teeth when the merciful disappearance of the sun gave way to an unmerciful bite of cold. For the past half century, that has been my sentence; and in all that time not a solitary soul—certainly not one seated at this table—dared to lend me aid nor comfort in all that time. But perhaps that proved to be a good thing; for in all that deafening silence in which I was left, my ears, too, were pricked by unexpected rumblings. Faint, mind you; but rumblings none the less."

As Samael spoke, his gaze remained leveled on Miseri as though he were the only other person in the room, and while Miseri held the weight of the piercing glance without so much as blinking, he felt relieved when Arrestel, his unspoken partner in crime, who was seated directly across from him and to Samael's right broke the silence that followed with a clearing of his throat.

"You must know, it was never anyone's intention to abandon you in your hour of need," said Arrestel, whose glowering features were made even more severe in the flickering firelight in the confines of the room, particularly about the eyes which appeared sunken and shadowed beneath the ridge of his brow, but not enough to douse the glint reflected in them when they exchanged a quiet look with Miseri; again, something that did not escape Samael's attention. "By the very nature of your internment, as you so call it, we were each of us rendered impotent to offer you any aid or comfort, and saw our presence at your side as nothing but a vigil of pity which we were certain you, yourself, would rebuke."

"The important thing, my dearest Samael, is that you are no longer held by the shackles that bound you, or the sands of the desert which were welded into the bars of your Tartarean prison," Lilith, running her hand across the top of the table as she leaned her body forward, said. "Might I add, one would be hard-pressed to spy even the slightest blemish that would betray the hardship of your captivity."

Indeed, Samael resembled nothing close to the defeated creature who was left tightly tethered by the unmerciful binds of the Herrinsu vine in the pit of the inhospitable Infernal Desert to be savagely ravaged by the cruel elements and ignored by even the circling carrion birds. In place of the unrecognizable carcass left sand-blasted and distorted, both by nature and the extreme wrath provoked by his confinement, Samael was now a vision of flawless strength and, more importantly, menacing beauty; even more so, perhaps, than he had ever exuded before his captivity. His wavy, shoulder-length locks, no longer limp with the grime of sweat or caked with the dust of the desert floor, shined with health. Pristine perfection once more molded the features of his face and served as a dutiful mask to conceal, though never fully, the uncharitable spirit which resided behind it and brought to being the tell-tale scarring to the left temple by a well-aimed, not to mention well-earned bolt of lightning once upon a time.

"I most heartedly echo Lilith's words," Demitriel, a particular nasty piece of work of a Fallen who grumblingly abandoned the cesspool of his Las Vegas den of degeneracy, appropriately called "Purgatory," when he received the summons to attend the subterranean gathering, suddenly spoke out. "But I would think something far more consequential has been made known to us."

"And what is that, Demitriel?" Lilith inquired in an uncanny tone she had that was both pleasant and withering at the same time.

"You needn't play coy with me when it's more than apparent. The mere fact that we find Samael here in our presence untethered by the dreaded Herrinsu vine could only mean one thing: you've proven yourself successful in your scheme to lay your hands on the Sword of Destiny. For what else could have possibly released him from the cage to which there was but one key?"

The others seated at the table traded looks of incredulity with one another over the possibility of such a claim.

"You are correct to a point, Demitriel," Thaniel, who had been sitting in his seat quietly staring down into his lap, timidly made his voice heard. "There was, indeed, a successful swindling where the sword is concerned, only the swindler proved to be Gothamel and I his dupe, and is the unfortunate explanation of why you now find yourselves blessed with my company."

"Then...if the sword continues to remain elusive of our possessing it, how then do you find yourself...released?" a puzzled Demitriel questioned Samael. "I'm certain to think I'm safe in saying Gothamel wasn't struck with an overriding sense of mercy where you're concerned."

Samael said nothing in return, at first, and for a moment or two that followed there was an awkward silence when again Thaniel spoke.

"I, too, have been privy to some most peculiar rumblings of recent," he said, "and it would seem, unbelievable as it may sound, that it was not Gothamel who was behind the liberation, but rather Damiel."

The revelation brought a collective gasp of shock from everyone at the table, but none more so than Thaniel whose eyes suddenly widened in terror when, at the same time, his lips appeared to fuse together followed by his very mouth vanishing from sight.

"While I am always appreciative of when one of my brothers takes a header from that high divine place, none has filled me with the euphoria of your inspired pitch, Thaniel. Particularly since it came stained with the spilling of my jailer's blood," Samael remarked cooly over Thaniel's muffled cries. "You will aid me well with your service in this the dawn of my return to the helm of the Underneath. But at present, your mouth runs far quicker than that supposed superior mind our father gifted you."

As Thaniel struggled in his chair, his jawbones visibly seen through the skin forming his cheeks working in a desperate attempt to open what was no longer in existence to open, Miseri turned to Samael who was clearly amused by the sight.

"Damiel is responsible for freeing you of your binds?" he asked half laughing at such an absurd notion. "In what realm of reality is that even a plausible notion?"

"Whatever his reasoning, it remains known to him," Samael lied with the ease that it took to inhale a breath.

"You're telling me he paid you a visit in the Infernal Desert and severed the binds set in place by Gothamel while offering you no explanation for the gesture?"

"I'm telling you the moment I felt the bite of the Herrinsu vine go slack around my ankles and wrists I vanished faster than a handful of sand cast into the wind," said Samael. "Had you ever experienced an imprisonment as I have, you would know, when someone dangles the sole key that fits your shackles in front of your face, the last thing you are interested in is bartering over the terms of its use."

Miseri's gaze narrowed. "So you're saying there were terms."

"I believe what I stated is that I didn't barter over them," countered Samael.

The growing tenseness between the two angels brought a sense of unease to the others seated at the table who could be seen squirming noticeably with discomfort in their chairs.

"Intriguing as this all is, may I be so bold as to suggest we move along to more pressing matters behind the calling of this meeting," suggested Lilith who at any other time or place would have more than enjoyed the sight of two rival Fallen like Samael and Miseri facing off against one another like two cocks in a henhouse.

"As usual, Lilith, you are quite right," Samael replied with a brief flash of maliciousness caught in the hint of a smile as he and Miseri continued to lock the daggers imbedded in their stares with one another.

~ ~ ~

"I hold no grudges to anyone in this room, or outside the circle of this meeting, for that matter, for what's transpired during my unplanned-for absence," Samael, getting up from his chair and beginning a slow stroll around the table, announced. "The Underneath is a ravenous beast that requires feeding; when it can't, it begins to wither and grows weak. When that happens, the mortal world slips free from the binds of our ascendancy to which we've tethered them, and they are left to flourish in the Light.

"We cannot have that!"

As Samael continued in his path around the table, no one dared to settle their gaze upon him; no one, that is, except the unshrinking Lilith. The boldest anyone revealed themselves to be was as a timid glance out of the corner of the eye as Samael passed, as though the newly freed and rejuvenated angel might suddenly seize upon them and relieve them of their lungs with a penetrating punch into the very core of their body through their back.

"A rudderless ship is always in danger of running aground, so know I do not hold fault with those who took to the life boats, nor do I bear enmity to those of you who saw fit to assume the perceived vacancy of the captain's chair," continued Samael, and again he spied out of the corner of his eye a knowing exchange of glances between Miseri and Arrestel. "What is important from this moment going forward is that you all acknowledge and understand what my presence before you this moment means to the long-understood hierarchy of the Underneath going forward. Any action perceived as circumventing or defying this established reign will be seen as sedition, plain and simple.

"So, too," Samael was quick to add as he came to a pause behind Arrestel, "would an act of conspiring with the mortal populace."

Never one to be timid of making eye contact with Samael, Miseri rolled his gaze upward and fixed them with unblinking intensity on the gleaming glare locked on him.

"We've always found it beneficial to forge alliances with the mortals," said Miseri. "It's what ensures their enslavement to us."

"Alliances, yes; not armies," said Samael.

With those words, Miseri's jaw tightened as he suddenly came to realize Samael's captivity had not rendered him unmindful of the clandestine maneuverings taking place outside the Infernal Desert.

"When each of us were cast off our perch on high, we traded the realm of Light for that of the Dark. The Darkness has been the last refuge left to us lest we surrender ourselves to the unhinged jaws of oblivion in its attempt to swallow us whole," Samael, taking a seat once more in his chair at the head of the table, continued. "Perhaps, Miseri, if you were focused less on forging alliances, as you so call it, or preening like a peacock at masquerade balls, you might have prevented the sanctum of our asylum from being breached."

The assertion took Miseri aback, but before he could open his mouth to speak Demitriel sounded an alarm of concern: "What do you mean breached? Certainly, I've heard of no such thing."

"No, I wouldn't imagine the green haze cast over that den of iniquity of yours allows you to hear or see much of anything past that mortal cesspool into which you freely wade," Samael remarked without so much as a glance in Demitriel's direction.

"Then what exactly...is it you're circling?" Miseri questioned gruffly before softening his tone when the growing annoyance in it met his ear.

"Once upon a time, shortly after the one who delivered us from our indentured servitude to the Light, a pact was made between him and God," Samael began softly as if reciting a storybook tale to a child right before bedtime. "Neither the Darkness below or the Light above could lend any influence on the mortals in between over which of the two they would ultimately choose to pledge their allegiance. It was by this agreement, of which our deliverer had no intention of abiding by, that the seven tendrils which produce the life force that is the Darkness came to be entrusted in my hands. I, in turn, secured these powers in seven specially made urns–Scucca Urns–which were then placed in the custody of the Pithens who were created for the specific task of protecting this, our most precious asset. You can imagine then the feeling of consternation that visited itself upon me when sometime in the aftermath of my quarrel with Gothamel coming to a head in the Infernal Desert, I learned the existence of the Pithens and, of far more importance, the precious cargo they were tasked to watch over and safeguard with their very lives, if need be, were discovered."

"I think I understand where this history lesson is leading," said Miseri.

"Do you?" Samael deadpanned. Again, he got up from the table, and with leisurely steps walked a short way to a nearby corner of the room where two of the Pithens being discussed had been standing nearly unnoticed despite their sizable presence. "Then perhaps you are in a position to lend me an explanation as to why when I called for the Pithens, which was the very first thing I did when freedom was returned to me, it was only two—these two—who answered my summons, and neither was in possession of their urn."

"Undoubtedly, you asked them," said Miseri. "What did they tell you?"

"I'm asking you."

Miseri clenched his jaw. "After three of the urns were thieved, I directed the remaining Pithens into hiding with their urns and to stay put no matter what unless instructed otherwise by me."

"And yet only two Pithens to have lost possession of their urns stand before me. What of the third?"

"Destroyed," answered Miseri, "while trying to retrieve one of the stolen urns."

Samael stood silent for a long moment, his gaze remaining firmly on the two Pithens who looked like a couple of serpents trying to assume a human form with their flat faces and snakelike features and hovering like giants in the confined space that barely accommodated their lording heights.

"Three urns, stolen," he finally muttered. "But by whom?"

"Why not ask Zophiel?" Arrestel suddenly chimed in shooting an accusatory glance across the table where the angel had been placidly sitting until the mention of his name. "After all, it is his son who has been revealed as the thief."

"Zophiel's son?" Samael replied, with a look of surprise as he turned his head and settled his gleaming gaze first on the angel on the receiving end of Arrestel's accusation and then on Arrestel, himself. "How do you know this?"

Arrestel opened his mouth to speak, but it was Miseri's voice which made itself heard: "Because he was seen by several witnesses, myself included, in the act of trying to pilfer a fourth urn, during one of those occasions where my so-called preening peacock traits were on full display."

Zophiel felt the immediate weight of everyone's gaze turn and rest themselves firmly on him, none more so than Samael's.

"I've already attested to the fact that I've had no knowledge of my son's interactions with the Pithens or the Scucca Urns; that is, until very recently when I was confronted about the matter," Zophiel said, with a sneer of offense, before leveling a revenge-filled scowl on the two Pithens. "Of course, that didn't stop one of these murderous vipers from destroying my family's home in search of my son and killing his mother in the process."

"Is this true?" Samael asked, shooting a fierce glance Miseri's way.

"There is very little that will deter a Pithen from trying to reclaim that which is stolen from its possession," Miseri explained indifferently.

Samael could clearly see there was equally very little keeping Zophiel planted in his seat instead of settling what was visibly a festering score with the Pithens. Returning to his chair, Samael proceeded to reach toward him across the table with his perfectly manicured hand which he then turned to reveal the underside any palm reader would have a field day attempting to interpret the future etched within the roadmap of lines and creases.

"Take my hand?" he asked invitingly.

Zophiel answered by reaching forth himself and placing his hand in Samael's grasp which instantly but gently closed itself around his like a Venus flytrap. A series of glints and flashes erupted within Samael's eyes, and in a matter of a few moments his fingers unfolded themselves from around Zophiel's hand.

"He's telling the truth," Samael announced.

"He could also be deceiving you by manipulating his memories," argued Lilith.

"Zophiel has never given me reason to question his loyalty," said Samael, though his eyes remained locked on the angel in a puzzling manner. "There does, however, exist within your thoughts a considerable stretch of time where your son—Hunter, is it?—seems to have...vanished."

Zophiel sat quiet for a moment before answering. "Several years ago he left home and we've been estranged ever since."

"Estranged?"

"The day he learned I was a Fallen was the day I became an unforgivable traitor in his eyes. I haven't seen or heard from him since then."

An unsympathetic, almost ghoulish smile slowly unfolded itself on Samael's face. "It must be such a disappointment to have sired such a morally misinformed and misguided offspring," he said before his expression morphed into one more thoughtful. "The question is, what possible mission could the boy be engaged in with these urns?"

"I would think the answer couldn't be any more clearer if it was written in neon," offered Arrestel. "Obviously, he wishes to destroy them and the power residing inside."

"I think this Hunter will find any attempt in trying to destroy them far more difficult than the act of stealing them," Lilith said with a hint of morbid glee. "Besides, if on the odd chance he managed to accomplish such a feat, the reverberation within the Darkness would have been felt; which means he still has them, somewhere, hidden away."

"The first Scucca Urn stolen was done so by an old blind man–a Silencer, to be precise–who used the urns to aid him in exterminating Infectors," said Miseri. "We believe he passed on his skills to the boy before he perished along with the destroyed Pithen."

"Exterminating Infectors," Samael muttered to himself. He then returned to where the two Pithens remained motionless and asked them: "Which of you is responsible for the killing of the mother of Zophiel's son?"

The one standing nearest him answered with a submissive bowing of its head.

Samael shot a look to Lilith out of the corner of his eye, and a cunning grin came to the dark beauty's face. The cause of the subtle yet wavy movements seen in the mane of her jet-black hair suddenly revealed itself when the head of a small snake poked itself out from within the tresses near Lilith's left ear. With an almost hypnotic movement, she gently and gracefully brought her hand to the left side of her face, allowing the winding serpent to wriggle its way into her grasp which she then released onto the table.

The snake's tongue flicked the air and it appeared to survey those gathered in the dank room with its sinister, hooded yellow eyes. Slowly, the snake proceeded to slither its way across the table, its cold, scaly coils gleaming in the light like a living and breathing pair of expensive leather shoes, and the further down the table the snake made its way the larger the eyes of those watching it became as its size grew larger with each undulation of its reptilian body. What first emerged from Lilith's hair as a harmless garter snake quickly became a python. When the snake reached the end of the table, it had transformed itself into something quite sizable and frightening akin to a species of anaconda found only in the undiscovered reaches of the Amazon jungle.

With a heavy thud, the snake made its way from the table to the floor, and the few moments it had fallen out of sight proved unsettling. It quickly returned into view, and in a most horrific way when suddenly, and quite instantaneously, it wrapped itself fully about the body of the Pithen who had confessed to the killing of Hunter's mother. The Pithen managed to cry out once before all sound was strangled from it by the tightening of the constricting coils wrapped around its towering body like so many linen bandages used to form a mummy. Even Zophiel couldn't suppress a wince of sympathy when the room began to echo the unforgiving sounds of bones snapping like so many pieces of brittle kindling. Others like Arrestel and Miseri, and particularly Lilith, looked on with satiated expressions of pleasure as though relaxing before a crackling fire burning in a hearth on a particularly winter-chilled night.

"I trust this serves as an agreeable repayment for your loss, Zophiel, and that I can hold faith in your continued loyalty," Samael remarked when finally the snake loosened its death grip and the Pithen collapsed broken, pulverized but not yet completely dead onto the floor.

"Of course," Zophiel managed to croak in return.

It was not the end of the horrific sounds to fill the room as the snake proceeded to unhinge its massive jaw and begin the task of consuming the still breathing Pithen. And as the last lingering moans of suffering grew muffled before being extinguished altogether amid the feeding taking place on the floor, Samael turned his attention to the remaining Pithen who had gone pale from what it had just witnessed and said: "If you don't wish to be rendered the next meal, I suggest you prove yourself successful in retrieving for me undamaged and fully intact that which you allowed to slip from your fingers."

~ ~ ~

When it appeared the unpleasantness of the evening had come to a close, Samael turned his attention back to those seated around the table with a renewed glow of ire alight in his eyes.

"While we're attending to wrongdoings, perhaps you can convince me from forcing you onto a platter for another of the hungry pets Lilith has hidden away in her locks," he said.

Demitriel, who was still engrossed by the unsightly sight taking place on the floor on the other side of the room, nearly went white when he realized Samael's anger-filled gazed was focused with an uncomfortable intensity on him.

"Wh–what have I done?"

"It's what you set out to do," Samael hissed. "You dared to unleash a throng of Infectors into the streets of that modern-day Babylon you've chosen to inhabit in a hunt for my son."

The accusation finally succeeded in draining fully the color from Demitriel's face and, in the process, all inhibitions of thinking twice about throwing someone else before the clamping jaws of a second possible hungry serpent suddenly appearing.

"It was her!" he cried out suddenly, pointing an accusatory finger in Lilith's direction. "She sent word far and wide that the boy was a detriment to the Darkness and was to be dealt with accordingly."

Lilith offered nothing in her defense except a baleful stare even her beauty could not blunt.

"Since when, Demitriel, have you married your servitude to any directive other than that voiced by my own tongue?" Samael said with a displeased hiss.

"B-b-but I...I thought—"

"I would have assumed by now you would have arrived at the same conclusion as I have that it is not in your best interest to think," Samael retorted snidely, before turning his simmering if not curious gaze onto the specious apparition of loveliness seated at the opposite end of the table. "Lilith's displeasure—hatred, even—for the boy has been understandable and forgivable, to say the least. And while the revelation surrounding him has proven itself both staggering and unforeseen not only to everyone seated at this table, but myself included, I trust I have since fully and satisfactorily explained to her both the rhyme and the reason behind his clandestine coming to be."

The look returned his way from Lilith was doting, though one would be hard-pressed to catch even a glimmer of any assured semblance of understanding.

"To the rest of you I offer a one-time warning," said Samael, in a tone that was oddly soft in its delivery. "Tread mindfully when it comes to the Nephilim known as Jacob Parrish. Unless you wish to know the dolor of what it's like to be digested whole, keep to memory that he is my son. Whatever his fate, it will be decided by me. Do we understand one other?"

Demitriel half nodded and half exhaled a welcome breath of relief when he realized he had been spared becoming an unwitting entrée for some ravenous slithering creature.

"What news is there concerning the boy?" Samael then posed the question to no one in particular as he slumped down into his chair.

"They've brought him before the Iudicium Tribunal, as we speak," said Zophiel. "Apparently, not everyone is convinced of the rumors surrounding him about being the Light Bearer."

The response drew a hearty chuckle from Samael.

"Oh, Sandel, if only I could be a witness to the personal torment the prospect of my son being the newest arrival of the anointed one has brought upon you."

The moment of levity was quick to fade and it was replaced by a look of grave concern.

"It is just that, isn't it: a prospect?" Samael asked the table as a whole.

A nervous silence followed before Demitriel found the courage to be the first to answer.

"Just recently, when Damiel paid me a surprise visit at my nightclub in the heart of Babylon, as you prefer to call it, I gave a quick perusal of his thoughts. It would seem not only he but the other Watchers as well believe this Jacob Parrish is the promise of the Apocrypha come to life, despite the fact he is your son," said Demitriel.

"More importantly, Gothamel believes it," Zophiel was quick to add. "And in these days following his return to Heaven's good graces, his words carry a lot of clout; perhaps more so now than the days before his Fall."

Samael's keen gaze shifted to Lilith at the mention of Gothamel and saw quite clearly how the name brought a weakening to her glacial veneer despite her best efforts to conceal such a revealing crack.

"Yes, well...Gothamel was always one to espouse the virtues of faith much to his own detriment," Samael remarked sourly.

"And liberation," Lilith whispered aloud her thoughts before realizing she had.

"If I may be so bold," Zophiel carefully intervened on tiptoes and drawing his way the icy look Samael had leveled at Lilith.

When Samael replied with a nod to speak, Zophiel proceeded, all the while mindful of his choice his words.

"What is your plan in regards to your son?"

"Plan?" Samael asked, with a puzzling raising of his brow.

"Certainly you can't be content in learning of his coming into the protective custody of the Watchers."

"I believe what Zophiel is attempting to ask is, do you intend to allow him to stay on with our enemy and have him be polluted by their proselytizing ways?" asked Arrestel.

"Of course he doesn't!" Lilith replied vigorously, before Samael had a chance to answer. "The boy needs to be removed. Immediately!"

"Removed?" echoed Zophiel with a somewhat bemused look.

"From Havenhid, and in the most expedited of methods from that God-forsaken Eden."

"I have to say I agree, at least in sentiment, with Lilith's stance," said Demitriel. "If in fact the rumors prove themselves true, then the longer he remains there, the more perilous our situation becomes with that dangerous prophecy hovering ever closer over our heads."

Samael remained silent, carefully listening to everything that was being said, and in that quiet moment his ears pricked to the faint sound of muffled whimpering. His eyes shifted to the right and came to rest on Thaniel sitting motionless–and mouthless–in his chair, but with his eyes wide and fixed on Samael reflecting his distress.

"And just how do you propose we go about this directive to remove him, to use your word? Would you have us storm the gate with a battering ram?" Samael inquired with an unveiled facetiousness.

Lilith narrowed a spiteful glare Samael's way before offering forth a pleasant smile that managed to remain void of any pleasantness.

"The surest way to any mortal's soft spot is straight through the heart," she explained with a menacing purr. "Nephilim share in the same weakness, and as I've recently come to discover, this Jacob Parrish of whom we speak has developed a particular soft spot residing in the old, but quaint Craftsman-style house of his upbringing in a charming, but well camouflaged town named Cain's Corner."

"His grandmother?" Samael leveraged a guess after a moment to mull over the known possibilities.

"How he adores her so," Lilith noted with wicked delight. "And she him."

Samael drew quiet, and again his gaze migrated to Thaniel's chair where the muffled murmurings grew louder and more urgent.

"Do forgive me, Thaniel; I'd plain forgotten you were still with us," Samael feigned apologetically.

As quickly as it had vanished, Thaniel's mouth suddenly reappeared where there had been fashioned a blank canvas of skin between his nose and chin.

"You don't need a battering ram, nor bother traveling halfway around the world to some town most anyone would be hard-pressed to find on a map," Thaniel said, while exhaling several deep breaths of relief.

"And what, if I may ask, do you see as the key for getting Jacob out of Eden?" Lilith asked in a withering tone.

"I would think it'd be obvious as the mouth suddenly returned to my face. The Tribunal, of course," answered Thaniel to the raising of eyebrows. "And Johiel."

"Johiel?" Miseri, shooting a scrutinizing look in the direction of the angel, echoed.

"I must say I'm intrigued," said Samael with an inquisitive gleam. "Enlighten me, and perhaps I'll rethink my intention of finishing what Gothamel denied us so many eons ago: separating you from that brilliant orb contained inside your head called a mind."

"Alone," insisted Thaniel. Then quickly remembering his place, he added most subserviently: "If you wouldn't mind."

~ ~ ~

Night had fallen over the cemetery when those attending the meeting were summarily dismissed and emerged from the bowels of the mausoleum. Demitriel and Zophiel took to the skies in opposite directions, and Lilith exited the grounds in the exact same slithering manner as she arrived. And while Samael and Thaniel were left to their private conspiring, so too were Miseri and Arrestel amongst the tombstones and the angel statues that keep watch over them.

"He knows," Arrestel, finally able to utter aloud the words that had been reverberating inside his head from the moment he saw Samael seated at the table beneath the tomb, said.

"He thinks he knows," corrected Miseri, "or you and I would not be standing here this moment colluding our next move."

"What reason would Damiel have to cut him loose from the Infernal Desert?"

"I'm sure I do not know," said Miseri, his brightly cold eyes staring off into the cemetery in a search of the answer which alluded him. "One thing is certain: Damiel has been a thorn in my side for far too long, and it's high time it is finally removed once and for all."

CHAPTER THREE

DAMIEL'S BANE

There was a noticeable change in Damiel; of that, no one could argue. That is to say, in most everyone's eyes, the angel who went in pursuit of a band of truant Fledglings in the hideaway town of Cain's Corner and ended up embarking on an unplanned trek that stretched from the sinful playground of the Las Vegas Strip and the mysterious Old-World waterways of Venice before landing quite unexpectedly in a hellish pock marking an uncharted corner of the world called the Infernal Desert was not the same angel who returned to Eden.

While Damiel's demeanor more often than not leaned toward the serious end of the personality scale, there emerged an almost tangible aloofness that took up company with his already solemn manner. What warmth emanated from the gold pools that were his eyes now flickered with a molten pulse of fire promising to scorch anyone or anything that wandered into their focus. Indubitably, it was not a flare of ire sparked by anyone or anything in Eden as some would reasonably come to conclude, but rather the reflective reckoning of the inferno he had knowingly if not completely willingly unleashed back into the unwitting world.

The Infernal Desert...

Damiel could still feel the stifling heat licking his skin the moment his feet touched ground in that unforgiving, windswept nightmare of creation. His pupils all but betrayed the latent memory repeating itself in a loop inside of his head by taking on the image of the black, dusty shape writhing in enervated agony on the cracked, sun-baked terrain. He had vowed never again to step foot in the desolate slice of hell on earth, and for a moment—brief as it was in its visit—Damiel felt a tinge of sympathy for the wretched inmate who found himself captive in so inhospitable a prison as this.

Displays of pity, however, had no place in the Infernal Desert.

Vengeance, on the other hand, was its life's blood. Damiel was teeming with it when he stood over Samael, trussed up and disfigured, with the Sword of Destiny—the sole key to his deliverance—clutched in his grasp and asked: "If that stubborn vine which has held you prisoner to this place with its unyielding hold were to somehow lose its grip, what would you do with your newfound freedom?"

Unlike Gotham who took his thirst for retribution over the death of his son by the reins in the form of a deceptive-looking strand of Herrinsu vine, Damiel had been denied any merciful alleviation of his own crushing grievance. For more than a century, he had somehow managed to tamp down the grief he suffered over the tragic loss of his own son, as well as the all-consuming rage he held for the one responsible for burying the same bloodied sword into the very center of his heart; that is, until one recent night when he attended a masquerade ball in St. Mark's Square in Venice begrudgingly dressed as a blue djinn. There he came face to face with the most preposterous sight he'd never before expected to witness: the slayer of his son, looking like some sort of walking dark omen, donning a raven's mask and a massive flowing cape made from the waxy, black feathers plucked from thousands of the passerine birds.

It was by some unseen divine grace that Damiel did not stake Miseri then and there, especially when Miseri began to sadistically taunt him through the mimicry of his deceased son's voice, further testing the binds of the angel's willpower which eventually came to unravel when a sword was suddenly drawn and its blade came to rest against the throat from which the mockery came. Somehow, though, Damiel kept himself from doing what every fiber of his being beseeched him to do: kill Miseri. For even in the blinding rage that came over him in that moment, Damiel was granted the clarity of seeing through the red, pulsating murk which had come to cloud his vision that the impious mark branding Miseri's temple would instantly come to scar his own if he allowed himself to spill the blood his sword was itching to draw forth from the neck in such a wrath-filled manner.

And so the unpunished—and unrepentant—murderer of his son lived to see another day, and so, too, did Damiel's ire. Only now it had been resurrected from the hole in which it had been hastily buried, and the taste for justice long been denied Damiel became an unquenchable hunger. So great did it become that the angel feared existence would soon become far worse than if he had resigned himself to the fate of a Fallen. And it was while he was in the grips of such overwhelming despair that he was gifted with a glimmer of light revealing a path leading to the well of justice along with the elusive peace he had long been in search of without the threat of losing his divine footing and succumbing to the precipitous plunge of his Fallen brothers.

Such a path led to the Infernal Desert, and more specifically to Samael.

Of all the things Samael had been robbed of during his confinement, however, his acuity was not amongst them. And when Damiel laid out before Samael the terms to which he would free him from his miserable captivity–to produce the impending war between the Darkness and the Light which Miseri had been scheming to keep from happening to ensure his immortal reign–Samael spied the intent behind Damiel's bargaining chip.

"I see no sign of the Herrinsu vine entwined around your limbs, but you're just as bound as I am now, isn't that the case?" he inquired with a knowing grin. "You have the sword to free me from my binds and, strangely enough, I have the only sword that can free you of yours."

For only through the precept of war–that, or a hostile attack perpetuated by Miseri, himself–could Damiel ever engage in the taking down of his mortal foe without fear of committing a punishable trespass. Samael was only too willing to comply to the terms of Damiel's trade; not only to win back his freedom, but to place into Damiel's hands the tidy execution of a task he himself would be only too happy to oblige: ridding himself of the traitor actively seeking to depose him of his rightful place in the Underneath.

And so it happened that Samael and the Infernal Desert came to part ways when the blade of the Sword of Destiny barely grazed the Herrinsu vine, and the vine's grip, which all of Samael's strength and power failed time and again in undoing its merciless hold, was finally severed. In that instant, Samael vanished from sight before his freedom could somehow be rescinded, and Damiel breathed deeply a sigh of relief as well as one venting lingering misgivings he had in the prudence of what he had just done.

Certainly, his scheme would finally afford him the personal requital that had long been denied him without fear of being branded for some unforgivable sin. He would not, however, leave the Infernal Desert unmarked. It might not have been the telltale scar of the Fallen seared into his temple, but it was no less an unsightly mark: one of betrayal.

It wasn't Gotham he felt he had betrayed, as one might suspect, though he couldn't fully shrug off a sense of duplicity he had committed against his brother and good friend. After all, he had in his act of freeing Samael stolen from Gotham the vengeance he sought to obtain for himself. His feelings of betrayal instead rested with Jacob and the knowing that he willfully deceived the boy into handing over possession of the Sword of Destiny into his hands in order to see through his scheme by disguising himself in the transformative likeness of Gotham.

The deceptive act left Damiel with a profound feeling of shame and perfidy as he had come to forge a particularly strong bond with Jacob. And it was out of that guilt, and the icy realization of what the severed strand of Herrinsu vine lying limp on the ground at his feet meant, that the Angel of the Sword turned his brooding attention with a far more discriminating eye to Lions Bite and the young Nephilim boys he trained there.

~ ~ ~

"AGAIN!"

Damiel's voice rang out like cannon fire amid the clangor of the numerous swords clashing against one another that sounded similar to the crackling of fireworks exploding in a dazzling display of independence against a warm July night sky. Standing inconspicuously behind one of the slanted, domino-like stone pillars which formed Lions Bite, Gotham quietly watched while the group of young Nephilim known as the Shrikes had their swordsmanship skills put to the test.

It had been well over a year since the group of Fledglings first stepped foot into the ancient-looking arena where Damiel promptly demonstrated the sorry state of their unfit and ill-equipped selves with a swift, unseen attack from above which, in a matter of seconds, left all of them with a face full of dirt from the ground they had been left sprawled upon.

"It is my job to see to it that when the day comes for you to leave Lions Bite for the last time, it will not be as the boys who first entered it," Damiel had promised the group, "but as the fighting warriors you are destined to become. Of that, I assure you."

And so it appeared to anyone who might be observing from afar that Damiel had made good on his promise; for the boys now feverishly sparring with one another looked nothing like the naive band he had reduced to a pathetic pile writhing on the ground at his feet that first day. Damiel had made certain of that, by running them to the point of collapse through punishing obstacles formed by the surrounding Forest until the lanky, out of shape bodies stumbling and struggling to keep up with the rigorous regimen slowly began to grow fit and strong. One by one, Damiel molded each boy as though they were nothing but a lump of clay placed before him; and from such clumps of clay he formed not just boys brimming with new-found confidence and self-assurance, but a platoon of sleek jungle cats. And then he upped the transformation by giving each of his young lions the bite by which their training grounds were named in the placing of a sword into the grasp of each of his creation's hand.

Yet always a taskmaster when it came to training his pupils, Damiel was not impressed with the performance taking place before him; that is, the Damiel who had recently returned from his clandestine visit to the Infernal Desert.

With an intense, sharp-eyed look fixed in his watchful eyes, the angel ambled his way amongst the sparring boys, intently studying and assessing the flurry of battling limbs and swinging of blades pealing loudly in a ringing of steel brushing against steel. No minute detail escaped his attention; not the trickle of a droplet of sweat streaking a forehead, nor curl of a lip betraying the subtlest of grimaces.

Quite suddenly, Damiel spun into action. In an instant, he maneuvered himself between each of the sparring boys in lightning-quick movements where he disarmed each of them one by one with a masterful use of his own drawn sword. Then, with an equally nimble display of acrobatic skill, he stole the footing from each of the completely caught-off-guard boys, knocking them to the ground; all that is except Max who, with a grin pasted upon his face that was both complacent and taunting, showed himself adroit enough to avoid losing both his sword and his upright position.

Damiel, however, offered not so much as a nod of being impressed. Instead, he came again at the boy with his sword, only in a much more fearsome manner. And again Max fended off the merciless swings of the blade slicing its way through the air in his direction with the equally skillful maneuverings of his own weapon, together with a well-timed back flip or two. The competitive peacocking demonstrated by the boy, no matter that it was the result of Damiel's superior instruction over the past months, only made the angel's brow furrow more with a focused determination until finally, Damiel made a last and mighty swing in Max's direction severing the boy's blade in half with a disintegrating blow. Then, just to put an exclamation point on the outcome of their heated yet brief match, Damiel kicked Max's feet out from under him with an effortless swipe of his leg sending the boy onto the ground to join the rest of his classmates.

"Well, then...I think it's fair to say we're all, unfortunate as it might be to admit, familiar with this scene. Though I'd have thought by now some of you at least would have tired of languishing in the role of a brood of fresh-faced Fledglings with an odd propensity to resemble a rack of pins laid to waste by an incoming bowling ball, and instead make some kind of visible attempt at living up to the name of Nephilim," Damiel remarked with an unexpected cool tenor that, strangely, was far more unsettling to the boys than if he'd given them a roar of a tongue-lashing.

He then turned as if to leave when he paused and halfway glanced over his shoulder in Max's direction without looking at him.

"I'll find a replacement for your sword," he said, "though, I question myself what the purpose would be, at this present moment."

Damiel then proceeded to walk away, but Max, clearly fuming, wasn't about to be dismissed in such a brushed-off manner.

"Any ole sword will do just fine," he called out as he jumped to his feet. "No reason to dig into your dirty bag of deceitful disguises to hoodwink some other poor pigeon on my account."

The acerbic words stopped Damiel dead in his tracks and, when he turned his head to look back at the boy who dared to voice them, the hate-filled look that greeted him was almost enough to douse the visible eruptions of fire within his eyes.

Almost.

Clenching his jaw, Max dug his feet more firmly into the ground when the angel moved briskly toward him, and for a passing moment, fearless as his nature was, he lamented the fact his mouth had ever been gifted a tongue. So loud was the reverberation of his quickening heartbeat within the walls of his chest pounding away in his ears that Max failed to hear the drone of a trumpet sending out its call from Havenhid which at the same time acted as a sort of repellent to Damiel's unnerving advance.

"You best take your cue," Damiel grumbled under his breath. "It's rare when a bowling ball is slowed once it's sent rolling down the alley toward its target."

Max wasn't all that quick in heeding Damiel's advice until Leos, Kairo and Ethan rushed toward him and forcefully escorted their bristling friend out of Lions Bite and back to Havenhid with his broken sword in hand.

~ ~ ~

Damiel stood alone in the center of the arena with his steely gaze following the boys as they traipsed off after the rest of their classmates. Only when they fell out of sight behind the downward slope of the path guiding them did his frozen visage melt. He closed his eyes and exhaled a deep breath, and for a brief moment it appeared as if he was overcome by some invisible weight hoisted upon him as his rigid posture went subtly slack.

"A bit heavy-handed with them, don't you think? Even for you?"

Damiel's posture instantly straightened at the unexpected voice, and his gaze quickly clouded over the reflectively troubled and doleful look that briefly cracked his stony facade when he turned his head and caught sight of Gotham standing a stone's throw from him near one of the massive slanted slabs of rock forming the perimeter of the arena.

"Every Fledgling who passes through these walls come knowing they won't be embraced with kid gloves," grumbled Damiel.

"Nor, I think it's fair to say, do they expect to be on the receiving end of a morgenstern," countered Gotham.

"I think your memory has fallen lax in keeping straight Lions Bite and its role as a provider of the crucial tools a Nephilim will find himself in need of on his return to the outside world," said Damiel.

"Funny," replied Gotham dryly, "as I was about to offer forth a similar reminder, only having to do with your role as Guide."

Far from being in the mood to entertain an unsolicited lecture from Gotham concerning his teaching methods, Damiel grumbled sourly under his breath and briskly brushed past the angel. Neither was Gotham's purpose in visiting Lions Bite to give Damiel a dressing down; at least in regards to his training techniques.

"I would have thought to have seen you at the start of the hearing today," Gotham said, while trailing after Damiel as the two exited Lions Bite.

"You seem to forget, I have other obligations; obligations I came to neglect thanks to having to chase a band of runaway Fledglings halfway around the world," Damiel replied brusquely. "Besides, what good would my presence at Halcyon have on anything or anyone?"

"I spied him eyeing the few empty chairs left vacant this morning. I have a strong feeling it would have meant a great deal to him to see you occupying one of them," argued Gotham. "He's going to be in need of support in the coming days; from all of us."

"And did you also pay a visit today to Crescent Scar and Broken Earth to shame Zuriel and Eksel on their absence as well, or did luck just happen to find me at the top of your list?"

"It's not the same thing, and you know it, Damiel. After everything the two of you have been through I'm surprised you'd be so flippant on the matter."

Damiel said nothing in return and continued to make his way along a narrow path winding its way through forest and meadow in the direction of Havenhid separate from the route taken by his young pupils.

"Do you plan on ever speaking again to the boy?" Gotham suddenly asked bluntly.

"What would you have me say to him? Sorry? Forgive me for I knew not what I was doing?" Damiel answered with a contemptuous sneer. "It would be a flagrant lie if I did."

"He's hurt, but he will eventually forgive you."

The remark drew a dismissive chuckle from Damiel. "Sorry to disappoint you, Gothamel, but I have no immediate plans to visit the confessional box."

Frustrated with conversing with the back of Damiel's head, Gotham grabbed the angel from taking another step and spun him around until they were once again eye to eye.

"I understand, Damiel, what led you to the Infernal Desert and made you cut Samael free; truly, I do. And I hold no ill will toward you for it," said Gotham in a voice that was both firm and compassionate at the same time. "You'd be the bearer of the mark that once scarred me had there not been a nugget of good intent in your thinking. Deep down inside, you'll come to learn, Jacob understands just as much."

"What you seem to fail to comprehend, Gothamel, is that I hold no interest in being the recipient of remission nor seek understanding for my actions, from either of you," Damiel responded curtly. "What I did I'd readily do again without an ounce of remorse, even when cast in the reflection of some Fledgling's hangdog expression."

Hearing his own words as he spoke them, Damiel paused his tongue between his teeth, closed his eyes and took a quieting breath.

"I have come to care a great deal for the boy; truly, I have," the angel then said. "When it was believed you had been forever lost to the world in that horrible moment at Broken Earth, I remembered the day the two of us were walking through the Forest and you asked from me the promise that I would step in as Jacob's guardian should you be relieved of the duty. Since then I have lent myself to fulfilling that vow and have watched over him as though he were my own.

"But, now, my duty to my own son has come calling," he continued. "And, frankly, nothing or no one is going to keep me from answering."

~ ~ ~

As Gotham watched glumly as Damiel continued alone on his way back to Havenhid, Hunter Wylde could be found on an opposite edge of the Garden wearing an expression upon his face that was as long, and tall as the thunderous waterfall spilling over the lip of a mountain and careening into the River beside which he knelt.

Until that very moment, Havenhid's newest resident hadn't any cause to show even the tiniest leaning toward being glum. And if, in fact, he suddenly did, one would be inclined to presume such a troubled look most likely stemmed from the onset of cramps from having his mouth frozen in the state of a perpetual smile since the moment he emerged from the Gate hidden in the depths of the Dilmun Sea, and stepped foot upon the feather-soft sands of Eden's shores. After all, if there existed a place with the singular ability to clobber its visitors with an imaginary sledge hammer to the back of the head leaving them wandering about looking like a "stoned mullet"—an apt description Max had coined in the distinctive native Australian way of his — Eden was such a place.

It had only been a few days since Hunter's arrival at the heavenly Xanadu he had only heard tales of from his father while growing up, and almost immediately he felt more times than not that he was on the receiving end of more than a few blows to the head by said imaginary sledge hammer. As a young man just short of twenty, he was by far the oldest Nephilim to ever become a resident of Havenhid, and as such stuck out like a sore thumb in most gatherings where he appeared to be more like an older and bigger brother to the other boys and a far cry from a Fledgling,

A Fledgling, however, he most certainly was.

Yet, because of his age, his time at Havenhid began almost immediately at a hurried, whirlwind-like pace. Where the other Fledglings were given the luxury to ease into the paradise, along with all of the imagination-bending properties residing within its beauty, Hunter found himself perched upon the face of a clock attempting to stay ahead of the sweeping, fast-approaching minute hand that had slowly begun to close in and nip at his heels.

What time he had to settle into the splendor of the opulent citadel created magnificently by a small grove of trees rooted on both banks of the River which would serve as his new home, was brief, indeed. A flurry of introductions came next; first to Anahel, an angel of imposing stature yet warm eyes and even warmer smile who oversaw Havenhid and the entirety of the Garden in which it resided, and then to four other equally distinguished Guides who Hunter learned would come to serve as his instructors, one being a stately figure with raven hair and an enigmatic countenance named Zuriel who quickly took custody of the young man to begin the training regimen awaiting him.

"You'll forgive us for hurrying you along as we will be prone to do, but there is much to do if you are to be part of the lineage of Nephilim into which you've been born and little time to accomplish all that must be," Anahel explained to Hunter.

The dull but noticeable pain targeting the upper portion of Hunter's back where two unmistakable humps could be seen protruding beneath his t-shirt which had begun visiting him with increasing discomfort served as a constant reminder to him of the direness of his situation. A Nephilim had only so big a window allowed to him to come into his wings, and despite the tell-tale pain that periodically coursed deep within his wingless back urgently signaling such a window was close to being closed to him forever, Hunter continued to hold hope in the buoyant words Gotham offered him when the angel examined the lad's back with the aid of the moonlight while standing in the middle of a deserted cemetery on a small isle in Venice.

"Wings are like seedlings sprouting from the soil. Without the sun, they end up withering and dying," Gotham had told him. "Yours are craving desperately such sunlight."

Such sunlight, Gotham assured Hunter, could only be found in Eden; most notably a place called Broken Earth.

The path, however, leading to said sunlight, or Broken Earth for that matter, was not one a Fledgling, no matter his age, could just take off racing down no matter how urgently his feet might be inclined to do so, Hunter was quick to find out. It was a path paved with steps; the first of which Zuriel accompanied Hunter to take in the upward climb awaiting him by first escorting him to a peaceful and secluded pocket of nature located on a plateau of rock jutting out from the heights of a mountain nestling the northwesterly corner of the Garden called the Crescent Scar.

There, Hunter was introduced to a strange drawing, much like an ancient scrawl of early man etched on a cave wall, imprinted upon the ground. The image was similar to that of a crescent moon dissected into six sections, and Hunter immediately had a good idea of what it was he was looking at.

"This is the place where I find out which of the Graces I possess, isn't it?" he asked with a lilt of excitement in his voice.

Zuriel answered by producing forth the Blackstone; a smooth, round kiwi-sized rock that was nondescript in every way except for its deep, obsidian-like hue—and the fact it had the unfailingly ability to peer deep into the soul of any Nephilim boy and spy what hidden nugget of power inherited from their father resided inside. Hunter went to catch the Blackstone when Zuriel pitched the intriguing stone in his direction only to watch in awe as it stopped short of meeting his grasp to float motionless in midair. The pupils of his eyes then followed the Blackstone as it slowly began circling him. Around and around it went, mimicking a small orbiting planet and gaining speed with every revolution it made around Hunter until it became nothing but a dizzying blur of motion.

Finally, the Blackstone came to a screeching halt and dropped to the ground with a pronounced thud. Appearing far more tense than when he was being circled by the strange probe, Hunter stood stone silent with his bugged eyes fixed firmly on the visibly smoldering stone and where it had landed smack dab on the middle of a line separating two sections of the crescent shape, before turning his antsy gaze to Zuriel for some explanation of what had just taken place.

"It would appear your long wait has rewarded you with two Graces," surmised Zuriel. "Whispering and Drifting."

The assessment was indeed good news to Hunter, though hardly unexpected. After hearing about a couple strange occurrences Hunter had experienced as a young runaway living by his wits on the streets of the world involving a shiver of sharks and an even more stunning moment when he inexplicably disappeared from one place only to reappear seconds later in another, Jacob deduced quite correctly while the two were in Venice that Hunter, who until that time had never heard what a Grace was, aside from the few words of thanks he mumbled before each meal, was showing signs of someone who possessed the divine powers to summon nature's creatures, both known and unknown, with only a whisper, as well as pass through the invisible film of time as though it were a door.

In the days that followed, Hunter became familiar with the daily training regimen awaiting all Nephilim boys who eventually arrived in Eden. Yet unlike his younger counterparts who were afforded the luxury of taking the steps which formed the path leading the way to Broken Earth one at a time, and then over the favored course of several months, Hunter found himself forced to clear the same steps two, perhaps even three, at a time until, finally, on this day that found him kneeling beside the River and staring at his reflection in the water with a forlorn expression he made it to the top.

At any other time in his life, perhaps Broken Earth would have proven itself to be the one rare obstacle he came upon to give him pause when finally he found himself standing at the cliff's edge which served as the threshold of the impossible dare which would be laid at the feet of all Nephilim boys who ever expected to turn the twin humps on their backs into the one vital thing that made them the sons of angels: wings. Whether it was the intermittent pain pulsating with increased intensity deep within the muscle and bones of his upper back, or the haunting *tick-tick-tick* of the circling minute hand of the phantom clock ticking away incessantly inside his ears, whatever gleam of fear was betrayed within his eyes was quickly eclipsed by an even brighter glint of resolve as Hunter stripped off his shirt and faced the stomach-churning challenge before him as though preparing to wrestle a not-so-friendly bear he had the misfortune of crossing paths with on an otherwise pleasant mountain hike.

He turned a questioning gaze first to the two angels named Farrel and Nigel who were perched like two magnificent winged beings on twin overhangs of rock stretching out over the cloud and mist-filled gorge (and who had been called upon to step into the roles of life preservers previously held by two perfidious angels whose presence, along with Thaniel's, had been eradicated from Eden), and then to Eksel who could be found patiently standing nearby waiting for Hunter to get on with the task at hand.

"So what? Is that's all there is to it? Just jump?" he asked.

Gotham had assured Hunter all his back needed was sunlight; the brilliance emanating from the blue cloudless sky above, however, highlighted instead two disconcerting large patches of bruising covering both of Hunter's exposed shoulder blades that appeared almost gangrenous in nature and offered little hope to anyone who might have cast their gaze on the painful-looking affliction that Hunter's prospect of finally finding his wings at Broken Earth wouldn't end in inconsolable dismay.

"That's it...just jump," echoed Eksel while forcing forth a tight-lipped smile of support.

Hunter paused but a moment, and then only to take two quick, steadying breaths while focusing the willful stare fixated in his eyes on the terrifying sea of nothingness residing at the end of the stunted path upon which he stood.

Then, with a final breath, he bolted toward it.

~ ~ ~

Kneeling a short while later on the banks of the River where Hunter sought out a moment alone in order to fully take in the end result from his leap of faith, as it was known, he leaned in for a closer look at his reflection in the water. With a discerning eye, he turned ever so slowly the upper part of his body to the right in order to get a better glimpse of the foreign appendages now attached to his back just behind his shoulders.

Wings.

At least, that is what Eksel assured him they were.

They did not, however, share any similarities to any wings Hunter had ever before laid eyes upon; that is, they looked nothing like the magnificent and striking pinions he had witnessed affixed to the backs of angels: not Eksel's, nor those of the intimidatingly strapping Nigel and Farrel, and most distressing of all is they bore little resemblance to the spectacular plumage of gray endowed by his own father.

The so-called wings came to him a dozen or so seconds while in the midst of his terrifying plunge into the gullet of Broken Earth when, in a blinding flash of blue light that engulfed Hunter first in a spark of jolting pain followed immediately by a rushing wave of relieving bliss, they pushed their way out simultaneously through the cocoon of bruised flesh in which they were held captive. It was only when he managed to raise himself out of the cloud-and-mist-choked ravine and settle his feet once more on the cliff from which he had jumped did Hunter get his first look at the twin appendages that had been long in their arrival, and his expression immediately dampened.

They were delicate things, his wings were; not the virile displays of strength he was expecting. Along with being transparent, they resembled something one would find attached to a member of the insect family such as a grasshopper, or better yet a mayfly.

Eksel, who had witnessed more times than he could count the transformative moment that took place when his students leapt head-first into the cloud bank residing within the gorge only to emerge from the misty soup with their newly acquired wings flapping furiously to return them back to the safety of the cliff, had grown quite accustomed to the mostly glum looks of disappointment that followed each pivotal accomplishment. Hunter was no different. And while he did his best to convince the young man that the wispy, delicate-looking attachments to his back that looked better suited for some sprite conjured within the pages of a fairytale book would most assuredly transmute themselves into something far more impressive and worthy of an angel's son in the days and even hours to come, the troubled look remained firmly etched upon Hunter's face as he continued to study himself in the mirror of water before him.

It was then, much to his chagrin, that he was startled by the approaching voices of his friends heading back to Havenhid from Lions Bite. He leapt to his feet and tried to cover up the embarrassing sight of his wings by wriggling back into his shirt, but it was too late. Ethan was the first to spot him—and his wings—and made a dash toward him.

"You did it! You got your wings! And on your first try, too," he cried out excitedly.

"Oh, thank goodness," echoed Leos with a huff of relief, but for different reasons. "You don't know how ecstatic I, and more importantly my arms are in knowing I will never be forced to haul you around like some overstuffed sack of potatoes."

Hunter offered a weak grin in return as he recalled the unpleasant exertion Leos was forced to share with Kairo in flying his wingless self from Venice to the Infernal Desert.

"It's a good thing fate forced our paths to cross when they did or there's a good chance you might never have gotten your wings. You must be pretty relieved," said Kairo.

"Relieved...that's what I am all right."

"So let's see them!" Ethan squealed while tugging at the back of Hunter's shirt.

"If it's all the same to you, I'd just as soon wait a bit," Hunter replied, pulling away. "Maybe let them...settle in a bit."

"I hear you," Leos said with an understanding nod. "I wasn't too keen in showing off my wings when I first got them either. They're not exactly showroom worthy when they first pop out. In fact, they're kind of embarrassing."

"How long did it take before they became, you know...normal-looking?" Hunter inquired somewhat timorously.

"A day, two tops. You'll likely start seeing your first feathers come in by the time you go to bed tonight."

While Leo's words appeared to bring a sense of ease to Hunter, it brought a visible look of perplexity to Ethan.

"Really...a day or two?" he muttered to himself. "It took nearly a week before mine looked even halfway decent."

As Kairo and Leos proceeded to give their friend some good-natured ribbing, Hunter turned his attention to the noticeable pillar of silence in the shape of Max who was standing nearby staring off in the direction of Lions Bite with a simmering scowl fixed on his face.

"You're pretty quiet," Hunter noted, breaking Max's trance. "You alright?"

"Tops," Max replied in a manner that suggested anything but.

"He's just still steamed over his dust-up with Damiel," Leos piped in.

"Damiel? What's going on with Damiel?"

"You really have to ask?" barked Max. "Or have the Guides got you jumping through so many hoops in their training regimen to make up for your lost time that you've forgotten about what happened in the Infernal Desert."

"No...I haven't forgotten."

Hunter took a thoughtful moment and slowly circled around Max until he stood between him and the direction he had his sulking gaze fixed.

"Listen, I know I haven't been acquainted with Damiel for as long as the rest of you but it was clear to me in the short time we've come to know each other that all of you not only looked up to him but cared a great deal for him. Am I wrong about that?"

Max's refusal to answer forced Kairo to speak up with a meek "No, you're not," and neither Leos nor Ethan voiced any argument.

"Now, I'm completely sympathetic to how all of you view what happened in the Infernal Desert as an act of betrayal on Damiel's part."

"You're damn straight," Max, looking directly at Hunter, grumbled. "What else would you call it?"

"That I can't say," said Hunter with a shrug. "All I know is that for a long time I was certain someone very close to me had betrayed me."

"Your father?" guessed Ethan.

Hunter nodded. "I ended up running away from home with a heart filled with hate and the belief that I was the son of a Fallen. Because of that I nearly sabotaged my future in living life as a true Nephilim: no Graces, no wings. And as you all witnessed in that cemetery we visited in Venice what I thought to be a betrayal was far from anything of a sort."

"It's not quite the same thing, now, is it?" replied Max. "You were there; Damiel admitted to us what he did."

Of that, Hunter had no argument.

"Yes, he did. But as someone who's a little older and maybe a tad bit wiser, may I offer up some unsolicited advice that maybe, perhaps, it might better serve you to look past what he did and focus more on the why."

The suggestion, whether welcomed or not, was met with a marked pause of silence that was drowned out by the nearby waterfalls.

"Perhaps Hunter's right," Kairo was the first to speak. "Maybe it would help explain why he's become so... different."

"Have any of you ever happened to walk by the Library late at night just before bed?" questioned Leos. "I have a couple times and both times I saw Damiel there by the Witnesses; just standing there staring at the four books as if in a trance as the events of the day were written onto the pages. It's like he's waiting for something."

"Maybe he is," Ethan commented quietly.

Their pondering on the matter was suddenly interrupted when a high-pitched screech drew their collective attention skyward to the sight of a falcon swooping down towards the huddled group where it dropped an envelope from the grasp of its talons directly over Max's head.

"What's this?" Max wondered aloud after catching the air delivery and seeing it was addressed to him.

He paused to give the odd, unfamiliar red wax seal stamped on the back flap a curious glance before he broke it and proceeded to open the envelope.

"Well knock me down and steal my teeth..."

"What is it?" Leos pressed impatiently.

"I think I'm being summoned," replied Max.

"Summoned? To what?" asked Hunter.

"You are hereby instructed, Maximillian Cuma Kelly–"

"Cuma? What kind of a name is Cuma?" Ethan interrupted.

"It's an old family name on my mother's side. It means the one who bears Christ. You sure you want to take the piss out of me over it?" Max answered with a challenging snarl.

"I don't know about taking the piss out of anything, but I certainly want to pause a moment over the fact that you're a Maximillian," Leos interjected with a jovial snicker.

For a brief moment Max forgot the letter as his gaze narrowed itself on Leos, Ethan and now Kairo as the triad joined together for a hearty chuckle until Hunter redirected his attention back to the matter at hand.

"Deal with them later and continue reading," Hunter coaxed, delaying any bout of fisticuffs for a later time.

"You are hereby instructed...," Max began again though stopping short of repeating his name while shooting Leos, Kairo and Ethan a withering glare before continuing, "to make yourself present before this seated body of the Iudicium Tribunal on such and such a date to provide testimony pertinent in the hearing involving Jacob Samson Parrish and the unsanctioned Blessing which took place at Havenhid in his name declaring him the Light Bearer."

"It must be from Anahel, to testify in support of Jacob," wagered Hunter.

"I don't think so. It's signed by Sandel; he's the one who issued the summons. He actually wants me to testify against my best friend," The worry in Max's face deepened as he returned his gaze back to the document and continued to read aloud: "Failure to comply with this order will institute a directive calling for your immediate detention."

His face reddening with offense, Max spat, "That winged knob is actually threatening to have me arrested."

"I don't get it. What does Sandel think you have to say to warrant issuing you a summons to come and testify against Jacob?" Leos stated aloud what everyone else was quietly wondering.

Several more screeches sounded from above making the group look again to the sky where this time they found four more falcons descending towards them, each carrying an envelope identical to the one delivered to Max which they summarily left in the hands of Hunter and the other three boys.

"Correction," Kairo remarked as they each opened their envelopes. "I guess Sandel thinks we all have something worthy to testify about."

"What do we do?" Ethan, looking the most uncomfortable about the unexpected situation, wondered aloud.

The silence that followed made it clear none of them had an answer. And it was in the accompaniment of such silence that the group continued on their way back to Havenhid.

~ ~ ~

The Hall of Light, when they finally arrived, was alive with the familiar ruckus of young Nephilim boys trading stories of their latest adventures while enjoying with gusto the generous dinner spread waiting for them after a long day of studies and training.

However, no topic of gossip was on the tips of more tongues than the "Son of Sam" proceedings, and despite Jacob's conscious efforts to remove himself as best he could from the constant din of the rumormongering swirling about by segregating himself from the rest of the boys, and sitting alone at an unoccupied corner of one of the two curving long tables, he unfortunately could not keep his keen Nephilim hearing from picking up the tittle-tattle of the day like some revolving satellite dish.

As uncomfortable a position as it may have been, it was not the first time Jacob felt the unease of sticking out like a sore thumb as he nonchalantly allowed his gaze to survey the room where his fellow classmates congregated only to spy a sea of equally casual, yet probing glances being returned his way, accompanied by the incessant whispering and occasional sniggering. It had been the same thing day after day, night after night, since he returned to Havenhid. Only this day the buzz making its way around the Hall was like a swarm of hornets, and according to Jacob's own ears, seemed to be stemming from the news that he had been relieved of the Sword of Destiny. And no one appeared more upbeat by the latest bulletin than Creed Maggert who Jacob happened to notice was staring directly at him from the opposite end of the Hall and baring as big a toothy smile as his mouth could be stretched to form.

Jacob looked down into his plate to conceal both the embarrassment as well as anger that he could feel beginning to well up from the pit of his core. His mind drifted to Cain's Corner and he wondered why he had allowed himself to be talked into leaving his home and returning to Eden, especially when the welcome mat laid out for him came in the shape of a summons ordering him to appear before the Iudicium Tribunal and endure its dispiriting efforts not only to renounce him as the Light Bearer, but disavow him of any other identity except being the son of Samael.

Unable to take the chatter pulsating in his ears, or feeling like an orangutan being goggled at by a horde of peanut-munching zoo-goers visiting the primate exhibit, Jacob was about to skip the rest of his dinner and escape to the privacy of his room when Max and Ethan surprised him by suddenly hopping in the seats on either side of him as he was getting to his feet and ushering him back into his own.

"Where do you think you're off to in such a hurry?" Max, who appeared to be in a bit better spirits, asked.

"I was just heading back to the room," Jacob replied glumly.

"But we just got here, and it's still early. Look!" Ethan remarked, directing

Jacob's eyes upward to where the glowing colors of the fiery-streaked sky was beginning to dim from the setting sun and allowed the pinpricks of starlight to slowly burst forth one by one. But it was the branches of the surrounding trees which formed the architecture of Havenhid, and in this particular case the massive vaulted ceiling, to which Ethan was referring. For every morning the limbs forming the decorative construct would loosen themselves and allow the panels of the ceiling to fold back like the pedals of flowers to allow the sunlight to flood the Hall only to close again with the setting of the sun and bring together once more the splintered fragments of an elaborate mural like pieces of a jigsaw puzzle. Jacob observed that while the tree limbs were slowly coming together, there was still a bit of time left before the separated images would fuse together to form once more the stunning masterpiece chronicling the books of Genesis and Revelation.

"Yeah, well, it's been a draining day and I've still got homework that's been piling up that I still have to get to before I can even go to sleep," said Jacob.

"How can you even think of homework and sleep now when we have some celebrating to do?" said Leos.

"What are you talking about? Celebrating what?"

"I think they're referring to me," muttered Hunter, looking a touch flushed having the spotlight directed his way. "On a count me getting wings and all."

It was undoubtedly the only news that could have perked Jacob up as it did and bring forth an elated smile to crack his glum veneer.

"You're kidding me! You got 'em? When?" Jacob asked with a sudden enthusiastic jolt.

"Earlier today," Hunter said with a slightly bashful smile he couldn't fully hide. "It's really not a big deal."

"Not a big deal?" Kairo chimed in. "I don't know about the rest of you but I sure was worried you might not have made it here in time, especially when we all got a gander at how bruised up your back was from waiting so long."

"No foolin'," agreed Ethan. "Do you know how lucky you are considering what the alternative could have been?"

"Jeez, but the two of you really know how to deflate the mood. You should go and form an act and call it 'Storm Cloud and Rain,' " said Leos.

"What did we say?" Ethan replied cluelessly.

While he and Kairo exchanged arguments with Leos, Jacob leaned across the table and gave Hunter a congratulatory fist bump. "It's a big achievement. Take it from someone who needed nearly a year before earning my own. I'm very happy for you."

"Thanks, I appreciate it," said Hunter. "But enough about me; I want to hear about how everything went today at the hearing."

In the short while that Hunter's wings had become the topic conversation, Jacob had been given a brief reprieve from feeling the burdensome weight of his hearing hanging over his head. Yet, like his fleeting smile, it was short-lived.

"Yes, tell us everything that happened," said Kairo whose back and forth banter with Ethan and Leos had abruptly ceased as the three boys, along with Max, focused their full and inquisitive attention on Jacob.

"You mean none of you have heard yet?" asked Jacob. "From all the chatter going on around here tonight I'm guessing you're the last to find out."

"Find out about what?" Max inquired impatiently.

"They relieved me of my sword."

A hush fell upon the group as stunned gazes were quietly exchanged.

"When you say your sword, you don't mean..." Ethan paused a moment as if the words about to leave his tongue were too horrible to utter.

"The Sword of Destiny?" Jacob finished the sentence. "That's exactly what I mean."

"They can't do that!" Max exclaimed angrily as if he had been the one to suffer the slight.

"Well they did," Jacob snapped back before adding in a somewhat softer tone: "Sort of."

"What do you mean sort of?" asked Hunter.

"Sandel was the one who made the demand to the Tribunal that I hand over the sword."

"That Sandel...he sure is a piece of work isn't he? He's been after that sword since your Blessing," said Leos.

"Gotham intervened," continued Jacob. "He requested the Tribunal to allow the sword to be returned to his care during the course of the hearing since he had been its caretaker before he gave it to me, and the Tribunal agreed. Trust me, it's the only way I would have relinquished it."

"And you can trust me when I tell you it's a temporary arrangement."

All heads turned to the sound of the familiar voice and a collective groan left the group of boys at the sight of Creed suddenly found standing nearby eavesdropping on the conversation being had.

"Turd alert; everyone out of the pool," Max muttered quietly with disdain at the unwelcome intrusion.

"What do you want, Creed? None of us here are in the mood to hear anything you have to say," said Leos.

"Understandable," Creed replied, looking not the slightest bit offended. In fact, quite the opposite. "I'm actually quite surprised to see that any of you showed up for dinner. I would've thought none of you would have much of an appetite considering everything that happened today at Halcyon."

It was crystal clear that while Creed was not among the spectators at the opening of Jacob's hearing, he nonetheless was privy of what had occurred at the proceedings judging from the knowing smirk shaped by his thin-lipped mouth.

"What are you talking about? What's a temporary arrangement?" Jacob couldn't help but ask, even though he was far from in the mood to engage Creed this night.

"What do you think I'm talking about? The Sword of Destiny being placed back in Gotham's hands, of course. My father will see to that, I can promise you."

"It was Gotham's sword to begin with. I'm doubtful there's anything anyone could do about that, even your father. Or has it already slipped your memory that Gotham is no longer some Fallen you can look down on and cast stones at like before? He's been redeemed, perhaps to an even higher position than before his Fall judging from the pair of white wings he now has fixed to his back," argued Jacob.

"Then you obviously don't know my father," said Creed smugly.

"Trust me, we know enough," Ethan sniped under his breath.

"Then know this, pipsqueak, when my father sets his mind to something you best believe no stone will go unturned. Then again, you'll all find that out come tomorrow."

"Tomorrow? What's happening tomorrow?" Jacob, straightening himself in his seat, inquired.

Creed said nothing in return at first but, instead, reached into the back pocket of his jeans, all while keeping his unsettling gaze firmly fixed on Jacob before bringing into a light what at first appeared to be a letter he had received.

"What's that you got?" Leos was the first to ask with a tremble of nervousness when he along with Max, Kairo, Ethan and Hunter recognized immediately the envelope in Creed's hand was identical to the ones they had received from five mysterious feathered couriers shortly before arriving back to Havenhid.

"You don't know?" Creed questioned in a goading voice. "I would have thought by now you of anyone would have recognized it immediately."

He then proceeded to open the flap of the envelope and remove the written document folded away inside which he revealed to apprehensive stares fixed his way with a flick of his wrist.

"It's a summons; to appear before the Iudicium Tribunal," Creed announced. "Tomorrow my father begins calling forth witnesses for the prosecution whose testimony will be used to build the case against Jacob Parrish and ensure this Weed impersonating a Nephilim is finally revealed to be the charlatan he is. And you'll be happy to know I will be among the first witnesses called to testify against you."

"I'm not a charlatan!" Jacob replied cooly while doing his best to conceal from Creed that his revelation had managed to rattle him somewhat. "Besides, what could you possibly say at the hearing that would prove otherwise? And if you did, it would be a lie."

"I take offense to that," said Creed, though the grin on his face clearly stated otherwise. "Those summoned to testify before it are sworn to tell the truth and nothing but the truth. And if there is one thing I am not, it's dishonest."

"Please! You can't even lie straight in a bed," Max remarked.

Creed ignored the remark and kept his gaze glued on Jacob. "You can bet that when the Tribunal hears what I have to say your short-lived days as Light Bearer will be over, and more importantly you will never lay another finger on the Sword of Destiny," he said with a self-satisfied hiss.

"I don't get what's happening here," Hunter spoke up suddenly after quietly listening to the back and forth. "Why would you and your father want to come after Jacob like you are and try and discredit him? I mean, I thought we were all supposed to be on the same team."

"Same team? We're not even in the same league! But why am I not surprised to see one Weed sticking up for another Weed?"

The derogatory statement caught Hunter in the same way as if Creed and delivered a stinging smack to the back of his head.

"Don't look so surprised; we all know about that disgraceful excuse of a Fallen father of yours," Creed spat with contempt, even as Hunter's fierce gaze all but seared a hole through his skull as effectively as a welder's torch. "Zophiel's his name, isn't it? My father told me all about him; said he was one of the first to ditch his loyalty to Heaven and take up allegiance with the rest of the Underneath scum. Only one I can think of who's beneath the layer of toad vomit your father has proven himself to be is Jacob's dear old dad. Now, here you are the two of you—the son of Sam and the spawn of toad vomit—becoming bosom buddies. Gotham might well have found favor again with Heaven, but if I had my way he'd be struck down again just for the unforgivable act of inflicting upon Eden and the rest of us noble Nephilim a growing undercast of undesirables. Then again, I guess the old saying proves true: Birds of the same feather flock together."

Hunter slowly but without a hint of reservation rose from his seat, and Creed, smartly taking notice of Hunter's larger size, both in height and brawn, not to mention simmering anger that all but escaped his ears in puffs of steam, took several mindful steps backward and out of reach of the pair of hands he spied being balled up into sizable fists.

"If I were you, Creed, I'd make like a bad check and bounce," advised Leos.

"And if I were you, I'd get myself plenty of sleep. You'll need it starting tomorrow," Creed shot back, before turning on his heel and retreating to the other corner of the Hall.

~ ~ ~

"Well, he's a pleasant one, isn't he?" Hunter remarked when he lowered himself back into his seat and proceeded to find his sunny disposition momentarily lost to him.

"You haven't seen the worst of it, trust me," said Jacob.

"He's about as useful as a third armpit, that drongo is," Max commented as his gaze continued to burn its way into the sight of Creed congregating with his friends at their table. "Not to mention a book short of a library."

"I can't believe he's actually going to be offering testimony against me tomorrow at my own hearing," said Jacob.

"What worries me is the why; what could he possibly have to say that could be so damaging in regards to you being the Light Bearer?" Kairo chimed in.

Judging from the shared looks the boys exchanged with one another, it was quite clear they each were more than well-acquainted with the depths to which Creed Maggert would stoop, especially when it came to his intense dislike of Jacob Parrish.

"It gets worse," Ethan suddenly blurted.

"What do you mean?" asked Jacob.

Ethan drew quiet for a moment when Max, Leos and Kairo turned a collective glare his way to zip his lips, something which didn't go unnoticed by Jacob.

"What's going on?" he asked.

"We have to tell him sometime. Might as well be now," Ethan said to his friends who slowly appeared more or less to agree with him.

"Tell me what?" Jacob pressed.

"Creed wasn't the only one who received summons to appear before the Tribunal," Max finally managed to croak out.

"You're kidding me. Who else?"

Jacob was clearly caught by surprise by the answer when one by one he watched as each one of his friends revealed an envelope tucked away in their pockets; envelopes identical to the one Creed had revealed only moments earlier.

"You've got to be pulling my leg," Jacob mumbled with disbelief.

"I wish we were," Kairo replied.

"And were any of you planning to tell me about this, or just let it be a big surprise when Sandel called you out before the Tribunal for questioning?" Jacob, growing noticeably more perturbed by the news, said.

"We just found out about it literally on our way back to Havenhid," answered Max. "We had every intention of telling you, it's just...we're still trying to figure out what possible reason there could be to issue us a summons."

"You gotta know there is nothing on earth—even that wormy Sandel—that could make any of us say anything bad about you," said Kairo.

"That's right! We are the five Musketeers after all," Leos added before quickly correcting himself when he took account of Hunter sitting next to him. "Make that six Musketeers."

56

"For reals!" Ethan seconded.

Such upbeat assurances appeared to do little to lift Jacob's mood, and when he promptly got up to leave the table Max reached out and took hold of his arm in an attempt to get him to stay.

"Don't be like that."

"I'm not mad, really," said Jacob, flashing his friends a half-hearted smile. "It's just...just when I think things can't get any worse, it somehow manages to do just that."

For the first time, he paid no mind to the sea of gazes and trail of chatter that followed him as he crossed the stretch of the Hall on his way to the privacy of his room.

CHAPTER FOUR

SEEDS OF DOUBT

The task of presenting to the Iudicium Tribunal evidence proving Jacob to be the anointed one heralded in a little-known Apocrypha detailing the coming of the Light Bearer began the following morning and, with the irrefutable proof he had in hand, Anahel believed quite rightly it was an open-and-shut case.

Standing before the jury, Anahel directed the dour members' gazes to the area of floor residing at the foot of the large crescent-shaped table at which they were seated. The floor was made of marble and so perfectly polished it appeared mirror-like, and it was within that gleaming reflection images began to surface and reveal themselves to the curious members of the Tribunal.

"The Apocrypha in question, with which you each are well acquainted, is vague on some details but pointedly clear in others when it comes to the prophesy of the Light Bearer," said Anahel. "The most telling of those factors in identifying who this anointed one might be is quite simply the possession of all seven Graces inherent in all angels."

He then directed the eyes of those seated at the table back to the floor where a sea of ghostly images began to surface one by one in flowering blooms of clarity and color. They would come to reveal what happened shortly after Anahel was visited early one evening by Gotham with a noticeably muddled Jacob in tow and informed of the shocking incident that occurred at Lions Bite when Jacob was witnessed to healing another boy whose leg had been sliced open in a sword mishap. The first image to emerge like a giant lily pad floating upon the still waters of a tranquil pond, showed Anahel and Gothamel along with the other summoned Guides looking on anxiously from a corner of Anahel's chamber as Zuriel set out to test what Graces, which had so far remained undetectable, Jacob might unwittingly possess. None of the members of the Tribunal appeared all that impressed as they looked on and watched as Jacob eventually managed to reveal himself in possession of the Grace of Cloaking by transforming himself into that of a chimpanzee. Nor did they seem all that impressed when the first image retreated with the appearance of a second image revealing Jacob demonstrating yet a second Grace—the Grace of Summoning—to eclipse from sight the massive full moon hanging over the Garden.

It was only when the third vision unfurled itself, followed by a fourth, a fifth, and still yet a sixth that a gradual look of consternation came to rest upon each of the Tribunal members as Jacob was witnessed to demonstrate somewhat awkwardly, yet undeniably, that he held each of the Graces that could be passed down from father to son at his fingertips. When the final image emerged, however, showing Jacob standing waist-deep in the River of Life whose flowing waters had been turned black by Azrael—the Angel of Death himself—the great room became quiet as a tomb. It was then everyone whose eyes were fixed on the floor watched in disbelief as the boy resurrected the dried-up waterfalls and swept away the shroud that had momentarily stilled the beating heart of Eden with a simple laying of his hands upon the surface of the River.

The deafening silence continued well after the final vision faded and retreated from sight into the depths of the marble, and Anahel, recognizing from the expressions on their faces that the Tribunal had been staggered by what they had just seen, left the jury to contemplate on their no-less-than-jumbled thoughts.

He retreated to where Jacob was quietly sitting and motioned the boy to his feet. Jacob then gave a somewhat nervous, self-conscious glance around the room before proceeding to strip off the t-shirt he was wearing when Anahel gave him a subtle nod.

"Let it not be overlooked, for those among you who might still find themselves skeptical, that along with the seven Graces, there is one other brand mentioned in the writings by which the Light Bearer will be marked," Anahel's commanding voice echoed off the high vaulted ceilings.

Slowly, in an almost timid manner, Jacob extended into view his left wing revealing the inside of what was an impressive cape of dark gray quills and, more importantly, a single white feather which appeared almost as a large birthmark, and instantly noticeable to anyone who was offered a glance. The reveal brought a collective hush to the room as awestricken looks were exchanged. The only one who looked noticeably unmoved was Sandel; if anything, the sight of Jacob and his telltale mark of a feather only seemed to make him glower all the more at the boy.

"Quite the odd circumstance, isn't it?" the albino-looking angel suddenly remarked softly as if speaking to himself, yet loud enough for everyone to hear clearly his words. "That something so simplistic as a solitary white feather nestled away in the underside of a wing could hold such consequence in determining whether a prophesy foretold is suddenly upon us, or a false prophet."

"Odd as you may find it to be, you cannot deny the words of the Apocrypha and that which your own eyes have seen," Anahel responded sternly.

"To the contrary; far be it for me to even attempt to deny what my eyes, as well as everyone's in this room, have just been shown in so clear a light," Sandel replied in a cordial manner that Anahel found immediately to be oddly out of character. "And yet I can't help but wonder, Anahel, if you might ever look upon me and entertain the notion that I, too, could be in the running for Light Bearer."

As he spoke, a great pair of gray wings slowly unfolded themselves from Sandel's back and emerged into sight from the two strategically placed slits in the loose-fitting garment he wore. Anahel's face twisted into a grimace when he saw instantly the wings were a mirror image of Jacob's, white feather and all.

"What kind of game is it you're playing, Sandel?" questioned Arafiel who looked no more amused than Anahel.

"Simply proving a point, elementary as it may be; a point, if I may be so frank, one would think would not need demonstrating before such a percipient group." Sandel's acidulous tone had returned to his tongue mirroring the glowering gaze he held fixed on Jacob. "Really, Anahel...I'm rather disappointed in you; one would think you to be oblivious to the existence of the Grace of mimicry and all the uncanny ways it could be put to deceptive uses, particularly when wielded by an especially deceptive possessor of said Grace."

With that, Sandel gave his wings a shake and the gesture appeared to cast from them the deep gray coloring from off his quills as if it were a dusting of chalk, and the single white feather revealed to all was immediately lost from sight amid a carpet of white as the angel's wings returned to their normal snowy appearance.

"I would have expected someone of your elevated stature to be somewhat more...skeptical on this matter," Sandel remarked haughtily. "Especially, concerning your history with purported Light Bearers."

Never one to take lightly to being addressed in such a pejorative manner, particularly by someone as impudent as Sandel, Anahel responded thusly:

"I'm quite aware of the wiles associated in the manner in which any Grace can be wielded, Sandel, just as I came to this inquest fully prepared to navigate the questionable contrivances and unscrupulous maneuverings for which you have well-earned your reputation during your tenure of serving on this noble Tribunal."

Jacob brought a fist to his mouth to muffle the snicker he couldn't help from escaping him at the sight of the light of superiority beaming forth from Sandel suddenly dimming noticeably from Anahel's verbal clout.

"That said," Anahel continued cooly, "odd as you may find the marking on Jacob Parrish's wing as being as worthy as an offering of pyrite in proving him to be the recipient of a divine prophesy, you act as if I have laid before this body a collection of evidence in the shape of a singular, dismissive quill. Trust me when I say, I'm most intrigued as to the kind of floorshow we will all be entertained by you next in disproving the boy's inarguable demonstration of possessing fully the seven Graces."

Sandel returned to his seat, and as he slowly sank into his seat an unexpected smile unfolded itself from his thin-lipped mouth looking something like a Cheshire cat sunning itself in a box window.

"Well then, that makes two of us who are eager to proceed," he stated ominously.

~ ~ ~

Zuriel was the first to be called by Sandel before the Tribunal. Taking a seat facing the rest of the room in the space surrounded by the half-circle table at which the Tribunal members sat, Zuriel maintained a dignified poise, even as his nose remained out of joint due to the inconvenience of having his daily tutelage with his students at Crescent Scar interrupted.

"Before the night in question presented before this body just a few moments ago in which Jacob Parrish allegedly demonstrated before you and the other Guides at Havenhid his ability to invoke six of the seven divine Graces—"

"There's no allegedly about the matter," Zuriel interrupted Sandel with a hint of impatience. "I can attest to you and this governing body that the boy most certainly holds the ability to wield the power of those Graces at will."

Zuriel, who much like Eksel, though not as disinclined, had been slow in warming to Jacob, glanced over in the direction of the boy seated quietly beside Anahel. And while Zuriel's youthfully handsome yet expressionless face appeared even more severe with his black mane of hair pulled tightly back and fashioned into a single thick braid decorated with a vine of emerald ivy that ran across the top of his head and down to the center of his back, Jacob could make out what appeared to be the twinkle of a supportive smile directed his way.

"Yes, well...we'll address your competency at deciphering such things momentarily," quipped Sandel who made it all too clear with his icy glare his displeasure with the angel's unsolicited commentary. "The only answer I wish to have forthcoming is to the following question: Did you, before that night, witness any anomalies to these so-called abilities?"

"Anomalies?"

"Yes...anomalies: irregularities, aberrations. I had assumed when it came to someone of your prestige that I wouldn't be relegated to paring down my vocabulary to that of only two syllables or less during my examination of you today."

Zuriel responded to the insolent slight with a glare that surprisingly to everyone seated in the room didn't bring the immediate formation of icicles to the ceiling.

"I'm quite aware of what an anomaly is," he hissed as civil-mannered as possible.

"Excellent!" Sandel replied with a celebratory clap of his hands. "Now then, it has become common knowledge that when Jacob Parrish first visited the Crescent Scar on his first day of instruction there was a so-called a-no-maly. Would you please refresh the minds of those here today what that anomaly was?"

At first, it looked as if any recollection might be momentarily delayed until after Zuriel got up from his chair, took Sandel aggressively by the collar and proceeded to give him several well-earned backhanded smacks. However, whatever internal tundra that resided within Zuriel and threatened to decorate the ceiling above with icicles, managed to put a deep freeze to such impulses.

"The Blackstone was unable to ascertain the presence of a specific Grace residing within the boy," answered Zuriel, instead.

"Unable to ascertain?" Sandel echoed the angel's words, bringing a slant to Zuriel's mouth.

"Perhaps it is I who failed to receive notice before my testimony to keep my responses at a more remedial level," Zuriel remarked dryly.

The comment didn't appear to rile Sandel; strangely, in fact, he seemed to take pleasure in facing off against someone who came armed with his own bat.

"Enlighten us, if you will, and explain exactly what happened," instructed Sandel.

Zuriel proceeded then to describe in simple enough terms how the Blackstone, when it came time to lob it in Jacob's direction once it became his time to be read by the mysterious rock, revolved around the boy at a blinding speed as it normally was known to do before abandoning its orbit and casting itself far from Jacob and the six divided sections denoting the various divine powers at his feet.

"I could only assume you made repeated attempts to right this rather strange reaction by the Blackstone," said Sandel.

"I did...several times, in fact, over the proceeding weeks, but with always the same result," answered Zuriel.

"Cast itself away from the boy as if he were a plague," Sandel surmised from the response. "And what, exactly, did you come to make of such a thing?"

"Just as their Civilian counterparts, it's not uncommon for some Nephilim who come to Havenhid to be what we often refer to as late bloomers when it comes to their physical, mental and emotional development."

"Is that so?" Sandel responded with overt intrigue.

"I assumed, quite naturally, that whatever Grace or Graces he had inherited were latent and therefore simply nonexistent at that point for the Blackstone to detect. Only–"

"Only what?" Sandel was quick to ask before Zuriel could finish his thought.

"Usually, in such cases, the Blackstone is known to make a few revolutions around such a boy before simply dropping to the ground with a thud and steering clear of any of the six quadrants representing the six Graces. The casting of itself clear across to the opposite end of the Crescent Scar was rather unusual," said Zuriel.

"Unusual, indeed," Sandel echoed with an air of suspense as if it had been the first time he had been made privy to any of Zuriel's testimony thus far, which of course wasn't the case.

"Tell me, is this the first time you witnessed the Blackstone to perform in such a way, or had it happened before?" Sandel then asked.

"It has happened before...once," Zuriel answered somewhat hesitantly while giving a fleeting glance in the direction where Gotham sat listening intently.

"And do you mind revealing with whom did it occur?" Sandel pressed.

Zuriel was reluctant at first to answer.

"Gothamel's son, David," the angel finally replied drawing from Sandel a subtle smirk.

~ ~ ~

The great room became very quiet for a minute or two except for the sound of Sandel's steps as he slowly paced the floor in front of Zuriel while appearing deep in thought.

"You said you believed the reason for the anomaly that occurred with Mr. Parrish at the Crescent Scar was the result of...being a late bloomer. Is that correct?" asked Sandel, finally.

"It is."

"Late bloomer," Sandel muttered as though he were thinking aloud to himself. "A rather odd deduction of something far more elementary–and frankly, in my opinion, obvious–don't you think?"

Zuriel's gaze closely followed Sandel's slow deliberate pace back and forth as though he were observing a poisonous white snake slithering across the marble floor. "You know the saying regarding opinions," he commented cooly.

"Explain to the room, Zuriel, if you will, the difference between a Nephilim who is the offspring of a sitting angel and one who is fathered by a Fallen," Sandel, ignoring the remark, inquired..

"The difference between...," Zuriel replied with a frown of confusion. "I'm not sure I understand the question."

"Come now, Zuriel; I find your repute as the sagacious pedagogue of Graces at Havenhid sorely lacking this day," Sandel barked with a sudden wave of impatience. "Perhaps if the two of us put our heads together we might just well come up with an alternative reason besides latent blooming as to why the Blackstone would have such an adverse reaction when confronted with reading the soul of an offspring of a Fallen, much less two."

Before Zuriel could answer, Anahel rose to his feet and made his voice heard.

"Might I inquire what specifically you're all but attempting to wring from your own witness' larynx?" he asked.

"I'm curious to know the answer to that question myself," said Arafiel.

"I believe I now understand the direction of discussion Sandel's spurs are nudging me toward," said Zuriel as his gaze narrowed with suspicion on Sandel. "Scourges. That is what you're hinting at, are you not?"

Sandel simpered at finally hearing the words pass through Zuriel's lips. "Finally! I was beginning to think this line of questioning would require engaging in a game of charades."

"Scourges!" echoed Anahel. "And what, pray tell, do Scourges have to do with what's being debated today?"

"Indulge me, and it will become more than abundantly clear," Sandel commented offhandedly over his shoulder before focusing his renewed attention back onto Zuriel.

"Now then, Zuriel," he said, "imagine those of us present in this room to be a gathering of naive, impressionable students on our first day of learning at the Crescent Scar, and explain to us as succinctly as you can what exactly Scourges are."

Anahel turned to Gotham and the look returned his way was as questioning as his own.

"Simply put, the Scourges are a perverted transmutation of the seven Graces," explained Zuriel. "Whereas the Graces are the divine powers manifested from the seven Virtues inherent in all angels and inherited by their offspring, the Scourges are the corrupted alteration of those Graces. When one of our Fallen brethren releases his hold of the Light in order to embrace the Darkness, so too do his Graces eventually mutate into a cache of powers birthed by the seven Vices or, as they are better known. the seven deadly sins: Envy, gluttony, lust, pride, greed, sloth and wrath."

"And like Graces, are these Scourges passed down through the bloodline?" asked Sandel.

"They are," answered Zuriel while glancing over at Jacob who was appearing more uncomfortable as the questioning continued.

"Help me to understand then, if you will, how the Guides of Havenhid came to believe that not one, but two scions of Fallen came to be born under the beatific starlight announcing the prophesy of the Light Bearer," Sandel questioned pointedly, "when, in fact, a far more rational and realistic origin resided simply in the prestidigitation that comes from the wielding of Scourges residing at one's fingertips."

The notion drew a murmur of whispers to circulate about the room.

"It's not that simple a deduction," Zuriel was quick to respond.

"Not that simple a deduction?" echoed Sandel with a dismissive guffaw. "Please enlighten us with the complexities."

"In the case of Gothamel's son, David, the suspicion of Scourges at play was not even considered."

"And why not, may I ask? Gothamel, at the time, had long been branded a Fallen."

"True," Zuriel conceded. "But he was not your requisite Fallen; that is to say, while he was meted out a punishment that exiled him from Heaven's grounds, he did not betray the Light to wade willingly into the realm of Darkness. And it was because of his unyielding repudiation of those dark things which had ensnared those who had fallen before him that during his banishment he never came to be infected by the seven malefic powers from which the Underneath and all things which inhabit it come to be, and the seven Graces remained alive and intact within him."

Sandel shot a sideways glance at Gotham and his colorless pupils could not conceal the disdain-filled air of judgment they directed at the angel despite the redeemed and scarless presence staring back his way.

"Yes, well...things have most certainly changed," he muttered before quickly shifting his sights to Jacob. "What I'm more interested in at this moment, and the reason we find ourselves gathered here this day, is the boy. Surely you, Zuriel, are knowledgeable enough in your position not to have entertained the blasphemous notion that the spawn of the second most Fallen to be purged from our ranks holds within him a single divine gift of a Grace, much less seven."

Zuriel, for the first time, grew visibly tentative as he shifted with slight discomfort in his seat.

"It's complicated," he grumbled softly after a quiet pause.

"Please, then, enlighten us," Sandel, his eyes all but shaping themselves into shanks of ice, coaxed.

"I wish I could sit here and tell you everything there is to know about Scourges, but the fact of the matter is we know very little about the extent of these powers which mirror our own. There are, however, a couple things I can say regarding the subject with absolute certainty."

"Go on," Sandel, his left eyebrow arching itself higher across his forehead, urged.

"All Nephilim newborns, including those sired by a Fallen, come into the world adorned with untainted Graces," explained Zuriel. "As such, they are given free rein equally in deciding to whom they will pledge their allegiances. Even the offspring of the most nefarious Fallen does not inherit an inescapable fate. The choice is a conscious one, and should one make the decision to shun the Light in favor of the Darkness then whatever Graces they possessed within themselves will go cold like a dying fire, like those of their fathers before them, and in its place will bloom a Scourge."

Try as he might, Jacob could not completely hide the terrifying weight of Zuriel's words as he listened; something of which Sandel instantly and most assuredly took note.

"And how might one conclude whether Graces or Scourges resides within a particular Nephilim?" question Sandel, his penetrating gaze firmly locked on Jacob.

"Scourges, by their very nature, are derived from the core essence that makes up the Darkness, just as the Graces are fragments that create the Light. And while we have come to discover the powers held within some of the known Scourges are similar in nature to several Graces, they each carry with it an unmistakably diabolical mark when exercised," answered Zuriel.

"No doubt, your next question for me will be whether I witnessed any such revelation when I was summoned by Anahel on the night in question to examine which, if any, Graces Mr. Parrish was suspected to unwittingly possess," the angel was quick to add before Sandel was able to address him first.

"And what would your answer be?" pressed Sandel.

"I did not."

The answer drew a most curious expression from Sandel.

"A most lackluster appraisal," the angel noted as he proceeded to slowly step his way toward Zuriel, all while holding him in the grips of his suspicious gaze. "I have left what may be the single most important, and dare I say pertinent question I've yet to ask you this morn: based on what you've witnessed and the attestation you've provided us, can you as the utmost authority on the matter state unequivocally to this body that Mr. Parrish does indeed possess Graces and, more importantly, that you believe him to be the Light Bearer?"

The question, for the first time, caused a noticeable crack in Zuriel's otherwise steely visage as he looked first to Anahel and then Jacob. The room became deathly quiet until, for a moment, it appeared Zuriel might not have heard the question posed to him.

"I cannot," he mumbled in a firm yet lament-laced tone. Zuriel immediately mouthed an apologetic "I'm sorry" to Jacob following his answer that stirred a mumbling of surprise to whirl about the room. Jacob, in return, offered Zuriel as much of a heartening smile as he could. Zuriel's long-lasting aversion to the boy since the moment he stepped foot in Havenhid had only begun to thaw in recent months, and Jacob knew the angel's response was voiced in honesty rather than spite or disdain; and for that, he could not hold resentment toward him.

Sandel, on the other hand, was clearly elated with the damaging two-word answer and, with a most contented look on his face, he ended his questioning of Zuriel and returned to his seat just as Anahel rose from his.

"If I may," he petitioned Aradiel with a gesture to Zuriel who remained seated.

Aradiel offered an accommodating nod, and Anahel turned his attention to Zuriel.

"I have always retained a high admiration for both your knowledge as well as your counsel when it comes to matters that we find ourselves debating today because I know it resides in a well of thoughtfulness and rectitude," Anahel said in an affable voice to which Zuriel returned a nod of appreciation.

"You stated earlier," the angel then continued, "that amongst the relatively few characteristics we know of them, Scourges are the perverted alterations of the Graces derived from the Darkness and, unlike Graces, carry with them, and I quote, 'an unmistakably diabolical mark when exercised.' "

"That is correct," Zuriel replied.

"In your expert opinion, do you think it possible a Nephilim in possession of any of the known Scourges would have the ability to conjure life—life, that is, as we know to be created by our father, not some deviant abomination bred in the Underneath—with a touch of his hands?" Anahel inquired.

"Absolutely not," Zuriel answered steadfastly without so much as a hesitation. "The very nature of the Darkness would make the notion of any power to heal, much less provide a renewed breath of life, completely preposterous."

"And yet you were present the morning following Azrael's visit to Eden when the entirety of Havenhid was not only forced to bear witness to the unsightly discovery of the River struck dead where she once flowed peacefully, but look on with shared amazement as Mr. Parrish here stirred her back to life by laying his hands upon the black surface of its waters and turning them once more blue."

"That I did," Zuriel concurred.

"How then, may I ask, do you account to be a witness of such a thing only to doubt the likelihood that the prophecy of the Light Bearer has visited itself on the boy seated before you?"

The great room held an unwavering silence broken only by the rustling that made itself heard when Zuriel shifted slightly in his chair.

"To the contrary," Zuriel remarked pointedly. "It's the single thing that has kept me from completely disregarding any such possibility."

The statement drew a renewed murmur of whispers and Anahel, shooting Sandel who appeared a tad nettled a content-filled look, said simply: "That is all."

"I should thank you, Anahel," said Sandel, rising from his chair, "for providing the appropriate preamble for my next witness."

~ ~ ~

All heads turned when Sandel gave a subtle nod to two sturdy-looking angels positioned like twin statues of marble on the far edge of the room, who proceeded to open the massive wooden doors over which they were standing guard.

"Who's that?" Jacob whispered to Anahel with instant curiosity at the sight of the towering figure with the unfamiliar face revealed to be patiently waiting on the other side of the entrance.

"I tend to forget you've been away from us for a spell and have still yet to meet your new Guide for Study," Anahel answered in reply. "Vessel came to us shortly after you took your leave for Cain's Corner to fill the vacancy left open by Thaniel's unfortunate departure."

Thaniel's replacement?

Jacob refocused his gaze in even more scrutinizing fashion on the stranger who made his way unhurriedly down the aisle to the awaiting seat positioned in the vacant gulf of space surrounded by the Tribunal. And while it was apparent Vessel belonged to the ranks of angels, judging from his potent stature not to mention manner of dress and movement, he appeared nothing like the angel into whose shoes he had been summoned to place his feet. Suddenly, Jacob found himself confronted with the excruciating pangs of sympathy and sorrow for his friend Thaniel whose fall and banishment from Eden, he had come to learn, was in fact a covert act of self-sacrifice, and in knowing that, Jacob couldn't help but feel a semblance of resentment toward the angel seated before him who now oversaw, whether maliciously or not, everything Thaniel had spent his entire existence curating.

"I'm more than a little curious to get your perspective on what has become a topic of debate, especially from one that some would consider to be amongst the finest minds within our ranks, second only to his now-Fallen predecessor," Sandel noted as he came to stand before both Vessel and the Tribunal.

"Some would—yes," Vessel replied with a cool edge to his voice, noting a touch of offense to Sandel's backhanded flattery

Sandel's cold stare then drifted downward to settle upon Vessel who was drumming his fingers upon the arm of the chair in which he was seated while waiting—and with a growing muster of patience, at that—for the start of the inquiry for which he had been summoned.

"Explain, if you would, what constitutes a soul," instructed Sandel.

The request drew a peculiar expression from Vessel. "Surely, I was not called away from my daily duties to lend forth an explanation of such a rudimentary concept, least of all to this gathering," he said.

Sandel, who had begun to languidly pace the floor, paused momentarily in his steps.

"Please, indulge me. Pretend, if you must, that those of us in this room are no more evolved than that of the stunted defendant seated before you," Sandel implored, while making a dismissive gesture of his hand in the direction of where Jacob was sitting.

Vessel returned Sandel's request with a glare of annoyance as he uncrossed his left leg from his right only to cross his right leg over his left while shifting himself in his chair.

"A soul," Vessel began his explanation, accompanied by a nettlesome sigh, "is the spiritual essence of a living being that resides within the immortal core of a mortal body."

"Of which living beings are you referring?"

"Man. Beasts."

"And rivers?"

71

Vessel shot Sandel a perplexed look with a cock of his head. "Rivers?"

"Rivers. You know, a channel of water?" explained Sandel.

"Yes, I'm quite familiar with the appellation," Vessel noted coolly in the face of the angel's unmistakable air of condescension.

"The defense, here, would lead us to believe, and with a notable amount of gall, that not only does the one River which flows through Eden's Garden harbors and hides within its waters a soul," continued Sandel, "but that this Nephilim has revealed himself a messiah of sorts by resurrecting that which cannot be resurrected in the true sense of the word."

Vessel shifted his gaze toward Jacob and assessed the boy for the first time while remaining expressionless.

"I'm well aware of the intriguing details that have made themselves known from that morn on the banks of the stricken River, yes," replied Vessel.

"And tell me, if you would, how many apparitions of rivers, streams and rills have you brushed shoulders with in our father's realm?"

Vessel responded to the sardonic inquiry with a subtle smile.

"You of all should know it's not exactly an easy task to unravel so complicated and intricately wound ball of yarn," Vessel began to answer. "Souls are a curious and mystifying creation. They each and every one require the domicile of a life form within which to dwell; not all life forms, however, possess a soul."

The answer was like a fish hook that had snagged Sandel's right eyebrow and slowly caused it to draw itself upward across his forehead. "Then you agree the notion of a river having a soul and, therefore, being resurrected is, to put it rather bluntly, ridiculous at best."

"It's quite possible," Vessel concurred much to Sandel's appeasement.

"That said," the angel was quick to add, "we are also not talking about any ordinary river."

Again, Sandel's brow caught the barb of the invisible fish hook. "Meaning?"

"Some would put forth the compelling argument this river—this River of Life—is the portal from which all living things came to be and exists as it does as the womb through which all souls first pass on their journey into the world."

Before Sandel could open his mouth to reply to such a hypothesis, Anahel rose to his feet to make his voice heard.

"I must protest to this entire line of questioning," he stated adamantly. "The argument of whether the River has or has not a soul is irrelevant in every manner, for nowhere in the words of the Apocrypha being debated before this body does it state the Light Bearer prove himself to be so by recreating the divine act of bringing Lazarus back from the dead; only that he reveals himself to wield the unmistakable faculties encompassing the Seventh Grace."

"The words of the Apocrypha reads in part, and I quote: 'He will draw into his very veins every affliction; his right hand will carry the lantern radiating the flame of Life, and his left the scythe of Death.' Have these words been lost to you?" said Sandel.

"Like a precious diamond, there are many facets to the power in question, as you well know," argued Anahel.

"With dominion over life and death being its crowning hallmark, would you not agree?" barked Sandel.

The echo of rising voices dueling one another as the argument grew more heated gave way to a return of quiet when Anahel took a calming breath.

"And what of Azrael?" he asked finally in a more composed tone.

" Azrael?"

"You appear to let slip from your mind that neither myself nor any of the Guides established or oversaw the test put forth in determining the true nature of whether or not Jacob Parrish, indeed, was anointed with such a gift. Rather, it was into Azrael's hands we surrendered such responsibility, though it was not without a helping of wariness on our part," explained Anahel.

Jacob, who remained in his seat quietly listening to the proceedings, couldn't help but shiver slightly at the unwelcoming reminder of Azrael—or, as he was better known, the Angel of Death—and the unpleasant image that suddenly forced its way to the front of his head of the ghoulish-looking angel who descended the heavens atop a black horse into Eden's fair garden and, with a massive scythe gripped by the fingers of his corpse-white hand, fouled the waters of the River with the one thing of which he held plenty in reserve: death.

"Surely, our brother would have no cause to do anyone, much less the boy, any favors by placing at his feet anything less than a challenge that would unequivocally dispel any doubts this matter which has been placed before us," continued Anahel. "Or are you attempting to discredit Azrael's methods as being dubious?"

Sandel appeared at first to ignore the question as he turned abruptly on his heel and returned to his place at the table where he retrieved a scroll from a line of four he had brought with him to the proceedings.

"Isn't it true," Sandel began as he unrolled the scroll and closely scanned the contents of the handwritten notes contained inside, "you first learned of the concomitants of Azrael's visit to Eden when you and Mr. Parrish emerged from Havenhid on the morning in question?"

"That's correct," answered Anahel.

"I can only assume, you were quite bereaved at the sight of discovering the River in such a befouled state."

"I can only hope I am spared from ever witnessing such a sight again."

"And so naturally your first order of business was to direct the boy into the water in the hopes he could pull from somewhere within his sleeves whatever magic elixir you imagined him to possess to remedy this unsightly blight," said Sandel.

Anahel's gaze narrowed itself with suspicion, and rightly so, on his albino inquisitor.

"My first order of business, as you put it, was to oversee that which needed to be overseen," Anahel responded with a measured tongue, "and, in the process, keep the death shroud from being pulled over a vital piece of Eden."

"And yet according to your own account of that seemingly miraculous day both Gothamel and Damiel advised you after surveying the entirety of Eden that Azrael's presence extended well beyond the River's reach," pressed Sandel. "In fact, Death had crept its way over the River's banks and was slowly extending its way across land."

"I'm sure you are inferring something with your line of question; what it might be I have yet to ascertain," said Anahel.

"Did it ever occur to you at any moment that, perhaps, the River was merely a means to disburse the so-called challenge laid down by Azrael, as you put it, and the revelation you were so desperate to lay bare like so many gold nuggets mined from the riverbed resided not in its waters but upon the land where souls are plentiful and varied."

For a moment, Anahel stood silent as it was clear the speculation put forth by Sandel was one he had not considered; neither could he dismiss it outright.

"Whether it be the River or land, the boy proved himself without question before all of Havenhid that he holds within him the ability to hold sway over the stain of death," the angel said finally.

"Did he?" Sandel replied with a lilt of condescension. "Pity such a feat comes marred with a stain of doubt for the rest of us."

Taking note, along with Anahel, that seeds of doubt had most definitely been planted judging from the dubious expressions staring back from around the Tribunal table, Sandel glanced over at Vessel and, with a smug smirk of victory said: "I have no further use of this witness."

~ ~ ~

A murmur of intrigue greeted Sandel's next witness when he was promptly called forth shortly after Vessel's dismissal.

"Did you know anything about this?" Gotham leaned over and whispered to Anahel when Eksel entered the hall and approached the Tribunal.

"No," Anahel replied, in a low tone that failed to camouflage his own surprise, "I did not."

"What is it you suspect Sandel hopes to gather from Eksel for his benefit?"

"Of that, I most certainly haven't a clue," answered Anahel while returning the cordial nod Eksel extended as he passed.

Eksel appeared every bit the vision of the formidable angel dressed in an all-black ensemble made of hard, leather-like material that molded to his powerful body like armor and crackled noticeably as he took his seat in the witness chair.

Without a word, he greeted the members of the Tribunal encircling him with the same amiable gesture he gave Gotham and Anahel by turning first to the left and nodding, then to the right, before looking once again forward and settling his stony-faced gaze on Sandel.

"I wish to first touch upon the day Jacob Parrish was brought by Gothamel to Havenhid unannounced," Sandel said when finally he addressed Eksel. "Would it be fair to say you were angry about the situation?"

"That would be putting it mildly, to say the least," Eksel answered bluntly. "I was incensed. Nor was I the only one, as my other brothers who were present at the time would readily attest."

"And could you explain to us here what about it infuriated you?"

"Do you really have to ask?" Eksel replied with a chortle. "We had a spawn of a Fallen being brought into our midst; not just any Fallen, mind you, but Samael, himself. How could any of us be remiss in forgetting the tragedy that occurred the last time we opened Eden's gate to a marked Nephilim? And while I tried to be a voice of both reason and warning, I was met with deaf ears. It was decreed the boy would stay at Havenhid and be schooled by us Guides. Needless to say, at the time, I found Anahel to be demonstrating a severely gross lapse in judgment by his decision."

Listening to Eksel, Jacob was reminded of the unwelcoming—hostile, even—attitude the angel heaped upon him from the moment he found himself in the crosshairs of his gold-radiating yet steely gaze. He had harbored a hatred for Eksel and his demeaning, unpleasant attitude he was forced to suffer from the angel for so long; a hatred which eventually wilted and reshaped itself into a compassion of understanding when Jacob discovered the hidden truth of his being. Suddenly, he found himself holding sympathy for his tormentor as he himself had come to know intimately a hatred for the son of Samael–for a brief while, at least.

"Was there anything Mr. Parrish came to reveal about himself, or do, to reinforce your initial feelings regarding him?" Sandel continued with his questioning.

"Broken Earth," Eksel replied without so much as a pause of thought. "I have been bringing young Nephilim into their wings and introducing them to the realm of the skies since the Gate was opened to the first Fledgling to pass through it, and recognized immediately when Jacob Parrish stepped foot on that sacred cliff, that he was missing in his core the one thing required in which to rise up from the maw from where the clouds come to rest. And just as I predicted, the boy failed each and every time he attempted the leap and has only recently, long after his fellow Nephilim, sprouted his pinions."

"Forgive me, if I come across as bovine," Anahel spoke up suddenly while rising to his feet, "but what may I inquire do the constraints of a timetable Eksel has obviously tethered to his pupils when it comes to their wings have anything to do with the argument before this body?"

"If you will allow me some leeway; I assure you there is a point," Sandel implored Aradiel who appeared as if he shared in Anahel's interest as well.

While Anahel voiced his displeasure with the line of questioning, Gotham leaned over to whisper into Jacob's ear: "I thought the enmity between Eksel and yourself had been laid to rest."

"So did I," Jacob muttered in return.

Once Anahel returned to his seat with an aggravated huff, Sandel turned once again to Eksel wearing a tight-lipped smile that was anything but friendly.

"Since you brought up Broken Earth, I'd like to revisit the day that saw Gothamel's unfortunate demise; or what was believed to be his demise," Sandel, his cold colorless eyes giving a furtive glance in the angel's direction just off his right shoulder, said. "You stated in your account of the events that occurred there that you had just dismissed your students for the day and had returned to Havenhid when a raven delivered to you a message from Thaniel to meet him at a specific time at Broken Earth."

"That's correct. We all of us received the same message."

"And when the time came for you to meet Thaniel, did you find him to be by himself?"

"No," answered Eksel. "Jacob was present with him."

Sandel cocked his head. "Didn't you find that to be, for lack of a better word, odd?"

The question appeared to catch Eksel slightly off guard. "Not especially. After all, Thaniel had summoned all of Havenhid, both Guides and Fledglings. Not only that, I had come to notice on more than one occasion that the two of them had come to develop a close bond. They spent quite a bit of time talking for great lengths, mostly in the Library long after Study had ended. Jacob was always picking Thaniel's brain about something or other," said Eksel. "It was only when Thaniel shocked us all by revealing the purpose for the gathering that day at Broken Earth that I came to believe something far more nefarious was at hand."

"How so?" Sandel growing noticeably more intrigued pressed.

"The Thaniel who stood before us at Broken Earth that day resembled nothing of the brother I knew. The things he said; what he eventually would come to do; It was as if some unseen evil had come into him and taken possession of his body. I was certain, sure as water is wet, that the boy had finally proven me right by revealing his true colors and had twisted Thaniel's mind like the dark monster I always knew him to be to commit such an unspeakable act," said Eksel, and as he spoke his eyes flared with rage and the tenor of his voice became laced with repugnance at the memory that came rushing back to him.

"By 'the boy,' I presume you to be referring to Jacob Parrish," Sandel, pointing a long, damning white finger at the very seat where Jacob sat with growing discomfort, said.

Eksel said nothing in reply at first, until the nightmarish recollection and the wrath that came with it broke instantly from him like a fever that had run its course.

"Do not misunderstand me," Eksel, suddenly taking notice of Sandel leering down at him like some prowling jungle cat, replied apologetically. "I am simply recounting my state of mind at the time. I do not at the present time hold this notion, nor any of the detestation I once held for the boy; for Jacob Parrish."

The subtle grin of mastery that had unfolded itself upon Sandel's face like a lithe sunbather stretching one's self upon a warm, soft patch of powdery beach slowly faded to the incoming tide of Eksel's clarifying words.

"And what exactly, may I inquire, brought about your profound conversion?"

"I witnessed what he did for Havenhid, and in extension for all of us the night following Gothamel's death. He went out at his own peril into the Silent Forest where he not only cast Thaniel to his deserved fate, but rid Eden of the dark gate that had long existed as a threat to this paradise," answered Eksel. "I cast away the perception I allowed to cloud my vision where the Fledgling was concerned and forced myself to see, instead, the boy who sits before me now in this room and not the contemptible father from whom he came to be."

Jacob couldn't help but feel heartened by Eksel's affecting words, especially when he saw the undeniable sincerity glistening in the angel's eyes. And as the two looked at one another the boy recalled sitting alone in the chapel at Havenhid the night following Gotham's death where Eksel, consumed with grief, offered Jacob an awkward apology, but an apology nonetheless, and the first kind words since his arrival at Eden by saying: "When I'm wrong, I readily admit it."

Sandel, however, was not one for such sentimental moments. "I'm quite curious," he said while directing the uncomfortable points of his gaze upon Eksel like a brandished dagger, "if asked this very moment if you believed Jacob Parrish to be Light Bearer foretold, what would you tell the ears listening intently to your answer?"

"My reply would be: I most certainly do believe it!" Eksel replied without a hint of wavering.

"You are telling this court here and now that you believe this Nephilim to be favored; this son of Samael, by whose hand Heaven has lost yet another of its celestial sons by most assuredly twisting the mind of our dear brother Thaniel to kill Gothamel and then sealing his fate to the eternal horrors of the Underneath by sending him into the deceptive snake pit residing within the Silent Forest?" Sandel's voiced roared with the authority of a church preacher spewing fire and brimstone to his congregation during Sunday services. "You would actually come to believe this serpent wearing the cloak of a boy has come to hold within himself the power of the seventh Grace and the divine anointment that comes with it?"

Sandel had barely spit out the last of his words and the bile that came with it when Anahel, unable to listen anymore, leapt to his feet.

"I most fervently protest the malicious calumny that has just been voiced before this court," Anahel argued with vigor equal to Sandel's. "The witness made it more than clear in his testimony the perception he had that Jacob was twisting Thaniel's mind was just that, and a false one at that. Now, your duplicitous inquisitor puts it forth as a maligning statement of fact, as though this Tribunal has already overseen such a trial which came to conclude the boy to be guilty of such a crime."

Before Aradiel could respond, Sandel cupped his hands before him and, with a contrite smile, said simply: "I withdraw my remarks."

As he turned to retire to his seat, apparently finished with his questioning, Sandel paused in his steps and slowly returned his focus to Eksel.

"One more question, if I may," he said, to which Eksel sank back into the witness chair. "The night of the unsanctioned Blessing at Havenhid I attempted to dictate that the Sword of Destiny be placed in my possession until the dispute over the matter of the Apocrypha had been settled. Do you recall what Mr. Parrish's response was to me?"

Eksel sat silent for a moment as he thought back to the moment in question.

"I believe he said you could have it," Eksel answered finally. "All you had to do was come and take it from his hand."

"That is correct," Sandel grumbled sourly as he himself darkened visibly at the recollection. "And what do you suspect would have occurred had I done just as he instructed?"

"There's no suspecting to be had. You'd have perished, instantly, and wholly," Eksel declared in no uncertain terms, and only after he had spoken did he realize the gravity of what he had said.

"An overt threat of annihilation directed at a heavenly host, and by the son of Samael no less," Sandel uttered with a quiet disgruntlement simmering inside him.

"In light of all that has occurred in these past few months and the testimony you have provided today, I would argue it is you, Eksel, who has shown himself to be demonstrating a severely gross lapse in judgment, and dare I say faithfulness."

The assessment took Eksel aback, but before he could open his mouth to respond Sandel turned away from him abruptly while announcing in a most dismissive tone: "I am through with this witness."

It was then Anahel came to realize Sandel's endgame wasn't just to prove false the idea the ancient Apocrypha had resurrected itself in Jacob Parrish, but to completely blacken the boy's entire existence.

CHAPTER FIVE

A GAME OF SLANDER

Jacob was all too eager to bolt from the grand room where the hearing was being held when Aradiel called for a recess following Eksel's testimony. His feet led him along several unfamiliar corridors and then, much to his relief, through an archway leading outside into the tranquil embrace of a spacious yet quaint courtyard.

Once he had allowed himself a deep and much-needed breath of the fresh air, he opened his eyes and was at once taken by the beauty into which he had stepped. It may well have been the most beautiful courtyard he had ever laid eyes upon, Jacob quickly surmised. Towering pillars carved from the white rock of the mountain which formed the architecture of the rest of Halcyon surrounded him as well as paved the ground upon which he stood. They gleamed brightly like crystal in the sunlight and were made all the more beautiful by the bursts of color coming from the blossoms of the flowering emerald vines entwined around each of the columns like strings of jewelry crafted by nature itself. Several Japanese magnolia trees provided shade with their smooth, bleached, outstretched branches adorned with large budding flowers whose radiant shades of pink and purple were not only dazzling to the eyes but enticed any visitor to turn their nose higher to breathe more deeply the air which they perfumed with their sweet, inviting fragrance.

More than the splendor of the lush grounds or the bouquet of the redolent blossoms, however, it was the lulling trickle of water coming from an ornate three-tier fountain sprouting from the center of a large, rectangular-shaped pond, also carved from the same white rock of the mountain in which Jacob found solace. The gentle thrum cast an invisible blanket of tranquility across every inch of the courtyard and was able to drown out even the maddening echoes of the day's depositions that had followed Jacob out of the hearing room.

Much to Jacob's chagrin, the peaceful respite was soon broken by the sound of approaching footsteps.

"The way you tore out of the hearing just now, I almost expected to discover you be halfway to the Gate in a mad dash to get back to Cain's Corner," came Gotham's voice, though Jacob already knew without so much as a glance it was the angel who stood behind him.

"Not a bad idea," Jacob grumbled tepidly at having his quiet moment alone suspended sooner than he would have expected. "Matter of fact, I was just standing here wondering what possessed me to agree to come back to this place."

The percolating fountain kept the courtyard from falling completely silent as Gotham took several slow and pensive steps forward until he was standing beside the boy.

"Quite beautiful, isn't it?" the angel remarked while sharing in the lush scenery. "Would you believe me if I were tell you it wasn't always so. In fact, earlier when Sandel was questioning Vessel on whether a soul resides within the River, I couldn't help but recall a time when this very spot was barren of any life. Looked quite similar to what you'd imagine a dry dusty rock quarry to be, if you can imagine it."

"If it's alright with you, I just want to have a moment alone to clear my head," Jacob groused, as the last thing he was interested in at that moment was a schooling in Halcyon's history.

"Spectacular as Halcyon was when its facade emerged from the white stone of the mountain from which it came, it was Dalquiel's desire this inapposite corner of his dwelling mirror the heavenliness of the Garden surrounding Havenhid," Gotham, seemingly paying no mind to Jacob's gripe, continued. "And so he set forth to construct this courtyard, starting, first, with the pillars, then the pool and elaborate stonework paving the ground around it, and, finally, the creation of the fountain itself. When it was finished, the courtyard, while striking with its embellishments, was just as lifeless as before Dalquiel began his labor of love. And so one day he made his way to the River with a silver chalice in hand which he used to retrieve a cup of water and returned with it to the courtyard. He emptied the chalice into the top tier of the fountain, and he waited.

"Almost immediately, there was heard the unmistakable sound of the breath of life taking its first gasps as the cup of water poured into the fountain by Dalquiel was seen to slowly fill the remaining top portion of the fountain. Soon, the water began to spill over the sides in a decorative veil and proceed to fill the middle tier until that, too, overflowed and started to pour into the bottom basin, and from there into the pool. It took a day and a night, and when Dalquiel finally returned to the courtyard the following morning even he who was used to such unfathomable splendor was left speechless where he stood at the sight of the vast, lush landscape of orchids, birds of paradise, bromeliads, bougainvillea, passion vines, to name a tiny few, that had sprouted overnight to create this heavenly oasis we find ourselves imbibing this moment."

"No doubt there's a point to this," Jacob responded with a huff of impatience.

"I've been watching you during this hearing," said Gotham, turning to face the boy. "The testimony so far has slowly been pressing its weight into you; of that I'm not surprised. Sandel has proven himself quite proficient in sowing seeds of doubt where they need to be planted."

"You think he's convincing the members of the Tribunal I'm everything he's suggesting I am? A fake?" Jacob asked with a touch of worry in his voice.

"It's not the Tribunal I'm worried about; it's you," replied Gotham.

"Me?"

"Sandel knows to his core—just as Dalquiel did when he walked to its banks with a chalice in hand—that the river which flows through Eden—the River of Life—does so with an indubitable, if not visible, heart from which beats forth the germ of creation. He knows when you resuscitated the River from the black shroud Azrael laid across its waters you proved yourself to possess the one Grace that only the one to be known as the Light Bearer could hold in the palms of his hands, and so he made it a point to argue the River was just a river, just as you are nothing more than an average Nephilim. Only his aim was not to convince the Tribunal, but yourself; for if he is successful in solidifying such uncertainty in you, then most assuredly you would reflect it in spades to the members of the Tribunal who are quite easily swayed by such cues."

The words at first appeared to trouble Jacob who turned away from the angel and walked a few steps to the edge of the pond.

"I admit I was beginning to second-guess whether what happened that morning at the River really proved anything or if maybe, like Sandel said, we failed to recognize Azrael's real test," said Jacob. "But if you want to know the truth, what really proved upsetting to me was when Eksel spoke about that day at Broken Earth when you died, or supposedly died, and he testified how he thought everything that happened was my doing; that I had somehow twisted Thaniel's mind into becoming a murderous traitor."

Even though the boy's back was turned to him, Gotham couldn't ignore the tremble of emotion in Jacob's voice as he spoke.

"Eksel didn't know you at the time, nor did he wish to," Gotham offered with a sympathetic tone.

"No, he didn't. But you did," Jacob blurted as he spun around once more to face Gotham who at first appeared taken aback by the charge.

"When did I ever—?"

"The night you caught me in the Silent Forest and told me the truth about who Lilith was and the Through Thaniel tricked me into believing led to another Heaven," Jacob continued before Gotham could finish his question. "I can understand Eksel's feelings toward me then. But you spent weeks training me; I looked up to you as the closest thing to a father I've ever known; I told you things about myself I've never shared with anyone before; and still your first instinct when you caught me speaking with Lilith was to assume I was conspiring with her to do harm upon Eden. How do I even begin to convince nine total strangers, not to mention myself, that I'm this...anointed one, when the person I'm most closest to once believed me to be the offensive portrait Sandel's attempting to paint?"

Gotham offered a contrite nod of understanding.

"You're quite right; but only partially," Gotham readily conceded. "It's true when I came upon the terrifying sight of you standing at the edge of the Through with your hand held out to Lilith my initial thought was one too horrible to voice aloud, even now. What you need to take away from this moment we find ourselves sharing is my admission that it was a mistake, and a fleeting one at that. More importantly, you must know I never would have bequeathed into your hands the most powerful weapon known to man or angel as I took my final breaths at Broken Earth if I didn't believe you to be of the stock worthy of such a gift of consequence."

"You did do that, didn't you?" Jacob muttered quietly, almost shamefully, as though it were the first time he fully considered the magnitude of that horrible yet fateful moment the two had shared.

"Nor am I alone in my judgment, as Eksel, being amongst them, has proven," said Gotham. Then, as he was prone to do whenever a moment became too entwined with sentiment, the corner of his mouth curled upward and he remarked in jest: "Though I dare say, I wouldn't hold your breath that Sandel will be joining your fan club anytime soon."

The comment drew a faint smile from Jacob, but only momentarily.

"He really has it out for me, doesn't he?" the boy asked. "Why does he dislike me so much?"

"Because he refuses to see you past the image he holds of you in his mind," answered Gotham. "I trust, like Eksel, the fog clouding his vision will one day pass. Until that time, get used to him being a particularly intolerable thorn imbedded in your side."

Gotham knew his words offered little, if any comfort to the boy. He also knew the days of treating him with kid gloves had come to an end.

"You pondered aloud just a little while ago why you had agreed to come back to Eden," Gotham, his piercing golden gaze penetrating deeply into Jacob's, said. "I think you already know the answer to that question. Because you had to; because you knew you had to confront this face to face no matter how unpleasant it might be."

There was something reassuring in the angel's words and how he spoke them that returned to Jacob his waning composure as he nodded with understanding just as Anahel's voice was heard to call out to them.

"Come, come; the Tribunal is reconvening," he announced.

Giving Jacob a supportive clasp to the shoulder, Gotham escorted the boy to where Anahel stood waiting near the entrance to the corridor leading the way inside.

"Everything okay?" Anahel, looking first to Jacob then to Gotham, asked.

"Just enjoying a bit of fresh air," Gotham replied.

"Has Johiel shown up yet?" Jacob asked suddenly before the three made their way back.

"Johiel?" replied Anahel.

"I haven't seen him at the hearing today," said Jacob.

If there was one thing that helped hold Jacob's composure together in the tense moments during the proceedings, it was the sight of Johiel sitting a few feet away with the rest of the observers and always at the ready with a reassuring wink or convivial smile. This day, however, he glanced over to find the usual chair where Johiel had sat since the beginning of the hearing empty.

"I wonder where he could be," Jacob muttered to himself.

"Perhaps he was delayed by something in need of his attention at Akdamar Island," said Gotham.

Whatever it was, Jacob knew it would have to of been something far more important than serving as an elderly docent to tourists visiting the ancient Turkish church Johiel called home just outside the Gate to Eden.

~ ~ ~

No matter the misgivings with which Jacob found himself plagued, nothing could have instantly straightened his back with resolve more than the sight of Creed Maggert when the proceedings resumed and Sandel called forth his next witness.

Dressed in a pastel-colored polo shirt, khakis and loafers with tassels, Creed looked more like a privileged student enrolled in a New England prep school than a Nephilim in training at Havenhid as he took a seat in the center of the room before the Tribunal. He gave not so much as a glance in Jacob's direction; Jacob, on the other hand, all but bore a hole straight through his rival in anticipation of his testimony.

"Your relationship with Mr. Parrish," Sandel addressed Creed with his first question, "how would you describe it?"

"Cordial," Creed answered. "That is, I do my best to keep things cordial."

Oh brother! Not even out of the gate and already he's lying, thought Jacob while exhaling a sigh of disbelief.

"By your answer, one would assume you to be implying your experience with Mr. Parrish to be less than friendly."

"That would be a polite way of putting it considering the unprovoked physical attacks I've endured from him on numerous occasions," answered Creed.

Sandel pivoted on his heel to face where Jacob sat between Anahel and Gotham to level a condemnatory glare with his icy white pupils on the boy, and it was then that Jacob took notice of how much father and son looked like one another down to Sandel's albino white hair, a striking trait which had gradually, and thoroughly, begun bleaching away the chestnut tint to Creed's thick locks as though he had been stricken with a freakish malady similar to male pattern baldness.

"And of what reason would Mr. Parrish have to lay even a finger upon you?" Sandel asked cooly, though to Jacob it felt, especially with Sandel's steely glare firmly fixed on him, that the question had been directed at him.

Beats me," Creed answered with a shrug, before adding in a put-on sheepish manner: "But, honestly, if I were to wager a guess—and, frankly, I'm almost too embarrassed to say it out loud—I'd say he harbors a deep resentment of me that stems mostly from...well, jealousy."

Had Jacob been taking a sip of his water at that very moment, he most certainly would have found it impossible to keep from choking and sending it spraying forth from out of his mouth (and very possibly his nose as well). He could not, however, keep quiet the chortle that escaped him upon hearing Creed's outlandish boast.

Ignoring Jacob's dismissive snort, Creed proceeded to prove his assertion by recounting for all who were listening the day he and the rest of his Nephilim classmates at Havenhid were summoned to Lions Bite where they were presented with their swords. Specifically, he recalled how Damiel called forth both him and Jacob to try out their newfound weapons, and with them the fighting skills they had so far honed under the angel's instruction, in a friendly match against one another. Only, in Creed's telling (or rather retelling) of events, it was Jacob who was painted as the underhanded competitor who resorted to an aggressive onslaught of dirty, unsportsmanlike tactics which Jacob instantly recognized as a grossly blatant distortion of what had actually taken place.

"He's lying!" Jacob grumbled under his breath to Anahel as he struggled mightily to contain his composure and keep himself planted in his chair.

Such restraint proved increasingly difficult the more Jacob was forced to listen to Creed continue in his shameful perjury; especially when the topic turned to the prestigious hunt for the Illume competition that Jacob, Creed and three other top Nephilim competitors won a spot to face off against one another during Illumination.

As Creed told it, and rather believably so, he was in pursuit of the mythical and elusive Illume—a deceptively beautiful bird who ventures out of hiding during a narrow sliver of time once a year in search of a mate—and was just about to capture the creature and emerge as the victor in the coveted contest when, out of nowhere, Jacob pounced upon him in a particularly nasty and unprovoked attack.

"Attack? He was the one on the attack. I was trying to protect the Illume," Jacob voiced to both Anahel and Gotham with increased irritation to which Anahel gave the boy's leg a tightening squeeze in an effort to quiet him.

"You have stated Mr. Parrish proceeded to threaten you, strike you, and on more than one instance throw you bodily against the trunk of several trees," Sandel made note, as he continued his slow walk back and forth before his son and the Tribunal. "Can you relay to the court what would warrant such a feral attack?"

Creed shook his head slowly, masterfully feigning the meek and defeated look one would spy in the face of an assault victim still shaken by the traumatic experience.

"At first I assumed it was because he saw I was on the cusp of winning the contest, and I knew he wouldn't stand for such a thing. But, if I were to be completely truthful with this court, I feel a responsibility to confess that I may have had a hand in what happened; at least partly," admitted Creed.

"Are you saying it was you who instigated the fight between yourself and Mr. Parrish?" asked Sandel.

"Heavens no; I have no beef with Jacob, not now, not then," Creed lied with aplomb. "Truth of the matter is I've tried on more than one occasion to extend my hand to him in friendship but for whatever reason he refused to take it. You see, I recognized the difficulty he faced at Havenhid being the only son of a Fallen amongst the rest of us Nephilim who are not disgraced. The sad truth is some kids can be so cruel. All I wanted to try and do was embrace him and help him to not feel like the outsider he is, and in doing so, well, I may have spoken out of turn."

"What do you mean speak out of turn?" nudged Sandel.

Jacob narrowed his glare on Creed as he waited for the next breath of fibs to make its way through his teeth.

"That day Jacob attacked me in the forest during the hunt I could see he was angry, even more so than usual; and I knew why," continued Creed. "It had to be difficult not knowing who his father was, especially on a day when all of our fathers had come to Havenhid to celebrate with us the start of Illumination. For the life of me I couldn't understand why Gotham, Anahel and the rest of the Guides purposely kept the truth from Jacob. I thought it was cruel; unusually so, and I couldn't stomach watching him continue to suffer over the not knowing. So in the middle of him pummeling me in the forest I decided to reveal the secret to him thinking— rather, hoping–it would bring him some much-needed peace, or at the very least calm him enough so his fists would cease delivering blows to my face. But it only made him madder."

Jacob had finally heard enough. "That's the biggest load of garbage I've ever heard in my life!" he spat while rising halfway out of his seat.

Aradiel promptly, and quite boisterously, called for order, and Anahel did his best to try and comply.

"Sit yourself down!" he huffed while struggling to pull the boy back to his chair.

"Are you going to let him get away with lying like this?" cried Jacob, before looking to the members of the Tribunal. "You all have the power to go back in time. Why don't you go now and see for yourself what really happened and who attacked who."

"If you can't control the boy, I will be left with no alternative than to have him removed from these proceedings," Aradiel directed the terse to Anahel.

Mad as he was, Jacob was somewhat surprised by the unexpected demonstration of strength Anahel revealed when the grip he had on his leg suddenly tightened and with a firm yank planted the boy back in his chair.

"I think that just about covers it," Sandel remarked aloud with a grin of satisfaction before turning his attention to the Tribunal. "I have no further questions."

As Sandel turned on his heel to make his way to his seat, Anahel took a calming breath and rose from his.

"I must say, I found your testimony to be quite...eye-opening. In all the time you've been at Havenhid, I was unaware of the depths of your regard for Mr. Parrish," Anahel addressed Creed in that calm and soothing way of his that made everyone who knew him question whether or not he was being facetious. "As a matter of fact, it makes me think back to another thuggish altercation that took place between the two of you one morning not so long ago in the Hall of Light when it was made known that Mr. Parrish's journal had somehow come into your possession."

Anyone who was looking closely enough would have noticed Anahel's broach of the incident caused Creed's Adam's apple to bob ever so slightly.

"Tell me, Mr. Maggert, where did your reserve of sympathy for your classmate for whom you voiced the desire to extend the hand of friendship just a few minutes ago when you purposefully, and might I add quite cruelly, not only read aloud to everyone within earshot who was gathered in the Hall Mr. Parrish's personal and private thoughts from his journal, but then proceeded to mock the circumstances surrounding the death of his mother?" Anahel asked pointedly.

Creed sat quietly for a moment or two staring ahead with a cold and unaffected look.

"I haven't the faintest idea of what you're talking about," he said finally.

"I have nearly a dozen boys I questioned at random shortly after who witnessed firsthand the unfortunate spectacle who I am sure could refresh your memory," Anahel shot back measuredly without missing a beat.

"I take exception with this entire line of questioning," Sandel, rising to his feet, barked in protest. "My son's action in relation to some journal, inappropriate or not, is not being weighed by this body."

Before Anahel could argue the matter, Creed's voice once more made itself heard.

"Suppose I did what it is you're trying to accuse me of, I doubt anyone in this room would find any fault in it; not after the underhanded shenanigans I observed Jacob taking part in," he blurted.

"And what underhanded shenanigans would those be?" questioned Anahel.

"There was one night when I couldn't sleep. I happened to be looking out of my window and out of the corner of my eye I caught something running through the darkness across the ground below. When I took a closer look I could see it was Jacob. 'What was he doing out in the Garden in the middle of the night?' I wondered to myself. That's when I realized, when I recognized the direction he was going, he was headed for the Silent Forest."

"The Silent Forest," echoed Anahel. "You saw Mr. Parrish go into the Silent Forest."

"No, I didn't actually see him go into it, but there are only two things in that corner of the Garden: the Silent Forest and Lions Bite. I hardly expected him to have a dueling match with himself at Lions Bite in the middle of the night. Where else would he be going knowing his history with the place?" answered Creed. "And then shortly afterwards that same night I spied Thaniel dressed in a dark cloak headed in the same direction."

"Didn't you have any inclination to follow either one of them to see if what you suspected was actually true?"

"Hardly! You've told us many times entering the Silent Forest is strictly forbidden, and my father instilled in me the importance of adhering to rules," Creed noted while looking dutifully to his father who replied to his son with a proud nod of approval.

It was all Anahel could do to keep his eyeballs from rolling in their sockets.

"Then your inference that some clandestine conspiratorial act was afoot is nothing but a theory, is it not?" asked Anahel.

"It's not a theory when I witnessed it with my own eyes," Creed argued defiantly.

"You just got through saying you didn't see either Jacob or Thaniel enter the Silent Forest.

"I didn't. It's what I saw later," said Creed. "The night before the start of Illumination I was passing the Library when I heard whispering. I peeked inside to see who it was coming from and found Jacob and Thaniel huddled at a table engaged in a deep conversation. I didn't think anything about it at first; Jacob was always in Thaniel's ear. I just chalked it up to him being the brown-noser I believed him to be."

"It would hardly be a strange sight to see the two of them conversing, particularly in the Library. Thaniel was Mr. Parrish's teacher, after all, and I happen to know he was quite fond of the boy," said Anahel. "For all you know, Jacob could have been seeking help from Thaniel over a recent lesson."

It appeared Anahel had finished his cross-questioning of Creed and was about to return to his seat when Creed again spoke.

"I couldn't hear exactly what it was they talking about, but there was one bit of their conversation I heard clearly: it had to do with the Spear of Destiny," he said.

The mention of the spear froze Anahel instantly in his place.

"I didn't think much about it until the night after Thaniel summoned the Guides and the rest of us that day to Broken Earth," Creed mentioned ominously.

The great room became silent as a tomb, as if the grenade Creed had just detonated had incinerated all existence of sound.

"Did you say you heard them conversing about the Spear of Destiny?" one of the members of the Tribunal named Basquel inquired, and it was clear by the tense expressions fixed upon the faces of his colleagues that he was not alone in his suspicions. "Are you certain of that?"

"Beyond certain," Creed replied.

"And what about the Spear of Destiny were they conversing about?"

"Beats me. I'm not in the habit of eavesdropping on private conversations," Creed replied virtuously, before noting, "Strange kind of a coincidence, isn't it, considering what ended up happening to Gotham at the edge of that cliff that day? I can't help but replay what Eksel said earlier when he was sitting up here about what ran through his mind seeing Thaniel and Jacob together on the top of that mountain. What if? When you think about it that way, a part of me wishes I wasn't always so mindful of trying to do what is right and listened in on that conversation. At least then, maybe I could have sounded the alarm on what was coming."

Anahel looked suddenly as if he had been struck by something that had stolen the wind from him, and in a quiet voice announced he had no further questions.

Creed, looking noticeably refreshed, as though he had just had his face spritzed with a cool spray of water on a sultry summer's day, got to his feet and for the first and only time since taking the witness seat he looked directly at Jacob. When Creed saw the hate-filled eyes glaring back his way, he smiled; the most content-filled and self-satisfied of smiles Jacob had ever had the displeasure of seeing.

~ ~ ~

Insufferable as Creed and his slanderous testimony was, the hearing became even more unbearable to Jacob when Sandel proceeded to call forth his four closest friends.

One by one Leos, Kairo, Ethan and Max were summoned into the great room before the Tribunal where they were instructed to take a seat in the intimidating witness chair. They each appeared to be wrestling with various degrees of discomfort, especially when they found themselves in the crosshairs of Sandel's penetrative icy pupils when he stepped forward to begin his interrogation of them.

He grilled each of the boys in roughly the same manner, peppering each with a list of questions centered around the course of events which took place inside the Silent Forest following Thaniel's betrayal at Broken Earth. Specifically, Sandel was most curious about the moments leading up to Thaniel's horrific fall into the watery Through. As each boy shared their nearly identical telling of Thaniel's end as they witnessed it, Jacob couldn't keep the memory of that fateful night from resurrecting itself right before his very eyes as he sat listening.

He could still feel the dampness of his rain-soaked clothes hanging heavy on his body and the trickle of water dribbling down the blade of his drawn sword and across his hand gripping its hilt for dear life as he stood in a battle stance against Thaniel. Nor could he forget the chill that ran through him when his ears caught the familiar howl of a wolf hidden somewhere amongst the night shadows of the surrounding forest trees.

"So...the beasts have decided to turn on their master," Jacob recalled Thaniel uttering scornfully when a wolf with a mane black as pitch stepped forward into the light while the numerous reflective gazes of the rest of the pack could be seen peering out from darkness all around them. Thaniel turned his sword in the direction of the black wolf hunched low to the ground and said threateningly: "I shall start with you, then."

Then, as he started to come at the wolf with his sword, a white blur burst through the trees and to Jacob's surprise—and horror—he saw it was his faithful companion Mist. It all happened in an instant: a bright flash from Thaniel's blade as Mist pounced upon the angel and caused him to stumble backward into the forbidden waters of the pool from which there was no escape from the clawing hands of the demonic creatures called Feeders lying in wait for the smallest of missteps and swiftly pulled him under to the hidden horrors residing beneath the inky surface.

"What happened after Thaniel disappeared into the Through?" asked Sandel.

"We celebrated," answered Kairo when asked the question.

"We realized the threat Thaniel held over Havenhid and Eden was over," came Leos' reply when it came his turn in the witness chair.

"But then Max called all of our attention to this white shape lying on the ground surrounded by the black wolf and the rest of the pack," Ethan, who appeared the most tense testifying before the Tribunal, noted dolefully. "That's when we realized Mist had been badly wounded by Thaniel's sword before he fell into the pool."

"Tell us, if you would, what occurred then," pressed Sandel.

"Jacob ran to Mist's side. He was beside himself; he loves that wolf," Leos replied.

"We all knew right away what he intended to do," said Kairo.

"Which was?" asked Sandel.

"Heal Mist, of course," said Kairo. "He said something to the effect of, 'I refuse to let anything take you...I'm going to make you good as new, I promise!' "

"And?"

"Max tried to stop him," said Leos.

The answer appeared at first to catch Sandel off guard, "But for what reason would he do that?" questioned the angel. "Here was his beloved companion sprawled on the ground with its life slowly draining away before his very eyes. For what reason would his best friend attempt to stop him from using whatever supposed power he had to save this brave creature?"

"Because of the rules," Ethan explained meekly, and appearing quite conflicted in doing so. "It's forbidden to turn the tide of history, especially when it concerns death."

"I see," Sandel remarked, as if it was the first time such an edict met his ears. "And what was Mr. Parrish's response to his friend's reminder of such a rule?"

All three boys sat hesitant to answer the question until pressed further.

" 'Screw the rules!' " they finally each answered much to Sandel's gratification.

Jacob looked first to Gotham and then to Anahel and was confused to see the same sullen shadow clouding each of their expressions. After all, the whole point of the hearing was to determine whether or not he was indeed this entity known as the Light Bearer; and what better way to prove such a farcical idea than the indisputable claim of what happened the night in question in the Silent Forest when he placed his hand on the mortally wounded wolf and before the eyes of everyone present made the creature take a renewed breath and rise up from off the ground and stand good as new upon her feet?

It was only when Max was called forward to testify that Jacob finally clued in to that of which both Gotham and Anahel were already quite aware: Sandel wasn't interested in disproving whether or not Jacob possessed the one Grace unobtainable to Nephilim, but to paint a portrait of an insurrectionary boy for the members of the Tribunal as being unworthy of such a divine anointment. In short, it was a blatant attempt at character assassination.

"You recently were found to be truant from Havenhid when you finagled for yourself an opportunity to sneak away from the supervision of the Guides outside Eden's gate and traipse halfway around the world to a place called Cain's Corner to where Mr. Parrish had run away without permission some days earlier," Sandel addressed Max. "Can you explain to us the reason behind your decision?"

"Because he's my mate," Max answered matter-of-factly with his thick Australian accent "I also wanted to explain to him what a boofhead he was being, and try to convince him to come back to Havenhid."

For a minute, it looked as if Sandel had taken a shot to the noggin with a baseball. "Boofhead?"

"Yeah, boofhead. You know, an idiot."

With an exasperated roll of his eyes, Sandel continued: "For what reason would Mr. Parrish need cajoling to return to Havenhid. For that matter, why did he choose to run away in the first place?"

"You're yanking me, right?" Max replied with a snide snigger. "Look what we're doing here. Would you want to stick around for this witch hunt?"

The angel shot the boy a disquieting look and Max smartly reeled himself in somewhat. Sandel then asked Max about the day he accompanied Jacob and two of his mortal friends–Wray Bliss and Ty Wrenwood–to a place called Penuel Point. More specifically, he inquired about a near fatal accident that occurred when Jacob and Ty partook in one of their favorite outdoor activities: BASE jumping from a ledge at the top of the mountain.

Max recalled instantly that which Sandel was referring.

"I decided to stay with Wray whose job was to monitor the jump from her Jeep at the bottom of the mountain and then race over to pick up Jacob and Ty as quickly as possible before the rangers got to them, seeing as their little thrill-seeking activity was illegal inside the park," said Max. "Personally, I think you have to have a few loose kangaroos in the top paddock to go leaping off a perfectly good cliff with anything short of a good strong pair of wings soldered to your back. And Jacob's mate Ty sure proved that when he made his jump and Wray and I watched in horror when he pulled his ripcord and released a chute that was all tangled up in a useless ball. We thought for sure he had seen his end in a most gruesome manner, but never fear. Good 'ol Jacob who was watching the entire mishap from the safety of his own deployed chute had flown into action and rescued Ty from certain death at the very last second when Ty slipped out of our sight behind the tree line at the base of the mountain. When

Wray and I finally reached the spot, we found Jacob helping Ty out of the wooded area and into the clearing looking a bit dazed and confused, but with all limbs and bones in one piece."

"Heroic, indeed," Sandel muttered indifferently. "But it would seem you left out a crucial part of the story. That is, the reason for Mr. Parrish's friend's noticeably dazed state."

Max suddenly appeared to grow noticeably uncomfortable in his seat.

"Come now, Mr. Kelly," urged Sandel, "it was certainly important enough for you to address your 'mate' about it later that evening once you had a moment alone with him."

Max grew visibly uncharacteristically more uneasy and glanced anxiously in the direction of where Jacob sat when Sandel vociferously reminded him of the oath he had taken to recount the truth.

"Like I said, Jacob saved his friend from certain death," Max began finally. "Problem was in the process he also ended up revealing the one big secret he had purposefully kept hidden from Ty. I can only imagine Ty's reaction to seeing his best friend standing over him with a pair of giant wings growing out of his back."

"And how did Mr. Parrish handle it?" asked Sandel.

"I assumed he used his resources to help Ty temporarily forget what had happened."

"You're speaking of Mr. Parrish's ability to utilize the Grace of Bending which he possesses, I assume," said Sandel, to which Max nodded.

"And did that prove to be the case?"

Again Max hesitated to answer and looked to Jacob who gave his friend as encouraging a smile as he could muster and assured him in a voice that only Max could hear: *'It's okay. Don't lie on my account. Go ahead and tell him what happened.'*

"I repeat," barked Sandel, "did that prove to be the case?"

"No. Not completely, that is," Max confessed softly when finally he answered. "He told me he didn't so much bind Ty's memory as scrub it permanently clean."

"And what was your response to learning what he had done?"

"I reminded him that he wasn't allowed to do that."

"Can you expound on your answer?" pressed Sandel.

"One of the first things Zuriel makes a point of teaching us at the

Crescent Scar is what we can and cannot do with our Graces," Max explained with a disheartening sigh. "When it comes to Bending, we're not allowed to permanently erase or alter another person's memories or thoughts. To do so would violate the golden rule forbidding us to knowingly tamper with the course of human history."

"I see," Sandel remarked with a slight curl visible on his lips. "And at the time of this incident was Mr. Parrish cognizant of what inarguably is a very important dictate to which all Nephilim must adhere?"

"He told me he panicked," Max muttered, "But, yes, he knew."

Sandel stood looking quite gratified as a flurry of whispers were traded both amongst the members of the Tribunal as well as the spectators who were observing the proceedings. And Max, who looked about as forlorn as a person could be, glanced again to his friend whom he felt he had done nothing less than betray simply mouthed: "I'm sorry!"

However, before Jacob could answer with a nod of encouragement, the familiar creak from one of the twin giant arched doors swinging open was heard to reveal the sight of Johiel. He moved with hurried urgent steps to where Sandel remained standing and, apologizing for the abrupt interruption, requested permission from Aradiel to approach his seat in order to deliver news of an extremely urgent matter to which Aradiel motioned him forward in reply.

Whatever the news Johiel was delivering, it appeared to be of vital importance and brought an unsettlingly grave expression to Aradiel's face when it was whispered into his ear.

"The witness is excused," Aradiel suddenly announced, much to Max's relief, followed by a directive to Sandel that he retire to his seat for the time being. Then to Johiel, Aradiel instructed: "Show him in."

Turning on his heel, Johiel paused before making his way back to the doors through which he entered and locked eyes with Jacob, and in that moment Jacob was filled with an inexplicable sense of dread when not so much as a hint of the familiar smile that usually greeted him was seen on the angel's face.

"What's going on?" Jacob wondered aloud when Johiel finally hurried on his way.

"I'm sure I have no idea," Anahel answered with the same tone of confusion as the boy's.

When the arched doors were finally opened again by the two guards standing dutifully at their posts there was heard a collective gasp throughout the room.

"It's Thaniel!" Jacob exclaimed at the unexpected sight of the now-Fallen angel seen at Johiel's side.

So surprising was it to see the angel who had served as architect of Havenhid before becoming one of its most influential teachers that Jacob failed to pay much mind to the stranger accompanying Johiel and Thaniel as they made their way towards the grand U-shaped table where the members of the Tribunal were seated and looking equally as stunned as Jacob. It was only as they walked closer that Jacob finally took notice of the stranger, and the stranger likewise took notice of him in return. Immediately, Jacob recognized something oddly familiar about the man—particularly around the striking eyes that were staring back at him—though he was certain he had never before crossed paths with him.

"Who is that with them?" he asked both Anahel and Gotham.

"You had best brace yourself," Gotham replied in what sounded like, and was intended to be, a dire warning. "It's your father; it's Samael."

CHAPTER SIX

The heavy and ominous silence that instantly settled itself upon the room was broken only by the echo of footsteps upon the glassy marble floor as Johiel escorted the two unexpected guests to stand before the Tribunal. Jacob sat frozen in his seat, looking on with mixture of horror and intrigue deep-set within his unblinking eyes. Aside from the nightmares that stalked him growing up, and the brief moment the Through inside the Silent Forest presented itself as a window revealing the Infernal Desert and the dark figure tethered tightly with a rope of Herrinsu vine imprisoned there just before he destroyed it with the Sword of Destiny, Jacob had never before had the pleasure (or rather displeasure, as far as he was concerned) of coming face to face with the notorious Fallen angel who also held the inescapable moniker of 'father'–his father.

Try as he did, Jacob couldn't turn a blind eye to the obvious family resemblance. It was quite striking, in fact, and immediately the boy came to understand the halting reaction other angels were prone to demonstrate when they came to lay eyes on him for the first time. And yet surprisingly, Samael looked nothing like Jacob expected now that he had him in his sights. In his nightmares, the dark, bound figure imprisoned in the harsh, intolerable grasp of the Infernal Desert existed as a ghastly looking embodiment of fathomless and inextinguishable rage. There was nothing ghastly looking about the Samael Jacob studied closely making his way toward the Tribunal. Quite the opposite, Samael revealed himself to be a surprisingly dashing figure dressed in a smartly tailored gray suit, monochromatic tie and camel's hair overcoat, looking more like a worldly financier than Fallen angel. With his dark hair impeccably trimmed and combed straight back, and aside from the couple remaining blemishes from the deep disfiguring burns he suffered from the merciless scorching desert sun which had yet to fully fade, there was no denying Samael was a handsome individual possessing a visage that was both pleasing and severe in its beauty, not to mention he exuded a youthfulness from within which a glimmer of a far-reaching and untold age could not be completely hidden. Nor could Samael conceal fully the flicker of something sinister residing just beneath the surface of his being which revealed itself in a brief flare in his eyes when he gave a passing glance at Anahel and Gotham.

"Outrageous!" Sandel's voice suddenly broke through the tense silence with a thunderous roar as he jumped to his feet. "I don't know what my eyes find to be more incredulous; the sight of Heaven's sworn enemy fouling these hallowed halls with his wretched presence, or the unmitigated offense of Eden's trusted gatekeeper acting as his personal escort."

"Please, Sandel," Aradiel said in a quiet yet firm tone accompanied by an even more silencing stare.

"It may please you to know that we were accompanied by three Powers, which as you are well aware is far and beyond the reserves needed in the handling of such a delicate situation as this," Johiel remarked bluntly in reference to the band of angel known for their fierce prowess who kept a constant vigil outside Eden's gate against enemy threats. "I do, however, apologize for this abrupt and unannounced visit. As it happened, I, too, was caught quite off guard when Samael paid me what can only be deemed an unexpected visit at Akdamar Island with Thaniel in tow. Once I learned the purpose of his call I was bound by law to present him post-haste before this body in order to air his, uh...grievances."

"Grievances?" Sandel spit curtly at Samael. "What possible grievance could you dare voice to any member of this Tribunal? And even then, by what measure could you entertain the notion any one of us would be interested in listening?"

It was then that Thaniel timidly stepped forward as if to address the Tribunal, and instantly Jacob's heart sank at the sight of the angel looking noticeably meek and reticent. However, before Thaniel could open his mouth to speak Samael silenced him by simply placing a hand on his shoulder and, like an obedient dog made to heel, Thaniel receded without protest to stand quietly behind his master.

"It seems as though a stretch of eternity has passed and, at the same time, but a single day since I last stood before this prestigious, if not unforgiving body," Samael began his address while his steely eyes purposefully and uncomfortably lingered on each and every face staring back his way. "You have each had the fortune to render upon me your judgment—some more than once."

Samael gave a pointed glance at Gotham out of the corner of his eye, with those last words, and he was met with a glower of unmistakable contempt.

"I have carried the oppressive weight of your jaundiced punishments in the saddlebag you placed upon my back like some pack mule. Before you I stood accused of the crime of insurrection though there existed not one instance you could prove where I had drawn my sword during that unfortunate uprising."

"You better than anyone knows insurrection is not raised by the rattling of sabers but by conspiracies shaped by wily tongues," a member of the Tribunal named Karel suddenly spoke out, who like the rest seated around him sat silently listening to Samael with a mixture of disinterest and scorn.

"And it was based on your conjectural ways that you decided my fate and opened the floor beneath my feet, casting me from my rightful home and down into the wormhole where the fires of damnation never go cold," Samael continued in a tone strangely devoid of the bitterness that shaped his words. "If that weren't enough, I was made to endure these past fifty-plus years the unjust penance for a trespass I did not commit; an especially heinous trespass for which my brother Gothamel, by all accounts, is in fact guilty of committing."

It was only by the grace of God—not to mention the combined effort of Jacob and Anahel taking hold of him—that Gotham remained rooted where he sat.

"Don't misunderstand me," Samael noted with a sinister smile that unfurled itself in the face of Gotham's growing ire. "I did not come here to rehash bitter disputes or settle old scores better left bound and forgotten in the folds of an inhospitable desert. What matters today is that my rightful freedom to roam the world unhindered has been restored to me."

Samael's unabashed crowing only served to unsettle Gotham all the more.

"Yes, we had all come to hear the whispered rumors that you had somehow managed to free yourself of the shackles of the infrangible Herrinsu vine which came to bind you," Aradiel was quick to interrupt, when he recognized even God's grace might not be enough to hold Gotham back from Samael's taunting. "Pray tell, if you would, how it is the door to the makeshift prison fashioned from the sands of the Infernal Desert came to be unlocked."

"Your guess is as good as mine," Samael answered coyly. "Perhaps my unforeseen savior came to recognize that the so-called shackles into which I was placed were unjustly secured to the wrong limbs, and I was gifted with his pity."

"Damiel would be the first to make clear it was not pity that guided him to the Infernal Desert with the Sword of Destiny of hand, but rather the madness only unfettered revenge is able to incite," Gotham, unable to remain quiet a single second further short of having his tongue cut out, cooly corrected Samael.

"Perhaps," Samael noted amiably. "After all, if anyone here was familiar with the madness of revenge, it most certainly would be you."

"If I had chosen to quench my thirst for revenge, I would have had it that day in the Infernal Desert by fixing your severed head atop a stake marking the spot of your end, and we would not be suffering the immense displeasure of your presence this day," Gotham spat assuredly.

"Pity for you that you didn't," Samael replied with marked iciness. "All the more pitiful is the sad realization that all these years later you still cling to the delusional idea that I am somehow to blame for the death of your son."

"You are to blame for his death!" Gotham bellowed in a voice akin to a lion's roar.

"Yet strangely it was not the blade of my sword that came to be stained with his blood, now, was it?"

Gotham was about to come at him, and neither Jacob nor Anahel would have been able to stop him, when Sandel was once more upon his feet.

"We're certainly not going to delve into relitigating that which was long ago put to rest," he bellowed before focusing his growing agitation squarely on Samael. "Now, you stated upon your arrival that you had a concern to bring before the Tribunal. Well, out with it then. As you can see we're already occupied with a far more pressing matter of which I'd like to resume."

"Ah, yes, the intriguing case of the reappearing Light Bearer," Samael, his face growing instantly brighter, said. "Is he or isn't he? That has become the question captivating the masses far and wide. Whispers of it managed to even worm their way into my ear as I rotted away upon that insufferable desert floor."

As he spoke, his gaze came to rest on Jacob, and for a good long moment it was hard to determine from his expressionless face whether the sight of his son was found to be a pleasant vision or quite the opposite. For Jacob, it was most certainly the latter as he squirmed with discomfort in his chair from being looked upon in such a rapt and studious fashion by a stranger he not only detested with every fiber of his being, but whose existence he wished to permanently scour from his brain.

"It's a good thing I arrived here when I did," Samael continued suddenly, while turning abruptly on his heel to once more address the Tribunal, "so that I can help ease the burdens of this most prominent court by informing you all that you need no longer bother with this case nor handing down a pronouncement to the question that has been laid at your feet: Is he...or isn't he?"

"Why should we not continue with these proceedings?" Karel inquired with a chuckle of puzzlement.

"Because I–to put it as bluntly and succinctly as I can –will not permit it."

Samael's matter-of-fact response brought a hushed silence upon the room.

"Not permit?" Sandel echoed angrily, even as his face strangely betrayed the crack of a smile. "And what imagined notion has led you to conclude that you have any authority regarding the business of this court?"

The question appeared to tickle Samael, at first.

"The notion–far from imagined, as you quickly are about to be reminded– rests in the indisputable fact that I am the father of the one who sits before you awaiting your judgment, and that by itself gives me every authority."

The room became deathly silent. No one dared, at first, to speak a word in argument against the brazen statement, and Samael reveled in the unmistakable glint of unease his presence sparked at that very moment.

"Let it be known that I intend to exercise to the fullest extent this God-given right," he continued, though pausing briefly as he visibly and overtly shuddered with revulsion at the mention of God. "And in doing so, my first order of business, aside from bringing these proceedings to a halt, is to present to the members of this Tribunal this petition," he continued, reaching into the confines of his suit jacket and bringing into view for all in the room to see a rolled-up document secured with a red seal.

With a subtle fling, he tossed the document in the direction of the Tribunal, and the document–as if it sported a pair of invisible wings–fluttered through the air the short distance needed until it came to land on the table before Aradiel.

"I trust, under the circumstances, you will render a judgment on the matter in expedient a manner as possible, for I've a fair amount time in which to make up for; and make up for it I have every intention."

If it were possible, the room grew even more silent and all eyes watched in eager anticipation as Aradiel broke the seal marked by an imprint of a large "S" and carefully began to survey the contents of the mysterious document.

"Well?" Karel groused impatiently. "What does it say?"

"It is indeed a petition," Aradiel confirmed. "Samael is seeking a judgment from this court to return the physical custody of Jacob Parrish back into his care."

~ ~ ~

The babel of incredulity that swept through the room following the brazen pronouncement diminished when Thaniel once again stepped forward from behind Samael's shadow where he had quietly and most subserviently positioned himself, and this time Samael did not signal for him to remain in his place.

"The law, as you well know, is unambiguous and, equally important, quite settled when it comes to matters concerning Nephilim children: in this case parental rights and wardship," Thaniel, sounding and looking at once redoubtable where moments earlier he was anything but, began. "To be clear, for the past sixteen years the child in question in the dispute before you—that being Jacob Parrish—has been illicitly and with malice aforethought kept from his father by Gothamel. Not only did he spirit away the child's mother to parts unknown while waiting to give birth, he kept both mother and child hidden away for the next fifteen years where at that time he asserted himself, quite unlawfully, guardian of said child and brought him to Havenhid where he has remained ever since."

"This is absurd!" Gotham's voice cut its way through the room like a clap of thunder as he took to his feet in offense, followed by Anahel who motioned to the enraged angel to mind his tongue.

"I must echo Gotham's sentiment," Anahel injected, but with a far calmer voice. "There has been no attempt to keep Mr. Parrish's presence at Havenhid a secret. And why should it be? He is, as you so stated, a Nephilim child and, as such, has the right like all Nephilim children to spend his formative years learning from the Guides at Havenhid those things necessary to exist."

"Not only do you fail to note Samael was denied his parental rights in any decisions made when it came to his child's formative years, you speak of Jacob Parrish as if he were a normal Nephilim. But a normal Nephilim he is not; he is the offspring of a Fallen, and, as such, he should never have been allowed entry to Havenhid, much less Eden itself," Thaniel indicated in a calm and measured tone. "Samael never would have allowed his child to be brought through Eden's gate; but you knew that, didn't you? I know, because I was there."

Both Anahel and Gotham could not believe the words, nor the sentiment that accompanied them, coming from Thaniel's mouth.

"Then by your own admission, I find it especially astounding how you purposefully fail now to recall the only reason by which the boy came to be here is his mother," said Gotham. "It was she who made me promise with her dying breath that when the time arrived I would assume the role of guardian and bring the boy to Havenhid, and I have abided by those wishes."

"Yes, I do call to mind you sharing to the Guides that touching exchange," Thaniel replied impassively. "Sentiment, however, does not supersede law and, thus, let me remind this court that the statutes which oversee children in the mortal world have no bearing when it comes to Nephilim. Where it is usually the mother who is favored to hold guardianship of her child in the mortal world, it is the father who assumes all custodial rights in the case of Nephilim. And the law, as they say, is the law."

It was then, for a split second, Anahel noticed the indifferent look set deep in Thaniel's eyes that was almost too unbearable to behold give way to a surrendering of contrition. Then, as if he realized his momentary tell, Thaniel shook it away.

"We have made our intent clear," he then said as he turned to address the members of the Tribunal, "and we await for the matter to be settled as expeditiously as possible."

Jacob, who sat looking more and more staggered while listening to the back and forth taking place, followed Thaniel with his gaze as he quietly retreated back into the background where he came to lean against a massive marble pillar and, strangely enough, appeared to be speaking with some unseen person hidden on the opposite side of the column. Perhaps the angel was arguing with his conscious over his effective performance as co-conspirator in the dirty scheme he was taking part in, Jacob thought to himself. Yet despite all that Thaniel had debated on behalf of Samael and, more unfortunately, against Jacob himself, Jacob could not help but look upon the visibly wilted angel with a deep sense of pity.

Likewise, the weight of what had been voiced was readily apparent on Aradiel's face.

"Much has been put forth before this court; all of it quite unexpectedly," he remarked thoughtfully. "It should go without saying that we will each of us need sufficient time to take into consideration the merits of the petition put before us and weigh it against the applicable written law."

"With all due respect, time is a luxury you do not have at hand," said Samael. "I trust you all still suffer from that unfortunate defect known as righteousness which causes you great offense whenever you witness anyone in the willful engagement of breaking one of those ten pesky little rules handed down by our despotic father called, um...oh yeah, sins. If memory serves me correctly, the eighth commandment forbids the act of theft in all its forms. The past sixteen years of my son's life were purposefully and willfully stolen from me; you'll understand when I tell you this minute that I will allow not a single day more to be lost to me."

"And you'll understand," countered Aradiel, "when I tell you I am not prepared to make a judgment one way or the other on this matter this day."

Samael replied with an unnatural if not cordial smile. "Maybe it's the recent trials I've suffered that have made me soft, but to demonstrate I am reasonable, I will allow you three days—nay, make it four—to resolve this issue."

The compromise appeared agreeable to the members of the Tribunal, but Jacob felt otherwise and quickly made his feelings on what was transpiring known when he leapt to his feet.

"Wait a minute! Isn't anyone going to ask me how I feel about any of this?" he cried in frustration before leveling a hate-filled look at Samael. "I don't care what anyone says; I'm not going anywhere with you. I don't want anything to do with you. The reason I came to Havenhid in the first place is to learn everything I needed so when the time comes I'm ready to do battle against you and all the other Underneath-dwelling scum."

Not one to take kindly to being publicly spoken to in such an impudent way, especially by his own son, Samael feigned a dismissive smile even while his ire was beginning to boil inside him.

"Now you understand my desire for expediency," he said to Aradiel. "With every day that he remains here in the care of the Guides, the more time they are allotted to twist his mind against me."

"This is asinine!" Gotham spat, while at the same time taking reign of Aradiel's and the rest of the Tribunal's attention. "This court was convened for the sole purpose of determining whether the boy seated before you has been anointed by our father above as the long-awaited Light Bearer. Am I now to believe you actually are considering, instead, handing him over like a lamb to slaughter to this, this...fiend?"

"Did not Thaniel state it clearly enough for you, O risen phoenix?"

Samael, clearly and with great disdain mocking Gotham's return to Heaven's embrace, was quick to reply with a most condescending and antagonizing sneer. "The law is the law."

"To hell with the law!" Gotham bawled in return.

"To hell with the law, indeed," said Samael. "You demonstrated as much when you imprisoned me in the Infernal Desert so many years ago, and then again when you stole from me my son after taking a sword to your own. Only now the tide has turned, hasn't it? And Karma, in all her delicious irony, has taken the unbreakable Herrinsu vine with which you long ago bound me and secured it to your own limbs."

Gotham slowly but in no less a threatening manner made his way toward Samael until the two stood nearly nose to nose with one another.

"You are by far the most despicable presence I've ever had the displeasure of crossing paths with," he growled while clenching his teeth. "How naive it was of me to think that perhaps, just possibly, in the time you were left to your deterioration while in solitary confinement in the Infernal Desert the scorching sun, from which I see you still bear the blistering scars, would have forced you to have an awakening of sorts. But there are some blights even the healing powers of nature are incapable of reclaiming. So let this be understood between the two of us: If you think I would ever watch you walk out of Eden with the boy in tow, then for your benefit it's high time I reintroduce myself to you. And you should leave here today knowing I would gladly take leave of Heaven a second time before I would ever allow such a thing."

The pointed threat appeared to cause not the slightest bit of worry to Samael.

"Not only will you watch me leave Eden with my son," Samael said in a whisper spoken loud enough for Gotham's ears alone to hear, "but the second coming of the fabled Light Bearer that died the instant you ran your blade through your son will once more be snuffed out. And in its stead you will see a kingdom unmatched in power rise up, and the boy you so valiantly defend this moment with your reclaimed position in our father's house you will see seated proudly at my right hand."

It was now Gotham's turn to smile.

"Kingdom?" he echoed with a chuckle. "How long I've been awaiting this so-called kingdom since the day you first crowed about it when you were first dragged before this Tribunal in shame."

Just as quickly, his smile faded and a grim look returned to his face.

"What I failed to impress upon you then I will do so now: Whatever kingdom it is you attempt to build, do so knowing this: it will be nothing more than a kingdom of sand built on a stretch of beach. And rest assured I will be the incoming tide."

~ ~ ~

It was clear by the grave look in his eyes that the threat spit forth by Gotham was neither empty nor veiled, and he may very well have proceeded to demonstrate then and there the seriousness of his words in order to remove all possible doubt Samael may have been entertaining had Jacob, clearly distraught by what was taking place, not suddenly jumped to his feet and charged his way out of the room.

Jacob, feeling his throat closing up tighter and tighter and Halcyon's towering walls appearing to slowly be closing in upon him from all sides, ran as fast as his feet could carry him down numerous winding halls and across the steps of several staircases. All the while it felt as if the oxygen in the air was slowly being sucked out of existence, and with every step he took he found his lungs slowly beginning to collapse as they struggled to take a much-needed breath. When finally he found his way outside the walls of Halcyon and felt the warmth of the sunlight on his face, Jacob collapsed to his knees on the soft green grass. There he struggled with gratitude to fill his starved lungs with the clean crip air scented with cedar and eucalyptus from the surrounding Forest.

No matter how many breaths he took, however, nothing seemed able to calm the overwhelming maelstrom of rage that had somehow been unleashed inside him. Its uncontrollable presence was instantly upon him, threatening to turn him inside and out and then proceed to swallow him alive in one quickening instant.

When Anahel and Gotham finally came upon Jacob, they found the boy pacing about blindly like a seething caged animal.

"Come, Jacob," Gotham said with a calm and soothing voice while holding out his hand to the clearly enraged boy. "It's all going to work okay."

"There's no way I'm going with him!"

"No one has said you have to go with anyone."

"Do you hear me? I'M NOT GOING WITH HIM! And there's not a court powerful enough to force me!"

There was a wild look in Jacob's eyes made all the more feral in appearance by the transformation of his irises into rings of fire more commonly witnessed during a once-in-a-lifetime solar eclipse and not aflame in the confines of someone's skull.

"You need to take a breath and calm yourself," Gotham said, though he could see readily the inconsolable boy was in need of far more than a breath.

"Calm down? How do you expect me to calm down? Did you not hear what occurred just now inside?" Jacob cried. "He wants to take me down in the Underneath!"

"We are not going to let that happen," Gotham tried to assure Jacob.

"Oh, sure, and how exactly are you going to stop him?" Jacob spit with near contempt at Gotham's useless attempt to extinguish the inferno burning out of control inside him. "You heard what Thaniel had to say: the law is the law. If anyone would know, it would be him."

"Jacob, please...come inside with me and Anahel. We'll find a solution to this."

Jacob paid him no mind and continued with his ranting. "He's never going to leave me be, is he?" he rambled aloud though it was unclear whether he was posing the question to Gotham or to himself. "At first it was in my dreams when I was a little kid. Now he's climbed out of my dreams and inserted himself squarely in the middle of my life. No matter what I do or where I go, I can't seem to shake him.

"I HATE HIM!" Jacob suddenly cried out venomously. "I hate him with every fiber of my being! So help me God if I had my sword with me now I'd run him through with it."

Gotham attempted to grab hold of the boy and embrace him with a hug but, in a show of force that caught the angel completely off guard by its sheer strength, Jacob pushed him away and in doing so sent him tumbling across the ground for several feet. Overcome by the ire pulsating through him, Jacob collapsed to his knees while at the same time driving his fist furiously into the ground causing the earth to form a sizable split similar to an earthquake fault. Then with his eyes ablaze he looked to the sky and, once more, made his hatred of Samael heard in deafening scream. Much to the horror of both Gotham and Anahel, the scream appeared to knock loose the sun as it suddenly began to plummet from the place where it hung in the sky. Larger and brighter it become swallowing the sea of blue that surrounded it in its terrifying plunge, and as it drew closer the tall trees of the Forest began to wither, brown and finally combust in flames while balls of fire erupted from the blinding orb and took aim at Eden's pristine lands like bombs released from some unseen plane.

Anahel jumped into action, and with his hands raised to the sky it looked at first as if he might actually attempt, quite impossibly, to catch the falling sun as though he were a centerfielder going for a pop fly. His own eyes erupted with their own illumination of gold, and just as quickly as the sun was sent hurtling from the heavens, it was returned to its reigning position. With the crisis averted, Anahel breathed a much needed sigh of relief, but a most troubled look returned to his face when he turned to find Gotham kneeling on the ground embracing Jacob, and the boy in turn allowing himself to be consoled while sobbing in the angel's arms.

"Well, then," Samael, who had witnessed the heartbreaking incident as he stood inconspicuously nearby with Thaniel at his side, muttered indifferently, "so much for the happy father and son reunion."

"I don't mean to spoil things by voicing any pessimism," Thaniel voiced gingerly, "but have you taken into consideration the possible chance the Tribunal might not rule in your favor?"

The corner of Samael's mouth curled upward in a most unsavory way.

"I would have thought you knew me well enough by now to know that I have never been one to count my chickens before they are hatched," he said in a tone that somehow had the ability to be as pleasant as it was unpleasant.

Thaniel then watched with a quiet uneasiness as Samael brought one of the sharp talons that were his fingernails on his right hand to the inside of his left wrist and then, in a most discreet manner, and without so much as a wince, punctured a vein concealed within his flesh with a lacerating motion as easily as if he had taken a razor blade to it. Blood, black as tar, dribbled from the wound onto the ground where it quickly seeped into the earth and disappeared out of sight.

"Whether the boy is sent packing from Eden and is returned to his place at my side, or the often unwise members of the Tribunal choose instead to keep that which is not theirs, one thing is most certain," said Samael. "The promise of the Light Bearer will finally, and permanently cease to exist."

Thaniel knew it was a vow Samael had every intention of keeping.

~ ~ ~

"I'll start packing my things tonight," Jacob announced to Gotham and

Anahel later that afternoon when the trio returned to Havenhid where they retreated to the private confines of Anahel's living quarters to ponder the next course of action following the day's unexpected, and most certainly unsettling, developments.

"Packing? And where may I ask are you planning to venture?" inquired Anahel who along with Gotham cast a look of surprise at the boy.

"Cain's Corner, of course," answered Jacob. "Obviously I can't stay here any longer, not when there's a chance I could he handed over to Samael like some dog in the pound going to its forever home."

"I understand your instinct to flee, truly I do," said Anahel with subtle smile of compassion. "But I think you're smart enough to know, even as you sit here conspiring in planning your escape, that this is not something from which you can run. And though it has done well in protecting you in the past, Cain's Corner you will soon come to learn will be unable to provide you refuge if in fact the Tribunal decides in favor of Samael."

"Then I'll go somewhere else; someplace that few people have ever heard about and...I'll disappear," said Jacob.

The orange flickering light coming from a crackling fire in the fireplace next to which Anahel was seated in a large overstuffed chair illuminated a look of empathy etched in the angel's face as he listened to the boy.

"Is that how you wish to spend the rest of your days; burrowed away under a rock like some timid shrew?" he asked.

"No...not especially. But it sure beats the alternative," Jacob answered meekly. "I was given an up close glimpse of the Underneath when I looked down into the Through in the Silent Forest. I saw what a horrible place it was and worse, the hideous things that live there. I couldn't imagine ever having to step foot inside it willingly."

"Then why do it; imagine it, that is? It would seem to me that it is a needless source of torment fretting over something which has yet to materialize; not to mention exhaustive."

An easy thing for you to say, Jacob mumbled to himself quietly inside his own head.

"This whole thing makes no sense to me," Gotham, who was occupied with his own thoughts, was heard to say as he worked to wear a path into the floor with his ceaseless pacing from one end of the room to the other. "What motive could Samael possibly hope to achieve by petitioning for custody of Jacob? He can't possibly think this move would ignite the war he promised

Damiel he would start. Certainly, it's not a bid to fulfill his fatherly obligations."

"No, of course not," Anahel was quick to agree. "Whatever scheme he's concocting to fulfill his promise to Damiel, he knows well enough to first neutralize the one looming threat which has cast an uncertain shadow over his future. Samael cares nothing about Jacob except for the simple fact that he shows all signs of being the Light Bearer. By gaining guardianship over Jacob, he hopes to stamp out once and for all the prophesy which has long haunted him. The only interest Samael has in the boy is in ensuring his own self-preservation, not to mention that of the Underneath, and nothing more."

As soon as he had spoken the words, Anahel regretted the blunt and insensitive manner in which he had wagged his tongue when he happened to glance over and noticed Jacob wearing a wounded look that revealed itself ever so faintly, but wounded nonetheless, and he silently chastised himself for his thoughtless insensitivity.

"I did not mean for that to sound as it was spoken," the angel said regretfully.

"No biggie! I mean, after all, it's the truth, isn't it?" Jacob replied through a forced half-smile. "What do I care anyway? It's not like I'm sitting here with the warm-and-fuzzies for him any more than he is for me."

Yet despite the boy's attempt to brush away the matter, he could not fully conceal the obvious sadness the realization of Anahel's words brought him. And how could he? For what child does not crave the feeling of being loved and wanted by the ones who brought them into the world; even when one of them is discovered to be the very antithesis of paternal love?

"Curses to Damiel!" Gotham was suddenly heard to exclaim in a renewed rant. "Had he the self-control to keep his taste for vengeance in check, Samael would still be wasting away in the Infernal Desert and we would not find ourselves burdened with this quandary."

"Admittedly, I cannot come to Damiel's defense, as his actions have proven themselves to be both disappointing and dangerously impetuous," Anahel said with a weighty sigh. "That said, I'm certain no one will feel the crushing weight of guilt more so than he will when news of what has transpired today reaches his ears."

The angel then spoke directly to Jacob.

"Despite whatever ill-will you are feeling–and goodness knows you are warranted of them–do not allow a misguided decision cloud the fact that

Damiel cares a great deal for you and would never knowingly bring a moment's unpleasantness to you."

If Jacob was embracing of such sentiment, his stony expression betrayed not a hint of his feelings.

"If anyone's to blame for any of this, it's me," he said, instead. "Maybe if I had been better prepared, more astute, I would have seen through Damiel's scheme and realized the Gotham who asked me to hand over to him the Sword of Destiny was nothing but Damiel wearing a Halloween costume. Now, thanks to my stupidity, my fa—that is, Samael has been set loose, and who knows what else he has in store."

"My dear boy, you are but a youngling taking his first steps as a Nephilim while Damiel has been mastering his skills since the world was in its infancy. Don't take this the wrong way, but you stood not a chance when Damiel put his ploy into motion," said Anahel.

"Thanks, that makes me feel a whole lot better," Jacob muttered sullenly in reply, as he slumped further in the chair upon which he sat.

"What I'm still having difficulty in understanding is Thaniel," said Gotham who abruptly ceased his pacing to address Anahel and Jacob.

"What of Thaniel?" asked Anahel.

"Why was he at Halcyon today? Specifically, why was he acting as counsel for Samael and arguing his case before the Tribunal? After all, this was the same Thaniel whose dispiriting act of betrayal when he severed my wings from my back and ensured the Sword of Destiny found its way into Jacob's hands when he sent me to my death at Broken Earth was later unveiled to be the mastermind of an inconceivable act of selfless love and sacrifice," Gotham recalled with a twinkle of gratitude in his eyes. "How then is it possible he would now forge an alliance with the very powers he purposefully schemed to undercut?"

"Ah, yes, I know what you mean. I was pondering much the same thing earlier today," said Anahel. "I found myself recalling the wondrous night of your return to Havenhid after such a horrendous departure, when you shared with me the details of Thaniel's unexpected and, dare I say, heart-rendering confession inside a church residing amid the headstones and crypts of a cemetery on a remote island in Venice. Oh, how I wish I had been there that night to embrace my brother and beg his forgiveness for the scornful thoughts I had come to hold for him. Yet seeing him today, and listening to his remarks spoken with such fervor, I found myself questioning the veracity of the repainting of his portrait as a sacrificial lamb."

The topic of Thaniel brought a grave expression to Jacob, even more so than when his own fate was being discussed.

"I'm not so sure Thaniel had much of a choice when it came to what he did today," he said.

"What makes you say that?" Gotham asked curiously.

Jacob replied, at first, with a simple shrug.

"Just a feeling I got when he showed up with Samael at Halcyon," answered Jacob. "I remember having so much hate for him when I saw him in that church at Venice. How could I not, after watching what he did to you. There was nothing he could say to make me believe he was anything less than the monster he revealed himself to be at Broken Earth. But I listened, and I quickly learned, quite shamefully, how badly I had misjudged him."

"You're not alone in feeling such remorse. We have all of us come to share the blame in assuming the worse when it came to Thaniel," said Gotham.

"The point I'm trying to make is that I was consciously keeping the memory of that night in the church in the back of my mind and, while Thaniel was addressing the court about Samael's petition demanding custody of me, I tried to look into Thaniel's mind and read his thoughts. He must have been purposefully keeping them guarded—most likely from Samael—because there was nothing there I could detect but a blank slate. But there was one brief moment when his mental walls gave way and I sensed a great amount of angst and regret for what he was doing."

"Then why do it, Thaniel?" Gotham questioned aloud as if Thaniel was present in the room eavesdropping on the conversation.

"Isn't it obvious?" answered Anahel. "Self-preservation. It's the one, and likely only thing Samael and Thaniel have in common at this particular moment in time. In Thaniel's case, he's been thrown into the vipers' den, or rather quite willingly stepped into it of his own accord. There are many who dwell in the Underneath who would not look kindly upon Thaniel—Samael being amongst them. After all, it was Thaniel's superior intellect that helped guide the forces of the Light to thwart numerous malevolent deeds attempted at various times throughout the ages by the Darkness. Now that he's been cast down into the depths and no longer possesses Heaven's shield of protection, there are undoubtedly those entities who will be looking to exact their pound of flesh from him. One cannot fault Thaniel for doing what he can to stem the tide of revenge rolling towards him."

"There must be something we can do," said Jacob.

"Do?"

"To help Thaniel."

Anahel could see clearly Jacob's distress over Thaniel's unfortunate situation, and a distressing feeling of helplessness came over him when all he could offer in return was a shared look of sympathy.

"Unfortunately, when it comes to matters such as this, there isn't much, if anything, that can be done on our behalf."

"But there must be," Jacob, unwilling to accept such an answer, argued. "You saw the way he looked today. There was a noticeable void in his eyes; as if the light that once burned inside him had all but been extinguished. When Gotham was a Fallen, you allowed him into Eden. Certainly you can do the same for Thaniel now that you know the real intent behind what he did. Please, promise me you'll do something to help him."

At first, all Anahel could do was answer with a hearty smile and reach over to give the boy's knee an appreciative squeeze, for it warmed him to see such genuine concern on display, considering the magnitude of his own issues.

"Thaniel would be quite touched to know the regard you hold for him," Anahel finally remarked.

Before Anahel could acquiesce to Jacob's plea, however, Gotham made sure to remind the two of the far more pressing issue that demanded their immediate attention: Samael's custody petition.

"Where are you going?" Anahel inquired, when Gotham suddenly made his way to the door to leave.

"I've got some homework to do," announced Gotham. "Our best hope to beating this is to play Samael's game. If he's able to use a statute of law that allows someone like him to gain custody of Jacob, then I will leave no stone unturned to find one that will stop him cold."

Once Gotham had gone off to begin his hunt, Jacob began to feel the onset of fatigue from the long eventful day and decided to head off to his room. As Jacob got to his feet and was about to bid Anahel a good night, the angel expressed a desire to have a quiet word with the boy, now that they were alone, and politely asked him if he would stay a little while longer.

"Sure," said Jacob. "What's up?"

"Come!" instructed the angel, as he rose from his chair just as Jacob reclaimed his. "Let us make our way out onto the terrace where we can enjoy the approach of the end of the day."

~ ~ ~

Jacob followed Anahel onto the large balcony where they were greeted by a spectacular view of the Garden looking to the north. The sky above them was slowly surrendering its blanket of blue for a bolt of fiery oranges and yellows that the setting sun was beginning to unfold. Everything, from the vast fields of green intermingling with large patches of vibrant wildflowers to the towering mountains in the distance were Broken Earth resided, was bathed in an ethereal shimmering of gold. Even the picturesque waterfalls appeared as if they had suddenly become firefalls during the stunning moment when the passing day handed its reign over to the arriving twilight and, in the exchange, it appeared as if the last remnants of sunlight had been cast into the falls transforming them into roaring columns of blinding molten orange.

"That was quite the display you put on earlier," Anahel remarked casually as the two stood at the railing of the terrace to share in the beauty of the falls of fire.

"I take it you're referring to the little outburst I had," Jacob recalled after a thoughtful moment.

"Little outburst?" echoed Anahel with the raising of his eyebrows. "I'm not quite sure causing the sun to spit fireballs down upon Eden or creating a fracture in the earth where there previously was none constitutes a 'little outburst.'"

Jacob exhaled a half-hearted chuckle before quickly taking note of the absence of levity in Anahel's demeanor.

"You're pulling my leg, right?"

One look at Anahel, however, and it was clear he was not engaging in the pulling of legs, or any limbs for that matter.

"I know I sorta lost it when I stormed out of the hearing, but after that..." Jacob's voice trailed off as he struggled to search the fragmented pieces that existed of the incident floating about in the confines of his memory, "I remember being so angry; angrier than I've ever been in my entire life; and having that anger come spewing out of my mouth at Gotham before everything just turned to red. Next thing I knew I was on the ground sobbing and Gotham was hugging me telling me everything was going to be okay."

If he recalled anything further, he didn't say so aloud but, instead, looked

116

to Anahel both apologetically and with a small measure of embarrassment. "I hope I didn't do anything that can't be repaired or fixed."

"The Forest suffered a few scorched acres, but nothing that couldn't be made good as new with Zuriel and Eksel's assistance," said Anahel.

The boy grew silent as he turned his attention back to the beauty of the falls, but Anahel could see, watching out of the corner of his eye, that the boy remained troubled by the idea that his angry outburst could have unhinged something as substantial as the sun itself.

"It's becoming a bit more commonplace, isn't it? These fits of rage?" Anahel posed the question when he finally parted his lips to speak.

"What do you mean?" asked Jacob.

"I can recall several instances offhand where you have surrendered yourself to your anger and come to blows with Creed Maggert. Granted, I've no doubt Mr. Maggert provoked the outcome of each instance, as he's sufficiently proven himself quite gifted and more than capable of doing. Then again, wrath has never been discriminatory when it comes to circumstance," said Anahel. "Then there was the time you vented your rage in the Silent Forest. True, it manifested in you driving the Sword of Destiny into the Through leading to the Underneath and obliterating its presence in Eden, but I wonder if you ever stopped to ponder what if it had not."

A confused look slowly crept over Jacob. "I'm not sure I'm following."

"I know one of the first points of instruction Damiel drills into the psyche of his young students is in recognizing the incapacitating effect anger can have when it is not controlled."

Jacob nodded in agreement. "He taught us anger is a vain emotion; that it clouds one's judgment, and that if it is not kept tightly leashed it will lead us to our end."

"You would be quite wise to heed Damiel's words," said Anahel. "Though I would respectfully correct Damiel on one point: Anger is much more than a vain emotion; it is a dangerous one."

Even as Jacob listened intently to what Anahel was saying to him, his mind remained a jumble of thoughts.

"Is it really true my hissy fit earlier caused what you said it did?" Jacob asked while sounding noticeably unnerved at the prospect.

"For what reason would I have to tell tales about such a thing?" said Anahel in return.

"But how? That's what's so unsettling. I don't recall doing anything close to what you described, nor could I ever imagine contemplating the idea of doing it; especially to Eden."

"You've heard of blind rage, haven't you? The mortal world of which you are from is teeming with countless stories of men and woman who end up committing horrific crimes—usually murderous—when they find themselves engulfed in a tempest of uncontrollable anger from which they cannot escape. It steals from its hapless victims the capacity to reason and leaves them with an insatiable desire to destroy everything around them without mercy or conscience," explained Anahel. "What makes it particularly dangerous for Nephilim resides in your inherited Graces and the stealth-like way anger taps into these powerful tools in the commission of such crimes in order to cause the most collateral damage."

Anahel's words proved to be most unnerving to Jacob; that much was visibly apparent. And while it was not the angel's intent to send the boy off to bed that night with such unpleasant visions dancing in his head, he knew his impromptu lesson was one which needed to be heard.

"Just as the Graces are powerful weapons for those who have sworn our loyalty to the Light, so, too, are Scourges for those who have chosen to dwell in the Dark," Anahel continued. "But nothing has proven itself more dangerous or malignant than Wrath. It devours all who it infects, and it is the teat from which all other maladies are nursed: envy, greed, pride, and most notably hate."

Despite the angst-inducing conversation, Anahel attempted to smooth the crinkles of worry that had begun to etch themselves upon Jacob's forehead by offering forth a comforting smile to accompany the hand that reached out and gave the boy's shoulder a reassuring squeeze.

"I tell you all of this not to fill you with panic or distress, only to help make you more mindful," said the angel. "I fear, with the reemergence of Samael, that you might be entering a particularly precarious time where the anger that has already visited you will stop at nothing to steal your sight from you."

"So then what do I need to do to ensure what occurred today doesn't ever happen again?" asked Jacob.

The grave look that slowly made itself seen on Anahel's face offered little encouragement.

"That, I'm afraid, is not so simple a solution," replied the angel.

It was not the answer Jacob had hoped to hear.

CHAPTER SEVEN

THE GREAT SWORD CAPER

Long after the bellow of a distant horn announced the hour for lights out, Jacob found himself lying wide awake in his bed. He wasn't alone in his restlessness as Leos, Max, Ethan, Kairo and Hunter—the newest roommate for whom the others had happily squeezed their beds together a little bit closer in order to make room in their tight quarters—were also stretched out on their backs staring up at the ceiling where they watched as the numerous night shadows fluttered about and twisted themselves into a captivating array of shadow puppets.

"Does this remind anyone of something?" Ethan's voice cut through the silence mingling with the rustling of the gentle breeze responsible for making the shadows sway as it came through the window.

"From here it looks like a large cat stretched out on tree branch," Kairo answered, after studying the black shapes moving about above Ethan.

"I'm not talking about the ceiling, but tonight in general," Ethan clarified, before his attention returned to the ceiling above him with renewed focus. "And where do you see a cat in a tree?"

"What about tonight?" Leos asked more out boredom than from any genuine interest.

"It just made me think back to that time not so long ago when Anahel announced a curfew for Havenhid in anticipation of you know who paying a visit to Eden," said Ethan.

"And who exactly is 'you know who'?" Hunter, reminding everyone else in the room of his new arrival status, asked.

"He's talking about Azrael," answered Kairo.

The utterance of the name caused Hunter to rise up onto his elbows and peer across the moon-lit room to the neighboring bed upon which Kairo was sprawled.

"Azrael? You're kidding. As in the Angel of Death?" he inquired.

"That would be him," said Leos. "You see, Jacob here accidentally discovered he had the Grace of healing which theoretically meant he had been chosen to be the Light Bearer. The White Circle, however, was a bit more skeptical about the matter so they summoned Azrael to come here in the middle of the night and basically create a test for Jacob to prove it one way or the other if, in fact, he was quote-unquote the anointed one."

"One thing's for sure: I never want to live through another night like that again, for reals," said Ethan. "Aside from Anahel warning us to keep all the lights out and stay out of sight, none of us knew what to expect. We ended up staying up most of the night, sitting in the dark and talking just like we are now. But, man, was it ever a nerve-racking experience."

"I'll sure say it was," Max, who had been quietly listening from his bed, finally commented. "When the first clippety-clop from the horse Azrael rode into Eden upon made itself heard, 'ol Ethan here went from unshakable Jedi knight to human chocolate factory in the blink of an eye."

"I did not!" Ethan barked in offense, amid a sniggering of giggles.

"Please! Whatever force was strong in you instantly turned into a bad case of the Hershey squirts."

"Ha, ha, very funny!" Ethan offered in retort of the snickers which quickly evolved into full-on hearty chuckles.

"So what happened?" Hunter asked, when the moment of levity began to die down.

"When we woke up the next morning and went outside we discovered the River and everything that lived in it—the fish, the frogs, even the turtles—had been struck dead," Kairo jumped in to continue the story. "The waterfalls had dried up, and the crystal clear blue water that used to flow in the River had turned black all the way to the Dilmun Sea."

"And?"

"Anahel and Gotham forced Jacob to wade into the water which, for the record, you could not have gotten me to stick even a toe into that stinking foul swamp which even now I can still smell," Leos recalled with a look of revulsion. "But kudos to Jacob for holding his nose and taking the plunge, so to speak. The rest of us gathered along the bank and watched with anticipation as he tried again and again to breathe life, for lack of a better phrase, into the River. And to be honest, I was beginning to have my doubts about the whole thing when after a good long while nothing appeared to happen. I think we all did. And then there came this deep rumbling and, right before our eyes, the waterfalls suddenly reappeared; and the black water slowly began to disappear and turn blue once again. Then came the most amazing thing: the fish and frogs and other creatures that lived in the River and were lying dead on the surface of the water for as far as the eye could see all started to come back to life and returned to frolicking in the water as though nothing had happened."

Visibly impressed by what he had just heard, Hunter shifted his gaze to the bed on the other side of the room where Jacob lay propped up against two pillows with his large furry wolf companion Mist stretched out next to him, who was enjoying quite immensely the thorough scratching she was being given to the top of her head and ears.

"No kidding," said Hunter, "Now, that's something I certainly wish I had been around to witness."

Jacob said nothing in return; in fact, the moonlight showed him to be staring off into space and completely oblivious to the conversation taking place.

"You okay over there, Jacob?" Leos inquired, and again there was no answer until he repeated Jacob's name again, and then one more time.

"I'm sorry," Jacob apologized when his trance finally broke, "I must have been caught up in my own thoughts."

"Are you thinking about the bomb Samael dropped on everyone when he showed up out of the blue today?" asked Ethan.

"That is scary eerie; I was having the exact same feeling," Max noted while looking quite taken aback. "We best alert Zuriel and let him know there might be a possibility we have a hidden Grace inside us we never knew about: the Grace of Swami-ism that allows us to read the minds of others."

Ethan grabbed his pillow and hurled it across the room in an effort to knock the mocking smirk that suddenly beamed forth from Max.

"And me melon thanks you, mate!" Max said, catching the incoming pillow as if it were a football and placing it atop his own before resting his head upon it with a gratifying sigh.

"What I meant was it must have really caught you off guard, even more than the rest of us," Ethan turned to Jacob and continued once again.

"It's not just what happened with Samael; it's the hearing," said Jacob. "Having to sit there and watch as Sandel calls up person after person to testify in a way that twists things that actually happened in order to paint a picture of me that is so far from accurate...well, it's just a bit hard to take."

Putting aside his wisecracking, Max grew suddenly serious—rueful, even—as he rose up onto one elbow and looked squarely at Jacob.

"I just have to say again how bad I feel for spilling the tea about what happened with your mate Ty," he said. "Can't help but feel guilty, like I betrayed—"

"No, you didn't!" Jacob said before Max could finish his sentence. "You answered how you should have to the questions you were asked. End of story."

"I should have lied, or at the very least feigned ignorance."

"Then I would have stood and told the truth myself," argued Jacob. "This is a hearing to determine if I'm really the Light Bearer. No way am I going to allow the outcome to be shaped by a lie or omission of truth."

Whether or not Max agreed with his friend or felt any measure of relief for his own guilt following his apology, it was impossible to tell as he fell back onto his pile of pillows.

"So, what happens now?" asked Kairo.

"We wait," Jacob replied. "The Tribunal has recessed the hearing until they have come to a decision on Samael's petition. And Gotham is working with Vessel to try and find something—anything—to counter Samael's claim."

"What if they don't find anything?" Ethan asked with a marked timidity. "Does that mean you're going to be forced to leave Havenhid and go with Samael to...to the...Underneath."

The pillow Ethan had lost moments earlier suddenly came hurtling back across the room, hitting Ethan squarely in the face.

"What's the matter with you?" barked Max.

"Well...it is the elephant in the room," balked Ethan, before looking to Jacob once more with both sympathy and fear. "Aren't you...scared?"

At first, Jacob said nothing.

"Enough to turn me into a human chocolate factory," he said finally, forcing forth a light-hearted grin.

"There's no way Anahel or Gotham are going to allow anything like that to happen, and neither are the rest of us," Max declared forcefully.

"I appreciate the sentiment. Unfortunately, if the Tribunal comes back in three days with a different decision, there's not a whole heck of a lot any of us can do about it," said Jacob.

The cynical outlook put an instant damper on everyone in the room; everyone that is except Hunter.

"That's not entirely true," he stated in the heavy silence that followed.

"What do you mean by that?" asked Leos.

"What if I were to tell you there just may be a very effective way to get Samael out of your hair, and we're holding it in our hands right now?"

"Well...are you going to keep us in suspense?" Max pressed with increasing anxiousness.

Hunter's roguish gaze shifted to each of the five pairs of peepers peering eagerly back at him through the silverly light of the moon as though he were second-guessing whether or not to share his secret.

"Two words: Scucca Urns," he said finally.

~ ~ ~

Scucca Urns.

The room suddenly became illuminated with a warm white light as if a switch had been thrown, and Jacob sat up in his bed.

"What do the Scucca Urns have to do with any of this?" asked Jacob whose curiosity, along with everyone else's in the room, was instantly stoked at the mention of the mysterious objects.

With everything happening since their return to Eden between the Tribunal hearing and Hunter being enrolled in a crash-course training regimen in order for him to get his wings in the precious little bit of time he had left to do so, the existence of the urns had momentarily receded from the forefront of everybody's mind, with the exception of Hunter.

They were, however, far from forgotten.

In fact, all it took was the mere reminder of the Scucca Urns by Hunter to cause Max, Leos, Kairo and Ethan to rise up from their reclined positions as they were each of them instantaneously revisited by the memory of when they were first given an up-close look at a Scucca Urn when Hunter went to retrieve not one, but three of the strange objects he had stashed away in a sack, and covered in five pounds of salt in a secret hiding place beneath the floor boards of the loft where he had been living, up until his newfound friends showed up quite unexpectedly at his door one night accompanied by an angel named Damiel.

The urns were as peculiar in appearance as their name. Made from what looked and felt to be a clear crystal of some sort, which radiated with a jade-colored iridescence, the spherical, medium-sized container was reminiscent of a vintage lava lamp created in another age where a black, inky plume-like shape could be observed inside in a constant state of morphing in its green glowing surroundings. It was Gotham who revealed the mystery and, more importantly, the purpose of the urns which proved to be as nefarious as the small demon-like creatures seemingly cast out of gold, and affixed to the top of each container. They told the story of a long-ago time when God and Satan agreed to a five-thousand-year-truce, and how Samael ended up with the reign of the Underneath in his hands when Satan, seeking a loophole in the truce, relinquished his power to Samael who in turn came up with his own scheme to possess it in perpetuity through the creation of the Scucca Urns.

Now it was Hunter who had come up with his own scheme where the Scucca Urns were concerned.

"Remember the night when we stopped by my place right before coming to Eden, and I revealed to you the three Scucca Urns I had stashed away?" Hunter started, with every eye intently fixed on him. "I told you about a man named Ben."

"That's the guy who used the Scucca Urns to draw Infectors out of people they have infected, and he ended up training you to basically be the sniper in waiting who annihilates those demon scum," Leos recalled. "They're called...they're called..."

"Silencers," Hunter filled in the blank. "If you recall, I told you how Ben was a devout believer that the Scucca Urns held the key to destroying the Darkness, and why after his death I became obsessed in tracking them down. Gotham all but confirmed Ben's hunch when he explained to us how there exists seven urns, and each one holds one of the seven Scourges from the which Darkness came to be. And that there, my friends, is the key to beating Samael."

The room became quiet as a tomb as each of the boy's traded puzzled looks with each other.

"I don't get it!" Ethan was the first to remark.

"Don't you see? We have three Scucca Urns. Granted it's not all seven, but it's nearly half. That would undoubtedly deliver a significant wound if we were to destroy those three; significant enough, at least, to force Samael to retreat into hiding back inside his wormhole," Hunter explained with an unmistakable enthusiasm. "Now, personally, I'm all for smashing all three Scucca Urns to smithereens. But, in this case, I think the smarter option would be to destroy only one of them—just to make Samael feel the sting—and then use the remaining two as bargaining chips to ensure he backs off on his claim to Jacob."

"That's a crackerjack idea," Max remarked approvingly. "In fact, I think it's crazy enough to actually work."

The plan seemed to entice Jacob as well, though he didn't say so one way or the other at first.

"Aren't you forgetting one tiny detail? How do you plan to destroy even one of those Scucca Urns?" asked Kairo. "Best I can remember, you had every tool and weapon known to man scattered across the floor of your loft, that you used to try and smash, hack and blow apart the urns, and they all ended up in broken mangled pieces. The Scucca Urns on the other hand suffered not a scratch."

"Right you are, Kairo," Hunter conceded, "Then again I didn't have the Sword of Destiny in my possession like Jacob here does. And if legend about the sword proves itself to be true, then the urns are as good as dust."

"But we don't even have the Scucca Urns. Remember, Anahel confiscated them the minute he learned you had them in your possession," Leos noted while recalling Anahel's face alight with delight at the sight of Gotham and the Nephilim in tow upon their return to Havenhid, only to darken when he was advised of the maleficent contraband they had in their possession.

"True," Hunter again conceded. "But I know where they are. I watched Anahel stash them away amongst a bunch of old books and scrolls, and dusty relics at the very top of the Library. Should be a cakewalk to go in there when Vessel is away and grab them."

"I wouldn't set my hopes on it," said Max.

Hunter waited for clarity and Jacob's reply proved to be even more cryptic when he said simply: "Greffiers."

"Greffiers?"

"Picture a mixture of Pitbull, Rottweiler and Doberman pincher all rolled into one and infected with an extremely nasty case of rabies, but instead of a mutant dog it's actually a bird: a very large and extremely mean bird," offered Max.

"Their job is to guard and protect the things kept in that highest and secluded region of the Library from anyone and everyone, and they are very good at their job. Anyone who even attempts to access any of the records, or items kept there, risks getting a serious flaying by some dangerous looking talons," warned Jacob.

"I take it there's more than one?"

"Three."

If anyone thought the description of the Greffiers painted by Max and Jacob would be cause enough for Hunter to take his plan back to the drawing board, they would have been mistaken.

"Definitely sounds like a challenge. But if I can manage to swipe a Scucca Urns from three separate Pethens and live to tell about it with all my limbs intact, then we should be able to come up with a plan to create enough of a diversion to allow one of us to get past the flesh-ripping talons and grab the urns," he said with an air of confidence.

Ethan, however, clearly didn't share the same optimism. "I not too sure about any of this," he whined. "It's starting to sound pretty risky."

"You want to chance the alternative?" questioned Max.

Ethan looked sheepishly to Leos and Kairo and then to Jacob.

"Look, I don't want anyone doing anything they are uncomfortable doing on my behalf, and I promise no hard feelings if you choose to bow out," said Jacob. "I, on the other hand, can't leave my fate in the hands of the Iudicium Tribunal. So I'm in."

Getting up from his bed, Jacob made his way over to Hunter and, in a show of solidarity, placed his hand on top of the one extended out to him. Max followed suit along with Leos and Kairo. The group then peered over at Ethan who still remained indecisive sitting on his bed until, finally, with a heavy sigh of surrender, he pushed his way into the circle formed by his friends and, with some lingering reluctance, placed his hand on top the others.

"That's my loyal chocolate factory," Max teased with smile.

Before they could break their huddle and get to planning, a troubled look suddenly descended upon Jacob.

"I hate to throw a monkey wrench in the works, but I just realized there's a major problem with your plan," Jacob, who went from hopeful to deflated in a matter of seconds, announced.

"What are you talking about?" asked Hunter.

"We failed to take into account a rather important detail, which is, I don't have the Sword of Destiny," said Jacob. "Remember, Sandel argued to the Tribunal that I be stripped of it during the course of the hearing. It's in Gotham's care now."

Just as before, with the disclosure of the Greffiers, Hunter didn't appear all that fazed by what was an obviously big fly in the ointment where his plan was concerned.

"Well then, I guess we have no choice but to get a little creative," Hunter muttered in response, after pausing a moment to think. He then shifted his gaze to Leos and, with a grin that was slightly mischievous, he asked: "The question is how creative are you willing to get?"

~ ~ ~

The following afternoon found Jacob standing outside a familiar door located in a secluded corner of Havenhid. How long had he been standing there he wasn't quite sure, for every time he went to make his presence known with a knock, he paused, only to bring his hand to the door once more after a moment of careful consideration, and then again stopping himself. Again and again he repeated the odd course of gestures as if trying to perfect the steps to a dance when finally, after nearly a dozen attempts, Jacob allowed his knuckle to rap on the door.

"Enter" a voice from inside answered.

After taking a steadying breath, Jacob gave the knob a turn to open the door and stepped inside a rather large sun-drenched room. It was, in fact, quite typical and expectant of the type of living quarters belonging to an angel where the space far outweighed the furniture. There was no bed to be found, for example, since angels had no need for them. Nor was there a table for dining (or for that matter, a kitchen) seeing as how angels had about as much need for food as they did sleep.

What furnishings there were included, in part, a couple of large easy chairs where one could sit and read next to the warm glow coming from the nearby fireplace. There was also a coffee table to place a saucer and cup during those quiet times spent with one's nose inside a book because, while angels had no need for sustenance, it did not mean they did not occasionally enjoy the soothing warmth that comes from sipping a particularly favorable cup of tea. In one corner of the room stood a large and intricately carved wooden armoire and, strangely enough, an even more beautiful brass clock residing on an otherwise bare mantle above the fireplace.

Intrigued, Jacob made his way over to get a closer look at the striking time piece; particularly the hypnotic sight of a brass ball bearing rolling its way along a zigzagging track set on the surface of a rectangular-shaped polished brash plate that slowly tilted from one side to another in accordance to the trajectory of the ball bearing. When the ball reached the end of the track, it struck a lever causing the plate to reverse its slow tilt while sending the ball zigzagging in the opposite direction. With each mesmerizing pass made by the ball bearing across the tilting plate there came an audible *Click!* as the hands on each of three porcelain time faces noting the seconds, minute and hour moved forward.

So captivated was Jacob by the ballet-like movements of the inner mechanical workings of the clock that he momentarily forgot where he was until he heard Gotham's voice. Taken aback, he looked to a far corner of the room not visible to him when he first walked in, and saw the angel seated at a large ornate desk piled high with books and various documents that he was busily studying.

"I was just admiring this clock of yours," said Jacob. "I don't think I've ever seen one quite like this."

"It's a replica—and quite a beautiful one at that—of the Congreve Rolling Ball Clock invented by Sir William Congreve in 1808. It got its name from the fact that it uses a rolling ball instead of a pendulum to regulate the time. I believe the original is housed in the British Museum," Gotham offered a brief tutorial, even as his attention remained glued to the pages of a book he was busily scanning.

"Pretty cool," noted Jacob. "I wouldn't think an angel would have much use for a clock, especially one as fancy as this."

"Personally, I've always been quite fond of clocks. I find the rhythmic pulse of the seconds ticking away to be particularly soothing to the ears; much like the sound of a heart beating," said Gotham. "As for the clock itself, it was a gift to me from your grandmother, which by itself makes it something I have long treasured."

Jacob proceeded to cross the room toward the desk where Gotham was seated, and as he did he casually, yet studiously, gave the armoire a hard, lingering look in passing. Whatever his eyes were searching for, they failed to spot it, and it was then he found himself forcing his feet to continue forward instead of giving in to their desire to abruptly change course and retrace his steps right out the door.

"Everything okay?" Gotham asked, when he allowed his eyes to briefly leave the clutter covering the top of the desk and settle their sights on Jacob who slowly lowered himself into a chair shaped exquisitely by the same tree branches which gave form to the rest of the chamber, and yet looking as though he was about to settle his backside upon a seat of nails.

"Sure!" Jacob replied a little too chippy. "Why do you ask?"

"I don't know; you just have a look about you I haven't seen since the day I introduced you to a lesson in overcoming your deepest fears using a simulation of an Infector."

Revisiting the memory of that unnerving face-off he had with that baleful apparition of the Underneath which proved itself that day to be a far more malevolent entity with its deceptive ability to transform itself into visions of the people he cared most about in the world was the last thing Jacob was interested in doing. And yet, strangely enough, he was certain if given the choice he'd happily travel back in time to face the menacing mirage rather than be seated before Gotham at that moment.

"Guess I'm still just a bit edgy with everything that's been going on," Jacob said instead.

"I certainly can't fault you for that," the angel said in a preoccupied tone. "Neither can I help but feel partially responsible for this worrisome situation of which you now find yourself in the middle."

"Why should you feel any responsibility?" questioned Jacob. "It's not like you were the one who set Samael free."

The comment caused Gotham to pause and give the boy another fleeting glance before continuing with his shuffling of papers in his search for whatever it was he was looking to find.

"No, I did not. I was, however, the one who convinced you to return to Eden and present your truth to the Iudicium Tribunal," he continued with a lilt of regret in his voice. "Perhaps, had I been less selfish in my feelings about proving yourself to be the Light Bearer and let you instead return to the quiet safety of Cain's Corner, you'd be much better off today."

"I'm not going to lie; the hearing has been no walk in the park, and I think I'd sooner have bamboo shoots driven underneath my fingernails than to continue on with it another day when it ends up resuming again. But you were right about me needing to come back and facing this whole Light Bearer thing—and you know what a bad taste it leaves in my mouth having to admit you are even the tiniest bit right." Jacob said, drawing a faint smile from Gotham. "Besides, as Anahel said last night, it wouldn't have made much difference whether I was here or at Cain's Corner; if the law is on Samael's side, it doesn't matter which side of Eden's gate I'm on."

It was at that precise moment Jacob heard a quiet but distinct *"Psst!"*—not in his ear, but inside his head. Slowly, and as inconspicuously as he could, he turned his head to glance over his right shoulder and look once more to the armoire several feet away and near where he sat. As he did, one of the doors to the armoire slowly opened and a hand Jacob knew belonged to Leos emerged through the crack to offer a quick wave before disappearing back inside as the door slowly closed again.

Jacob swiftly spun his head forward and took a deep breath when he heard Leos' voice echo inside his head: *"Let's put this Great Sword Caper Plan into motion already so we can finish it. I've been in this armoire so long I think I'm starting to develop the onset of claustrophobia."*

The Great Sword Caper Plan, as it was deemed, was concocted into the late hours the previous night, immediately after Hunter posed the cryptic question to Leos "How creative are you willing to get?" after it was reminded to everyone that Jacob had been forced to relinquish his Sword of Destiny into Gotham's care for the duration of his hearing before the Iudicium Tribunal. On paper, the plan itself appeared quite simple. Leos–who was volunteered for the assignment on the basis of elimination since he was only one aside from Jacob who possessed the Grace of Bending–would have the dicey role of sneaking into Gotham's chamber while the angel was away and hide himself away in the armoire, which was suggested to be the best concealment, and later use his special talent to affect the angel's thinking.

Jacob would later pay a visit to the room upon Gotham's return and engage the angel in conversation which was critical in helping to camouflage the guile involved in influencing and reshaping the thoughts of another, especially one as sensitive and mindful to such things as Gotham.

Simple as it may have seemed, however, Jacob knew full well the peril involved when it came to trickery and angels.

~ ~ ~

"What is all this, anyway?" Jacob asked as nonchalantly as he could muster about the stacks of books and the array of what looked to be various types of aged documents scattered across the desk.

"At the moment, the source of what is slowly becoming one giant headache," Gotham replied. "The breadth of laws which govern angels alone consumes three full floors of the Library. From that, I was able to procure all I could ascertain as being pertinent to Samael's petition to the Tribunal. It is my hope that residing somewhere in this collective clutter is the answer to our problems."

"You really think it's possible...beating Samael in his case, that is?" asked

Jacob.

"I refuse to believe otherwise," Gotham remarked defiantly, as his riffling through the papers grew suddenly more urgent.

"Where is it?" The angel suddenly grumbled aloud impatiently.

"Where's what?" asked Jacob.

"I had some important notes Vessel had scribbled down for me. They were written on a yellow piece of paper so it wouldn't get lost in the shuffle and here I've gone and lost it, though I could have sworn I just saw it shortly before you knocked on my door."

Then to Jacob's unbridled horror, Gotham suddenly announced: "Perhaps I left it in the pocket of my shirt I was wearing last night."

Before Jacob could think of anything within reason to say to stop him, Gotham rose to his feet from behind the desk and began making his way toward the armoire.

"Uh, mayday...you need to think of something! And quick!" Jacob heard Leos's voice sound off in panic inside his head.

Do? Do what? wondered Jacob who was equally, if not more panicked.

Frantically he began searching the desk, for what he hadn't a clue. Desperately he pushed aside a pile of documents followed by several books.

"Do something!" Leos' voice screeched urgently. *"ANYTHING!"*

More papers went flying into the air until quite miraculously Jacob caught a glimpse of a vibrant yellow piece of paper peering out from between the pages of a particularly age-worn book.

"I found it!" Jacob all but screamed at the top of his lungs, and as he spun around with the yellow paper clutched in his hand he nearly surrendered to the onslaught of a stroke at what he saw.

Standing at the armoire was Gotham who thankfully had turned his head to look back over his shoulder at Jacob just as he was opening one of the doors to the wardrobe and so far was oblivious to the exposed presence of Leos who was frozen with fear hiding away inside. When Gotham proceeded to close the door to his armoire without so much as a glance back, Jacob could almost hear Leos drop down to his knees to pray in thanks for being allowed to see another day.

"Okay...that was way too close to death for my liking," Jacob heard Leos comment. *"Now can we just do this so we can be done with it?"*

Jacob couldn't have agreed more with Leos, and when Gotham sat down again at his desk he was finally given an opening to get the ball rolling to their plan.

"While we wait for word from the Tribunal, it might be a good idea for you to return to your training. Goodness knows it's been awhile now, and you more than anyone need to stay at the top of your game," suggested Gotham.

"I'd like to and all, but..." Jacob began.

"But..." echoed Gotham. "Does the reluctance I hear in your voice have anything to do with your continued squabble with Damiel?"

Jacob had done well in keeping any hint of Damiel out of his thoughts, now the passing mention of him instantly ignited a flame of resentment.

"It's a little more complicated than a squabble," argued Jacob. "Besides, I would not continue with my training just because of Damiel. In fact, I was planning to head out with Max and the others to Lions Bite, only..."

"Only..." Gotham again echoed with a faint huff of wavering patience.

"Well for starters, you can't do a whole lot at Lions Bite without a sword and, if you'll remember, you sort of put mine under lock and key."

A look of clarity emerged from Gotham and Jacob followed the slow shift of his gaze to a far wall where he spied his sword gleaming in the golden light cast down from the afternoon sun resting on its point.

"You still have your old sword. Use it instead," suggested Gotham, before returning his attention to the scribble of notes scrawled across the yellow piece of paper for which he had earlier been searching.

"I can't go back to my old sword, not when I've finally started becoming used to the Sword of Destiny," argued Jacob. "Couldn't I just use it for a little while this afternoon. I mean what's the big deal? The Tribunal has recessed the hearing until further notice."

"I'm sorry, Jacob, but I just can't do it. I gave my word to the Tribunal that I would retain possession of it until the hearing was concluded."

As Jacob watched Gotham read over his notes, he proceeded to have a telepathic conversation with Leos as quietly as he could.

"He's not budging. What's going on?"

"Give me a minute. It's not like waving a magic wand," answered Leos. *"Go ahead...keep pressuring him."*

Taking a breath, Jacob worked up his next argument.

"How about if you come with me then?" said Jacob. "It'd be like the old days when you used to train me. The two of us could even spar a little. And you wouldn't really be breaking any rules, at least not blatantly. I mean, you'd be right there with me; the sword wouldn't even leave your sight."

Jacob's gaze bore its way into Gotham as he searched for any hint, any sign of a change of heart, even if it was coerced by (literally) hidden forces. But again he was met with no such luck.

"I wish I could, Jacob," Gotham replied. "Even if I wanted to, what favor would I be serving you by squandering such needed time when I've yet to find the thing needed to deter Samael?"

Jacob gave Gotham a surrendering nod and got up to leave the angel to his work when Leos' voice once again sounded inside his head.

"What are you doing? Where are you going? You're giving up too quickly."

"Just forget it. You're not going to get him to budge," Jacob answered back dismissively.

Suddenly, just at that moment, Gotham called out to him. "You know something; you're right. There's no reason you shouldn't be allowed access to your sword in order to continue with your training," said the angel. "It's only for a couple hours, and you'll return the sword to me afterward, right?"

Jacob couldn't believe what he was hearing, or better yet what he was seeing when Gotham got up from behind his desk and crossed the room to grab the sword and place it in his hands. Then before there was any change of heart (or in this case mind), Jacob went to make his exit but, just as he was one or two steps short of reaching the door, the angel again called out to him and Jacob was certain this time whatever mind-bending spell Leos had managed to cast on Gotham it was short-lived and already beginning to dissipate.

"I spoke to Damiel today and he feels real bad about what Samael is doing," said Gotham. "I just thought you might want to know that."

"Good! He should feel bad," Jacob replied indifferently.

It wasn't exactly the response Gotham had hoped for in return.

"How long are you going to hold this grudge?" he asked.

"Let me ask you first," countered Jacob, "have you forgiven him for what he did?"

Gotham appeared to consider the question for a moment or two before answering.

"I have empathy for his reasoning," he said finally.

Whether Jacob was surprised by the answer or not he did not let on.

Instead, he replied, "To answer your question, I hold no grudge against Damiel. But neither do I trust him. And I'm not sure I ever will."

Gotham said nothing further in return as the boy turned to leave the room. It was only when Jacob was halfway down the hall with the Sword of Destiny in hand that he remembered Leos, and the only thing he could do was hope his friend would be able to stay quietly hidden until the coast was clear to tiptoe his way out of the armoire and out of the room before Gotham felt the hankering to slip into a fresh shirt.

CHAPTER EIGHT

THE SECRET KEYS

With the Sword of Destiny in hand, Jacob, Max, Kairo and Hunter assembled inside the Library to launch the second part of their plan: The Great Scucca Urn Caper. There still, however, remained a couple hurdles standing in their way; the most immediate being Havenhid's newest Guide and steward of the Library, Vessel.

For some time, the group remained tucked away out of sight behind an arrangement of bookshelves watching as Vessel thumbed his way quite leisurely through several books as he prepared the following day's lesson plan.

"At this rate, it's going to be morning by the time he's through and clears out of here," Jacob grumbled impatiently.

"I think I might be able to get him to move along," said Kairo.

"What exactly do you think you're going to do? Clear the room with one of your ghost turds?" Max, painting a crass, if not humorous flatulence image in everybody's mind, asked.

"First off, eww!" Kairo replied. "Second of all, if I say it out loud I'll likely chicken out."

Before anyone could press him further, Kairo stepped out of the shadows that cloaked them.

"What's he going to do? Ask him to chaperone us?" Max wondered aloud as they watched Kairo casually walk over to where Vessel was seated.

It was then that someone suddenly came up behind them nearly causing Max, Jacob and Hunter to come out of their skin before seeing it was Leos out of breath and quite elated that he managed to finally free himself from the confines of Gotham's wardrobe.

"You trying to give us a collective heart attack?" whispered Jacob.

"Yeah, well, it would serve you all right for not coming up with something to get me out of there sooner. I was beginning to feel like I had been transformed into a Keebler elf and that old wardrobe was going to my new home," Leos grumbled sourly. "What's going on anyway? Did I miss anything?"

Max motioned with a nod of his head in the direction of where their attention had been focused, and they watched intently as Kairo approached Vessel. At first, it was clear from the look on Vessel's face that he was surprised to see the young boy in the Library at so late an hour. Even with their acute Nephilim hearing, they failed to catch a word of what Kairo was saying to Vessel but, much to their surprise, they watched as Vessel ended up getting up from the desk where he was sitting, grab a few of his things and leave the Library.

Once the coast was clear, Jacob and others rushed over to Kairo.

"What'd you say to get him to leave?" asked Jacob.

"Easy. I just told him Anahel had been looking for him," answered Kairo, before quickly adding defensively when he noticed his friends' eyebrows slowly rise up in unison in a collective show of judgment, "What? It wasn't a lie! Anahel did ask me if I had seen Vessel. Granted it was early this morning, but who knows, he might still be looking for him."

"We better step on it then," advised Hunter. "It won't be long before Vessel comes back once he discovers he's been sent on a wild goose chase."

"It wasn't a lie!" Kairo repeated his guiltlessness, though no one seemed to care one way or the other.

In a flash, the boys stripped off their shirts and tucked them into the waistbands of their jeans, and the familiar susurrus of wings unfurling themselves into view followed.

Ignoring the twin spiral staircases on either side of the room which led the way to Library's numerous floors, the boys chose instead the path of convenience and speed: straight up. One by one they launched themselves, and with tremendous speed they sailed upward with the same ease and rapidity of someone surrendering to the pull of gravity after diving off a cliff.

Upward and onward their wings propelled them toward a massive dome which capped the Library some forty-plus stories above them. They had less than half a dozen floors to go when Jacob made an abrupt diversion to one of the numerous balconies surrounding each and every floor of the Library as a precautionary measure to what awaited them. With the rest of the boys following behind, he led the rest of the way up a winding staircase to the upper most floor of the Library where the steps came to an end at the threshold of a large platform.

Standing beneath the dome that unfolded itself overhead like some giant architecturally exquisite umbrella, it was extremely hard deciding where to focus one's overwhelmed senses which were immediately pulled in different directions. First, there was the dome itself; impeccably formed by the trees that gave shape to the rest of Havenhid, the intricacies of the interwoven branches were such that the dome at first glance appeared to have been constructed out of an earthy brown marble. The inside of the dome was lined with numerous shelves, and housed upon those shelves were countless scrolls and old dusty parchments stacked one upon another along with an assortment of old relics and antiquities. Anyone wishing to satisfy their curiosity by browsing through the contents on the shelves, however, were met with an instant head-scratcher, as there was no feasible way for anyone who ventured to this rarely visited spot in the Library to get their hands on any of the treasures. The platform upon which the boys stood extended only about a quarter of the way beneath the dome before yielding to a sheer drop leading straight back to the bottom floor of the Library stretching some forty-some floors, and the steps to the spiral staircases leading to the platform continued no further.

Ultimately, though, it was the impossible-to-ignore presence of the three raptor-like birds, each perched on one of the large arched openings along the rim of the dome through which could be seen the orb of the full moon hanging high in the night sky whose gauzy silvery light pouring forth into the Library only served to make the dark shapes appear all the more menacing.

One only had to be offered a glimpse of the menacing feathered creature to know instantly why a Greffier would be chosen to serve as guardians of this restricted corner of the Library much less three. For starters, they were sizable creatures more on par to that of a bear than say a Wandering albatross or an Andean condor, not to mention fierce-looking. It was the kind of offspring one would expect to emerge from a nest of eggs if a member of the eagle family waded into the vulture pond. What sat poised and ready on the rim of the dome against the backdrop of the full moon had the powerfully built and sleek body of an eagle, but its face was all vulture with its bare featherless head, large hooked beak and the most unfriendly of eyes that, strangely enough, appeared to assume an even more sinister look as they unveiled their faces that were tucked away inside their wing to stare down from their perch at the group of Nephilim who made the unfortunate mistake of disturbing them.

~ ~ ~

Even though it had not been Jacob and Max's first visit to the upper reaches of the Library, their expressions were no less as dumbstruck as their friends' when they suddenly found themselves standing in the presence of such intimidating creatures.

"I take it those would be the Greffiers," Leos was the first to comment.

"What gave it away? The fact they are giant menacing birds, or the fact that they are giant menacing birds?" Max asked drolly.

There came unexpectedly from behind a loud stomping of feet that caused everyone to turn their head in unison only to find Ethan charging up the spiral stairs to the platform where his feet came to abrupt halt while his eyeballs proceeded to all but pop out of their sockets.

"Oh boy!" he gasped with dismay at the disquieting sight of the three Greffiers whose backs hunched and necks stretched forward even further in order to fix their black glassy eyes on Ethan's sudden arrival.

"Where've you been?" asked Kairo.

"I-I-I told you," Ethan stammered while doing his best to keep his feet from making a one-hundred-and-eighty-degree-turn at the ankle and retracing his steps back down the stairs he had just ascended in quick order.

"I was going to go do a quick search to see if I could find any information on the...on the...on those," he said, motioning nervously to the three Greffiers who continued to look at him as though he were an especially tasty looking rodent who had emerged from its hole at the most inopportune of times.

"And?" Leos pressed impatiently.

The question managed to knock free the stunned look Ethan had fixed on the Greffiers and turn his attention instead to the book he had clutched in his hand.

"Oh yeah...well, I found this book. It's all about different animals who have served as guardians of the Light," Ethan said as he furiously flipped his way through the pages until he finally found what he was looking for and held the book out for all to see. "It has a whole chapter on these Greffiers."

"And? What does it say?" Max barked testily.

"Alright, alright...jeez, don't have a coronary!" Ethan mumbled as he spun the book back around and began to earnestly scan through the pages. "It says the Greffier is the only species of its kind within an order of birds many scientists now believe never existed except in lore and mythology."

The boys all turned their heads slowly in unison to take another glance at the three feathered beasts leering down at them.

"I'm no scientist," said Hunter, "but I think it's safe to say we have clearly debunked the notion that Greffiers are the stuff of fairytales."

"The Greffier has long established itself as the most fearsome of all raptors," Ethan continued with his reading, pausing a moment to mutter under his breath, "You can say that again!"

"They are also the largest of all bird species, with a wing span that can easily reach twenty feet, and weighing northwards of fifty pounds. The Greffier is a carnivore who swallows its prey whole. It feeds on a number of small to mid-size animals including wild boar, foxes, young lambs and even calfs, though ancient Roman legend holds that the monstrous-looking birds had a penchant for slipping through open windows when couples had retired for the night and carrying off newborns left unguarded and asleep in their bassinets."

As if the Greffiers weren't frightening enough, the image of them as an ancient boogeyman stealing sleeping babies from their beds to enjoy as a midnight snack brought a renewed look of horror to the group.

"We're running out of time so let's cut the chase already," Jacob, growing more uptight with each passing minute, said. "Is there anything we need to know about besides the obvious?"

Ethan didn't seem to find anything noteworthy as he quickly scanned the remaining pages, when suddenly a look of alarm came over him.

"What is it?" asked Kairo.

"They're venomous," answered Ethan. "It says here their talons secrete a poison that causes complete and permanent paralysis the instant it is injected into its prey."

Closing the book, Ethan looked to his friends with a deepening worry.

"I sure don't like the sound of that. For reals."

He wasn't the only one.

"Maybe we need to rethink this whole thing," suggested Hunter.

"You're not wussing out on us now, are you?" balked Max.

"It has nothing to do with wussing out. I just think it bears reassessing whether going through with this is worth chancing the possibility of making the wrong move and living out the rest of your days as a piece of petrified wood."

"Hunter might be right," Jacob said in agreement. "I don't want anyone risking their lives or their ability to move on my account."

"She'll be apples! You said it yourself: there's three of them and there's six of us," Max said to Hunter before looking to Jacob. "As for anyone taking any risks, you know I'm always more than happy to be the red flag that's waved in a snorting bull's face."

Before anyone could stop him, Max's wings unfolded themselves into view from behind his back and, as he swiftly took the air, he called out to his friends: "All I need you to do is create a diversion and keep these baby-eating buzzards off my tail."

~ ~ ~

The three Greffiers craned their heads forward as far as their necks would allow, making them appear like a clowder of felines ready to pounce upon an unsuspecting bird that's chosen unwisely to come to rest on a low fence, and they let loose an ear-splitting screech of rage at the sight of Max willfully crossing the boundary of the platform and entering the restricted space inside the dome with his sword drawn and in hand.

In a flash, the Greffier perched in the center opened its massive span of wings and lunged towards Max with its eyes aflame.

"Look out!" Jacob cried out in warning.

The Greffier dive-bombed Max whose lightning reflexes managed to steer himself clear of the razor-sharp talons that slashed their way at him narrowly missing his shreddable flesh and, instead, sliced the air with a wince-inducing whooshing sound.

When the other two Greffiers rose up higher on their clawed feet and stretched open their wings in preparation to join the attack, Max looked to his friends for assistance.

"That whole creating a diversion thing I mentioned earlier would really come in handy right about now," Max cried out.

Jacob and Hunter were first to begin hollering at the top of their lungs and waving their arms and were soon joined by Leos, Kairo and, eventually, Ethan. The ruckus drew the attention of all three birds and, with their raptorial eyes momentarily diverted, Max made a brazen dash for a section of the guarded shelves where he spied the familiar sack used to hold the Scucca Urns. He had nearly reached his target when the first Greffier turned its head suddenly and, with a shriek of rage, swooped in with lightning speed to block his victory. The Greffier's wings sounded like the blades of a thousand swords cutting through the air as it flapped them, and with its eyes flaming with anger fixed uncomfortably on Max, it let loose another terrible screech that made itself felt to one's very bones.

The other two Greffiers quickly abandoned the attention they had focused on the other Nephilim screaming and jumping wildly about on the platform and flew off to join the first despite the boys' frantic attempts to keep them engaged.

Suddenly, Max found himself surrounded by the unfriendly creatures that began to circle him like a kettle of vultures eyeing the fresh carcass of a deceased cow. Despite his best attempt to keep up a brave and unintimidated face, Max could feel his heart thumping inside his chest. His right hand clutching tighter the grip of his drawn sword, as his unblinking eyes attempted to keep each of the circling beasts in his sight and, more specifically, the unnerving claws attached to their feet that gleamed every so often when the moonlight hit them just so.

It was while he was cautiously eyeing those claws and hearing the echo of Ethan's voice in his head revealing what a dangerous weapon they were, that one of the Greffiers caught him by surprise by buzzing uncomfortably close past him. As he spun around to face his attacker, a second Greffier took advantage of his blind spot by swooping in and delivering a powerful strike from behind with its wing. The blow not only knocked the wind from Max, it caused the sword to slip free of his hand and fall out of sight in its irretrievable plummet to the ground floor of the Library.

"We gotta do something!" Leos cried, as he and the others looked on in horror at the sight of their friend levitating in the air like a doomed sitting duck ready to be feasted upon by the three circling Greffiers.

Again, they bellowed and waved their arms about in a desperate attempt to draw the attention of the giant birds which largely went ignored until, much to the surprise to everyone who witnessed it, Ethan took a running jump off the platform and into the forbidden airspace inside the dome.

"Come and get me buzzard beaks!" he called out to them while flapping his way toward a section of shelves filled with secret documents and relics on the opposite end of the dome.

Two of the Greffiers squawked loudly and flew full speed in pursuit of Ethan whose brief moment of bravery instantly dissolved into panic.

With the threat surrounding him momentarily gone, Max saw a clear avenue to the sack containing the Scucca Urns open itself to him and he made a lunge for it, unaware that the first Greffier who first held him in its sights still remained but a hair's breadth away. Max was just a few feet away from grabbing hold of the sack when the Greffier was suddenly once more in front of him screeching its deafening cry. With a look of terror alight in his eyes, Max caught sight of the Greffiers clawed foot viciously swipe its way toward him. Instinctively, he held up his arm to protect himself from the lacerating talons and, as he did, the inside of his wrist came into contact with the reach of the moonlight pouring through the arched openings lining the dome, and the invisible sigil branded onto his skin with the fiery tip of the feather plucked from the most rarest and beautiful of birds—the Illume—to mark his and Jacob's victory during the Illumination competition, was instantly visible in a vibrant display of iridescent blue radiance.

In an instant, the Greffier retracted both its assault and its talons, and Max watched in amazement as the bird docilely returned to its perch in one of the dome's arched openings. Not sure exactly what he had just witnessed, Max turned to the other two Greffiers who had cornered Ethan and were about to permanently incapacitate the boy.

"Hey! Look this way you oversized bin chickens," Max called out.

The birds swung their heads around and just like the first Greffier who had retreated to the sidelines, they immediately became submissive and abandoned their attack on Ethan when they got a glimpse of the glyph radiating from Max's wrist that he held out in front of him for all to see.

"Ripper!" Max muttered to himself once Ethan was safely back on the platform and the Greffiers had surrendered their attack and returned to their perches.

"Did you see that? Did you see what happened?" he asked, clearly excited, as he returned to his friends and looked to Jacob. "I told you I suspected these sigils weren't just some cool-looking brand; I told you they had to serve some other purpose like being a key to something. Well, now we've discovered the lock to the door these things are able to open."

"I wonder why Anahel never told us," Jacob wondered aloud, while studying his wrist which, outside the touch of the moonlight, showed no sign of the veiled symbol.

"Go ahead," Max urged Jacob. "Give it a burl!"

Jacob looked upwards to the rim of the dome where the Greffiers sat in an unthreatening manner yet continued to keep a watchful eye on the group of boys. Then, with a touch a hesitancy, he opened his wings and gingerly rose up off the platform and into the guarded open space. The Greffiers immediately became alert and unfolded their wings in preparation to go on the offense against the intruder they held locked in their menacing sights. Before they could launch themselves, however, Jacob quickly raised his arm so that his wrist came into contact with the glow of the moonlight and instantly the mark hidden on his flesh surfaced in a brilliant flickering of blue flame, and the Greffiers, upon seeing it, abruptly receded back into submissiveness.

When he saw the Greffiers no longer posed a threat to him, Jacob swiftly flew himself over to the section of shelves lining the inside of the dome and snatched up the sack for which they had placed their lives on the line, or at the very least the use of their limbs for the unforeseeable future. Then returning to the platform, Jacob held the weighted sack over his head as if he were an athlete presenting the torch at the start of the Olympic Games. As he was greeted with cheers of a job well done from his equally elated friends, Max turned to look for Ethan and, when he finally spied him, aimed a pointed finger his way and barked: "YOU!"

Ethan was still too shaken up from his too-close-for-comfort face-to-face with the Greffiers to worry about what he may or may not have done.

"What exactly do you think you were doing performing a dill stunt like that?" Max asked, though it came across far more like an accusation.

"You dropped your sword and those Greffiers were coming at you. Weren't you listening when I read from the book that they're poisonous?" Ethan replied meekly.

"So you just took it upon yourself to prove yourself a Wally by throwing yourself in the middle of a blue you had no business getting involved in. Don't you know how close you came to getting yourself hurt?"

"You're one to talk. Why else do you think I'd risk doing such a stupid thing?" Ethan grumbled sourly before muttering under his breath: "Sue me for caring."

Of course, Max already knew deep in his gut the reason behind Ethan's uncharacteristically brave display, and he couldn't help but be profoundly touched that, despite having to endure times of humiliating razzing–some might say incessantly–not to mention be on the receiving end of routine noogies, Ethan had managed to find the goolies needed to dangle himself like bait in front of two seething Greffiers, and on his behalf, no less. In response, Max did the only thing he could: he grabbed Ethan up in his arms and gave him a big old–and very much genuine–bear hug.

When he had finished, he kept Ethan in a headlock and, with the warmest of affection, gave the top of his head a good rubbing with his knuckles because there were some things–like routine noogies–which were impossible to resist.

From that day forward, the two boys would come to share an unspoken, and unbreakable bond.

~ ~ ~

"So...now what do we do?"

Leos asked the question, but they were each wondering the exact same thing as they huddled together on the platform moments later staring at one of the Scucca Urns they had removed from the sack and set on the floor while above them the Greffiers looked on with quiet intrigue.

"What we came here to do," answered Hunter. "Destroy it."

All eyes then slowly turned their way to Jacob who was unusually silent.

"I guess that's where this comes in, huh?" he said finally, while raising his right hand which held the Sword of Destiny.

"If you'd rather, I could do it for you," Max volunteered.

For a moment, it looked as if Jacob might take his friend up on his offer.

"That's okay. This is my problem; it's best I deal with it," he said, instead, though it was more than apparent he was less than gung-ho about the task before him.

"What exactly do I do?" he then asked.

"You take that sword in your hand, and you drive it home would be my best estimation," instructed Hunter who, despite being the one who conceived the plan at hand, looked in more ways than one to be second-guessing the wisdom of his scheme.

"And I'd say if you're going to do it you better make it quick," Max was quick to add. "With all the ruckus we made in here trying to get our hands on these things, I'm surprised we're not in the middle of getting out hides tanned by the Guides."

Jacob took note of the warning and nervously he adjusted his grip on his sword. Just as he was about to raise it, though, Ethan voiced the second question that was at the front of everyone's mind.

"Has anyone considered what could happen when Jacob strikes this thing with his sword?"

"What do you mean?" asked Kairo.

"Hello...it's a Scucca Urn; a devil urn. If it's true what Gotham told us about these things—that they carry pieces of what makes the Darkness the Darkness—then whatever is in there is going to come out," said Ethan.

"He's right," Leos said in agreement. "What if we end up unleashing some demon that makes these Greffiers look like cuddly kittens?"

No one answered, but the looks that were exchanged between everyone in the group said more than enough.

"Nothing's going to happen," Hunter finally blurted.

"How can you be so sure?" asked Leos.

"Because we have the Sword of Destiny. Nothing's going to survive a blow from that blade. You can take that to the bank."

As assured as Hunter's words were, as well as the voice that spoke them, no one appeared any more confident. Yet despite the continued wavering, Jacob stiffened himself while taking a steadying breath.

"Alright, no more lollygagging," he said, and upon hearing his own words, he immediately chastised his tongue for unconsciously allowing one of Gotham's archaic choice of phrases he joyfully chided the angel for using regularly in conversation to pass through his own lips.

Again, he tightened his grip on his sword before slowly raising it over his head. Closing his eyes, his took another deep breath then squeezed his eyes tighter still when, finally, he mustered the goolies (to coin a phrase from Max) to bring the blade of his sword down upon the Scucca Urn with a firm and determined swing. A loud *CLANK* echoed inside the dome, and the stinging thunderbolt of what felt like a jolt of lightning shot through Jacob's hand and up his arms. When he opened his eyes, he found the edge of his blade resting against a still-intact urn which betrayed not so much as a nick from the blow.

"Maybe you didn't hit it hard enough," said Kairo.

"Sure sounded like it was hard enough," Ethan argued, while rubbing his left ear which rang from the clangor caused by Jacob's sword.

"Give it another go," Max urged with a nod of his head.

Again Jacob raised his sword and again he brought it down upon the Scucca Urn, only this time with all the strength he could muster. Another loud *CLANK* sounded. Only this time Hunter barely managed to duck out of the way and keep from getting pegged squarely in the head when the blow from the sword sent the urn airborne. It sailed like a shot across the platform and, quite unexpectedly to all parties involved, into Anahel's left hand which proved to possess the same lightning-quick reflexes as Hunter's ducking responses just as he climbed the final step of the spiral staircase leading to the platform.

A deathly silence followed as Anahel studied momentarily the object that was suddenly in his clutches. Then, with an expression most grave, he looked to the group of Nephilim huddled together and slowly approached them.

"Unless I'm mistaken, I do believe this belongs to you," Anahel addressed Max in a cool and collected voice while extending his right hand in which was held the boy's sword. "Strange thing to leave one's sword abandoned on the floor of the Library."

"Little bugger! I must have dropped it," Max replied with a nervous laugh, as he took the sword and quickly put it away in the hidden sheath inside his left wing.

"Yes...I've no doubt," Anahel said.

His gaze then drifted upward to survey the dome where the three Greffiers were calmly residing. Another quiet and uneasy moment or two passed as Anahel again gave the urn in hand a curious once-over before turning a suspicious eye on the group again.

"I'm certain the explanation regarding this will be equally as...forthcoming," he remarked.

~ ~ ~

Looking like a pack of troublesome pooches with their tails tucked firmly between their legs, the group of boys obediently followed Anahel as he led the way to the ground floor of the Library—not the short and easy route by wing but the far more tedious and arduous track down the spiral staircase.

Without speaking a word, they then followed the angel to the study area of the Library where they found Vessel, looking none too pleased about the wild goose chase he had been sent on by Kairo, seated at his desk. The boys found their own seats as instructed at the three tables forming the first of four rows arranged in front of Vessel's desk. Once they had settled themselves, Anahel placed the Scucca Urn along with the sack where the other two remained concealed in the middle of Vessel's desk for all to see and demanded brusquely: "Explain."

The boys traded hesitant, if not nervous glances with one another, until Jacob cleared his throat and declared as fearlessly as he could muster that what had taken place earlier in the evening was on his account and he would take full responsibility for whatever repercussions were coming.

"That remains to be seen," replied Anahel who appeared not the least bit impressed by the boy's valor as he folded his arms in front of himself while leaning back against Vessel's desk with his left eyebrow cocked in an unmistakable show of his growing impatience.

And so Jacob proceeded to disclose to both Anahel and Vessel the plan concocted by the group of six while lying on their beds in the dark, staring at the night shadows clamoring about the ceiling of their room. He conveyed how the desperate scheme was hinged to a very desperate fear of the Iudicium Tribunal siding with Samael and forcing him against his will to succumb to a life in the Underneath, and in that fear, using the power of Scucca Urns as a bargaining chip to impel Samael to relinquish his rights to the boy.

Try as he might otherwise, Anahel couldn't help but allow a watering of sympathy to douse at least a tad bit the fire of his anger as he listened to the boy, and when Jacob had finished and reverted his eyes to his lap as he awaited whatever punishment was coming his way, the angel sat in silence quietly marinating in what he had just heard.

"One would think a lesson would have been learned from the unfortunate circumstances that guided your feet across the threshold of the Silent Forest and the illusory lair where Lilith once dwelled," Anahel finally spoke in a thoughtful voice. "Out of sight, out of mind. I believed at the time, keeping the existence of such dark things secret and unspoken helped to make the world around you and to the other Nephilim who have left their footprints in Eden's soil before you a safer place. Ignorance, however, is not bliss, but in fact quite dangerous as I, not to mention all of you, have come to learn. And so I cannot deny my own culpability for that which has brought us here to this very moment.

"When you returned to Havenhid with these Scucca Urns in your possession, I cannot convey to you the irrepressible feeling of dread that came rushing over me like a tsunami. I recognized instantly what they were and, more so, what they contained, and I was overcome by an almost suffocating sense of foreboding of what the presence of these objects of Darkness meant for Eden and all who call her home. It's a moment most rare which found me in such an incapacitated state, yet it had visited me, and is the reason why my reaction was blunt in its muteness. All I could focus on was to secrete these urns out of sight and out of reach until I had time to deliberate the next course of action.

"As it happened, the hearing before the Tribunal became much more involved than any of us could ever have anticipated, and is about the only thing which could have possibly caused me to push these Scucca Urns out of my thoughts, that is, until this moment. This matter should have been brought to the forefront and addressed long before this night, and for that I acknowledge my error in judgment, not to mention extend my apology."

It was not the reaction Jacob and his friends expected from Anahel, yet they readily welcomed it and felt themselves relax in their chairs. The moment of relief, however, proved itself to be short-lived.

"That, of course, does not release you from the barb of the hook upon which you now find yourself wriggling," he scolded in a voice once more curt. "When I think about what could have happened had you found yourselves successful in your plot. Do you have any sense of comprehension what it is you might have unleashed inside this Library had you managed to breach the shell of this urn, not to mention the immediate danger you may have brought upon the whole of Havenhid or your unsuspecting classmates?"

No one said a word in response; not even Ethan who couldn't help but feel a little vindicated for being the only one in the bunch who had attempted to be the voice of reason by trying to make the others question the possible outcomes of striking a Scucca Urn with the one sword capable of destroying it.

A high-pitched scraping sound made itself suddenly heard when Vessel pushed his chair away from the desk at which he was sitting and rose to his feet. His presence, like other angels, was most notable in his towering stature, and Jacob found himself eyeing the angel with both interest and greater curiosity. It was, after all, one of the first opportunities he had being in the same room with Vessel aside from his appearance at the hearing to be questioned by Sandel and, as Jacob casually looked the angel over and studied him, the more he realized how much unlike Thaniel he was. To begin with, Thaniel's less imposing presence was deceptive in cloaking a tightly wound coil of unexpected strength residing inside him, while Vessel wore an aura of intimidation in much the same way as his shirt. Where Thaniel evoked the image of an angel as half Roman warrior and half carefree nymph depicted in numerous Italian Renaissance paintings, Vessel was reminiscent of a superhero attempting to hide his identity behind the guise of a professor that failed miserably in concealing the image of a warrior angel, with sword in hand, smiting demons left and right, even when surrounded by walls of books. It wasn't that Vessel didn't emit an air of intellect and acumen like

Thaniel; to the contrary, one only had to engage in even the briefest of conversations with Vessel and walk away in the realization that he was appropriately christened. But where Thaniel represented "The Republic" by Plato, Vessel was a living embodiment of Niccoló Machiavelli's "The Prince."

"I must confess I'm still rather confused somewhat by this so-called plot. What exactly was it you were attempting to achieve by destroying the urn?" Vessel asked, while casually strolling the length of floor before the tables where the boys sat while following him with their gazes.

"I can answer that," said Hunter. "I appreciate Jacob trying to lay the blame for all of this squarely on his shoulders, but the truth of the matter is, it was me: I came up with the plan and talked everyone here into going along with it."

With the hours of night ticking away, Hunter then proceeded to fill in both Vessel and Anahel on the backstory of how the Scucca Urns found their way into his possession; the details of which neither angel had yet to fully hear since the young man was first introduced to them upon his arrival at Havenhid.

Hunter told about a certain stormy night several years back when he was living life by his wits on the streets and, while digging through garbage cans in a darkened alleyway in search for food, being drawn to a strange house from which he had heard a woman scream. It was there while investigating by peering through an upstairs window that he first came face to face with an Infector, and befriended the man named Ben in whose hand he first witnessed a Scucca Urn that was used to lure the ghastly specter of the Underneath to its death.

"This Ben...I take it he was a disciple of the Purgatores?" Vessel asked, when Hunter had finished.

"That would be an appropriate way to put it; he was a Silencer."

Hunter replied with a tone of sadness while being reminded of the last unbearable memory he held in his memory of Ben in the death grip of a particularly vengeful Infector and the unfortunate demise that met his friend, not by the black demonic shroud, but an arrow drawn from his own quiver.

"What's a Purgator?" Ethan inquired curiously.

"The Purgatores were...*are* a personal prelature of the church tasked with the cleansing of the uncleansed in the world. To put it simply, they are what many today would classify as exorcists; eradicators of ungodly entities," Vessel explained. "I wasn't aware they still existed in this day and age, and if they did

I would guess their numbers to be quite small. They first emerged in centuries prior, but it was during the Crusades that this small and very elite band of skilled and gifted warriors made itself known. When eventually the Crusades came to an end under the smothering weight of the Protestant Reformation, so, too, did the Purgatores; but not altogether.

"The group, consisting of able-bodied men trained to go up against the maligning forces of the Underneath, such as Hunter's friend Ben who did so as a Silencer, continued to exist out of sight if not out of mind, but exist they did, waging their invisible war against the enemy of Darkness and passing on the weapons used in their relentless battle to generations who followed in their path."

Vessel turned a discerning eye onto Hunter who had been quietly staring off ahead while listening. "I've noticed you to be the rare–dare I say exceptional–Nephilim who favors the weapon of an archer over the more proficient sword while training at Lions Bite."

"I'd argue which is more proficient at Lions Bite or anywhere else for that matter–a sword or bow and arrow–is dependent upon whose hands they are placed," Hunter replied.

"Particularly if that person is a Toxotai, wouldn't you say?" asked Vessel.

It was clear by the apprehensive expression on Hunter's face that the astute observation caught Hunter off guard.

"Ben trained me to be his Toxotai, if that's what you're asking," Hunter replied finally with a renewed confidence.

"And from what I've observed at Lions Bite, he's proved himself to be a most effective teacher," said Vessel to which Hunter nodded in acknowledgment.

"Tell us, if you would, how you came to your beliefs about the Scucca Urns, and more importantly, how these three came into your possession," Anahel, who was anxious to get to the crux of the matter, asked.

"Everything I know about the Scucca Urns I learned from Ben," answered Hunter, before motioning with a nod of his head to the one residing in full view on the desk in front of him. "That one there belonged to him, and he had it with him the night we met. He knew they were an important key to the existence of the Darkness; he just didn't know to what extent in the way Gotham later explained to us when I showed them to him at my loft."

"That there are seven of them; each holding one of the seven Scourges from which the Darkness was created as part of a devious scheme devised by

Samael to retain in perpetuity dominion over the Underneath placed temporarily in his hands following a covenant set in place between God and the Dragon," said Anahel, to which Hunter nodded agreement.

"Ben was certain that by destroying the urns you could, in fact, destroy the Darkness. Figuring out how to destroy something that proved itself to be indestructible, however, was another matter altogether, not to mention locating the other six and wresting them away from their Pethen caretakers," said Hunter. "And so, in the meantime, Ben did the next best thing by using the sole Scucca Urn he had in his possession as an instrument to lure Infectors from the people they infected and destroy them one by one."

Hunter then went on to explain how he came to have the other two urns which resided inside the sack: the first being the bittersweet remnant he recovered from the pile of ashes that were once his friend Ben and the Infector Hunter had caused to spontaneously combust with a well-aimed arrow; and the second he brazenly absconded with in broad daylight in a pristine upscale London neighborhood where one would never suspect a nasty unsightly Pethen to reside.

"A lot of good it's done. I've been trying, to no avail, to destroy them ever since, including tonight," Hunter grumbled with frustration.

"I wouldn't fret much over it," said Vessel. "Even if you somehow had managed to find success in destroying the urns, you'd quickly realize you would have fallen quite short of your objective."

The statement drew the collective focus of confused gazes from the boys.

"What do you mean?" asked Max.

"If destroying the Darkness is your aim, then know such an ambitious feat will not be wholly accomplished by the obliteration of these pernicious objects."

"You have to be kidding me," said Jacob. "Then all of this was for nothing, and these Scucca Urns are completely worthless to us."

"Then...Ben was wrong," Hunter muttered with disappointment.

"Maybe a bit a mistaken in his belief, but not completely wide of the mark," said Vessel.

Leos gave his head a vigorous shaking like he had just come up during a dip in a swimming pool with an ear plugged with water. "Is this supposed to be some kind of riddle or something?"

"Even if you had been successful tonight in you mission to destroy this Scucca Urn, you would have found it a futile, and dare I say unnerving effort to exterminate that which resides inside. The Darkness, like the Light, is an enduring force of immense power that cannot simply be snuffed out with a swing of a sword," said Vessel. "When Samael created these adamantine urns and placed inside them the seven hearts which pump life into the Darkness, he forever and wholly secured in his grasp the maligning power of the Underneath. His scheme, however, was not without its Achilles heel. Should someone come to possess any single Scucca Urn and find a way to destroy it, the Scourge concealed inside would return itself to its true master, the Dragon, and the power that came with it would be forever lost to Samael. And so–"

"And so, to prevent any possibility of something like that happening, Samael put the Scucca Urns into the only hands he could trust–those of the Pethens, and he disbursed them to opposite ends of the earth with one sole directive: keep the urns safe, and at any cost," Hunter interjected to finish Vessel's thought.

~ ~ ~

The group took a moment of silence to absorb all they heard, and none of the gears turning inside each of the boys' heads was grinding away more than Jacob's.

"There's just one thing I don't understand," he wondered aloud, both to himself as well as those seated around him. "Why the need for the Pethens?"

"I thought it was made pretty obvious," replied Max. "To safeguard them from people like Ben and Hunter who were on a mission to destroy them."

"That's my point. We just tried to destroy one of them, and with the Sword of Destiny to boot, and we didn't even leave a nick on it," said Jacob. "If the Sword of Destiny is known to be the most powerful weapon in existence and it failed to destroy a Scucca Urn, what else is left to protect it from?"

The question sparked a rumble of intrigue from the other boys.

"Yeah, how about that? I thought the Sword of Destiny was able to lay waste to anything and everything in its path," Leos said to both Vessel and Anahel who looked equally as perplexed.

"That is the question at the moment, isn't it?" Vessel said in reply. "Unfortunately, it is one I do not have an answer to at this precise moment. To say I am quite flummoxed by this revelation would be an understatement, and I am most anxious to begin the hunt through the fields of books housed in this Library for some clue in solving this intriguing mystery."

"I find myself equally bemused, though for slightly different reasons," noted Anahel whose penetrating gaze came to rest itself squarely on Jacob. "Dare I ask how it is you came to have the sword in question for this escapade? If memory serves me correctly, the last I recall is Gothamel taking ownership of it from you at the beginning of the hearing at Sandel's bequest."

Jacob instantly felt an uncomfortable heat begin to radiate from his reddened face.

"Oh, uh, he...he agreed to let me borrow it...for a short while," the boy stammered awkwardly.

"Did he now?" the angel replied with feigned surprise punctuated with raised eyebrows.

Jacob, however, knew better than to try and put one over on Anahel and smartly confessed: "That is, he agreed with a little outside influence."

"Well, then, I'll leave in your hands the pure joy you are sure to reap when you confess to him your chicanery while returning the sword back into his care," Anahel calmly instructed in a way that ensured precise obedience. "Immediately, I might add."

Jacob replied with an obedient if not hesitant nod. Then, with an upward glance, Anahel remarked on the late hour and advised his charges the time had come for them to retire to their room and into their beds.

"There's just one more thing I'm curious about," Jacob said, as he walked alongside Anahel towards the doors to the Library. "Why didn't you tell us about the sigils?"

"Sigils?" echoed Anahel with a puzzled look.

"You know...the mark you placed on my and Max's wrist with the feather from the Illume when we won the final Illumination competition."

"And what exactly is it you're implying I kept from you?"

"That they're secret keys; at least, that's how Max refers to them," said Jacob. "He tried to convince me about the idea before, but I thought it was a bit far-fetched. Then we discovered completely by accident that when the spot on our wrist came in contact with the moonlight and revealed the hidden sigil branded there, it made the Greffiers back off on their vicious attack and allow us total access to all that stuff they're guarding. I don't think I ever would have been able to successfully grab the sack holding the Scucca Urns if it wasn't for this sigil.

Anahel's gaze followed Jacob's to the inside of his wrist he held up revealing the strange mark which was again brilliantly aglow under the gauze of light from the moon being cast down from above them.

"Ah, yes, now I understand; and so you've come to satisfy another curiosity within me on how you managed to do what no other could possibly manage no matter how skilled, and that is, to get past the Greffiers in a manner that kept you bodily intact," said the angel. "As for your sigil being a key of sorts to the one area of the Library restricted to all, I can assure you it is not. That it helped guide you past the Greffiers' talons while you were attempting to seize the Scucca Urns is nothing more than coincidence in that regard.

"That's not to say the mark you carry on your arm is not as mysterious in its nature as the luminous bird from which it came," continued Anahel. "It is believed by some –and I'm not saying I am among the converts–that when one is marked by the blue fire of the Illume, the flame of the marking delves deep inside that person to where the soul resides. It illuminates it wholly and based on what is revealed serves as a guide, for lack of a better word, to ensure the person carrying its mark sees himself past any hurdles that might block the way to the destined fate residing at the end of life's path."

"Then perhaps what happened tonight wasn't a coincidence," Jacob mused. "Perhaps the sigil was removing a hurdle for me by making the Greffiers back off."

"Perhaps," Anahel, not sounding convinced one way or the other, replied.

"But then why would Max's sigil do the exact same thing and cause the Greffiers to stop attacking?"

Anahel pondered the question for a moment. "Perhaps, the two of you hold fates that are tightly intertwined; fates that, somehow, passed together as one through the dome above us that the Greffiers guard so rabidly."

Jacob followed Anahel's gaze as it rolled upward to peer thoughtfully at the highest point of the Library which looked to be hovering miles away, and he found his tongue suddenly weighted with more pressing questions when who should enter the Library but none other than Gotham.

"A little late in the hour to be burning the midnight candle, isn't it?" Gotham, looking as surprised to find himself face to face with the group of Nephilim as they were of him, remarked.

"You're absolutely right about that, which is why we were just on our way to bed," Jacob replied, as he tried to make a clean getaway, and likely would have succeeded had Anahel not been quicker in grabbing him by the arm and keeping him firmly in place beside him.

"It would appear these Fledglings were in demolition mode tonight," said

Anahel.

At first, Gotham didn't appear to have a clue as to what Anahel meant until the angel held up the sack clutched in his right hand containing the three Scucca Urns.

"Demolition mo—" Gotham began, before narrowing his glare on Jacob. "And here I was feeling like a louse after you came to my room earlier trying to entice me to give you back the Sword of Destiny to supposedly get in a little training at Lions Bite. There's something to be said about listening to that little voice that now and again buzzes in your ear, and I'm sure glad I lent it both ears and kept the sword safe and sound in my care or goodness knows what trouble you might have caused."

"You quite certain about that?" Anahel inquired, and again a puzzled look briefly came over Gotham, until his eyes roamed downward and caught the surprising sight of the sword in question in Jacob's hand.

"That's impossible!" Gotham muttered in disbelief. "I clearly remember you sitting across the desk from me pleading with me to lend you the sword for a couple hours. You even tried to get me to come along with you to Lions Bite to spar. 'It'd be like the old days when you used to train me,' you tried to coax me. And as tempting as it was, there is no doubt in my mind that I said no—"

Again Gotham's voice stopped suddenly, as though a lightbulb suddenly turned itself on inside his head, and yet what looked to be a dark shadow suddenly descended upon him, and Jacob felt himself shrink slightly when the gaze fixed upon him narrowed even more. One could almost catch wisps of steam coming off Gotham as he slowly stepped toward the boy in a way that looked as if he was mustering every bit of control he had to keep from pouncing on Jacob.

"I—" Jacob attempted to croak, but he was instantly silenced when the angel held up his hand and all but reached out and pinched closed the boy's lips.

Taking a steadying breath, Gotham held out his opened hand and, with eyes ablaze, he stood waiting for Jacob to timidly relinquish the sword back into his custody.

Then without utterance of another word, Gotham turned on his heel and quietly left the Library. When the angel was gone, Jacob took a breath; not one of relief, but rather dread. He had known full well the danger involved when it came to trickery and angels. He was now going to learn in spades the repercussions.

CHAPTER NINE

THE CRUCIBLE

Hardly a day passed when Predmore LeDuc didn't find himself mulling the most nagging of questions: How was it that he came to be alive?

To be clear, it wasn't a question of biology that sooner or later visits itself upon young boys who eventually come to learn there are more to birds and bees than meets the eye. Rather, it was a literally pondering of how it was he came to be drawing breath at any given moment when he became conscious of the routine function his body performed without thought.

It was a haunting question which would come to pursue Predmore relentlessly since the day it first began its echo inside the boy's head the year before he came to Eden. He was fourteen years old then; a shy and awkward kid who, unlike Jacob, knew exactly who his father was growing up and, equally important, what he himself was. Neither, however, left him with an adequate sense of confidence regarding his footing in the world. Hence, his days were often spent alone, and at no time did such a solitary existence make itself felt more than during the lunch hour at school when he could be found sitting by himself in the cafeteria surrounded by the incessant drone of his teenaged peers buzzing about from table to table in a social frenzy.

That's not to say Predmore was without friends. His best friend, in fact, was his brother Trevor who was four years older than him, was very much embedded in the social hubbub of high school life and, most markedly, was not a Nephilim, having been the product of Predmore's mother's brief marriage to a mere mortal man before setting her sights on higher plains. Strangely enough, it was the differences between the two brothers that helped to forge their strong bond, and even though Predmore would be the one who would eventually come to have them, it was Trevor who spent the better part of their young lives together taking his younger brother under his wing, metaphorical as it was.

And so it came to happen one chilly fall afternoon that Predmore found himself at his usual spot in the cafeteria watching his schoolmates mingling with one another as though he was observing chimpanzees through the bars of a zoo exhibit, when Trevor suddenly appeared and plopped himself in the seat directly across from him.

"How's it goin' there, Sprout?" Trevor addressed his little brother with the pet name he coined when they were younger to go along with the one Predmore had given him: Giant, which is how Trevor existed in Predmore's eyes in more ways than one.

Helping himself to the bag of chips sitting on the table in front of Predmore, Trevor gave his brother a thoughtful look as he nibbled.

"Don't worry about it. It's okay," Predmore said quietly.

"What's okay?"

"You changing your plans to go with me to the movies after school."

Trevor froze a moment with his jaw unhinged. "How did you know I was coming over to tell you that?"

Predmore gestured subtly to his ear and Trevor understood instantly.

"I know I promised," Trevor explained. "It's just...Derrick finally managed to buy himself a used car and, sadly, it's a real hunk of junk. So a bunch of us are going to head over to his place to see if we can at least get it to run without sounding like a cat being fed through a paper shredder, which I'm not sure quite how that's going to turn out since none of us, as far as I know, have wands."

Predmore turned his gaze to where Derrick and the rest of Trevor's friends were seen cavorting on the opposite side of the cafeteria where he first spied them earlier and overheard them pressuring Trevor to "ditch the shrimp."

"Tell you what I'm gonna do to make it up to you, though," Trevor's voice once more grabbed Predmore's attention. "Tomorrow we'll go to movies, and afterwards I'll even throw in a game of miniature golf at Putters. Maybe I'll finally get lucky and beat you for once."

It sounded like the perfect way to spend a Saturday, but Predmore failed to show his usual excitement when such offers were extended his way.

"That's okay, I don't want to rope you into wasting a day by spending it with me," he said with a touch of gloom.

"Does it look like my hands are tied?" Trevor replied holding out his arms and flashing an infectious smile. "Besides, I hardly think of spending time with my little brother as a waste of any day. Believe it or not—and if you tell anyone I said this I'll wring your scrawny neck—unlike most brothers, I actually enjoy hanging out with you."

One couldn't blame Predmore for being skeptical that a popular senior like his older brother would even acknowledge his nobody-of-a-freshman sibling, much less spend any time hanging out with him, unless it involved the delivery of wet willies and the random public pantsing.

The smile on Trevor's face gradually receded. "You know, I bet you there's a lot of kids your age in this cafeteria who would also enjoy hanging out with you if you just gave them a chance to get to know you," he said.

The suggestion caused Predmore to visibly withdraw within himself.

"Listen, I understand why you're so hesitant, really I do," Trevor said in a quieter tone while leaning in from across the table. "Everyone here feels awkward in some way, shape or form, myself included. You're really no different than anyone else."

Predmore didn't need to respond; the look he shot his brother was more than enough.

"Alright...your differences are a tad bit more complex," Trevor acknowledged. After all, it was safe to say Predmore was more than likely the only one in the cafeteria dealing with the pangs of not only puberty but the subtle and not-so-subtle changes that comes with being a Nephilim on top of it.

"All I'm saying is," Trevor offered his brother in the nicest way possible, "if you want to make friends, you have to be a little bit more inviting than sitting here alone by yourself looking like one of those kids from 'Children of the Corn.' "

"What if they end up not liking me? What if they discover I'm...weird?" asked Predmore.

"Newsflash: you are weird! But if it helps boost your confidence, I've known you've been weird for some time and, strangely enough...I like you," said Trevor. "And again, if you tell a soul, I'll be coming for that neck of yours."

The two brothers shared a hearty laugh together, but the levity was short-lived when Predmore's attention was drawn suddenly to the entrance of the cafeteria and the sight of tall young man dressed all in black, and his smile instantly faded when he watched the stranger pull from the confines of the long, heavy overcoat he was wearing a semi-automatic rifle as he strolled casually toward the buzz of students oblivious of the approaching nightmare.

Predmore looked back to his brother who was still in the midst of laughter and, with terror flooding into his eyes, he fought to sound a warning but found himself gripped by a sudden and completely immobilizing paralysis that left him frozen solid like a block of ice in his seat. The *RAT-TAT-TAT* of gunfire finally voiced what Predmore found himself unable to release from his throat as the gunman sent a spray of bullets into the unsuspecting groups of teenagers eating their lunch while indulging in the latest hot gossip of the day.

The cacophony of screams that sounded was unlike any herald of horror Predmore could imagine, and in the bedlam that followed the boy remained glued to his seat, his petrified gaze fixed on the shooter.

RAT-TAT-TAT!

RAT-TAT-TAT-RAT-TAT-TAT!

When the reality of what was happening kicked in, Trevor leapt to his feet, and as he did Predmore watched in horror as the shooter paused his massacre quite abruptly and turned his attention to the table where he was seated. An evil, monstrous smile unfolded itself on the shooter's face, and much to Predmore's disbelief his acute hearing caught the shooter whisper *"Nephilim"* before aiming his rifle directly at him.

More bullets sounded just as Trevor cleared his way around the table before making a last desperate lunge at Predmore and tackling him to the floor in a hit that stole every bit of breath the young boy had in his body. Everything went black, though the screams and gunfire continued to ring out unbearably so inside his ears, and for a moment Predmore found an inexplicable sense of safety and security that came from the heavy weight of Trevor's body on top of him as he lay pinned to the floor. It quickly gave way to unimaginable dread when he suddenly became aware of something warm and sticky dribbling down onto him. And only when he managed to see that the wetness was crimson in color did the real terror swoop down upon him.

~ ~ ~

How was it that he came to be alive?

The question posed itself in a whisper as it usually did to Predmore, this time while he was taking a break from training at Lions Bite. Why the inescapable memory of his brother's death chose to visit him at that precise moment, he hadn't a clue.

Perhaps it was because the place where swords were unsheathed to sing their battle cries from the arena floor only served to stoke the all-consuming guilt he felt not only in what he believed was his failure to help save his brother's life, but the knowledge in knowing his being a Nephilim may very well have led to Trevor's death.

It may also have been the fact he was observing Hunter showing off his fighting skills under Damiel's watchful eye. There was something Predmore found quite striking about Hunter that reminded him of his late brother. It was not so much the way he looked–though Hunter did bear the same dark, laidback athletic look as his brother–but rather the self-assuredness wrapped in a healthy helping of considerateness that revealed itself in the nod of recognition Predmore received whenever their paths crossed that paid a reminder to Trevor. Not to mention the willful, headstrong streak which was subtle in its existence, and blunt when prodded out into the open for all to observe.

From the day Hunter first stepped foot in Lions Bite, he and Damiel had clashed like the blades of two swords engaged in a fierce duel. Their wrangling stemmed mostly from Hunter's unwavering stance in favoring his trusty bow and arrow as his weapon of choice over the prerequisite sword every Nephilim eventually comes to acquire when the time is right.

"You cannot sufficiently defend yourself from the forces of the Darkness with anything less than a sword," Damiel argued for the umpteenth time in his weeks-long attempt to convince Hunter otherwise.

"Let me ask you this: Isn't the whole point of arming us to ensure we slay the very thing that might come looking to attack us?" asked Hunter.

"It is," Damiel grumbled surly.

"Then thank you very much, but I will choose my bow over a sword any day of the week."

"You are being pigheaded on this matter for pigheadedness sake," said Damiel.

"Why are being such a tyrant about this? I've tried to explain it to you; it's not that I have anything against swords, in fact I find them to be quite nice, when they're not pointed in my direction, that is. But I am more comfortable with, and, might I add quite skilled at using my bow." A thought then illuminated itself inside Hunter's head that caused his gaze to narrow itself on the angel in a devious manner. "In fact, I'm willing wager I can perform just as well as you and your sword. Maybe even better."

Just as Hunter suspected it would, the challenge sparked a glint of intrigue in Damiel's eyes.

"And what, exactly, is your wager?" the angel inquired.

"If you win, I'll ditch the bow and give the sword a try," Hunter proposed, before quickly adding: "But if I win, you have to promise to get off my back about it."

"Fair enough," the angel grumbled.

"And..." Hunter was prompt to add, "you allow me and the rest of my classmates to have a go at The Crucible."

The mention of The Crucible was quick to draw Damiel's full attention.

"You've been here but a few short weeks, and only recently come into your wings. What makes you think you're even close to being ready to set foot in The Crucible?" Damiel questioned with a dismissive chuckle.

"I know you let the Shrikes compete there recently, not to mention the Harriers. Overheard Creed Maggert the other day crowing about making it through on his first attempt, and if that little frosted flake can do it, you better believe I can too, wings or no wings."

Annoyed as he was with Hunter, Daniel couldn't help take pleasure, albeit in a sneering way, in the measure of brazenness with which the young man chose to highlight his gumption.

"They say fortune favors the bold. Myself, I've witnessed more times than naught such intrepidness, when not reigned in, has an unwelcome habit of piercing daring young lads such as yourself right about here," the angel noted matter-of-factly while gently tapping the center of Hunter's chest where his heart beat with two fingers, "and deflating them instantly where they stand."

"Do we have a bet?" Hunter, paying no mind to Damiel's comment, asked.

Hands were shook, and Predmore watched with heightened excitement along with the rest of his classmates who had gathered in closer to watch what promised to be a thrilling spectacle as Damiel and Hunter positioned themselves a respectable distance from one another in the center of the arena. All was quiet but for a gentle breeze whistling its way through the behemoth slanted slabs of stone forming the walls of the arena when suddenly they revealed themselves.

Infectors.

They emerged from the patches of shadow and dark corners of the stone slabs. First came two, then four, then eight, and soon an entire swarm. Naturally, they weren't the real versions of the fiendish wraithlike creatures of the Underneath, but rather uncomfortably realistic simulations used quite effectively in training Nephilim to address their fear. Yet neither were they harmless mirages; in fact, they were almost as dangerous as the genuine articles, as most Nephilim who eventually came to take part in the harrowing exercise soon learned. Even Damiel understood the challenge he had accepted was not one to take lightly.

Keeping a sharp eye on the circling figures shrouded in their hooded cloaks, Damiel drew his sword from the sheath formed by the plumes on the inside of his left wing. Hunter followed suit, first by placing a single arrow firmly between his teeth, then reaching behind to grab three more arrows from the quiver strapped to his back. When the Infectors finally attacked, they did so with blinding speed and intensity.

Damiel was the first to strike, cleaving in two the first apparition to swoop down upon him and instantly rendering it a cloud of ash that quickly dissipated into the air. Hunter, however, quickly upped the stakes of showmanship when he nocked all three arrows gripped in his hand at once, took aim and sent them whizzing through the air like bullets from a gun where they simultaneously stuck three Infectors and created a far more impressive display of three clouds of ash.

"Showoff!" Damiel grumbled to himself at the feat.

In a flash, Damiel proceeded to demonstrate the true mastery he commanded with his sword as he set about cutting down Infectors left and right in spectacular fashion while Hunter followed in step sending arrow after arrow at their targets at a speed that needed to be seen to be believed. All the while Damiel watched closely out of the corners of his eyes Hunter's progress, and to ensure the mounting death count remained in his favor.

One by one the Infectors' numbers dwindled until only seven remained. With lightning speed and equal devastation, Damiel beheaded three of the ghastly specters with three swipes of his blade. Then, to secure his all-but-declared victory, he set his golden-eyed sights on a fourth Infector, drew back his sword and sent it hurtling toward the demon, but Hunter proved himself quicker. After downing three of the last Infectors himself he spun around, took the arrow still clutched between his teeth and sent it squarely into the head of the last remaining Infector leaving nothing but a lingering gasp of ash for Damiel's sword to pierce.

It was nothing less than an exhilarating showing of fighting prowess for the group of Nephilim watching from the sidelines, and they erupted in a chorus of cheers for Hunter's unexpected victory. Even Damiel couldn't ignore the ability it took to squeak out a win against his unmatched skills, yet he refused to betray even a smidgen of admiration deserving of such a display of adeptness.

"Just so we understand one another; that's as close as you'll get to receiving a passing mark from me for your time at Lions Bite," the angel declared brusquely, before walking off to retrieve his sword resting on the ground where it had fallen some distance away.

~ ~ ~

Hunter stomped off to a patch of grass near where Predmore was sitting where he cast aside his bow and quiver of arrows while grumbling angrily to himself before dropping down onto the ground in a huff.

"That was pretty impressive," Predmore offered meekly. "I don't think I've ever seen anyone go up against Damiel and come out the winner."

Hunter acted as if Predmore wasn't even in earshot of him and said nothing in return.

"You certainly were adamant about not using a sword," Predmore said after an awkward silence. "How come?"

"Weren't you watching just a minute ago? I thought it was made pretty obvious." Hunter snapped back angrily.

The curt response caught Predmore by surprise, not to mention Hunter who immediately bowed his head and took inside him a quieting breath.

"I'm sorry, Predmore; I didn't mean to snap at you like that," he glanced back at the boy over his shoulder and offered apologetically. "It's just...Damiel can be so frustrating sometimes. I thought the whole point of this Lions Bite was to turn us into the best fighters we can be. For some reason he just refuses to recognize that this...THIS makes me the fighter I am," he said grabbing hold of his bow.

"All I know is I wish I had your courage. You didn't even look one bit afraid of those Infectors. I mean, I know they weren't real Infectors, but they were real enough. Me, I've been terrified of those things ever since one killed my brother," said Predmore. "I've tried to have courage...that is, the kind of courage Damiel says one needs to go up against something like an Infector. Truth is, I've ended up injured more times than anyone at Lions Bite. I think maybe I'm not cut out for this Nephilim thing."

The matter-of-fact manner in which Predmore spoke, absent any trace of self-wallowing, inexplicably tugged at Hunter.

"Can I let you in on a secret? I'm not really all that brave as you think I am. To be perfectly honest, I'm scared to death of Infectors. Every time I see one. I'm this close to having an embarrassing Depends moment," Hunter confessed before quickly adding, "And if you breathe a word about what I just said I'll wring your neck."

The playful jab met Predmore's ears with a pang of familiarity when, in that brief moment, it was as if his brother was suddenly present speaking to him.

"You know, I've watched you go up against some of the guys here and you are not nearly as inept as you make yourself out to be," said Hunter. "But, if you're looking to be better, the first thing you have to do is change your perception when you step out into the arena and overcome your fear."

"How do I do that?" asked Predmore.

"Admit you're scared to death and face it head on by being the first to step up to any challenge, no matter how much you might not want to."

It sounded simple enough, but Predmore still had his doubts.

"Do you think...that is, would you mind one day teaching me how to use that?" he asked somewhat timidly, motioning to the bow lying on the ground where Hunter had deposited it.

"You bet," replied Hunter with a smile.

Drawn by the clamor of swords clanging loudly, the two turned their attention in unison to the floor of the arena where several of the boys were engaged in one-on-one bouts with each other. Predmore, however, continued to look as if something was gnawing at him as he glanced every now and then at Hunter as though something lingered on the tip of his tongue.

"Can I tell you a secret?" he finally asked apprehensively.

"Sure," Hunter answered while continuing to remain focused on the dueling.

"I think Jacob might be in danger," Predmore blurted out, causing Hunter's gaze to shift his way.

"Danger? What makes you say that?"

"His soul...it's blank."

Hunter's body straightened itself from its relaxed state. "Blank?"

"Don't misunderstand me; it wasn't like I was prying," Predmore was quick to explain. "For the past couple years I started seeing...visions, I guess, is the only way to describe it, whenever I looked at people. When I came here it was confirmed at the Crescent Scar that my Grace is Gazing."

"The ability to peer into the souls of others and see their lives both past and present as though it were a sort of scrapbook," said Hunter.

Predmore nodded, looking more like someone who had been gifted a curse rather than a divine gift. "I'm only telling you this because I'm afraid of what might happen if I don't. But I also don't want to spook anyone."

"Go on."

"It's like I said: whenever I look at Jacob, all I see is a black slate, completely void, as if his soul had eyelids and they were closed tight." Predmore grew suddenly more sullen. "The same thing happened with my brother. Two days later he was killed by an Infector."

Hunter sat quiet for a moment looking quite troubled by what he had heard.

"You haven't told anyone about this, have you?" he asked finally.

Predmore replied with a simple shake of his head.

"Good. I think for the time being we should keep this just between the two of us until I can figure out what is best to do," said Hunter, before giving Premier a renewed glance. "That's a pretty powerful weapon you have."

"Not sure I see what's so powerful about it. It's just a bunch of pictures I'm able to see," Predmore scoffed. "Changing yourself into something else or controlling the elements of the earth...now those are powerful weapons I'd trade my Grace for in heartbeat."

Hunter spun himself around until he was fully face to face with the boy.

"You know, I once met this man who wasn't a Nephilim, or an angel, nor did he possess the Grace of Gazing, but he had the ability to do things similar to you," said Hunter. "His name was Ben and he was a blind man, yet he could see things a man with twenty-twenty vision couldn't. And he was responsible for sending more Infectors to their deaths than I can count."

Hunter's words, spoken in a quiet tone, almost as if he were revealing a secret he wished no other pair of ears to hear, instantly intrigued Predmore.

"Trust me when I tell you the Grace you hold is equally as powerful as any of the ones you secretly wish you possessed, if not more," said Hunter. "The blind man I spoke of is responsible for how I just performed against Damiel. He trained me how to use my bow, and more importantly how to use it against Infectors. If you're interested, I can teach you everything he taught me as well as how to make that Grace of yours as dangerous as your sword."

The unexpected offer brought a light to Predmore's face.

"All I ask is that we keep our training regimen off the radar," said Hunter. "Last thing I need is for Damiel to think I'm usurping their territory or converting his students to the evils of the dreaded bow and arrow."

Predmore agreed and Hunter turned himself back to the action taking place inside Lions Bite when he paused suddenly, glanced back at Predmore over his shoulder and asked, "If you don't mind my asking, whatever happened to the Infector who killed your brother?"

It was the one question in regards to his brother's demise Predmore had no trouble answering.

"My father showed up out of nowhere just as the shooter who shot Trevor turned his gun on me and both the young man and the Infector who infected him were no more," Predmore explained without a hint of emotion in his voice. "I asked my father how he knew I was in trouble, and he told me he heard my soul cry out in terror."

Hunter opened his mouth to inquire more on the matter but was stopped when a voice called out. It came from a French boy named Matthieu waving wildly from the other side of Lions Bite for the attention of his fellow Ospreys.

"Damiel asked me to fetch all of you pronto," Matthieu yelled at the boys. "It's time!"

"Time for what?" one of the Ospreys yelled in return.

"The Crucible," came the answer.

~ ~ ~

It was both the sudden rush of excitement as well as an equal amount of trepidation that brought the boys to their feet and sent them running full speed across a plain of tall grass and a short distance into a stretch of forest that led the way to a small clearing where they came upon a nearly impregnable thicket.

It was in front of this wall of vegetation Damiel was found patiently waiting.

"It's assuring to see the vigor in which your feet answered my summons, as it most certainly will be the first thing to be tested in spades beyond the point where I stand," remarked the angel, and he watched as each boy's eyes looked past him and nervously attempted to peer into the thicket, as rightly they should.

"You mean we're finally going to get the chance to run The Crucible?" one of the boys asked to which Damiel nodded.

The whispers of excitement were traded amongst the boys as well as a few high-fives which caused Damiel's eyebrow to arch itself.

167

"I wouldn't be so quick to pat each other on the back," said the angel. "or do I need to remind you both the Ospreys and the Shrikes have already leapfrogged over you by a good distance in standing where you now are?"

There were several pivotal moments which marked a Nephilim's time at Havenhid: The reveal of Graces at the Crescent Scar, the presenting of swords at Lions Bite, and the baptism into wings at Broken Earth. Receiving a lesser-known summons to the little-known secluded spot of forest known as Deep Thorn would most certainly be amongst them; for it meant Damiel believed he had taught his chosen pupils all he could and the time was finally at hand to put to the test each boy's readiness by making them face their greatest and most punishing challenge to date: The Crucible.

As Damiel proceeded to explain to his enlivened students, Deep Thorn came to be known as Ground Zero of man's fall to sin. It was the place where God discovered Eden's first mortal inhabitants, Adam and Eve, after they had shown themselves disobedient by eating from the Tree of Life. It was there the two were found hiding in the brush desperate to conceal their nudity of which the conscius—the forbidden pear-like fruit grown by the Tree of Life, of which they ate—made them suddenly aware, as well as escape the voice coming from the clouds; and it was there they received their punishment in the form of exile from the Garden.

"What once was a short-lived sanctuary to the doomed mortal inhabitants of this once-earthly paradise now exists as a domicile where the remnants of temptation breathed forth by the Serpent intermingling with God's wrath continue to reside, and from whose energy The Crucible came to be," said Damiel. "For those of you pondering the obvious, Deep Thorn most certainly would have joined the Silent Forest and the Northern Lands as one of the rare places Fledglings are forbidden to trespass were it not for the impregnable thicket of brush which fully surrounds this area of forest and virtually seals it off from the rest of Eden. Or, to put even more succinctly, just as nothing is able to emerge from the other side of the thicket, so, too, is no one free to enter Deep Thorn at will; that is, until after he receives divine permission, which in this case comes from me."

The angel intently scanned the faces before him and the corner of his mouth curled itself upward. He had their attention.

"Color me stupid, but like, what exactly is this Crucible thing anyway?" one boy blurted out. "Like you said before, some of the Harriers or Shrikes have already gone inside, but when I've asked them to describe exactly what the challenge is they all have different answers."

"That's because The Crucible presents itself differently to everyone who faces it; neither does it reveal the same face to those who do not succeed in their first attempt and seek a rematch, as is the case with most," explained Damiel. "The Crucible is, by its very definition, a moment of extreme trial and tribulation that will make every test you've endured so far during your time in Eden, seem like a walk in the park. When the time comes for each of you to enter Deep Thorn, you will do so in pairs. Not only will you be competing with one another, you will be pitted against each other in a series of severe and exacting challenges targeting such things as strength, mental acuity, loyalty, and even faith, in ways untested at Broken Earth.

Damiel paused a moment to allow for the murmuring of pensive consideration over what he detailed being traded amongst the boys to die down.

"There's just one more thing," he said finally, waiting for the perfect moment to voice a very crucial footnote he had yet to reveal. "There are two caveats that must be followed when competing in The Crucible: you are not allowed the use of your wings, nor that of your Graces, at any time, under any circumstances. If, at any moment, you fail to oblige by said conditions, you will instantly be expelled from Deep Thorn and deposited somewhere in the vicinity of this threshold in a manner that will likely make your head spin."

"What about our swords?" the question arose from somewhere amongst the boys in a somewhat timid manner.

"Fortunately, that's one thing you will be allowed to take with you, and most undoubtedly will find use for," Damiel answered ominously.

"And a bow?" Hunter was quick to ask, drawing a stern look from Damiel.

"I guess we shall find out, as you will be the first to do so," the angel grumbled.

Then, turning his attention back to the gathering of boys standing before him, he asked: "Who amongst you wishes to go first?"

~ ~ ~

The woods grew markedly quiet as not a single Nephilim so much as cleared his throat for fear of having it being mistaken by Damiel as an equivalent of eagerly raising one's hand. Several uncomfortable minutes passed with Damiel's weighty gaze pressing itself with growing intensity on the fidgeting group, when Hunter looked over at Predmore who was standing next to him.

"What do you think? Feeling lucky?" he whispered. The question caught Predmore by surprise.

"You–you want me to volunteer to go first?" he asked, as his eyes grew wide at the prospect.

"Remember what I told you about the perception of fear?" he reminded the boy of their conversation not too long ago while huddling together at Lions Bite. "Might be the perfect opportunity to face it head on."

Before Predmore could respond one way or the other, Hunter faced forward once more, raised his hand and announced, "Seems only fitting I go since it was my wager that brought us here."

Damiel appeared neither surprised or particularly happy about his first volunteer as Hunter stepped forward and stood beside him.

"Very well," he conceded with a sigh. "Who would care to face off against Mr. Wylde?"

Again, silence followed. And then, despite every fiber of his being trying to convince him otherwise, Predmore meekly raised his hand and stepped forward, much to everyone's surprise.

"Well, this should be interesting," Damiel commented under his breath.

After both boy's wings had been tethered with a rope of vine to keep them immobile, Damiel then led the boys to a particular spot along the wall of brush and wished them luck. Gripping his bow in one hand, Hunter retrieved an arrow from his quiver with the other, and Predmore gripped all the more tightly his own sword.

There came the unmistakable rustling of leaves and Hunter and Predmore each took a steadying breath as they watched the branches and vines forming the dense barrier that closed off Deep Thorn from the rest of Eden begin to move of their own accord and slowly disentangle themselves from one another.

Before long a patch of the brush had untwined itself enough to form the mouth of a dark opening in the dense vegetation which looked much like the entrance to an inhospitable cave.

Without a semblance of urgency, Hunter and Predmore made their way inside, the grips on their weapons growing ever tighter with every step. Once they had fully entered the awaiting murkiness, the branches and vines that had cleared the passageway quickly wove themselves together and, in a flash, the entry vanished from sight, as did Hunter and Predmore

"What happens now?" several boys asked Damiel in unison.

"We wait," the angel answered.

Waiting, however, proved to be as much a trial for the Nephilim gathered outside Deep Thorn as what each boy quietly imagined what might be taking place out of sight on the inside. Minutes felt like hours, and each passing second that followed grew more and more unbearable with every passing tick. Not a single Harrier uttered not so much as a whisper as they stood with their eyes glued to the spot where the passage into Deep Thorn had briefly revealed itself when suddenly, after what had seemed to be an eternity plus a day, there was heard a cry.

"What was that?" came the obvious question.

Before anyone could venture a guess, there was heard another cry. It was distant and muffled, but there was no mistaking it was a cry. A human cry. A cry for help.

"It sounds like...Hunter."

All eyes turned to Damiel who looked gravely to the wall of brush where the entrance lay hidden and he drew his sword as though he were about to cut his way through with his blade.

Before he could take a step, however, the vegetation began to once more move with life and again the branches and vines unraveled themselves allowing the dark opening to reappear from within the thicket. As it did, both the Ospreys and Damiel searched desperately the murky gloom inside and were relieved at first at the sight of Hunter's silhouette making its way quickly towards them. Relief turned to dread, however, when Hunter came in reach of the light as he raced out of Deep Thorn with Predmore's unconscious and limp body dangling in his arms.

CHAPTER TEN

THE BIRTH OF SILENCE

"**W**hat happened?"

The gruff and pointed question came from Anahel while watching with grave concern as Zuriel attended to Predmore who was still out cold lying in a bed inside a sun-filled room set aside for Nephilim who occasionally found themselves on the receiving end of an injury requiring more than just the healing touch from one of the Guides. Anahel's gaze shifted immediately to Damiel who was found standing quietly by himself in a corner of the room mindlessly rubbing his chin as he stared at the boy sprawled out unconscious in the bed, but it was Hunter who eventually spoke.

"He saved me."

"Saved you? From what?" asked Anahel.

"A...well, a flower," answered Hunter, drawing an even more confused look from Anahel.

"Perhaps you should start at the beginning," the angel suggested.

Hunter obliged and began by telling Anahel how he and Predmore had volunteered to go into Deep Thorn prompting Anahel to look once more to Damiel, only this time with a look most unpleasant.

"Go on," Anahel said in a withering tone.

Hunter proceeded to describe the gloominess he and Predmore suddenly found themselves surrounded by when the entrance to Deep Thorn closed behind them except for a window of sun-lit forest they spied several yards away, and he and Predmore began making their way towards it.

"As we were walking, we became aware that the air was becoming thin; so much so that we started having difficulty breathing," said Hunter. "We moved faster and the air grew even thinner. We began panting as we struggled harder to breathe. Finally the air became void of oxygen. We started racing in a panic toward the sunlight, and as we did the distance between it and us stretched itself longer and longer right before our eyes. To make matters worse, I felt something slowing my feet and making it increasingly difficult to run, and when I looked down, I saw that the ground had mysteriously turned into a path of unforgiving sticky mud into which my feet sank past the ankles. I fought to carry on but my lungs were empty and burning.

"Predmore was faring worse than I and eventually collapsed. I considered putting my wings to use; at least we'd be thrown out of Deep Thorn and live to see another day. But that stubborn streak I have that, more times than not, gets me into trouble kicked in, and I grabbed Predmore and managed to drag us into the safety of the sunlight where the return of air greeted us."

With parts of him still caked in the mud described in his ordeal, Hunter continued, "Once we had a minute to recover, we found ourselves in a setting as beautiful as any other part of the Garden. But there was something markedly different about it, too. I couldn't tell you exactly what it was, but I could feel it. And then I could hear. There was something lurking out of sight, camouflaged in the beauty surrounding us. An animal of some sort, or maybe something more nefarious? Whatever it was, I had my bow at the ready."

"What about the flower?" Gotham, who was also in the room, inquired with a hint of impatience.

"I'm getting to it,' said Hunter. "It appeared out of nowhere; rising up from a patch of fern like the periscope of a submarine," said Hunter. "It was beautiful; probably the prettiest flower I've ever seen before. Predmore on the other hand looked like he'd come face to face with a twelve-foot rattlesnake. He was more wary of that flower than whatever it was that continued to stalk us, and as I quickly discovered rightly so. Whatever kind of flower it was, it had a second bulb of bright red petals that slowly opened like a giant mouth, and inside was a half dozen or so barbs shaped like tiny knives and covered in golden-colored pollen. Before I knew what was happening, Predmore suddenly dove at me knocking me to the ground. Once I regained my bearing I found him out like a light on top of me with one of those barbs the flower had obviously intended to shoot at me, now imbedded in his neck."

Hunter paused a moment to check his emotions as he continued to stare down at Predmore looking all but lifeless.

"Kid tries to overcome his fears and risks his life for my own in the process," he mumbled before looking to Zuriel. "He's going to be alright, isn't he?"

"That remains to be seen," came the less-than-optimistic reply. "Whatever toxin was secreted through that barb, your friend was shot with an extreme dose."

"But you're an angel. How come you just can't place your hands on him and make him well again like you always do whenever one of us gets injured?" asked Hunter.

"I wish it were as simple as that. Truth be told, there still exists in the world certain elements outside the reach of our powers. Deep Thorn and the untold obstacles which make up The Crucible are among them," said Zuriel. "That said, I'm quite confident Mr. LeDuc will come through this just fine. When that will be is something I unfortunately can't provide you at this time."

Then to the others gathered in the room, Zuriel said, "All we can do at this point is pray, and wait."

"While we're waiting and praying perhaps someone here can explain to me how these two Fledglings managed to find themselves in Deep Thorn," Anahel said in a voice in which a very real anger could be heard coming to a boil within its calm and composed tone. "As I recall, I strictly forbad the use of The Crucible to be included in any curriculum the last time we found ourselves assembled in this room under similar, albeit less dire circumstances."

"The Crucible is a very potent and invaluable teaching instrument," Damiel grumbled in response, while staring straight ahead as though he were fitted with a pair of blinders.

"I've no interest to engage in a debate with you over the merits of The Crucible," Anahel shot back. "What I am interested in is finding out how long Fledglings have been granted entry to Deep Thorn under my nose without my knowledge and, more importantly, consent."

"There are far worse things a Fledgling can suffer than the spore from a flower," argued Damiel. "In case you've let it slip your mind, the dogs of war are beginning to gather. As one of their Guides, it is my job to ensure these younglings are prepared for the coming battle and to stay one step ahead of the enemy, and far worse."

"Is that what we're doing here; bearing witness to the prowess one acquires at Lions Bite of sidestepping Death?" Anahel inquired sarcastically before stepping his way closer to Damiel while wearing a most serious expression. "Now you are to listen to me, Damiel, and listen to me good. It's been as plain as day from the moment you returned from your excursion to bring Jacob back to Havenhid that you have been wrestling with some inner turmoil. When you're not riding your pupils like some steer wrestler saddled upon a bull, you spend hours on end in the Library with your eyes hypnotically–obsessively, even–scanning the happenings chronicled by The

Witnesses. If you wish not to share what exactly has caused you to be in this troubled state, that is your prerogative. What I will not tolerate, however, is a blatant disregard you, or any Guide for that matter, might choose to demonstrate against the boundaries I have put in place here at Havenhid. Choose to defy me again, Damiel, and I assure you the conversation to be had will be far less civil than the one we're having this minute. Do I make myself clear?"

"Crystal," Damiel stated cooly but with a glint of insolence in his flaming eyes of gold which he finally leveled at Anahel.

"If there's nothing further," Damiel then stated and, as he proceeded to take his leave of the room before Anahel could object, he addressed Zuriel in passing, over his shoulder, saying, "You'll be sure to keep me up to date on the boy's condition."

Anahel and Gotham exchanged exasperated looks with one another. Then, seeing as there was nothing left for them to do besides, as Zuriel offered, wait and pray, they suggested to Hunter it was time for them to be on their way and allow Predmore some peace to rest.

"I'm staying," Hunter was quick in his reply that was more a declaration than request.

Rather than argue with the young man, Anahel simply nodded his understanding and both he and Gotham left Hunter to his bedside vigil.

~ ~ ~

Upon leaving Predmore to what was hoped to be a speedy recovery, Anahel and Gotham made their way to the Library where they not so surprisingly, caught what had become the familiar sight of Damiel engrossed in the most recent happenings of the mortal world being mysteriously recorded onto the pages of the four massive books known as the Witnesses under the shade of the blossoming tree.

"What is it he's looking for?" Anahel wondered aloud.

"Come now, Anahel, must you ask the question after I shared with you everything that occurred in the Infernal Desert," answered Gotham. "He's waiting for a sign to reveal Samael has fulfilled the promise he made to Damiel in exchange for his freedom."

"What I meant was, does Damiel really expect Samael to keep such an asinine promise?" said Anahel.

"Personally, I believe Samael has already made good on his promise,"

Gotham surmised, drawing a confused look from Anahel. "The day he walked into Halcyon and made his claim on Jacob was the day he fired the first shot upon Eden. Whether it escalates into the War foretold is dependent upon the outcome of Samael's latest chess move when the Tribunal reconvenes and renders its verdict."

"And what then?" asked Anahel. "No matter the Tribunal's pronouncement, it's the thought of what comes after that preys on my mind."

The troubled look deep-set in Anahel's face receded suddenly as both he and Gotham were met by a distinct feeling they were no longer alone. In unison, they turned their heads and were greeted by a most beautiful, if not quite unexpected vision of loveliness quietly residing just outside the large arched entryway to the Library.

"Etirsa!" Anahel instantly beamed with delight as he briskly walked over to the beautiful figure dressed in a sheer flowing gown of radiant turquoise and warmly embraced her hand.

"You'll forgive me for not having sent word earlier alerting you of my arrival," Etirsa replied in a honeyed voice. "The Tribunal had news it wished to convey to you and, well, seeing as how it had been some time since I last ventured to this corner of Eden, I thought what better opportunity for me to deliver the message to you personally as well as pay a visit to your charming Havenhid that's been long past due."

"You know the doors to Havenhid are always open to not only you, but your equally lovely sisters as well. I only wish I would have known you'd be coming so we would have been better prepared to greet you," said Anahel.

Etirsa's smile dimmed noticeably at the sight of Gotham's approach over Anahel's left shoulder.

"Hello, Gothamel," she said in a most demure manner.

"Etirsa," Gotham, who was far more reserved in greeting than Anahel, replied politely while averting his gaze.

"I'm sure it's proven to be a trying time for you...for both of you, that is," said Etirsa.

"Let's just say we'd all sooner be happier to have this business with the Tribunal over so we can return to the normal business at hand," said Anahel.

The awkwardness suddenly surrounding themselves was thick enough to slice through with a knife.

"You can't imagine my surprise when I was called upon to fill Gothamel's seat when he recused himself from the proceedings," Etirsa noted before her gaze came back to rest itself on Gotham. "I can only hope I am as mindful in my deliberations in your absence as you are."

Gotham appeared to grow more uncomfortable with the idle back and forth and in return inquired, almost too brusquely, "You mentioned something about delivering a message from the Tribunal."

The terse reply finished scrubbing away what was left of Etirsa's polite and endearing smile.

"Yes...that's right," she said with a growing fidgetiness of unease. "The members of the Tribunal have reached a decision in regards to the claim of action put before it by Samael. They plan to reconvene the day after tomorrow and issue their judgment at such time."

"The day after tomorrow," Anahel muttered. "I don't know whether to be troubled by such an announcement or relieved that we'll soon be awakened from this nightmare."

"Is that all?" Gotham asked Etirsa.

Etirsa appeared to hesitate in her reply.

"I am restrained by my duty from voicing anything further in regards to the case, except to say the Tribunal weighed heavily both sides of this case and did not reach its decision lightly."

"And?" Gotham pressed, sensing there was more Etirsa's tongue wished to make heard.

"If there exists more evidence vital to this case; something important enough to sway the members of the court," said Etirsa, "I strongly suggest you find it."

"I see," was all Anahel said in reply, though it was clear by the looks of concern shared by both he and Gotham that Etirsa's advising words were clearly understood.

It was then that Gotham excused himself, but before he could slink off, Etirsa stopped him by embracing his forearm.

"I was hoping I might have a moment to speak to you alone," she said.

"Is it that important?"

"How important does it have to be?" Etirsa replied with a hint of offense at the angel's aloof manner.

"If the hearing is to reconvene day after next and the Tribunal is voicing a need for a more persuasive contention on behalf of the boy, you'll understand when I respectfully make it known that I suddenly find myself in a vigorous race with the circling sun," answered Gotham.

Etirsa's gaze slowly lowered itself like a pair of sailboat masts being retired for the day and she reluctantly released her hold on Gotham's arm.

"I wish you a safe journey back to Halcyon," Gotham said with a courteous, if not hasty bow, while ignoring the disapproving glare coming from Anahel before he quickly retreated into the bowels of the Library.

~ ~ ~

Meanwhile, as Anahel escorted Etirsa from the Library to the foyer where they exchanged final pleasantries before bidding goodbye to one another, Jacob could be found alone on a veranda attached to one of the common rooms overlooking the Garden. It wasn't often when one was able to find a quiet moment away from everyone and everything else in order to be alone with their thoughts; Jacob was grateful to have the opportunity to embrace such a moment. Lying in a hammock-like contraption formed by the same branches that shaped the veranda, and the rest of Havenhid, for that matter, with Mist stretched alongside him with her head resting on his foot fast asleep, Jacob stared out into the picturesque view unfolded before him of the Garden where the beauty of the tranquil blue waters of the River flowing past the grove of trees serving as home for Havenhid glistened with sunlight as it wound its way southward. Jacob's focus, however, was on Predmore.

Earlier, he had rushed over to the room where his unconscious friend had been brought to be treated by Zuriel when news of what had happened made its way predictably through Havenhid. It was with a sense of relief, then, that he caught sight of a heavenly figure out of the corner of his eye that made him sit up straight and, in the process, cast aside all thoughts of Predmore and his unfortunate encounter in The Crucible. In a flash, he grabbed hold of the veranda railing and propelled his body over it in the same fashion a gymnast clears a vault and glided his way to a graceful landing on the banks of the River below. He then sprinted across a stone bridge to the other side of the River until he once more had the beautiful female with red tresses cascading down her back and wearing a gossamery dress of turquoise back in his sights.

Stealthily, Jacob followed a distance behind her with growing curiosity as she casually followed the narrow path winding its way through the lush surroundings of the Garden as though she were enjoying an afternoon stroll through a park.

Only when the path took a noticeable turn to the right into a growth of

Giant Ostrich Fern did Jacob lose sight of the beautiful red-headed woman. He picked up the pace to catch her again in his sights which he quickly did while passing through the forest of feathery, jade-colored fronds when, suddenly, he came upon her standing in the middle of the trail as though waiting for him and found himself staring into one of the most beautiful pairs of eyes he'd ever looked into.

"Make it a habit of stalking unsuspecting wayfarers who roam this path, do you?" she asked.

"I, uh...that is to say, I–I wasn't stalking you. Honest!" Jacob managed to stammer. "I was looking out from one of the terraces back at Havenhid when I caught sight of you and, well...it's not every day we see someone of your...ilk taking a walk through the Garden."

His boyish reply drew a smile from the unexpected visitor. "Allow me to formally introduce myself. My name is–"

"Etirsa. I know. You're the one sitting in for Gotham on the Iudicium Tribunal," said Jacob. "I'm–"

"Jacob," Etirsa jumped in to finish the boy's introduction as he had done to her. "I know as well. You're the one who's been seated before the Iudicium Tribunal trying to convince us you're the Light Bearer."

Jacob replied with an awkward smile that quickly vanished when Etirsa remarked, "It would appear someone is a bit miffed at you at the moment."

No sooner had she spoken than there was heard a familiar barking in the distance. Jacob followed Etirsa's gaze which was fixed on the path they had just walked where Mist, not the least bit amused of being left behind on the veranda, was suddenly seen running toward them.

Ignoring Jacob, the white wolf went to greet Etirsa with a chorus of high-pitched squeals of excitement.

"This is Mist," said Jacob. "She doesn't take all that kindly to when I take off without her."

Etirsa knelt on the ground to embrace the wolf's enthusiastic greeting with an affectionate acknowledgment of her own, and when sufficient licks and pets had been exchanged between the two, Jacob asked finally, "So...what are you doing here?"

"I had some news to deliver Anahel from the Tribunal," Etirsa replied.

"What about? Is it important?"

Etirsa at first was hesitant to tell Jacob until she quickly realized he had a right to know as well, perhaps even before Anahel.

"The Tribunal has come to decision in the matter of Samael's case," she said.

Looking not one bit happy by the news, Jacob stood quiet for a moment with downcast eyes and grumbled a simple yet glum, "Oh."

Not wishing to upset the boy further, Etirsa quickly fumbled for a polite avenue of escape.

"Well, then, if you'll excuse me, I must be on my way," she said.

Before she could disappear into the forest of ferns, Jacob stopped her.

"Aren't you going the wrong way? Halcyon's that's way," he said, pointing to the south over his shoulder with his thumb, as though he were standing on the side of a road hitching for a ride.

"You're quite right about that. But, you see, it's been some time since I've set foot in the Garden and I'd much like to visit the Tree."

Naturally, Jacob knew immediately the "Tree" of which Etirsa was speaking, as there was only one "Tree" in all Eden, just as there was only one "River." He was also taken a bit off guard when Etirsa asked if he cared to accompany her on the walk; an innocent enough request he was more than happy to oblige, only–

"You're a member of the Tribunal and I have not one but two cases before you. Wouldn't you and I being seen together qualify as some sort of misconduct?" he asked.

Etirsa let out a giggle Jacob found quite charming.

"I have no plan to bring up either of your cases with you. Do you have any intentions of bringing them up with me?" she posed the question to Jacob who answered with a decisive shaking of his head. "Well, then, I think we'll be safe from any misconduct allegations."

~ ~ ~

The two walked for some time in silence, with only the chatter of birds and other curious forest creatures peering out at the passing visitors from the surrounding scrub accompanying them. They soon came upon an immense banyan tree with its mammoth limbs outstretched to all points of the sky like the arms of an octopus, and it was upon the easy slope of one of the boughs where they spied Haniel reclining on his back in the company of a slothful black panther whose swinging tail undulating slowly in the air mimicked the lazy sway of the angel's dangling leg. Both appeared to be enjoying the serenity of an afternoon snooze which Jacob instantly found to be odd.

"That's something you don't see often. Since when are angels prone to taking naps?" he whispered to Etirsa.

"We're not prone to taking naps," Haniel was heard to answer before Etirsa could part her lips, while remaining in his relaxed state with his eyes closed. "That doesn't mean we don't have a hankering now and then to indulge in the peacefulness one can find in a comfortable tree like this and bask in the resplendence of a perfect day.

"Besides," he added, opening his eyes, finally, and glancing in the direction of where Jacob and Etirsa stood, "it's quite the relaxing way to pass the time while I waited for you."

"You were waiting for us?" asked Jacob. "But how'd you even know either one of us would be walking this path?"

"Simple," Haniel replied, as he sat himself upright with both legs hanging off the same side of the bough upon which he was perched. "I caught wind that the vision of loveliness accompanying you was paying a visit to Havenhid, and as far back as I can recall, she has never ventured to this corner of Eden without paying a visit to the Tree of Life."

He proceeded to push himself off the tree limb and landed with effortless grace on the ground many feet below. Haniel was of lusty and sturdy stock; that much was clear to anyone who ever laid eyes on the striking angel. Not only was he Herculean in size, but an almost palpable intimidation radiated from his arresting countenance, and it was more than evident how he came to be the Guardian of the Tree, not to mention the protector of the Garden; for no one would doubt Haniel's ability to single-handedly snuff out any danger that might threaten Eden's lands whether it came in the form of a merciless incinerating conflagration, or something far more sinister and destructive lurking in the Northern Lands.

As he made his way toward where Jacob and Etirsa were standing, he picked a colorful flower with an effortless sweep of his hand without breaking his unhurried stride while passing a shrub blooming with a bouquet of radiant blossoms. Jacob was about to introduce the angel to Etirsa but it quickly became apparent such introductions were made long ago when Haniel presented Etirsa with the freshly plucked flower.

"It is always a pleasure whenever you honor us with your presence, not only to me but the creatures of the Garden, as you can well hear," said Haniel over a babel of excited voices coming from the treetops and deep within the surrounding forest where numerous animals roamed.

"Thank you, Haniel," Etirsa replied with a smile, while bringing the redolent flower to her nose.

Haniel then turned a more serious gaze onto Jacob. "I can't tell you how happy I was to hear of your return to Havenhid. I'd been wanting to call on you to tell you so. But after hearing all this unpleasant business before the Iudicium Tribunal you suddenly find yourself dealing with, I wasn't certain you'd be accepting of such company," he said.

"I appreciate it, Haniel. I'm handling it," Jacob replied in as upbeat a manner as he could, but not enough to completely shield from the angel the toll from the growing angst that had been slowly building since his return.

Returning his attention to Etirsa, Haniel inquired in a tone a touch less welcoming as moments before, "Just how long is the Tribunal going to allow this circus to go on?"

Whatever bliss Etirsa found in the heavenly fragrance contained in the velvety soft petals of the flower caressing the edge of her nose instantly dissipated.

"I assume you're referring to the two cases involving Mr. Parrish currently before the Iudicium Tribunal, but I would take issue with you characterizing the proceedings as a circus," she replied politely, if not firmly.

"You and the rest of the Tribunal can't possibly be considering, even for a single moment, placing the welfare of this boy into the hands of Samael," argued Haniel.

"Much as I adore you, Haniel, you will understand when I say it would be improper for me to voice what the Tribunal is and is not considering in this setting," Etirsa said cooly.

Haniel opened his mouth to speak further on the subject when Jacob, seeing how uncomfortable Etirsa was quickly becoming, spoke up first.

"Etirsa is right; speaking about this outside the presence of the entire Tribunal can only complicate matters more," said Jacob. "Besides, it's all going to be worked out the day after tomorrow. So I say let's just hold off on arguing over something until there's something to argue over."

Haniel did his best to oblige the boy, though he visibly struggled to stifle any further sentiment on the subject. Silently, Jacob couldn't help but be heartened by the angel's protective stance of him.

"Would you care to join us?" Etirsa said to the angel after several awkward moments of silence ticked by.

The tense crease in Haniel's forehead slowly receded upon hearing the invitation.

"No," he replied bluntly at first, but then more pleasantly added, "That is, I heard about what happened to Predmore and I wanted to go to Havenhid to check in on him. How is he doing?"

"Zuriel's hopeful he'll pull through, but it's too early to tell. To tell you the truth he didn't look all that great to me," said Jacob.

"What's this? A friend of yours is hurt?" asked Etirsa.

Jacob nodded. "At Deep Thorn," he said, and Etirsa seemed to immediately understand.

Haniel shook his head with dismay over the news. "It doesn't make sense. I thought Anahel prohibited any more rivalries in Deep Thorn after the last mishap. What was Damiel thinking?"

The mention of the angel's name caused a fog of disgruntlement to descend upon Jacob.

"I don't think Damiel is paying much mind to anyone these days," he said.

It was then Haniel announced it was time for him to part company.

"Godspeed to you," he wished to Etirsa, before turning his head and sending a whistle over his shoulder in the direction of the Banyan tree, and more notable to the black feline still stretched out across its limb who instantly sprang to its feet, nimbly leapt to the ground and followed after the heels of the angel as he started toward Havenhid.

~ ~ ~

Of all the beautiful gems which encrusted the crown known as Eden, none matched the magnificence that was the Tree of Life.

True it lacked the jaw-dropping impressiveness that was Broken Earth, the Sphinx-like presence of Lions Bite, or even the allurement of Havenhid whose inarguable mystique was the one thing that could not be cloaked by the trees in whose branches its existence was soundly concealed from sight. Even amongst other trees, of which every species known to man, and then some, shaped the acres upon acres of forests stretching from one end of Eden to the other, the Tree of Life was not the most stately. Neither was it the most striking. Yet, in a break in the woods that formed the small clearing where it stood rooted, the Tree exuded a regalness that was undeniable and existed like the most precious of pearls hidden away in the protective confines of the shell of an oyster.

It radiated a sheen of gold that hung in the sky in the form of rippling curtains of shimmering light above the reach of its branches like some heavenly aurora borealis. The stunning phenomenon, which remained present during the day as well as night, was caused by fine veins etched in the leaves of the tree which were gold in color and reflected brilliantly under the glare of the sun and, later, the illumination of the moon.

While it wasn't the first time Jacob had paid a visit to the Tree, he found himself filled with an overwhelming sense of awe as he followed Etirsa from the shade of the Forest into the sun-drenched clearing. Everywhere he looked beauty flourished, from the lush flowery vegetation, to the many species of equally dazzling birds dressed in their coats—or rather feathers—of many colors. Amongst them was a muster of peacocks rooting about the large white burial vault which contained the remains of Gotham's beloved son. Residing off to the side at the foot of the Tree and draped by a naturally growing vine adorned with thousands of delicate, tiny, white star-shaped flowers, the decorative crypt with its ornate etchings and detailed reliefs looked almost to have been carved from ivory rather than stone. It gleamed brightly, almost ethereally, in the sunlight, and Jacob was instantly reminded of the last time he stepped foot in this most sacred space of nature when he not only discovered a hidden compartment at the base of the crypt beneath the carving of the lamb etched upon the side of the vault where Gotham had stashed away the Sword of Destiny for protection, but also experienced a harrowing and nearly life-ending face-to-face with a terrifying creation known as a Cherub.

The drama of that rain-soaked night came flooding back to Jacob tenfold when, thankfully, he caught in his periphery as he mindlessly walked further into the clearing that he was about to step upon a carpet of red.

Immortalis!

The sight of the diminutive plant with its crimson-colored, bell-shaped blossoms didn't look any more dangerous than a cheerful sprig of violets. Jacob, however knew better, and the sight of the deceptively beautiful Immortalis growing in patches like clover and forming an encircling border around the Tree caused him to immediately freeze; that is, unless he had a tugging desire to summons forth from out of whatever mysterious ether it lived the frightening Cherubim, or Cherub, which, most certainly, Jacob had not the slightest aspiration to do. For you see, the Immortalis was a security system of sorts, and all it took was someone with mortal blood pumping through their veins to set but a toe on the other side of the boundary marked by the scarlet flowers for the blossoms to unfold their soft petals and release a high-pitched shrill of a cry which would immediately summon forth the Cherub and bring the weight of his wrath in the form of a flaming sword down upon the foolish trespasser who dared to step closer to the Tree than allowed.

The threat of the Cherub, however, didn't appear to bother Etirsa. Catching sight of her too late to cry out in warning, Jacob watched in horror as Etirsa stepped over the line of red flowers without pause or thought and braced himself for the inevitable wail to follow, but none came.

"What are you?" Jacob suddenly heard himself blurt out before he could block the words behind his clenched teeth, and drew from Etirsa a curious glance over her shoulder. Not that he hadn't been itching to ask the question since he first laid eyes on the strangely mysterious and beautiful woman, though in manner far more tactful.

"Er, that is, I asked Anahel who you and the other, uh, ladies were when I first saw you the first day of the Tribunal hearing, and he told me you were Witnesses," said Jacob. "What I was really wanting to know is what are you. If there's one thing I've come to learn it's that nothing is as it first appears, and seeing as how I watched you cross over the Immortalis just now and they didn't so much as twitch, I'm guessing the odds are pretty great you aren't a female of the mortal variety."

Etirsa gave the spray of red flowers on the ground a musing glance.

"What would cause you to speculate I might be a mortal?" she asked inquisitively.

"I don't know," Jacob replied with an awkward shrug of his shoulders. "Only things I seem to have crossed paths with since coming to Eden are angels and demons. The last woman...I mean, lady...that is, the last time I laid eyes on someone who looked like you it proved unfortunately to be the latter. However, seeing as how you live in Eden and currently sitting in Gotham's seat on the Tribunal, I'm guessing it's safe to eliminate that option from the list. That basically leaves mortal or angel as choices, and as far as I know, the only angels I know that exist are, well...dudes."

There was something undeniably endearing Etirsa had come to recognize about the boy in the short time since their paths crossed on the trail leading to the Tree, and it was a trait she didn't expect any offspring of Samael to possess in spades.

"I guess we haven't been properly introduced to one another, have we?" she answered, finally, with a smile most pleasing. "You are quite right in your assumptions; I am not a female of the mortal variety, as the Immortalis have proven. Neither are my sisters."

"Sisters?" Jacob's thoughts immediately took him back to the first day of the hearing before the Tribunal when he first saw Etirsa enter the great room at Halcyon where the proceedings were scheduled to take place, accompanied by six other visions of poise and loveliness.

"Our existence has been the crux to shaping many legends and mythologies over the centuries: The Muses, The Nine Sisters, The Nymphs," Etirsa said after a pensive moment. "And while such myths hold some truth to the roles we've come to play in the universe, they fail to fully paint for the world the portraits of who we truly are."

"Which is?" Jacob asked with growing curiosity that was hard to hide.

"When our father in Heaven brought into being the first and only two mortals who would call Eden home, it did not go unnoticed by him how the angels, who were already bristling and feeling slighted having to witness the adoration God heaped upon his newest creations, observed from a distance with great intrigue and fascination the interactions between Adam and the Lady Eve," said Etirsa. "And so, to help lessen the sting of no longer being the single apple of his eye, God did for his loyal angels what he had done for Adam, and brought into being for them companions."

"How about that!" Jacob exclaimed with a hint of disbelief. "Then you do exist. You are angels; female angels."

"We were the first nine—The Nine Sisters—to take a breath. We were also the last," Etirsa replied somewhat solemnly.

She abruptly turned her back on the boy and continued on her way with the edging of Immortalis guiding her footsteps to where the vine-covered crypt rested. Jacob followed her with eyes glinting with an arousal of fascination and, as she ran her delicate ivory hands along the top of the sarcophagi while looking intently at the relief of the lamb as well as that of the lion laying opposite it, he found himself studying her with a renewed interest, as if it was the first time she had ever entered his sights.

"If I didn't know better, I might think I had inexplicably sprouted a second head the way you are staring at me in such a rapt manner," Etirsa noted, suddenly, without shifting her attention from the carvings she was studying on the stone vault.

"I'm sorry...I don't mean to stare," Jacob replied apologetically. "It's just...you remind me of someone."

"Anyone with whom I'm acquainted?"

"I think that's highly unlikely. She's a horrendously hideous demon," Jacob replied with a chuckle before instantly being overtaken by a look expected of someone who'd been caught with his pants down. "Don't misunderstand me...I'm not implying in the slightest that you are horrendously hideous or a demon. Far from it, in fact. What I meant is you remind me of someone who happens, yes, to be a horrendously hideous demon, but who, believe it or not, is actually quite beautiful when she's not so...hideous."

He was rambling now, and the more he heard himself ramble the more he wanted to leap over the Immortalis in order to conjure the Cherub to put him out of his misery. Etirsa, on the other hand, didn't appear to have taken the slightest bit of offense at the clumsy comparison. If anything, she appeared subtly amused in observing the boyish manner in which Jacob attempted to remove his foot from his mouth.

"This beautiful demon, does she have a name?" she inquired.

"Lilith."

Jacob's reply caused Etirsa's smile to disappear.

"You're quite right about her. She is noticeably beautiful," she noted before quickly adding, "and equally as horrendous."

The comment caught Jacob off guard.

"You know her?"

"It's an unfortunate acquaintance," said Etirsa. "You see, she's my sister."

~ ~ ~

How long Jacob stood with his mouth hanging wide open like a freshly caught bass, he had no idea.

"Well...that can't be right," he said. "If Lilith's your sister, then that would mean she would be like you: an angel. Trust me, I've seen her up close and personal and there is no way in h–" he caught his tongue, took a breath and finished his sentence using a better choice of words, "there's no way possible she's anything close to being angelic."

Etirsa couldn't help but appreciate the boy's difficulty in comprehending what was in his mind, and the minds of most who might learn of such a thing, an outlandish notion.

"Hard as it might be for you to believe, she did not start off being the creation she is now. And if what you say is true about witnessing the stark contrast of her inner facade compared to that of her outside, I would imagine it to be quite difficult," said Etirsa.

When Jacob expressed a desire to know more, it was clear Etirsa was resistant of broaching the subject of Lilith and tried to steer the topic of conversation in a different direction, but Jacob was persistent.

"You said you were one of the first nine created, but also that you were the last. What do you mean by that?" he asked.

Realizing Jacob was not going to relent in his questioning, Etirsa succumbed to take a seat on the ground with the graceful movements of a butterfly across from the boy, with the vibrant yet delicate Immortalis flowers separating them. As he waited to hear whatever unspoken history Etirsa knew of concerning Lilith, Jacob couldn't help but realize he was sitting in exactly the same spot when Gotham revealed to him the history of the Sword of Destiny and, more importantly, the unfathomable tragic events that lead to the stone burial vault sharing this sacred plot of land with the Tree of Life. Where Jacob failed to prepare himself, however, was in not anticipating the words which were about to pass from Etirsa's lips–particularly when invoking as dark and odious a subject as Lilith–would not weave another equally, if not more diabolical yarn.

"Have you ever been in love?"

It was a simple question, yet one which caught Jacob off guard.

"My feminine intuition," Etirsa continued when Jacob showed himself reluctant to answer, "tells me that while you're still notably young to know intimately the intricacies of being enamored with someone, you've come to be acquainted with–quite recently, in fact–the strange and unmistakable bliss of having your heartstrings gently plucked."

The pointed, not to mention accurate, observation caused Jacob's thoughts at that precise moment to turn appropriately to the source of his plucked heartstrings: Wray Bliss. And while the boy felt an embarrassing burning sensation consume his ears, Etirsa took notice of the crimson glow that quickly blossomed across his face.

"Interesting thing love; it has the extraordinary power of cementing two souls together while just as easily completely destroying them," said Etirsa.

Confused about what exactly she was referring to, Jacob asked, "I'm sorry...are you implying love is what caused Lilith to become what she is now?"

"I wish I could say for certain one way or the other," answered Etirsa. "Perhaps the dark forces were always inherent in her, existing at first like a spot of rust on the bow of a boat before eventually, with time, it extends its reach until the corrosion consumes the entire hull. What memory I hold of her before such tarnish left its mark is someone who exuded light. She was kind and gay, but most of all she was beautiful; far more beautiful than myself or any of my seven other sisters."

Jacob may have been dubious about such claims speaking to Lilith's kindness and cheerful nature, but he could not argue any declarations concerning her beauty. His own eyes offered proof long ago that, despite whatever hideousness lurked beneath the surface, the chimera he spied wading in a midnight-colored pool of water inside the Silent Forest was one of the most heavenly creatures he'd ever come to witness, with her long raven-hued hair, nearly colorless alabaster skin, blood-red lips and eyes like deep dark wells that instantly hypnotized anyone who dared to gaze directly into them. Whether the breadth of Lilith's beauty was far more radiant than that of her sisters, as Etirsa so modestly claimed, was most certainly a debate that could be had, as Jacob found himself equally as enthralled sitting across from Etirsa and staring into a flesh-and-blood bust of loveliness and allure Michelangelo himself would be hard-pressed to improve upon.

"It should then come as no surprise when I tell you Lilith proved herself to hold an unmatched ability to reduce ranks of Heaven's otherwise commanding and formidable angels into servile admirers," continued Etirsa. "And while it was obvious to anyone watching that Lilith secretly enjoyed the inducing spell her beauty had on everyone except the blind, there was only one she longed to entice with her charms; one with whom she would very deeply and most completely fall desperately in love."

"Well? Who did she fall in love with?" Jacob was quick to ask anxiously.

"Gothamel."

~ ~ ~

While the revelation caught Jacob somewhat off guard, it didn't come as a complete surprise. Gotham, after all, was a living embodiment of mythos; strong, striking, a courier of justice and righteousness, he was Superman with a sword long before DC Comics gave birth to Clark Kent. Jacob also found himself reminiscing back to the night in the Silent Forest where he had his fateful face-off with Thaniel after the angel sent Gotham to his death atop Broken Earth. He recalled Lilith's reaction to hearing the news of Gotham's death; it was not one of glee or contentment, but rather anger. And, Jacob was most certain he spied a veiled, yet unmistakable glimmer of despair.

It was, however, what Etirsa would come to reveal next as she continued with her story that would prove to be a bolt from the blue.

"To Lilith, Gothamel was everything under the sun: he was beautiful, he was just, his strength and fighting skills were unmatched by any who formed the legions of God's army, but more importantly he held an unprecedented and envious position of favor in his creator's eye. If there was one thing Lilith would come to desire almost as much as matters of the heart, it was the heights of such power Gotham would come to evince," said Etirsa as Jacob listened on intently. "There was just one problem: Lilith's feelings of endearment for Gotham were not reciprocated. True, Lilith's beauty did not go unnoticed or unappreciated by Gotham; neither did the warmth which, at one time, inhabited her heart. Gothamel, in fact, was quite fond of Lilith and, for a time, held a soft spot for her. His heart, however, would come to belong solely and completely to that of another."

Naturally, Jacob assumed the recipient of the angel's declared devotion was his grandmother. After all, it was also in the very same spot he was now sitting where Jacob learned of the Sword of Destiny and the events leading to the death of Gotham's son that the angel also spoke candidly of his mindful avoidance of romantic entanglements while navigating his painfully long existence; that is, until fate caused his path to intersect with that of the famous opera singer Ava Delacroux, whose angelic voice proved to be the one weakness capable of bringing the mighty celestial warrior to his knees. To Jacob's surprise, however, it was not his grandmother Etirsa was referring to, but rather her sister—one of The Nine Sisters named Damira. And it was with Damira, Etirsa explained, that Gotham would come to sire a child.

"Whoa...come again!" Jacob instantly sat up straight, like a spooked rabbit who'd just caught sight of the stalking shadow cast upon the ground from an eagle on the hunt soaring in the sky overheard. "Are you telling me Gotham...that David isn't...he has another child?"

A dark cloud settled itself over Etirsa and she fell silent.

Appearing quite somber, she rose to her feet and for a moment it looked to Jacob as if she had resigned herself from speaking any further on the matter as she walked about the foot of the Tree of Life.

"As I said earlier, the creation of The Nine Sisters was meant to be a gift of companionship from God to his beloved angels. It was a gift, however, that unintentionally widened the gulf of emptiness between angels and mortals when the angels soon came to realize they had been neutered of the most affirming and uplifting joys that comes from such couplings: the miracle of creating a living reflection of one's love for another in the form of a child," Etirsa said while staring upward at the golden radiance created by the reflective sheen of the Tree's gold-etched leaves illuminating the sky. "How Damira longed to know firsthand the felicity she witnessed from the mortal women tending to and nursing their newborns; so much so that she eventually threw herself before God and begged him that she could know the bliss of motherhood."

Jacob leaned forward ever so slightly while listening with rapt attention as Etirsa impressed upon him the important fact that the life-giving miracle of birth was one God explicitly bestowed upon mortal women, and the pain all women would endure at childbirth was part of the suffering Eve helped to usher into the world as part of the consequence for the sin she and Adam committed.

"Always merciful, our father could not deny Damira's tearful appeal; there was, however, one caveat to granting Damira's plea," Etirsa continued. "If, indeed, Damira was as committed to wanting a child as she so ardently expressed, then it was God's unyielding condition she do so as a mortal woman."

"I can't believe Gotham never shared any of this with me," Jacob muttered to himself, looking quite overwhelmed as he tried to absorb everything he had just heard. "Your sister—Damira—she must have really wanted a baby to make a sacrifice as great as giving up being an angel, even if it was only a temporary nine-month-long change in status."

"It was her fatal undoing!" Etirsa declared, in a sudden burst of anger she was just as quickly able to extinguish by closing her inflamed eyes and taking a deep, calming breath.

"On the day Damira gathered her sisters to deliver the joyful news she was with child, I watched the light inside Lilith go out as unceremoniously as a breath puts out a candle, leaving only a cold, smoldering wick," Etirsa, her voice composed yet slightly quivering with emotion, continued. "What I witnessed at that exact moment was the passing of my sister and something quite hate-filled rise up in her place. I tried to warn Damira that something ominous was at hand, and when she scoffed at my forecast, going so far as to scold me for nurturing such thoughts about our sister, I went to Gothamel. Sadly, he, too, like Damira, failed to heed my warning, much to their detriment.

"So it came to happen, on the final day of her pregnancy, while Damira was sitting under the shade of a tree along the banks of River not far from Halcyon, enjoying her last hours of existing as a mortal, that Lilith paid her a visit. She arrived bearing a warm and pleasant smile as well as gifts in each hand: a beautiful bouquet of fragrant flowers, and a beautiful crystal bottle filled with some sort of clear liquid. I imagine the embrace they shared before the exchange of gifts left Damira with a passing thought of vindication over how mistaken she believed me to be in my assumptions about our sister. Nothing, however, could have been further from truth," continued Etirsa. "By all appearances, it was a most delightful visit the two shared sitting beside the peaceful flow of the River. Their joyful laughter filled the air as they spoke about such timely things as baby names and tried to make light of the inconveniences and discomforts that descend upon a mortal woman's body when expecting. All the while Damira would bring to her nose the bouquet of flowers Lilith had given her and inhale the heavenly scent that proved to be quite intoxicating.

"After a while of discussing all things under the sun about babies, Damira began feeling lightheaded. Lilith, telling her it was likely the toll of being out in Eden's bright afternoon light, grabbed the bottle she had earlier presented as a gift and told Damira a sip of the soothing elixir inside would do her well. Having no reason to question the gesture, Damira did as instructed. Almost immediately she was overtaken by an unpleasant feeling that slithered its way down inside her before erupting in what felt like an excruciating searing ball of fire in her belly. 'What have you done to me?' Damira asked in a panicked voice when she noticed the cold, unexpectant look on Lilith's face. 'That which you have already done to me,' Lilith replied.

"Damira attempted to get to her feet and retreat to Halcyon but was greeted by an almost paralyzing feeling encasing her legs brought on, unbeknownst to her, by the poison-laced aroma of the flowers she had been enjoying that afternoon," said Etirsa. "She fell to the ground and, with the world a spinning blur in her sights, and the pain overtaking her growing more unbearable, she became panicked. 'My baby! Please, don't hurt my baby!' she pleaded. Lilith paid her no mind except in the thorough enjoyment of witnessing the suffering taking place at her feet. When finally Lilith lent forth her hand it was to reach down and cruelly take hold of her suffering sister by her long silky blond locks. Damira's wails tore through Eden's ever-present serenity as Lilith savagely dragged her across the ground toward the water of the River and then, much to Damira's abject horror, into the water. The calm currents instantly began to churn and boil, much like a thousand ravenous piranha reducing a felled cow to a skeleton, as Lilith, proving herself to be equally if not more dangerous than any predatory fish. And with a villainous gleam alive in her cold, vacant eyes, went about the deed of committing the most egregious of all offenses."

The Garden became strangely still—deathly, even—when Etirsa had finished, and Jacob appeared as shocked as one could be from what he had just heard.

"Did she...Lilith, that is...actually kill her own sister?" Jacob was almost too timid to ask the delicate question.

"As well as the baby that was about to be delivered into the world; one by a lethal poison uncorked from a bottle, the other drowned in a river that until then had only produced life," Etirsa replied solemnly. "It's quite ironic, isn't it? My sweet, loving sister Damira chose to become mortal in order to bring forth life into the world and in doing so she left herself vulnerable to the one weakness that ultimately ushered in death."

Turning back around from the Tree, Etirsa returned to where Jacob remained seated and Jacob could see revisiting such a horrible memory had brought tears to her eyes.

"You asked why my sisters and I represent the only one of our kind amongst angels. Now you know," said Etirsa. "With Damira's demise and the tremendous grief it brought to every corner of Heaven, so, too, did any prospect of growing the ranks of our sisterhood come to an unfortunate end. Halcyon ended up becoming a home for myself and my remaining sisters; you can say it's become a sort of convent for us, and it is where we have come to live a quiet and secluded life.

"You also now know how it is Lilith came to be, what she is now and, more importantly, how it is her presence came to darken the Silent Forest for such a long period," continued Etirsa. "For you see, when Gothamel learned of the deaths of Damira and his yet-to-be-born son, there was no corner of the Earth she could have possibly found to escape the vengeance ignited by his wrath. How he managed the willful restraint not to end her I will never know. Thankfully, Thaniel—ever the wise sage—intercepted him before he left on his hunt, and succeeded in penetrating his ear with words of soundness and rationale. I am of strong belief it was Thaniel's words that kept

Gothamel's sword from skewering Lilith's heart when he finally caught up to her, and instead, condemned her to the realm of the Underneath by sending her into the Through created when God expelled the Dragon himself, from his once pristine Garden he tainted with his nefarious ways."

Jacob found it all to be a bit much to take in; so much so he wondered if his brain was physically large enough to absorb such a tragic course of events. Etirsa herself could see clearly how haunted the boy was over the troubling images her harrowing story had painted inside his head. She also recognized that, in the short time they had spent together, she had come to look upon Jacob in a light much favorable than she had before, and if the opportunity to speak bluntly to the boy served to protect his own good, then so be it.

"May I offer you a word of caution Jacob Parrish?" she asked.

"S-Sure," Jacob replied a bit apprehensively.

"If you ever have the bad fortune to cross paths with Lilith, do whatever is in your power to avoid her like the plague, for that is what she is, if not deadlier," said Etirsa. "You revealed earlier that you have already had the unfortunate privilege to coming face to face with her. Be grateful you were blessed enough to come away from such a meeting with your heart still beating. I would not dare to tempt fate a second time, if I were you."

Sensing Jacob might be misjudging the weight of her warning, she added more soberly, "If indeed you are the Light Bearer foretold, you are in grave danger for as long as you and Lilith walk the same earth. Heed what I say when I tell you many centuries have been littered with the scattered remains cast to the wind of those who were blind to the seasons of wickedness Lilith holds in her hand."

~ ~ ~

Etirsa's words stayed with Jacob when shortly after they parted company and he started back for Havenhid with Mist leading the way. So, too, did the nightmarish images of Damira succumbing to her demise in such a monstrous way.

Before his eye-opening talk with Etirsa in the comforting presence of the Tree of Life, Jacob had witnessed firsthand the devilish entity Lilith was, and she quite effectively seared that vision in the boy's mind. Yet even Jacob was a bit staggered Lilith could prove herself to be so fiendish to commit without batting an eye such a horrendous crime not only against her own flesh and blood but an unborn child. No matter how evil he once believed her to be, he now saw her as a thousand times worse. No longer was she some demon from the Underneath; she was the worst kind of monster all children believed at one time or another lurked beneath their beds or the dark confines of the closet.

It was Gotham, however, who remained at the forefront of his churning thoughts. And it was with an immense amount of compassion and regard that he did so for his close friend and mentor. True, he experienced a brief moment of having his nose pushed out of joint when Etirsa brought to light the bond of love Gotham and Damira shared with one another. It hurt Jacob to know such a love existed. After all, it was in the presence of the Tree that Gotham did what was quite rare for him to do: peel back his hard, steely veneer and reveal the inner vulnerable parts of himself sealed away from the rest of the world. And, in doing so, the angel conveyed the only love he had ever known was that which he found with Jacob's grandmother Ava.

Naturally, Jacob felt betrayed when he learned otherwise, and he was certain his grandmother would feel the same. Then, as he learned of the tragic circumstances that ended Gotham's relationship with Damira, he was met with pangs of guilt for his initial reaction. Suddenly, he came to realize how much more special Gotham and his grandmother's time was together; for it was Ava who ended up thawing the block of ice that had so completely encased itself around Gotham's heart for centuries that followed and allowed him to surrender himself not only to the great risk to feel love again, but to becoming a father once more. Jacob also found himself quite grateful for Thaniel's unfailingly good timing in catching Gotham before he stormed off half-cocked to deliver an eye for an eye to Lilith and injecting a dose of needed reason to help cool his heels. If he had not, it was highly possible Gotham and Ava's paths might never have crossed. And if so, he most likely never would have come to be born.

It was while he was being escorted along on his way with these thoughts that he was struck by something quite out of the blue which brought his feet to an abrupt a stop.

"Thaniel!" he muttered aloud to himself.

The light of whatever light bulb went on inside the confines of his brain made itself seen in an unmistakable glint deep within his eyes.

"Of course! Why didn't any of us think of this before?" he said, as if answering some voice only his ears were privy to hear.

If the voice had anything further to say, it caused a smile of glee to slowly unfold itself underneath Jacob's nose like the pedals of a freshly blooming flower and, in a flash, Jacob kicked up a cloud of dust as his feet made a mad dash back to Havenhid with Mist chasing after him.

"**T**haniel?"

The response rang out collectively from Max, Kairo, Leos and Ethan when Jacob finally managed to track down his friends, who were enjoying a rare moment of leisure in one of Havenhid's many common rooms, and proceeded to share with them the revelation he had on his return from the enlightening visit he had with Etirsa under the shade of the Tree of Life.

"Thaniel, naturally," Jacob answered, though quietly enough so as to not allow their huddled conversation to be eavesdropped upon by any of the other boys in the room. "Here we've been racking our brains trying to figure out the secret to destroying the Scucca Urns, while ignoring the one person who most likely knows the answer."

"I didn't know any of us were still racking our brains about that. That is, I haven't been; have any of you?" Ethan asked Kairo, Leos and Max.

"You mean to say your curiosity hasn't been piqued, even slightly, after the other night when we all witnessed something which shouldn't have been possible?" Jacob pressed, before any of the four boys could answer Ethan.

"What are you saying? You're not still entertaining the idea of trying to destroy those urns, are you?" asked Max.

"I just can't get out of my head how something like a Scucca Urn could survive a blow from the Sword of Destiny without even suffering a scratch," Jacob mulled quietly.

"Maybe you didn't hit it hard enough," Ethan suggested, and received a flick to his ear from Max for his contribution.

"Our mate Jacob here took out a Fury in his first scrap using that sword," Max was quick to remind everyone who may have forgotten the attack by one of the Underneath devils lying in wait outside Hunter's loft before the group's return to Eden. "I think he can muscle up the strength to turn a softball-sized urn into scrap metal."

"And you think Thaniel would be able to shed light on what happened?" asked Kairo.

Jacob shrugged with uncertainty. "He seemed to know everything about everything under the sun. If anyone had the answers needed to solve the mystery surrounding those Scucca Urns, Thaniel would be that person."

On that point, everyone stood in agreement.

"There's just one problem: Thaniel's not around anymore to ask," said Leos.

"That's not entirely true," Jacob noted, drawing curious expressions from each of his friends by his cryptic reply.

Before any of the boys could ask what he meant, they were interrupted by the sudden arrival of Hunter who plopped himself heavily upon one of the two sofas where the group was huddled.

"Well, well, well...look what the cat dragged in!" Max muttered while giving a slow once over to the slightly disheveled shape slumped beside him. "We've been wondering where you've been, cobber."

"I've been sitting with Predmore; keeping him company," Hunter replied with a weary sigh.

"You've been sitting with him this whole time?" asked Leos.

"Except for when I had to show up for Study in the Library earlier today."

"Is he still unconscious?" inquired Ethan.

Hunter nodded.

"You know you can't keep blaming yourself for what happened," Jacob attempted to soothe the visibly troubled young man.

Hunter, however, made it clear he wasn't in the mood of having any of the guilt he may or may not have possibly been harboring over Predmore's condition from being lifted off his shoulders and quickly looked to change the focus of discussion.

"What were the five of you discussing before I flopped myself in the middle of your conversation?" he asked.

"Ole Jacob here was just telling us he thinks he knows who might be able to provide the key to destroying those Devil Urns you pinched," said Max.

Hearing that, Hunter appeared to shake off momentarily the exhaustion weighing down the lids of his eyes as his body sat itself straighter on the sofa.

"Who might that be?" he looked to Jacob and asked with keen interest.

"Thaniel," came the answer from Ethan, instead.

"What makes you think he would know?"

"The fact that he's about the most brilliant angel ever created," said Kairo.

"He used to be our teacher here in the Library, and there wasn't anything he didn't know."

A glimmer of intrigue sparkled within the hazel-colored irises of Hunter's eyes as he continued to hold Jacob in his gaze.

"The only problem, as I was reminding Jacob right before you showed up, is that Thaniel's not around anymore to question about the urns," said Leos. Then turning to Jacob he asked, "What did you mean when you said that's not entirely true?"

"Only that when Samael showed up unexpectedly to petition the Tribunal for custody of me, Thaniel was with him," answered Jacob.

"And?" Max replied with a shrug. "Seeing as how that was nearly three days ago and Thaniel's no longer in Eden, I'd give you all of two chances of solving the Scucca Urn mystery: Buckley's and none. That is unless you've got a time machine stashed away somewhere that nobody here knows–"

Max hadn't managed to finish the sentence when the left side of his mouth slowly slanted upward like a teeter-totter.

"Well I'll be a drongo! Not sure what caused the circuits in my brain to short just now, but I think I'm powered back up," said Max, causing Hunter to lean all the more forward into the conversation with a look of confusion.

"What'd I just miss?"

"If you of all people have to ask, you need to double up on your training at the Crescent Scar," said Leos.

"Jacob obviously is alluding to using the Grace of Drifting to go back in time to when Thaniel was here and find out what we need to know about the Scucca Urns," explained Kairo.

The look of confusion on Hunter's face slowly gave way to one of clarity. Leos was right: if anyone in the group should have known what was being inferred, it was Hunter. After all, the first thing revealed to him when he arrived in Eden, when he was immediately taken to the Crescent Scar, was that, aside from the Grace of Whispering, he was blessed with the Grace that allows one to move from place to place and through the corridors of time in a blink of an eye, and with the same ease as walking through an open doorway.

~ ~ ~

"Not to be a wet blanket, or anything," Ethan piped in, suddenly, while preparing his ears for the likely retaliatory sting of another painful flick from Max, "but didn't we give our word to Anahel we wouldn't mess with the Scucca Urns after he caught us the other night?"

Surprisingly, no one took aim at his ears.

"And we're going to keep our word," assured Jacob. "All we're looking to do is try and understand what it is we're dealing with when it comes to these Scucca Urns, and find out what, if anything, can destroy them."

"He's right! Personally, I feel it would be a dereliction of our duty as Nephilim if we just continued to go about our days and ignore the fact that there could be three ticking time bombs hidden away in a sack in the rafters of the Library," Leos remarked ominously.

"What do you mean time bombs?" Ethan asked hesitantly with a glimmer of alarm in his eyes.

"How should I know? But festive ornaments for the Christmas tree they are not," said Leos. "I don't know about the rest of you, but I haven't had a good night's sleep since we got back knowing those three trinkets from the Underneath are under the same roof as us, and carrying three Scourges inside them no less."

If any of the other boys shared Leos' sentiment, they didn't voice it; nor did their anxious expressions require them to do so.

"There may be a far more pressing reason to act on this," Hunter noted out of the blue, drawing all eyes to focus on him.

"What pressing reason?" asked Jacob.

Hunter appeared hesitant at first to continue.

"I had planned on speaking to you about it before now, but then Predmore had that accident in The Crucible," Hunter began finally. "There's definitely something you should be made aware of."

Looking somewhat uneasy about what it was he was about to be told, Jacob listened intently, along with the other boys, as Hunter proceeded to recount a conversation he had with Predmore as the two sat on the sidelines of Lions Bite during a rest in their training. Specifically, Hunter noted how Predmore had voiced an ominous concern that Jacob might be in danger.

"Danger? What would make him think I was in any danger?" inquired Jacob.

"It has to do with what he sees in your soul; or rather in this case, what he doesn't see."

Seeing how his explanation only served to confuse Jacob and the other boys even more, Hunter revealed how Predmore had confided to him how he experienced seeing visions of certain people he was around when he was growing up. One particularly fateful vision would concern Predmore's older brother Trevor which would lead the two into the crosshairs of a mass shooting at their school where Trevor would lose his life in the hail of bullets sprayed by the assailant's gun while courageously trying to save Predmore.

"Crikey, that's horrible!" a stunned Max uttered with disbelief. "But what does any of that have to do with Jacob?"

It was clear the same exact question resided on the tip of Jacob's tongue as well.

"Predmore didn't understand why these visions would randomly flash before his eyes, or what any of them meant, until he came to Eden and, more specifically, went to the Crescent Scar," continued Hunter. "Once he learned his Grace was Gazing, he understood the visions were glimpses he had not yet learned to control; visions of souls belonging to whoever might have been in his presence at that given moment."

Then looking to Jacob, Hunter said, "However it came about that he caught a glimpse of your soul, whether purposefully or by accident, it apparently bothered him enough to bring it to my attention."

"So what was it that bothered him? What did he see?" Jacob asked with a touch of a nervous reserve.

"That's just it," Hunter replied. "There was nothing to see; for the most part, that is."

"I think you might want to lie down, mate. You're starting to slip into a dialect none of us here are able to follow very well. I believe it's called gibberish," said Max.

Ignoring Max, Hunter attempted again to explain.

"It's not so much what Predmore saw when he gazed into your soul, but that it ends abruptly. Goes black."

"What does that mean, goes black?"

"The way he described it was that it was like pulling the plug on a TV while you're watching a movie and the screen instantly goes blank." Taking note of how quiet and still Jacob suddenly became, Hunter considered refraining from going on but knew he couldn't. "The repeated glimpses Predmore had of his brother's soul played out the same way. He didn't know what he was seeing at the time, but they revealed the last moments Predmore and his brother would share together sitting across the table from one another in the school cafeteria before that horrible shooting happened. The visions always ended with Trevor throwing his body over Predmore to protect him from the onslaught of bullets before suddenly...going black."

The group sat in silence for a moment or two before Max leveled a suspect eye in Hunter's direction.

"What exactly are you trying to insinuate? Predmore gazed into his brother's soul and witnessed his death before it happened and now believes the same fate awaits Jacob just because whatever vision he saw ends in what? A fade out?" he grumbled surly. "Why's he even gazing into any of our souls in the first place without asking first? I don't know about the rest of youse, but I consider that a matter of privacy; like what kind of skivvies I choose to wear in the morning."

"I wasn't trying to insinuate anything," Hunter looked past Max and responded, instead, to Jacob. "For all I know this could be a heaping helping of coincidence. But I also think it's important to remember you've been revealed to be the Light Bearer, Samael has been released back into the world and his first order of business is to claim you, and you have your first kill of a Fury under your belt. If I were in your shoes, I would want to know what Predmore saw, coincidence or not."

"No, I'm glad you told me," Jacob, looking anything but relieved after learning about the premonitory revelation, replied while trying to put forward a brave face.

"I guess now it makes sense," Ethan was heard to mutter quietly.

"What's that?" asked Kairo.

"Why Predmore always looked like he was trying to bore holes into Jacob with his eyes; like the other night during dinner in the Hall of Light."

"So? What do we do now?" Leos wondered aloud while looking to everyone gathered in their huddle.

"We definitely need to go seek out Thaniel and hope he has the answers we need," said Jacob. "Predmore's a good kid, and I know he wouldn't have brought any of this up to Hunter if he wasn't genuinely concerned, but I hope this ends up being a huge nothing burger like Hunter said. I'm also aware recent events have placed me squarely in the crosshairs of not-so-nice people who would love nothing more than to see me take a header off Broken Earth Gotham-style, but there's no way I'm going to stand here like some sitting duck without taking some kind of action if Predmore's visions are meant to serve as a warning to me."

"Agreed," echoed Hunter. "It's honorable you want to keep your word to Anahel but, as far as I'm concerned, a threat to any one of our lives voids any such promises."

As he spoke, he leaned forward and held out his hand, and one by one each of the boys followed suit and placed their hands on top the other in a sign of unity.

"Well, then," Jacob began with an anxious sigh, after the moment of brotherhood shared amongst the boys had passed, "I guess there's no time like the present."

It was clear the anticipation of taking a walk back in time to speak with Thaniel was enough to bring a twitch of nerves to the surface of the skin. After all, it wasn't as if Jacob would be enjoying a pleasant moment of catch up with the newly Fallen angel over a serving of tea and crumpets. For all Jacob knew, he could very well be walking straight into the vision Predmore had warned Hunter about where an abrupt "fade out," as Max deemed it, was awaiting him.

"If you'd rather, I could go instead," Kairo, who also had the Grace of Drifting, offered.

"I'm fine to do it," Jacob declined politely. "Besides, if all goes well, I'd like a chance to see Thaniel alone."

He then sat back in his seat, closed his eyes and took several relaxing breaths. Once he was ready, he opened his eyes revealing irises alight with the glittering flakes of a shimmering, golden radiance.

And in an instant, he vanished from sight.

~ ~ ~

"Where it is usually the mother who is favored to hold guardianship of her child in the mortal world, it is the father who assumes all custodial rights in the case of Nephilim."

The sound of Thaniel's voice, distant and garbled at first, quickly became increasingly present and clear. Moving through the barriers of time, exhilarating as it might have been, was not for the timid. Disappearing from one place and reappearing in another was simple enough (simple, that is, if one was blessed with the Grace to affix time-traveling wings to one's heels like the Greek god Hermes). Being jettisoned at a high velocity through what appeared to be a long corridor seemingly constructed by numerous strands of celluloid film containing images of life past, present and future interwoven together in a distorted tapestry took an acquired level of endurance. When, finally, Jacob reached the end of the corridor through which he was hurled as though he were a rock launched from a slingshot, he took several gulps of air needed to steady oneself following the equally discombobulating, if not nausea-inducing jolt, stemming from coming to such an abrupt and whiplash-causing halt.

"And the law, as they say, is the law."

Again, Thaniel's voice made itself heard, and Jacob was quick to collect himself and survey his surroundings. In an instant, he recognized his feet had landed him inconspicuously in the back of the great room where his case before the Iudicium Tribunal had been taking place at Halcyon, standing near a giant pillar of marble which he quickly disappeared behind to hide his presence. Peering out from behind the pillar, Jacob looked to the front of the room and found the members of the Tribunal seated and listening intently to an argument Thaniel presented to the court days earlier. Then, shifting his gaze further to the right, Jacob was greeted by the strangely surreal, if not off-putting sight of his own self seated in-between Anahel and Gotham and looking none too pleased with the proceedings taking place in front of him.

"We have made our intent clear," Thaniel continued in his address before the Tribunal, "and we await for the matter to be settled as expeditiously as possible."

Careful that his presence not be revealed, Jacob watched as Thaniel receded into the background once he had finished speaking, leaving Aradiel to respond to the argument he had put forth on Samael's behalf. Despite his commanding and equally persuasive performance, Thaniel looked to be quite dispirited and moved like someone burdened with a heavy load saddled upon his shoulders as he slowly made his way toward the pillar which concealed Jacob. Leaning against the pillar with his head hung low, Thaniel breathed a sigh of anguish, and Jacob was certain his ears caught a mumbled plea leave the angel's lips asking some unseen entity for pardon.

Feeling more than a twinge of sympathy for the angel, Jacob hesitated to make his presence known and intrude on what was obviously a private moment. He also knew time was of the essence, and the grains of sand were quickly funneling themselves through the narrow neck of the invisible hourglass hovering above him.

"Thaniel."

His whisper appeared to go unheard, and so he called out again a little louder, "Thaniel!"

The second utterance of his name caught Thaniel's attention, and when he craned his neck to peer around the pillar he appeared most staggered at finding Jacob as the source of the whisper.

"Jacob!" he gasped with surprise. His head then swiveled upon his neck so quickly Jacob thought it might perform a full revolution as the angel peered back over his shoulder to level his gaze upon the sight of the Jacob that was seated between Anahel and Gotham before turning back to the mirror image of the boy standing in front of him.

"What is it you're doing here?" Thaniel inquired somewhat frantically, realizing instantly Jacob had utilized his Graces in order to perform what ordinary people would consider a smoke-and-mirrors illusion executed by a serviceable magician utilizing a large cabinet with a concealed trick door.

"Please...I haven't got much time," Jacob whispered urgently in reply. "If I remember correctly, Samael and Gotham are going to begin a verbal spar with one another any minute before I stand up and have my own outburst, and there's something I need to find out from you before Samael grabs you and chases after me."

Thaniel, however, didn't appear to be listening as a heavy look of sorrow suddenly swept over him.

"I'm so sorry for all of this...truly I am," Thaniel lamented, while gently cupping the boy's chin in his hand. "The last thing I would ever want is for Samael to gain any kind of control over you, especially in the role as your father. I'm ashamed to confess it's all I could do to stay in his good graces and survive this unfortunate existence visited upon me."

"You have nothing to be ashamed about, Thaniel. I understand." And most certainly Jacob was being truthful as he looked upon the once stoic angel with pity. "Whatever ends up happening, please know I don't hold any ill-will toward you. I know you are only doing what you have to, no matter your feelings."

If the boy's words helped to soothe Thaniel, it wasn't noticeable, at least at first. Nor did Jacob have the luxury to further console his friend.

"I apologize for being so abrupt, but my time is quickly running out, and there's something of vital importance I need your help with. Information, actually; and I'm praying you have it."

The urgency heard in Jacob's voice was enough to pierce through the glumness in which Thaniel found himself immersed. Obviously, a matter of great importance was at hand for the boy to step back in time in order to seek his assistance, Thaniel thought to himself, and the fog clouding his piercing gaze was instantly swept away as the angel resettled his gaze on Jacob with a renewed focus of attention.

"Are you familiar with what a Scucca Urn is?" Jacob asked Thaniel.

"Of course," came the reply. "They're the receptacles Samael created to house the seven Scourges in a particularly artful stratagem on his part to wrangle control of the Underneath from the Dragon."

No sooner had Thaniel answered the question than a faint frown appeared on his face. "How have you come to know about the existence of the Scucca Urns? If memory serves me well, I had not yet touched upon the topic in Study."

"You remember the young man named Hunter who was with us when we saw you unexpectedly at the church in the graveyard in Venice, right? Well, it's a long story I don't have time to get into, but the short version is he managed to steal three of them from the Pethens who guard them," said Jacob.

Thaniel's eyes widened. "Stole...three? So, he is the one."

"There's two things we need to know," Jacob continued with an increased urgency. "First, is it true that if you destroy the Scucca Urns that Samael's power is weakened? And second, is it actually possible to destroy these things? We attempted to destroy one the other night using the Sword of Destiny, and I didn't so much as even nick it. How is that possible?"

The words coming at Thaniel was almost too much for him to absorb all at once and he took a beat to make sense of what Jacob had spewed forth.

"Let me get this straight: you are in possession of three Scucca Urns, and now you seek my help to destroy them? Do you have any idea the torrential waters into which you and your impulsive companions are looking to wade?" Thaniel answered in an earnest voice he struggled to keep at a whisper.

"Please...!" Jacob pleaded, while glancing to the front of the room where he spied Samael and Gotham engaged in their verbal tussle.

Recognizing Jacob's desperation, as well as realizing the moment available to them to converse would be brief at best, Thaniel, dubious as he was to do so, acquiesced.

"It is arguable, though highly probable, that in destroying a Scucca Urn one would siphon from Samael a great measure of the power he possesses today," said Thaniel. "You see, the nucleus of the Darkness' strength comes from the seven Scourges which Samael conspired to assume from the Dragon by concealing them in the urns. By destroying any of the urns, one would set free the Scourge inside to reunite with the Dragon and, thus, rob from Samael the cutlass of strength said Scourge had placed into his hands."

"Then it is possible to destroy these Scucca Urns," Jacob said with a lilt of hope.

"Possible yes; easily is another matter altogether."

"Then how? With what? And how is it the Sword of Destiny wasn't able to leave even a mark on it? I thought it had the power to destroy anything and everything."

"There exists always a footnote regarding anything is deemed to be 'all powerful,' " answered Thaniel. Do you remember what happened when Moses came down from Mount Sinai with the tablets in his hands containing the ten laws of God?"

Jacob couldn't believe Thaniel was attempting to question him on a passage from Exodus as though he was back teaching Study in the Library at Havenhid.

"He found the Israelites dancing around a golden calf they had created to worship and, after he smashed the tablets, he used his staff to destroy the calf and throw it into a river.

"What has that got to do with anything?" Jacob replied with a frustrated huff.

"When Samael created his Scucca Urns, he did so quite shrewdly from the pulverized remnants of that pagan relic that brought to shape in a cast of gold the first and greatest sin man could dare to commit," Thaniel began to explain. "The Sword of Destiny, lethal as it may be, would be an impotent tool in destroying the Scucca Urns, as you so noted, simply because its great power was born from the blood of The Christ that came to stain its blade. To destroy something created from the remains of such a great offense would require a weapon baptized by the fire of God's wrath; and there is only one such weapon ever to have come into existence."

"The staff of Moses," Jacob said before Thaniel could reveal the answer.

Thaniel nodded knowingly and repeated, "The staff of Moses."

~ ~ ~

"Now that I have quieted your spirit of inquiry, you must listen to what I have to say," Thaniel said, suddenly, with an unmistakable tone that matched his equally grave expression. "Abort this foolish endeavor you and your cohorts have undertaken. You haven't the slightest understanding of the danger you are dabbling in when it comes to these Scucca Urns."

"But—"

"There are no buts!" Thaniel remarked brusquely. "Even I, in all my wisdom, couldn't tell you what might happen should you break the seal to one of those cursed vessels and set free the malignant smog inside known as the Scourge. My only source of solace at this moment is in knowing that, in this instance, the Sword of Destiny will be of no help to you."

The last thing Jacob had patience for was a lecture on the dangers of the Scucca Urn that had already been drilled into his head by both Anahel and Gotham; certainly not when he had a far more important question he desperately needed Thaniel to answer. When he opened his mouth to ask it, however, there was suddenly heard a ruckus that caused him and Thaniel to turn their attention to the front of the room. In a moment that proved itself to be strangely surreal, Jacob watched the reflection of himself from days earlier stand up from his seat and, in a burst of anger, storm past the pillar where the two were standing and flee out of the room. Gotham and Anahel quickly gave chase after the boy and, as they did, the future Jacob retreated further behind the pillar to ensure his presence escaped detection.

With his back against the pillar, Jacob attempted the impossible task of pressing himself even further into the marble when Samael also followed after only to pause in his tracks when he came upon Thaniel trying to appear casual leaning against the pillar.

"Why didn't you stop him, fool?" Samael barked at Thaniel.

Ignoring whatever reply Thaniel might offer, Samael immediately turned his probing gaze on the pillar itself which he eyed with notable suspicion, as though he sensed some unseen presence lurking out of sight on the other side.

Jacob, who could all but feel Samael's fire-lit eyeballs boring their way through the dense slab of marble like twin lasers, closed tightly his eyes and held his breath.

"Come, we better go and find Jacob," Thaniel suggested, while quickly stepping forward in the hopes of redirecting Samael's attention.

Samael, however, was not one to be easily distracted by shiny objects and motioned to Thaniel to stay put with a simple but halting gesture. With the slow stalking steps of a lion on the hunt, Samael crept his way around the pillar. Sensing every approaching step, Jacob felt his heart quicken in his chest.

Were it not for the one remaining question he was desperate to ask Thaniel, Jacob would have allowed the Grace that brought him through the threads of time to return him to the safe confines of Havenhid; and so he forced himself to stay rooted to the floor upon which he stood motionless, nerve-racking as it may have been to do so. Only when he spied the approach of Samael's shadow inching its way nearer, and he was certain the last grains of sand were about to pass their way through the hourglass guiding his journey, did his eyes ignite with a familiar golden shimmer.

When Samael came around the other side of the pillar expecting to catch whoever it was who thought they could pull such a childish trick on the ruler of the Underneath, his cocksure expression dropped like a weight at the unexpected sight of...nothing.

CHAPTER TWELVE

VESSEL

Jacob, at first, wasn't sure he had successfully navigated his way back from Halcyon to the common room at Havenhid or whether he had mistakenly taken an unplanned detour that had landed him smack dab in the middle of a car wash when his face suddenly came under assault by what felt to be a warm, wet shammy.

Through squinted eyes, he found the culprit to be Mist, who was happily greeting his return with an enthusiastic, not to mention extremely wet lapping with her chamois-like tongue.

"Okay, girl, I get the picture—I missed you, too!" Jacob chuckled.

As he returned the slobbery welcome with a hearty scratching of the white wolf's ears, he took notice of the five sets of eyes of his friends seated around him firmly fixed on him as they anxiously awaited a report back detailing his Drifting excursion.

"Well?" they inquired impatiently in unison, once Mist was satisfied with the acknowledgement she received and went to recline on the plush, roomy cushion of an oversized stuffed chair nearby.

"Well," Jacob replied, "I found Thaniel, and managed to have a word with him."

"And?" the chorus rang out again with increased eagerness.

"And I discovered I could have the strength of the Incredible Hulk and I still wouldn't have managed to destroy the Scucca Urns, at least not with the Sword of Destiny," said Jacob.

The news brought a hiss of disappointment from the others in what sounded like the escape of air from a punctured tire.

"So there you have it. I guess those Scucca Urns truly are, and will always be, indestructible," remarked Hunter who looked to be the most disappointed out of the group about the news.

"I wouldn't exactly say that," said Jacob.

"But you just said the Sword of Destiny was useless when it comes to destroying the Scucca Urn. Didn't you?" asked Ethan with a frown of confusion.

"That's right," Jacob, causing even more puzzled looks, answered. "Apparently, as lethal as the Sword of Destiny is against virtually every other thing on the face of the earth, it lacks one certain element needed to destroy a Scucca Urn. There is, however, one instrument in existence with that needed element and is capable of obliterating each and every urn as easily as shattering a glass by throwing it against the wall."

The group, listening intently, leaned forward collectively in their seats anxious to learn the identity of the mysterious instrument Jacob mentioned.

"Well...are you going to leave us hanging? Tell us already!" Leos bleated with growing frustration.

Jacob gave a cautious glance around the common room in order to ensure no one might be eavesdropping on the conversation, before leaning in to the group himself.

"The staff of Moses," he said finally.

"Moses?" Hunter bellowed incredulously as though Jacob had mentioned, instead, the name of St. Nick himself, before immediately lowering his voice and asking with no less bafflement, "As in the Moses from the Book of Exodus Moses?"

Jacob proceeded to recount his visit with Thaniel to his captive audience; particularly, he conveyed word for word what the angel had disclosed to him about the biblical staff in question and, more importantly, what made it the powerful instrument it was—even more so than the Sword of Destiny, at least in this one case—to be capable of turning to dust the mysterious urns which had so far proven themselves impervious to all other known means of destruction.

"Starve the lizards! We're talking about something that existed, what...thirty five hundred years ago? Is it even possible for a wooden staff from that long ago to exist today?" Max inquired with a great deal of built-up incredulity.

"And if it did exist, where would you even begin to search for it?" wondered Leos.

"If anyone knows, I'm sure it's Thaniel," Kairo chimed in.

All eyes once again shifted to Jacob, and all Jacob could offer in return was a sheepish smile.

"Here's where it gets a little complicated: I didn't ask him," he said.

"Didn't ask him? But that's like the most important question there was to ask," balked Leos.

"Actually, finding out whether the Scucca Urns could be destroyed, and if so by what were the far more pressing inquiries," Hunter piped in. "But it's definitely next on the list."

Jacob quickly explained the circumstances which prevented him from finding the answer to such a vital question. As well, he also offered a solution to make up for the unintentional bungle.

"I could always go back and make another attempt to find out the rest of what we need to know," he said.

"Actually, no you can't," Max was quick to argue.

"Why not?"

"Rules. You can't use Drifting to make repeated visits to the same moment in time. Something to do about creating a higher probability of affecting history that's played out. Besides," Max added, "you're already playing a dangerous game of whack-a-mole, with you being the mole, by tip-toeing around your own hearing. Last thing you need is to get caught. Then you'll really be hip-deep in roo dung!"

"So why not pay Thaniel a visit at some other more convenient spot in time?" asked Ethan.

"When might that be: before his fall when he was busy plotting Gotham's redemption by killing him, or after his fall when he spilled his guts to us in Venice?" Jacob replied.

The group sat in silence for some time, each one sifting through the innards of their skulls for some semblance of an idea to guide them forward in their quest, but not a one of them had a "Eureka!" moment.

"I think I might know of someone who could possibly help us," Jacob eventually was heard to mutter. "Not a hundred percent certain, mind you, especially after the other night."

"Who?" asked Ethan, before quickly taking a guess: "Anahel?"

"Zuriel?" Kairo hazarded his own guess.

Instead of answering, Jacob got to his feet, motioned to Mist before gesturing to his friends with the invitation, "Follow me."

~ ~ ~

The group followed the lead to the Library, which was silent as a tomb, as it usually was at that precise late afternoon hour, and just as empty, or so it appeared at first glance. As they made their way inside, however, they came in view of the large tree rooted to the floor near the center of the Library and Jacob's feet paused themselves when he spotted what had by then become a familiar sight of Damiel standing beneath the flowering canopy scouring obsessively the pages of the four Witnesses. Damiel allowed his gaze to briefly take leave of the day's events being chronicled in the pages of the books at the sound of the group's arrival, and his expressionless stare met Jacob's. The boy offered not so much as a nod or hint of smile in return before continuing along.

They proceeded to the corner of the Library where classes for Study were held and, as they rounded a corner, Jacob brought the train following him to a sudden halt when he spotted Vessel attending to his daily duties as he always did once his classes were finished for the day; in this case, it was returning a number of books to their proper spots upon the countless bookshelves coiling around and upwards like some unending snake throughout the massive vault of knowledge that was the Library.

"You sure this isn't a big waste of time?" Max whispered as they watched Vessel toss a rather large and aged book high into the air above him where it appeared to spring to life and, with the front and back sides of its cover flapping like the wings of a bird, fly itself through the air to the tenth story of the Library where it quickly found a vacant spot on one of the shelves and slid its way into it.

"He was given this job for a reason, so I guess we'll find out," Jacob replied. "Besides, what do we have to lose at this point?"

"Nothing good ever comes from asking that question," mumbled Ethan.

"Remember to just follow my lead," Jacob then instructed everyone.

"Lead on," Leos remarked in agreement.

This time, it was Mist who led the way, her claws tapping out what sounded like a Morse code message as her paws padded their way across the smooth, polished floor. Naturally, when Vessel took notice of the group of boys coming towards him, it wasn't without a touch of surprise.

"Well, this is an unexpected sight," the angel remarked while flinging another book high into the air where it hovered momentarily before fluttering with life and scurrying off to some unseen bookshelf. "It's not often the Library sees many visits from students at this hour of the day."

"We've still got a while before dinner is served. So we thought we'd kill the time to do a little research," said Jacob, before quickly adding, "If that's okay with you, that is."

The boy's choice of words caused Vessel's left eyebrow to arch itself slightly upon his forehead. "I'm not sure how to take any student of mine who approaches their homework as killing time," the angel grumbled. "But by all means."

When Vessel returned his attention to his pile of books, Jacob looked to his friends and shot them a guiding wink.

"Welp, this is your last chance, Max," he then proceeded to say in a voice that was a tad louder than how he would normally speak in order to ensure Vessel heard him, while slowly migrating with the rest of the group in the direction of the winding stairs. "Because in a few minutes you're going to be eating your words when I finally prove to you that aside from the Sword of Destiny there's never been anything more powerful than the staff of Moses."

Receiving an impatient and most unwelcome gesture from Jacob to jump into the improvisational performance argument, Max attempted to clear the sudden nerves clogging his throat before hesitantly answering in a voice that was even more stilted than that of his friend.

"Uh...I say you're out of your tree, I do. The staff of Moses, bah! What's so powerful about an old walking stick?" he replied awkwardly.

"Alright, Einstein, then name something more powerful?"

"Gladly! For starters, there's..."

Max's eyes suddenly grew large as his brain went blank and his tongue silent. "There's...um, well for instance there's..." he muttered like a blathering fool, while desperately looking to his friends for an end to his sentence before he blurted out "the Ark of the Covenant" with a question mark of a shrug.

"The staff of Moses was able to conjure up plagues of locusts and frogs as well as part the Red Sea," argued Jacob, after giving Max the A-okay sign.

"Yeah, well, the Ark of the Covenant was able to melt the faces off a bunch of Nazis and anyone else who messed with it. Ha!" Max, clearly beginning to lose himself in the make-believe argument, shot back in reply.

"Right! And let me guess: it's still lost in some unknown warehouse filled with thousands of other crated artifacts."

Max was just about to level Jacob with a zinger when Vessel's voice rang out calling for quiet.

"Need I remind you where you are," the angel said, before hurling a final book into the air. "Now, what is the cause of all the ruckus?"

"It's nothing. We're just having a difference of opinion about something, that's all," said Jacob.

"Yes, you've made that quite apparent to myself, and I suspect anyone who might be wandering the stacks for several floors above us," said Vessel, before adding dourly, "Not that I suspect that to be the case."

"Sorry," offered Jacob. "But you see, we were having a discussion about the Sword of Destiny and, well, it ended up becoming a debate over what other religious artifacts were comparable. In terms of power, that is."

"I see. And you believe the victor in this most intriguing argument is the staff once possessed by Moses," Vessel noted before his burrowing gaze slowly shifted from Jacob to Max, "while you contend, and quite astoundingly I might add, it's the face-melting Ark of the Covenant."

For a moment, both Jacob and Max couldn't help but wonder while held captive in the grasp of such an intimidating gaze if perhaps they had unwittingly offended the angel with their bogus argument. Needless to say, it came with a sense of relief when the boring intensity of Vessel's stare gave way to the twinkle of smile.

"Come," he instructed, suddenly, while sweeping past the two boys, "and follow me!"

~ ~ ~

Obediently, the group did what was asked of them and, without trading a single word amongst each other, they followed Vessel's brisk assent up several flights of stairs to the ninth level of the Library. There, Vessel continued his way along a narrow platform lined with numerous elaborate archways and ornate railings on one side, and shelves upon shelves forming what seemed to be an unending wall of books on the other.

At one point, Vessel paused in his steps and, unlike Thaniel's uncanny ability to instantaneously pull from any shelf anywhere in the Library the book he desired at any given time, the angel took a moment to survey the shelves in front of him before his eyes settled themselves upon a large book whose binding was noticeably worn and frayed. Snatching the book from off the shelf, Vessel resumed the procession along the platform a short distance more to a nearby alcove, which served as a quiet reading area, and tossed the book clasped in his hand upon a large wooden table in the center of the room where it landed with a clamorous bang that echoed throughout the Library.

All six boys stood frozen with startled intrigue staring at the book with no visible title or name of the author who had written it anywhere on its weathered binding.

"What is it?" Jacob finally asked the question that was on everyone's minds.

"You came seeking answers, did you not?" answered Vessel.

Looking no less fazed by the reply, Jacob approached the table and opened the book.

"You'll find, much like the divine spearhead from which your sword came to be, the staff of Moses is a loom from which many legends, both true and otherwise, have been weaved," Vessel remarked, as Jacob thumbed his way through several pages of the book which he quickly discovered was all about the ancient biblical relic.

The angel then proceeded to regale the group with some of those legends; legends that held belief the staff was no ordinary walking stick made of wood, but rather sapphire, while others claimed it was fashioned from the Tree of Life itself at twilight on the sixth day of Creation and bequeathed to Adam, from whom it would be passed down from generation to generation until it reached Moses' hand.

Another mythos told of the staff finding its way in the Pharaoh of Egypt's palace before making its way into the hands of one of Pharaoh's advisers named Jethro who one day plunged the staff into the ground of his garden where it instantly took root and became immovable. Immoveable, that is, until Moses one day paid Jethro a visit and expressed his desire for Jethro's daughter Zipporah's hand in marriage. Jethro, in reply, challenged Moses to pull the rooted staff out of the ground—a task that had proved impossible for all who had previously attempted it. For Moses, however, it proved to be an effortless test when he went out into the garden, read the ineffable name of God along with the 10 plagues of Egypt inscribed in Hebrew on the staff, and proceeded to do what others had failed.

"Like King Arthur when he pulled the sword Excalibur out of a stone that no one else could," Ethan commented like an excited youngster listening to his nightly story being read to him right before bedtime.

While some of the legends proved to be wholly new to the ears of the Nephilim audience who listened to Vessel with great intrigue, nothing quite captured their attention like hearing what most considered the official record contained in the Book of Exodus. It was a story the boys had come to know by heart from their earliest days, and yet it was like hearing a completely new tale the way Vessel told of the burning bush from which the voice of God came and revealed to Moses the power of the staff in his hands, first by transforming it into a fearsome-looking serpent when Moses was instructed to cast the walking stick onto the ground, and then aiding Moses in his mission to free the Israelites from the godless Pharaoh's enslavement by bringing upon Egypt the Ten Plagues and, finally, parting the waters of the Red Sea in the desperate escape to the Promised Land that followed.

Equally captivating to Jacob were the numerous paintings, drawings and imagined renderings of the staff revealed inside the book on the table whose pages he continued to flip through while listening to the stories shared by Vessel. Some of the illustrations depicted the biblical staff exactly as he imagined it inside his head as a large, curved, wooden walking stick a shepherd from a time long past would use to help tend his flock. Others presented the staff as a completely foreign instrument of an unexpected shape and inscribed with strange symbols and hieroglyphics, or encrusted with mysterious jewels and crystals.

"So, whatever happened to it?" Jacob asked, when Vessel finished his Exodus telling, while continuing to carefully study the pictures inside the book. "The staff, that is."

An answer was not immediately forthcoming, and only when Jacob felt the intense weight of the angel's gaze leveled at him did he turn his attention from the book to the twin golden orbs fixed upon him.

"That is the question of the hour, is it not?" Vessel remarked with a somewhat cryptic tone.

"Well? Is there an answer?" Leos asked impatiently.

"There are many answers, actually. Or rather theories." All eyes followed as Vessel then began a slow stroll around the table. "It was widely believed by some that the staff was buried with Moses upon his death. Others contend it eventually was used to fashion the cross on which the Son of God was crucified. Some claim the staff came into King David's possession who passed it on to the Davidic kings who followed him and used it as scepter until the destruction of the First Temple. Still others have theorized it resides with the Ark of the Covenant in a secret unknown chamber built by King Solomon."

"What you're saying then is it's basically been swallowed up by the world, and anyone hoping to find it would have a better chance of catching Big Foot, or the Loch Ness Monster," said Max.

"Perhaps. Perhaps not," replied the angel. "There are several museums as well as antiquities collectors who claim to own the staff. As well, there are one or two churches who have also professed ownership of the biblical rod. And if we are to be thorough in connecting all the dots that trace the journey of the staff since it left Moses' grasp, you might also include the Vatican, where still more theories abound pointing it's present day location as being deep inside the church's archive."

"But you're an angel," Jacob noted. "Don't you have the ability to know one way or the other?"

The question appeared to tickle Vessel.

"There is a reason I was chosen to come here to Havenhid and, more specifically, step into the shoes that, until recently, were filled by my brother, Thaniel," said Vessel. "Having said that, I'm most certain you'll understand when I tell you I need not have been blessed with a heightened level of intelligence to clearly recognize when my students are attempting to gaslight me into revealing something through a puerile, and might I add, badly acted squabble over an imbecilic wager."

While the angel's reproof was absent any anger or animosity (if anything, the subtle grin on Vessel's face betrayed a hidden amusement in the situation), the boys couldn't keep themselves from turning various shades of red from being called out in such a pointed manner over their silly ruse. It came as almost a relief when the familiar call from a distant trumpet pierced the silence of the Library.

"I believe the expression used for a moment like this is 'saved by the bell.' Or in this case, the dinner trumpet," said Vessel.

The group was more than happy to answer the call when Vessel finally dismissed them. But, as Jacob went to follow, the angel motioned him to remain behind saying—

"I'd like to have a word with you in private, Mr. Parrish."

~ ~ ~

Once they were alone, Jacob settled himself in a nearby seat, and Vessel watched with interest as Mist followed suit, positioning herself right beside the boy like the faithful companion she had become, and gently resting her head on the boy's knee.

"There's a saying: 'You can judge the true character of a man by the way he treats his fellow animals,' " said Vessel. "I would argue such character is better defined, in fact, by the manner in which an animal responds to the presence of any one man."

Jacob, not entirely sure how to respond to what seemingly was a compliment, quietly turned his attention to Mist and, as he gave the white wolf a loving scratch to the top of her head, was mindful of the angel slowly crossing the room in his periphery.

"No doubt, you're wondering why I wished to have a moment with you alone. Unfortunately, circumstances being as they are, the opportunity to get better acquainted has been fleeting at best," Vessel remarked, as he took a seat in the vacant chair beside the boy. "Even before I was summoned to Havenhid, I had come to hear a great deal about a certain Nephilim by the name of Jacob Parrish. There's but a noted few who've been able to make their names reverberate like a clap of thunder in both the celestial and Nether worldly planes; so you can be certain I have been looking forward to meeting your acquaintance."

"Thunder? I'd say that's a bit of an exaggeration. I mean, what's so special about me or my name? I'm hardly anybody," Jacob asked with an awkward chuckle.

"Hardly anybody? Could you possibly be that unwitting?" questioned Vessel with a curious tilt of his head. "You stand at the precipice of being named the Light Bearer, in what is undoubtedly one of the most consequential cases to be brought before the Iudicium Tribunal. As if that weren't enough, you do so in the unforeseen, and might I add most unexpected, guise of Samael's son. Either circumstance on its own would make you quite the person of interest no matter what side of the divide one might reside."

Jacob bristled at the second half of Vessel's assessment. "You should probably know I don't recognize Samael as my father, and I certainly don't consider myself his son," grumbled Jacob. "Up until recently, I've lived my life believing my father didn't exist, except as this faceless figure who mysteriously vanished from my life before I was born. As far as I'm concerned, nothing's changed."

Vessel could hear the cemented stance in the boy's voice, and replied with a simple and agreeable "That's completely understandable."

"As for the whole Light Bearer thing, well, I guess we'll be finding out one way or the other soon enough," said Jacob.

The angel sat quietly for a moment studying Jacob and his wolf companion, and taking particular note of the boy's sudden glum demeanor.

"If you don't mind me saying, you don't sound all that confident the Tribunal will rule in your favor," he finally said.

"It's not so much I'm concerned about the Tribunal coming back and declaring I'm not the Light Bearer. The truth is I'm much more anxious about the possibility of them stating outright that I am, in fact, the Light Bearer," said Jacob.

"I'm not certain I understand what you mean." The furrows that made themselves visible across Vessel's forehead punctuated his confusion.

"Everyone has been so focused on making sure I am named this thing called Light Bearer, I'm not sure anyone has stopped to consider if I'm actually the person capable enough to be the Light Bearer," explained Jacob. "Since all of this started, I keep thinking about the purpose of the Light Bearer; the supposed mission to deliver a fatal blow to the Darkness as the Apocrypha states. I haven't the first clue as to what that even entails. How am I supposed to be something, or do something I don't even understand?"

The frown lining Vessel's forehead slowly began to fade as he came to understand what it was that troubled the boy so.

Then, looking upon Jacob with compassion, he said, "Trust me, Mr. Parrish...Jacob. Most men who would come to leave their mark on history only knew the direction in which the path of destiny extended, and while paved before their feet, were in fact blind to what the path actually looked like."

Vessel could see his words did little to assuage Jacob, and so he decided it was time to touch upon the reason he had the boy remain behind from his friends to engage in this private chat.

"I don't want you to misconstrue what I'm about to say, but I was not exactly enlivened at the news that I would be sent here to fill the vacancy left behind by Thaniel," he began.

"How come?" Jacob inquired curiously.

"The idea of teaching a bunch of Nephilim was something, I must confess, I viewed as beneath my time. True, I may have been blessed with the wisdom and intellectual insight like my brother, but I don't share the bond he forged with this Library he built, or with the words making up the countless books which fill it," said Vessel. "Don't get me wrong; I have long been a subscriber to the belief that knowledge is power of untold strength and, as a Guide, helping to exercise the muscle which resides inside the young skulls of you and your fellow Nephilim is one of the greatest weapons I can hand you.

But the truth of the matter is, I have always been and will always be a warrior at heart. I cannot tell you the number of battles I have fought in defense of the Light, and be clear, my sword is marked to see many more. It wasn't until quite recently–the other night when Anahel brought you along with your young friends and the Scucca Urn you attempted to destroy, to consult with me–that I came to realize I am still very much a warrior suited up for battle, only the battlefield has extended its reach to Havenhid."

"I'm not sure I follow. As a matter fact, I'm quite sure," Jacob, looking visibly confused, said.

"It's like the men I spoke of earlier who would come to mark history; my own eyes have been blinded to exactly how the path upon which my feet have been placed will unfold itself. I have, however, come to discover–by whatever mysterious and divine manner in which it came to me–the direction the unseen bends of said path leads, and that is to Havenhid. And more specifically to you."

Then, with a marked seriousness fixed in his eyes, Vessel leaned in closer to Jacob as his voice receded to just above a whisper. "Understand when I tell you: you are not alone in this divine endeavor of which you have come to inherit by the simple act of coming into the world," he said. "The Light Bearer, by its very definition, is the bringer of the Light. We are all of us–the Guides, your friends and fellow Nephilim, both here at Havenhid and outside Eden's Gate, the Heavenly Host and a multitude of winged mercenaries spread throughout the mortal world–soldiers in the army you have yet to assemble; an army of Light. However it happens you come to deliver the Darkness' fate, we can rest assured knowing we will help to serve as couriers. I myself will do all I can to ready you for your destiny."

"Except tell me where Moses' staff can be found." The words sort of rolled off Jacob's tongue without him meaning them to do so.

"I'm coming to find that you are a persistent one, if nothing else. That can be a dangerous trait for a Nephilim such as you," Vessel, narrowing his gaze on the boy as if seeing him for the first time, remarked. "You would do yourself good to take heed in the warning Thaniel gave you about the Scucca Urns when you spoke to him."

Jacob was naturally taken aback at the mention of Thaniel. "I don't know what you mean," he answered coyly, in an unconvincing attempt to play dumb.

"Please," Vessel said with a smile, "even as I sit here, I can hear the echoes of Thaniel's admonition still ringing through your head. Though I must commend you for your quick-witted resourcefulness in uncovering the answer to the riddle concerning the Scucca Urns."

"I wouldn't quite call it quick-witted; not when I failed to ask the most important question, which is, where the heck is Moses' staff?" Jacob noted sullenly.

"Thank goodness for small miracles," the angel muttered under his breath.

"This is a perfect example of why I have the doubts I do about being this Light Bearer," argued Jacob. "If it's true destroying the Scucca Urns would render Samael powerless, I would think Anahel, Gotham–you–would have formed a search party the first night we returned to Havenhid and revealed we had three of them in our possession. Yet here we are with my gut telling me to get my hands on that staff ASAP while everyone's making me feel like I'm planning to use it to vandalize the Vatican."

"One does not simply destroy Scucca Urns, despite what signals their gut might be sending them; just as one wouldn't take a wrecking ball to a nefarious facility rumored to hold deadly lab-grown pathogens capable of wiping out mortals on a grand scale," Vessel replied calmly. "I would caution you before you attempt to navigate this minefield with the charge of a pachyderm, to hold at the very forefront of your mind the plain and sobering fact that the very presence of the Scucca Urns here at Havenhid has placed all of Eden, and those who reside within her gates, in the gravest of danger. For when Samael finally discovers who holds possession of these unholy curios, there isn't anything he won't do in order to get them back–to anything, or anyone."

"Which just goes to prove my point. Are we actually going to sit around and wait until he learns they're here when we can put an end to his reign before he even realizes what's happening?"

"Alas, your impetuous nature is getting the better of you. It would behoove you to be mindful of the saying 'fools rush in where angels fear to tread.' " The chastising manner in which Vessel spoke caused Jacob to clench tightly his jaw to keep himself from speaking further. Vessel, likewise, paused his tongue when the boy's frustration became evident.

"I recognize the place from which the fervor behind your words comes, truly I do," the angel offered in more sympathetic tone. "You have assumed the mantle of Light Bearer before it has even officially been handed to you. I am appealing to your forbearance to not allow a hasty act on your part to cause the Tribunal to render a decision that would bring about yet another burial of a most important prophesy."

With some reluctance, Jacob met Vessel's gaze with his own and he was immediately greeted with an embrace of tranquility and solicitude that came from the gleam of gold radiating from the intensely penetrating eyes staring back at him.

"Remember what I told you about the army of Light," said Vessel. "I promise you, once the Tribunal has rendered its verdict on the matter, we will have leave to pick up this conversation where we are forced to leave it today. You just have to trust me."

Except for the few times they had crossed paths, Vessel had been slightly less than a stranger to Jacob. Yet there was a cordiality about the angel to which Jacob found himself immediately drawn. In many ways, Vessel reminded Jacob of Thaniel, except for the fact he cast a far more sizable and intimidating shadow. And while recent events involving both Thaniel and Damiel had caused him to be less than one hundred percent trusting when it came to angels, Jacob discovered, as he got up to leave, no such distrust after speaking with Vessel. In fact, Jacob found himself, strangely enough, entertaining the notion he and Vessel might have just formed the beginning of a special tight-knit bond.

"By the way," Vessel called out as Jacob began to leave with Mist in tow, "in case you were interested, you were both wrong."

Jacob paused and glanced back at the angel who remained seated in his chair. "Who was wrong about what?"

"That spurious little wager you and Mr. Kelly were in engaged in earlier downstairs regarding the staff of Moses and the Ark of the covenant," explained Vessel. "The truth is neither the staff or the Ark is any more powerful than the other. Quite the contrary, they are both quite powerless."

"How can that be?" inquired a newly intrigued Jacob. "What about all the things Moses was able to do with the staff: cause numerous plagues to rain down on Egypt; part the Red Sea?"

"I'm not discounting any of those things. However, the power to do such miracles came not from the staff, but from God himself, which is why we prefer the name staff of God rather than staff of Moses when referring to it. The staff was but an instrument—a conduit—to the power which flowed through it. Had God not chosen to demonstrate his mighty power through the staff, then it would have continued to exist as simply an everyday walking sick," said Vessel.

"What about the Ark?" asked Jacob.

"A gold-plated wooden chest."

The angel could almost hear the chorus of questions beginning to percolate inside the boy, but before Jacob could open his mouth to voice a single one, Vessel bid a pleasant, "Good evening, Mr. Parrish."

~ ~ ~

Leaving the Library, Jacob made his way to the Hall of Light which was alive with the din of teenage boys gabbing about the day's events while feeding their ravenous appetites from the usual spread of sumptuous dishes laid out for them each evening when the dinner trumpet was blown. The buzz of chatter grew noticeably and abruptly quieter, however, when Jacob entered the Hall and, as casually as one could with all eyes suddenly fixed his way, he made his way to the section of table where he spotted his friends as casually as one could with all eyes suddenly fixed his way.

It was to be expected. Ever since the hearing to determine whether or not he was the Light Bearer began, Jacob had become quite the topic of conversation, or rather gossip. Now that he was also the center of a custody battle of which the deadline for a decision by the Iudicium Tribunal was fast approaching, Jacob had become the one thing he always feared: a sideshow spectacle for curiosity seekers. What's more, he had ignited, unbeknownst to him, a flurry of secret bets amongst his fellow Nephilim recognizing an entertaining way to put their money where their predictions were on the outcomes of both hearings.

As he usually did, Jacob did his best to ignore the whispering chitchat that normally accompanied his arrival, not only inside the Hall of Light, but most any room or area in Havenhid where more than two of his classmates were present.

Only when he plopped himself in the vacant seat next to Leos did he come to feel at least slightly less conspicuous to the sea of eyeballs watching his every move.

"Well?" Max asked in a tone matching the anxious expressions fixed upon Kairo, Ethan and Leos' faces before Jacob could take a much-needed drink from the glass of water in front of him.

"Well what?"

"Whattaya mean, well what? The staff of Moses...did you find out where it is?"

Jacob replied with a defeated shaking of his head. "If Vessel knows the whereabouts of the staff, he isn't saying. So I guess this means we have officially hit a dead end."

"Man, if only you'd have asked Thaniel when you had the chance," Ethan muttered. His eyes suddenly enlarged themselves when his words met his ears and he turned to Jacob with a hangdog look. "Not that I'm blaming you for any of this. It just...well, you know..."

"Trust me, I've been kicking myself over the same thing," said Jacob. "But it was either asking Thaniel where the staff was or having Samael discover me."

"There's got to be someone else we can ask. What about Anahel or Gotham?" asked Kairo.

"After what we pulled the other night trying to destroy one of the urns with the Sword of Destiny? I'd say the chances of them telling us are south of doubtful," said Max.

It was then a bird flew down from somewhere above and landed on the table a short distance away from where the boys were sitting. The boys paid hardly a notice to the avian visitor. It was, after all, quite a common sight for birds such as sparrows, finches, canaries and starlings to not only dart inside and pay the boys a visit when the morning sun caused the vaulted ceiling to slowly open itself to the world outside, but also the birds that existed as painted images in the numerous murals covering the ceiling who managed to magically emerge as living creatures to feed on the generous helping of crumbs left to them before returning to their colorful oil-painted landscapes.

This bird, however, was somewhat unusual. For starters, it was a large blue jay, and it was carrying what appeared to be an envelope in its beak. It hopped its way across the table and around the obstacle created by the various dishes of food laid out across it until it was poised in front of Jacob.

"Hello there, fella!" Jacob greeted the blue jay whose black markings around his eyes gave him a particularly fierce look. "What's that you got there?"

Jacob slowly reached out to take the envelope from the bird, and to his surprise the blue jay appeared to stretch his head forward and direct the envelope into Jacob's grasp before issuing a loud squawk and flying off into the soft lavender glow of the descending twilight.

"What is it?" Leos asked with noted curiosity once Jacob opened the envelope and unfolded the note sealed inside.

"That's weird!" Jacob replied after reading the contents. "It says, 'The person who can help you uncover the thing you are looking for is Cyprus Morgan of Morgan Antiquities,' and it gives an address somewhere in London."

"Maybe Vessel had a change of mind," said Kairo.

Jacob dismissed the notion with a shaking of his head. "It had to be Thaniel," he said after a moment of pondering. "He was the one who told me about Moses' staff being the one thing able to destroy the Scucca Urns, even though he wasn't all that jazzed about our plans. It must have occurred to him, like it did me, that I failed to find out where to find it, and so he made sure to send along this message."

"What I find way more weird is that the staff used by Moses to part the Red Sea and unleash all kinds of plagues on Egypt is in the hands of some guy named Cyprus Morgan in some antiquities shop," Ethan wondered aloud. "How do you suppose the staff ended up with him?"

"The note doesn't actually say this Cyprus Morgan has the staff; only that he could help in finding it," said Max. "The question now is: what's our next move?"

All eyes shifted to Jacob who remained quiet in his own thoughts while staring at the mysterious note in his hand.

"We don't make one; at least for the time being," he said finally to the consternation of his friends. "Vessel made a point of holding off until after the hearing is over to address what to do about the Scucca Urns. He believes a bad move on our part at this juncture could jeopardize the Tribunal ruling in my favor, on both counts. Frankly, I'm starting to think it might be in our best interest to listen to him and cool our heels for the time being. At least until he is able to lend us a hand, which he promised to do."

With that, it appeared the subject of the divine staff and destroying the Scucca Urns had been put on ice, and the boys quietly returned to their dinner.

~ ~ ~

Despite Jacob leading his friends to believe he was putting the subject out of his mind for the time being, the Scucca Urns and, more importantly, the staff of Moses remained very much front and center of his thoughts long after lights out and everyone else drifted off to sleep. Lying in his bed with the mysterious note delivered to him earlier by the blue jay clutched in his hand, Jacob was serenaded by the echoes of both Thaniel and Vessel's voices speaking of the dangers of trying to destroy the pilfered urns.

For what seemed the hundredth time, he raised the note into the silvery glow of the moonlight and studied the unfamiliar name and address scrawled on the paper with his scrutinizing eyes. Oddly enough, it was Ethan's voice–and more specifically a particular question he had pondered aloud which largely went ignored–that managed to push its way past the others to make itself heard. Who was this Cyprus Morgan? And how did he–a mere everyday mortal–happen to come into possession of not only one of history's holiest relics, but one which could severely wound the Darkness?

Unable to cogitate on the matter one minute longer, he got up from his bed and, as quietly as he could so as to not awaken his sleeping roommates who were busy sawing logs, rummaged around for his shoes and a nearby sweatshirt. He then motioned to Mist to stay put where she lay at the foot of the bed, and the wolf obediently did as she was told, albeit with a whimper of resentment, as the image of Jacob tiptoeing his way softly across the room and slipping out the door reflected itself in her soulful eyes.

Once in the hallway, Jacob quickly pulled on his sweatshirt and slipped his feet into his worn sneakers. The hour was late and, with the other Nephilim sound asleep in their respective rooms, the deafening quiet that had settled itself on Havenhid was as delicate as a sudden, high-pitched scream, Jacob found. So, when he reached the last step of the stairway he descended leading to the grand foyer, he nearly made leave of his own body when an unexpected voice called out to him from out of the blue.

"Well, well, well...going somewhere?"

Being as the need for sleep was one of several noted conditions reserved for those with mortal blood flowing through their veins, there were a handful of residents at Havenhid one would expect to find roaming its halls at such a late hour. So when Jacob spun around like a flash at the sound of the voice, he expected to find himself face to face with Anahel or one of the other Guides. Much to his relief–and rather surprise–he found Max with a half-eaten apple in his hand looking like someone who had been to bed only to rise back up a couple hours later.

"Sheesh! You scared me!" Jacob said with a heavy sigh. "What are you doing up at this time of night?"

"Doing what I normally do: grabbing a late-night tucker," said Max. "And you?"

"Oh, you know...feeling a little restless so I thought I'd give my legs a stretch."

"Yeah? Cause from where I was standing it looked like you were headed for somewhere outside Havenhid."

"Yeah, so? Is there something illicit with going outside and getting a little fresh air?"

Max replied by giving his friend a slow and suspicious once-over from head to toe before biting down on his apple to free his hand that he then used to grab the folded piece of paper he spied clutched in Jacob's fist.

"And perhaps pay a quick visit to one Cyprus Morgan?" Max inquired when he saw the paper was the mysterious message sent earlier that evening before his teeth finished through the bite they had on the apple.

"What are you talking about? You think I'm on my way to London?" Jacob argued quite unbelievably.

"Come off it, mate! We've bosom-buddied long enough now that I didn't even need the power to read your thoughts earlier at dinner to see the way the gears were turning inside that melon of yours," Max replied, crunching loudly on his bite of apple while wearing a cocksure grin.

Before Jacob could respond, another voice—this one a whisper—made itself heard. Both boys turned their heads to the sight of Kairo hurrying his way down the staircase towards them.

"What are you doing up?" asked Jacob.

"Something woke me up and I happened to notice both your beds were empty," said Kairo. "Just wanted to make sure another Silent Forest-type incident wasn't in the making."

"That remains to be seen. Jacob here was just about to sneak off and go on a staff-hunting excursion," explained Max.

The clock was ticking and, knowing Max as well as he did, Jacob realized his attempts to convince his friend of anything other than the truth was futile at best. At worst, the longer they remained where they were the more likely it was one of the Guides would happen upon their late-night kiki.

"Alright, fine, I admit it. I was on my way to go find this Cyprus Morgan, whoever he is, and hopefully come back with the staff," admitted Jacob.

"Why all the secrecy, then? I thought we were all in on this together," pressed Max.

"There is no secrecy. I just had a sudden change of heart while lying in bed upstairs."

"I don't get it. I thought you said we needed to cool our heels after your talk with Vessel," said Kairo.

It was apparent the more Jacob was interrogated on the issue, the more impatient he was becoming with the conversation.

"Look," he finally barked with frustration, "the day after tomorrow the Iudicium Tribunal is going to render their verdict on whether or not Samael is going to be given custodial rights over me, and at the moment things don't look that hot in my favor. Do you understand what that means? It means not only am I going to be forced to leave Havenhid against my will, but the Underneath will likely end up being my new home."

Both Max and Kairo were instantly crestfallen when confronted by the reality of Jacob's words.

"Now, I meant what I said about listening to Vessel and holding off on destroying the urns. But I can't just sit back twiddling my thumbs and hope for the best when my fate hangs by a thread," Jacob continued in a more composed voice. "If this supposed staff that belonged to Moses truly is capable of doing what Thaniel says, then we should at the very least have it in our hands for the moment when our agreed-upon cooling off period is over. And that could likely happen the day after tomorrow."

Neither Kairo or Max could argue their friend's stance; in fact, it made all the sense in the world to them.

"At least, let us go with you to help," implored Max.

Jacob responded to the gesture with an appreciative smile.

"Three of us going AWOL is certain to draw attention," he said. "Besides, I need the two of you to help cover for my absence. I'd leave it to Ethan, but we all know what happened when he attempted to stand in for you when you snuck off to Cain's Corner to come look for me."

The memory of Ethan's hapless attempt to transform himself into a Max clone in order to fool Damiel in which he managed to get the look right but grossly bungle the height brought a shared chuckle between the three boys. Max and Kairo then offered Jacob luck on his search and began to escort him to the winding stairs located at the end of the foyer leading the way to the hollow of the tree which served as the entrance to Havenhid. Just then, however, they were greeted by the unexpected sight of Eksel coming up those same steps.

~ ~ ~

"A bit late, isn't it, to be going for a stroll outside?" Eksel inquired as he slowly ascended the last few steps while his gaze fixed itself intently on all three boys.

Max was first to open his mouth and attempt a believable enough explanation, but Eksel quickly held up his hand and advised the boy not to strain his truth-stretching skills.

"I assure you it was quite unintentional, but your voices carried loudly enough to reach my ears as I was climbing these stairs just now; and I am quite well informed of the scheme you have brewed this night," Eksel said cooly.

"I don't think scheme is the appropriate word to use here," advised Max.

"Is that so? Leaving Havenhid in the dead of night to embark on an unauthorized excursion of an unknown nature outside Eden's boundaries without a single word to your superiors; you wouldn't classify such antics as a scheme? Perhaps ruse, ploy or stratagem would better suit your linguistic tastes," Eksel noted brusquely.

The boys attempted to argue their case, but the Herculean angel was not easily affected.

"Do you have any idea the trouble you could cause?" Eksel focused his question to Jacob. "Have you forgotten you are the focus of two major cases before the Iudicium Tribunal? Not only are they to decide if you are indeed the Light Bearer but, perhaps even more importantly, whether or not to place you in Samael's care. Already Sandel has been looking for the smallest thing with which to bury you. One misstep on your part and you may finally give him his victory by causing the Tribunal to sway to his side. Now, you might be willing to take that risk, but I can assure you I am not."

Jacob was instantly dispirited. Perhaps he had been wrong about the gruff and sometimes uncivil angel, he wondered to himself. Even though Jacob and Eksel had formed an affable bond after what had started out as a mutual contemptuousness for one another, the angel's far from amiable demeanor reminded Jacob of the Eksel of old, despite the fact his argument was clearly in the boy's best interest.

"I guess we might as well go back to bed," Jacob grumbled sourly to his friends.

As they turned to make the long, dejected climb back upstairs, Eksel spoke again in a tone that made them pause their feet.

"However," he said somewhat reluctantly, "I recognize fully the seed for such a scheme, as the last thing I would want is to have to bear witness to an unimaginable ruling by the Tribunal, particularly where Samael is concerned. And make no mistake, I would first serve as escort to the cretinous inhabitants of the Underneath wishing to step foot in our sacred Garden before I would deny you the ability to arm yourself for defense in the face of such an inconceivable prospect."

Jacob's face instantly lit up. "Then...you'll let me go?"

"Hardly," Eksel replied emphatically, once more dashing the boy's hopes. "As I said, I cannot and will not allow you to risk sullying your character Sandel has labored hard to dirty.

"But you just sa—" Kairo began before the angel cut him off abruptly.

"If, say, two of your schoolmates were to take it upon themselves to act in their friend's best interests and devise their own scheme to hunt down this most important staff, well then, I don't see how it could affect your hearing and, therefore, wouldn't cause me a moment's worry."

The three boys exchanged looks of uncertainty, as though searching for some sign of assurance from the other that their ears did, indeed, hear what they had heard.

"You're saying you'd be okay if the two of us went?" Max, gesturing to himself and Kairo, asked.

"Wait a minute. That's a stupid idea," said Jacob, suddenly alarmed.

"I appreciate the confidence, mate," Max shot back.

"I just meant there's a small obstacle nobody here seems to be taking into consideration called the Gate," explained Jacob. "If you two attempt to go through it on your own, there's a high likelihood you're not coming out. Trust me, I barely made it through when I attempted it.

"Jacob's quite right," Eksel agreed. "The two of you have about as much chance navigating yourselves through the Gate as trying to navigate a desert made of quicksand. And having two Nephilim boys consumed by the smothering nullity awaiting them would be a misfortune I'd rather not have hung around my neck."

For a moment, it appeared to the boys they had come upon an obstacle of which there was no way around, until Eksel spoke again.

"It would seem then the only option left would be for me to take the two of you through myself," declared the angel, much to the surprise of the three boys.

"Seriously? You would do that?" asked Jacob who looked to be the most taken aback.

Eksel stood silent for a moment, as though he was second-guessing the smartness of his proposal.

"Because I owe you that much, and not just for the inexcusable way I came to receive your arrival at Havenhid," said Eksel. "I meant what I said when I testified before the Tribunal: I firmly believe you to be the Light Bearer foretold. The fate of such a divine prophesy, however, cannot rest solely on the whims of belief; not mine, or anybody else's. And as much as I can understand somewhat the lens through which my brother Sandel has come to look upon you, it is not for him—or certainly not Samael, for that matter—to extinguish the wick of the Apocrypha when, finally, it is lit."

~ ~ ~

Jacob gave a final wave to Max and Kairo as they took off after Eksel into the moon-lit sky and started their trek from the secluded corner of the Garden southward across the vast reaches of Eden.

When finally they reached the Dilmun Sea, they continued on over the usually deep turquoise-colored waters that, under the silvery light of the moon, sparkled as if an infinite amount of diamonds were floating upon its surface. They soon came upon the familiar and eerie barrier of fog stretching along the water like a phantom wall that instantly cloaked from sight all signs of Eden once the trio passed over it. Then, a short distance further, they came upon the spot where the unseen Gate leading to the now-unseen biblical paradise resided in the watery depths.

Grasping a boy in both his arms, Eksel ascended higher into the black sky studded with the pin pricks of a million brilliantly burning stars. Then, like a pelican taking aim at a school of fish, Eksel turned direction and, after offering the boys an obligatory warning to gather their breath, dove headfirst into the water.

The Gate greeted the trio by completely and wholly engulfing them in an abyss of blackness capable of wiping out the entirety of everything in existence in an unnerving instant. Despite having traveled through the Gate on more than one occasion, both Max and Kairo soon came to realize traveling through the ominous passageway was something no one ever grew accustomed to; and what proved to be a nerve-racking and suffocating experience the first time either one met their acquaintance with the Gate, remained equally as harrowing this time around.

Undoubtedly, it was always with a great sense of relief when a Nephilim emerged from the belly of such darkness on the other side, and so it was again as the two boys followed Eksel upward in an almost desperate rush to break through the water's surface that was suddenly made visible to them and fill their straining, oxygen-starved lungs. Once they had breathed in their fill of the frigid night air, Eksel led the way not to Akdamar Island as expected but in the opposite direction to the mainland. It was best, the angel explained to Max and Kairo, that no one be privy to their mission, even Johiel.

"Now, listen to me carefully," Eksel said when the three had reached the shore. "You have the next twenty four hours in which to find the staff for which you're searching, and not a minute longer. Whether you are successful in your hunt or not, you will make sure you are back here at this very spot within that time frame. Do I make myself clear on that matter? I am placing my neck on the cutting block and I am not looking forward to the possibility of losing my head over this."

The boys nodded their agreement and, after Eksel wished them luck before disappearing into the night, they decided their first course of action was to find themselves a set of dry clothes.

CHAPTER THIRTEEN

THE FIRST SHOT

There are times when even an angel finds himself in the grip of an unfortunate affliction reserved for mortals.

One only had to gaze into Damiel's eyes to see he had succumbed to such a malady. They burned with the telltale fire of obsession; an all-consuming fixation that manifested itself whenever he was in the presence of the Witnesses. Except for when he was training his students at Lions Bite, the angel spent every second of the remaining hours of each passing day and night pouring over the numerous testimonies of happenings occurring within the mortal world which were randomly, yet purposively recorded within the pages of the four mysterious books.

Again and again, Damiel would move back and forth, and around and around, from one book to the other in an almost agitated state brought about by the near-constant scratching sound of what seemed to be coming from the tips of several feather quills dipped in ink furiously writing. Only there was not a quill in sight, nor ink well; and yet, words appeared on the blank pages of the books as though written by some unseen hand.

It was not, however, the manner in which the words surfaced in the pages, but rather the message they carried that fueled Damiel's near-manic state.

Since his return to Eden, the angel had been patiently awaiting the unmistakable sign that Samael had fulfilled his end of the bargain the two had struck in exchange for his freedom from the Infernal Desert. But as days stretched themselves into weeks, and with not a glimmer of the promise of a war yet to be found amongst the screed of revelations being added to the books, Damiel's patience was quickly wearing thin.

Had that viperous Samael made the decision to deceive him? Damiel found himself wondering on more than one occasion as his eyes managed somehow to shield the fire burning within them and keep the books from bursting into flames as they raked the pages with a growing feverishness whenever a new entry appeared. He had warned Samael in no uncertain terms of the consequences should he trifle with him, and Damiel had every intention of making good on his threat, even if it meant overturning every rock in existence in which such a reneging worm could hide.

It was then, as he fumed with anger and began plotting the means by which he would exact his revenge on Samael, that the damper was momentarily shut on the fire fueling his ire.

Suddenly, amid the never-ending bulletins announcing wars, gruesome crimes and other inhumanities mortal man unleashed on one other, Damiel caught a gleam of the very thing for which he had been desperately waiting, or so he thought. His looming presence leaned in closer as his gaze narrowed itself to burn its way through the dizzying, almost maddening swirl of words, and focus with increasing raptness on a single entry which had imprinted itself upon the pages of the book before him:

"Cardinal Thomas Menard, favored to be the next leader of the Catholic Church, as cardinals from around the world gather at the Vatican to form the conclave that will choose the next pontiff following the sudden and unexpected death of Pope Gregory XVII."

Cardinal Thomas Menard...

In an instant, Damiel's thoughts transported him back in time to a grand and elaborately decorated room inside the Doge's Palace in Venice. It was there he recently happened to attend a most eventful masquerade ball where he not only had the great displeasure of parading around in a periwinkle-colored Arabian costume that made him appear like a giant blue genie, but brought him face-to-face with Miseriel, the cretinous Fallen who had murdered his son along with several other young Nephilim in cold blood, and whose name had taken the form of a thorn imbedded deep in his side where it had festered ever since.

It also happened to be the place where Damiel first set eyes on Cardinal Thomas Menard, who was also in attendance at the masquerade ball dressed in a costume reminiscent of Friar Tuck, one of Robin Hood's Merry Men. The portly, gray-haired Cardinal was one of several other high-profile attendees Miseriel called out before the other invited guests in order to remind them of the servitude still owed him now that he held the deed to their bartered souls.

"You I saved from a humiliating, if not justifiable, defrocking by the holy church itself," Miseriel reminded the Cardinal as the memory of that night resurrected itself inside Damiel's head. "It was by my hand that you've traded your bishop's hat for the scarlet mozzetta of a Cardinal and enjoy the pomp surroundings of the Vatican."

Thomas Menard, in return, expressed his gratitude to Miseriel by raising the oversized golden goblet filled with wine in his hand, from which he had visibly taken one too many sips, and replied with a subtle slur: "And I bless you for your benevolence."

It was no secret that of all the earthly things in existence the dark forces roaming the world wished to corrupt and ultimately destroy, the Church–even more so than mankind itself–was at the top of the list. For without the Church, and more importantly, the foundation upon which the first stone was placed to give rise to it, man would slip from Heaven's grasp to wallow in the mud of its own oblivion. And so the wolves came, dressed in vestments, but wolves nonetheless, to infest along with other undesirable vermin, countless churches and holy sanctuaries throughout the world where they fed on the faith of the unexpected faithful.

Up until then, it had been a quiet clash between good and evil. The latest revelation concerning Cardinal Thomas Menard, however, who had proven himself to be more vermin than wolf was one which Damiel found difficult to digest. It was bad enough such a man perverted by the dark ways had befouled the sanctity of the Church with his vile masquerade as a man of the cloth; the idea he could now be elevated to the highest holy position was beyond revolting to Damiel.

He instantly began wrestling with the possible aims the Darkness would have to make such a move, and as he did, he suddenly became acutely aware that he was no longer alone. In three moves so swift they appeared as nothing more than an indecipherable blur, Damiel grabbed his sword inside his wing, spun around on his heel and introduced the cold steel of his blade to the neck of the unannounced figure standing behind him whose presence was as unfamiliar to Havenhid as Havenhid was to him.

~ ~ ~

"Zophiel!" Damiel exclaimed with surprise at the sight of the angel looking stiff as a board at the end of his sword.

"Not exactly the welcome I was expecting," Zophiel replied, cautiously eyeing the brightly gleaming blade pressed uncomfortably against his throat.

Damiel lowered his sword and returned it to its place within the plumes of his wing without so much as a grumble of an apology.

"To what might we owe this unexpected visit to Havenhid?" Damiel asked, while at the same time turning his back abruptly on Zophiel and returning his attention back to the Witness. "I would think coming here would prove quite dangerous for you and put in jeopardy your carefully cloaked guise as Heaven's spy."

It was also during that fated night of the masquerade ball at the Doge's Palace, Damiel had moments earlier been reminiscing about, that Zophiel, an angel long believed to have earned the mark of a Fallen during the Great War in Heaven, revealed himself to have been sent into the pits of the Underneath by God himself as a mole to both surveil and subvert the nefarious aims of the Darkness.

"You're quite right about that, it is quite dangerous; I've something of great import to speak with you about, however, and I felt it worth the risk," said Zophiel.

He then followed the line of Damiel's intense stare to the book at which it was aimed.

"I take it is safe for me to presume, finding you here glued to these books, the rumors I've heard are indeed true about your freeing Samael from his imprisonment in exchange for a war," Zophiel then said.

Damiel stood quiet for a long while, ignoring the question.

Then, he did something few if any have ever been privy to witness: he revealed a crack in his formidable self and hung low his head, as though the weight of holding it up proudly had finally exhausted his strength.

"Have you any idea, brother, the generations of Nephilim I have castigated for their impetuousness? Who would have thought I'd find myself at this moment staring into the maw of my own imprudence?" said Damiel when finally he spoke. "I've lost count of the hours I've spent staring at the pages of these four books since returning from the Infernal Desert, impatiently awaiting a message of some evil act perpetrated upon humanity as confirmation Samael had abided to his end of the agreement he made with me in exchange for his freedom. It's only in recent days, that my scouring of these books has become feverish, nay, desperate; for I refused to believe the sign I was awaiting would come as it did–fired like a flare from the heart of Halcyon to illuminate the skies over Eden in a burst of hellfire."

Naturally, Zophiel knew of what Damiel was speaking, as news of Samael's brazen act to petition the Iudicium Tribunal for custody of the boy rumored to be the Light Bearer had spread to every part of the world like wildfire. He also caught sight of how painful Samael's callous act was for Damiel when the angel tilted back his head and a tear was seen escaping the corner of his eye.

"Oh, Zophiel! What have I done?" Damiel lamented in quiet agony. "Never did it occur to me that our Fallen brother, despite all the vileness that infests his very being, would take aim and fire the first shot of the war for which I bargained at the boy. Yet, not only did I free his hands of the unbreakable vine by which he was destined to forever be bound, I placed in them the gun from which he would fire the bullet."

There was an unmistakable tone of despair resonant in his voice, and when Damiel turned his head to meet Zophiel's sympathetic gaze, Zophiel saw he had not imagined the rare tear slipping across the sturdy warrior's profile, as Damiel's eyes were brimming with them.

"It is no secret I have come to hold great love for the boy, as though he were my own. How will I ever come to absolve myself of such foolhardiness, much less expect a sliver of forgiveness from him for what I have unleashed on him, intentional or not?" Damiel wondered aloud.

Zophiel stepped closer to Damiel and placed his hand upon the angel's shoulder in a comforting gesture.

"I, too, have come to hold the boy in high regard. After all, it is because of him I now have my son back in my life," he remarked in reference to Hunter from whom he became estranged when Zophiel chose to conceal his covert role as Heaven's spy with the unforgivable and shameful guise of a Fallen; something his son as a teenaged Nephilim just coming into his own viewed as a gross betrayal, father or not.

"I have only known this Jacob Parrish for a brief while but, in that time we spent in Venice, it did not escape me his strong fondness for you as well. And it is due to that fondness that he will come to forgive you," continued Zophiel. "Unfortunately, you will each first have to weather this squall you now find yourself swallowed up within; as you are quite correct in recognizing Samael's calculated move in appealing to the Iudicium Tribunal for wardship of the boy to be not a shot across the bow, but a direct aim at you, Havenhid and the whole of Heaven itself."

Zophiel then shifted his gold-illuminated gaze onto the pages of the Witness before them; specifically to the entry concerning Cardinal Menard which had engrossed Damiel a short time earlier.

"I'm here to inform you Samael is not the only one moving pieces across the board," he said.

~ ~ ~

Damiel's moment of despair evaporated instantly by a sudden pique of curiosity that moved him to Zophiel's side and drew his attention back to the book.

"Then, you know about this?" Damiel asked when he saw Zophiel's gaze was fixed on the entry regarding the Cardinal.

"We're aware of something irreligious attempting to make its way across the threshold of the Church," Zophiel said in what Damiel found to be an oddly close-mouthed manner before adding, quite ominously: "And that is not all."

Damiel's intrigue grew as Zophiel began flipping his way backwards through the pages of the book where he referred the angel to several entries recorded days earlier. They were each familiar in their wording, noting the death toll caused by an unnamed and unknown disease emerging in several small pockets of the world.

"I'm familiar with these notations from when the Witnesses first revealed them. But what of it? The pages of these books are filled with a countless tally of plagues and diseases, as well as the unfortunate souls who succumbed to them, stretching back centuries," said Damiel.

"True. But then, none of the illnesses of which you refer where unleashed upon the populace by Miseriel," said Zophiel.

The name which left Zophiel's tongue greeted Damiel like a stinging slap across his face.

"Miseriel? Are you certain?"

"It's not a contagion expected to draw much attention at first, which is why it likely escaped scrutiny by you. In fact, it behaves much like the common cold or flu, yet the reality is, it kills more than eighty percent of those it infects," Zophiel said much to Damiel's horror. "I have only come to learn this small bit of it after accidentally coming upon Miseriel and Arrestel quietly conversing about it when they believed themselves to be alone."

It was clear by the stunned look on Damiel's face the revelation had caught the angel off guard.

"But why?" he asked finally when words returned to his tongue. "For what purpose would he have to do this?"

"That is the question now, isn't it? Not only in relation to this but the unforeseen emergence of this Cardinal Menard in the wake of the Pope's suspicious and sudden demise, of which I've no doubt Miseriel is readily playing a vital role."

Of that, Damiel was in sound agreement.

"There is more," Zophiel announced suddenly. "Something of a far more dire matter."

"Come now, then...out with it!" Damiel pressed impatiently, when Zophiel was not immediately forthcoming with whatever was visibly weighing on his mind.

He then looked on somewhat annoyed as Zophiel slowly circled about the platform where the four Witnesses were positioned across from one another, appearing like someone quietly at odds with himself over disclosing that which was coiled upon the end of his tongue as he made his way from one book to another.

"Miseriel, it may come to surprise you, has fermented within himself over his long existence a particular acidulous vintage of venom and hatred where you're concern," Zophiel finally said.

"And here I was left to believe all this time there was absolutely nothing me and my dear brother had in common," Damiel grumbled facetiously.

"He has only become more fervid in his disdain for you, now that you have released Samael from his imprisonment and muddied his plans to assume dominion over the Underneath."

"Poor Miseriel; a day late and a throne short!" Damiel remarked with a growing giddiness over what he was hearing. "I'm still waiting for the part you warned was dire."

"Miseriel is determined to destroy you, Damiel," blurted Zophiel. "He has made it more than clear that he will not rest until your days as Angel of the Sword are cast to the West with the setting sun. Specifically, he is bent on ensuring that the mark of the Fallen finds its way to scar your temple."

The threat drew a hearty chuckle from Damiel.

"The mark of the Fallen...on me? The sulfur must be eating its way through his brain," Damiel guffawed. "As to his zest in wanting to destroy me I say to Miseriel, 'Take your best shot!' "

"I believe he already has," Zophiel said in a reply that instantly snuffed Damiel's sniggering.

~ ~ ~

"What do you mean you believe he already has?"

Somehow, Zophiel's already sober demeanor became even more grave.

"I've wrestled with whether or not to bring this to you attention–"

"Please, Zophiel, for once just say what needs to be said," Damiel snapped testily.

"Very well," Zophiel replied agreeably. "Miseriel has recently seized several younglings."

Damiel became like a block of ice upon hearing the news, but never more so than when Zophiel cautiously, but pointedly added, "Nephilim younglings. Fourteen of them, to be exact."

A marked silence settled itself around the two angels, with only the constant scratching of writing coming from the pages of the four Witnesses being the only sound to pierce the tense stillness.

"What do you mean by seized?" Damiel finally asked quietly.

"Taken, kidnapped, abducted...however you wish to call it," answered Zophiel.

"Why didn't you stop him?" Damiel barked in a voice that began to reflect his growing fury with every passing second.

"By the time I came to learn of it, Miseriel already had the younglings in his clutches," said Zophiel.

"And you're saying you believe these abductions were committed because of me?" Damiel asked somewhat apprehensively.

"I would not be here speaking with you about it if I thought otherwise," said Zophiel. "Miseriel, in his heartlessness, may not fully know your weaknesses, but he realizes intimately the wound he left you with to suffer so long ago is far from healed. Venice demonstrated as much to him."

Damiel grew more agitated with each new detail he came to hear as he frantically paced the floor before stopping suddenly and brusquely asking Zophiel the identities of the Nephilim Miseriel had abducted. When Zophiel revealed to him both the names of the younglings, as well as their fathers, the anger coloring Damiel's face receded slightly.

"Why they're just about a year shy of reaching the age when they would be brought to Havenhid themselves," the angel noted quietly.

It was impossible for him, at that moment, not to reflect on the memory of his own son, as well as the thirteen other Nephilim boys who were tragically denied the long-anticipated journey through Eden's Gate when their young lives were snuffed out when Miseriel and his dark band of Furies stepped foot inside the sanctuary of the church on Akdamar Island.

"Where has he taken them?" Damiel demanded to know, after quickly shaking away the memory of that woeful day.

"That I do not know," said Zophiel.

Unflustered by the answer, Damiel noted simply, "Then I will simply have to find them."

When he abruptly turned to leave, he found Zophiel whose feet proved themselves far quicker blocking his way.

"This is exactly the response Miseriel is anticipating from you, and why I was hesitant to bring this to your attention in the first place," said Zophiel.

"Your concern is noted, Zophiel," Damiel acknowledged. "But if you think I'm going stand by and allow another repeat of what happened at Akdamar Island to occur, then you're right: you should have rethought your decision to reveal this matter to me."

"If you go off half-cocked—" Zophiel began while taking hold of Damiel's shoulder in an almost desperate grasp. "Well...let's just say I fear the next time I find myself face to face with you I will be greeted by the unsightly reality that I am no longer in the presence of the Angel of the Sword. And that, dear brother, saddens me greatly."

For a moment, it appeared to Zophiel his words had managed to pause the flight that had found the angel's feet and quiet the impetuousness stoked within him that Damiel had earlier lamented as the two stared deep into the other's gaze.

Yet it was only for a moment when suddenly the golden gleam of ire erupted from within Damiel's eyes like a sun flare. And without uttering another word, Damiel pulled himself free from Zolphiel's iron grasp and briskly headed for the door to the Library.

~ ~ ~

Damiel's swift departure from Havenhid was marked by his stark winged shadow cast down by the ethereal glow of the moonlight as it swept across Eden's landscape like that of a giant eagle. Yet his shadow wasn't the only one to be revealed by the waxing moon.

Just as he spied the glistening of the Dilmun Sea in the approaching distance, Damiel became acutely aware of the presence of someone trailing his movements. Naturally, his suspicions first led him to believe it was Zophiel seeking to make another futile attempt to persuade the angel to rethink seeking out Miseriel and return to Havenhid, at least until cooler heads might prevail. Zophiel, however, would have easily caught up to Damiel by then, and whoever it was following behind was doing so discreetly, and doing their best to remain hidden from sight in the process.

Soaring over the ridge of mountains where the corridor bridging the shores of Eden to its interior paradise called the Emmaus Passage resided hidden within the carcass of rock, Damiel took advantage of a momentary blind spot lent to him by the crest of the mountain and abruptly abandoned the sky and dropped out of sight. Perched inconspicuously on a shelf of rock, he fixed his acute gaze on the starry skies above and waited.

Soon enough, and just as he expected, the silhouette of another winged figure glided over the top of the mountain pass and was about to proceed onward over the Dilmun Sea. Damiel's eyes flashed a glint of gold before his wings once more unfurled themselves and aimed him with great speed and stealth at the figure fixed in his sights. In an instant, he pounced upon the unsuspecting stalker with a blow that sent the two into a tailspin from which neither could recover. In an explosion of sand, they hit the beach below them like two incoming cannonballs fused together, fired from the deck of some unseen pirate ship lurking offshore. When the dust finally cleared, Damiel was visibly taken aback to discover the lurker upon whose chest his knee firmly rested was not Zophiel, as he suspected, but rather his son, Hunter.

"What is it you think you're doing?" Damiel growled with visible irritability.

"At the moment, choking on a mouthful of sand, not to mention trying to breathe despite having what feels like a giant anvil resting upon my chest," Hunter croaked painfully.

Somewhat begrudgingly, Damiel offered relief to Hunter by removing his knee from his torso and rising to his feet, while at the same time he was quite deliberate in ignoring the hand Hunter extended to him to help him up from off the ground.

The angel stood quiet for a moment, eyeing Hunter as he slowly got to his feet and began to feel about his sides to check for possible broken ribs. "I suppose, if I were to inquire as to why it is I find you shadowing me at this late hour of night, you'd attempt to convince me it's but a coincidence. Would I be correct in such an assumption?"

"That all depends," Hunter, who was now busily shaking his hair and the plumes of his wings free of sand, answered. "Would you believe me if I did?"

"Not likely," Damiel replied cooly before he proceeded to launder his own soiled wings with one thorough and meticulous shake that sent the castoff blanket of debris directly onto a very much annoyed Hunter.

"But seeing as though I have neither the time nor the interest at this moment to wrangle the truth from you, you'll understand me clearly when I advise you this incident has a fair chance of being forgotten if you were to return to Havenhid this minute without argue and see yourself back into bed," said Damiel.

The angel turned his back to the boy and was about to take for the sky again when Hunter called out urgently, "I know about the Nephilim Miseriel's abducted."

Damiel's feet held their stance upon the sand.

"How do you know this?" Damiel inquired, peering over his shoulder and fixing a scrutinizing stare on Hunter, before he immediately took a stab at guessing the answer. "Your father told you?"

"I wouldn't say that, exactly," answered Hunter. "I actually had no idea he was at Havenhid."

"Then from whom did you hear of it...exactly?" pressed Damiel.

Hunter proceeded to tell the angel how earlier in the evening he was sitting with the still-ailing Predmore, as he was often inclined to spend whatever free time he had ever since the unfortunate incident inside The Crucible left the young boy unconscious and bedridden. When the hour finally arrived that he could no longer keep his eyes open, Hunter surrendered his seat in the chair where he sat beside the bed with the promise to return first thing the next morning. As he walked the long, winding hall on his way to his room, he passed the Library, and it was there he felt the pull of an unmistakable and familiar presence lingering just beyond the closed doors.

"It wasn't my intention to eavesdrop on the conversation you were having," said Hunter. "In fact, I was far more surprised to see my father at Havenhid and wondering why he hadn't let me know he was planning to visit. But then I understood when I happened to hear him tell you about Miseriel."

"I see. And now you wish to take up where your father failed in trying to convince me to stay put in Eden, instead of rectifying the situation," said Damiel.

"Quite the opposite, actually. More than a dozen Nephilim lives are in danger as we speak, so most definitely you should do whatever it is you can to save them; but with one caveat: that you not go it alone."

"Come again."

"That's why I'm here. I wasn't so much stalking you as I was tagging along. I want to go along with you and help."

Damiel stood silent for a moment staring blankly at the young man as though the words he had just heard were an indecipherable garble of sounds. Then, much to Hunter's chagrin, the angel let loose a hearty roar of a laugh that made itself heard from one end of the beach to the other, and then out across the Dilmun Sea.

It was not the reaction Hunter expected from the angel, and he did his best to ignore the sniggering, even as it caused his face to flush all the more with the color of anger and embarrassment, saying, "I figure if what my father says about Miseriel setting up a trap to get you to Fall proves to be true then it'd be a smart move to have me around as a backup."

The suggestion made Damiel throw back his head and release even more laughter from his chest.

"Do you mind explaining what you find to be so funny?" Hunter, his nose clearly out of joint, finally grumbled.

"Forgive me!" Damiel chuckled forth in what was far from apologetic. "Here you stand, a Nephilim, who until just a few short weeks ago was living by his wits—most notably by rummaging through garbage bins and the intermittent life-and-death battle settled by a tried and true bout of fisticuffs, and now feels emboldened enough to come face to face with the proverbial monster residing underneath the bed, even as his newly sprouted wings still carry the scent reminiscent of a new-born baby."

Hunter, bristling at the flippant characterization leveled his way, shot back, "You conveniently left out that same Nephilim had notched more than a dozen Infector deaths in his belt before he even stepped foot in Eden and began training, not to mention wrangle three of the seven Scucca Urns from protective grasps of some rather vicious Pethens."

"What I recall quite plainly was witnessing you make a foolish attempt to wrangle, as you so put it, a fourth urn in the middle of a masquerade ball inside the Doge's Palace, and instead wound up in the clutches of a rather miffed Pethen who took hold of you by the ankle, leaving you to dangle upside-down like some birthday piñata," countered Daniel. "Luckily for you, your father was at hand to save you that evening from what I suspect would have been an unfortunate and unsightly version of a taffy pull, so you could live to see Eden and receive the instruction you obviously were lacking in preventing you from being swept off your feet with such ease."

Then, to prove his point, Damiel placed his foot behind Hunter's right heel and a hand against his chest in a combination of movements so swift they went unnoticed, and before Hunter knew what was happening he was pushed backward and his feet were swept out from under him, sending him to the ground where he landed with a thud flat on his back.

"I rest my case!" the angel remarked smugly to the young man who was at once abashed at being caught off guard by such a juvenile tactic.

"Funny that." Hunter replied with not a hint of levity. "And here I would have thought the memory to burn itself into that brain of yours would have been what happened the other day at Lions Bite: you know, when I threw a challenge at your feet and beat you soundly."

Damiel's expression soured instantly at the unwelcome reminder of Hunter's impressive showing of his skills with a bow and arrow (though Damiel remained too pigheaded to admit it out loud) against the angel's mastery of the sword, while going head to head in the Infector simulation training exercise.

"Then again, if I were the Angel of the Sword and had just gotten smoked by a Nephilim newbie, I'm sure I'd be praying for a bout of amnesia myself," Hunter added with just the right amount of salt. Then for added emphasis, Hunter took a lesson from Damiel's playbook and swept his leg forward, catching the angel by surprise with a mighty and well-aimed kick to the calf that knocked him cleanly off his feet. The stunned expression that found Damiel when he landed squarely on his backside with a muffled thud that all but shook the entirety of the beach more than made up for Hunter's own embarrassing spill moments earlier.

"And that, if I may be so bold, is what is known as checkmate!" Hunter crowed while shooting Damiel a victorious grin.

In a flash, Damiel was back upon his feet with two shakes of his wings. This time, however, it was the angel who extended his hand to Hunter in what appeared to be a cordial gesture to help him off the ground, even as he stood glowering at the young man.

"Checkmate, indeed," Damiel noted quietly.

"That mean I can come along?" Hunter asked with a lilt of enthusiasm.

Damiel silently pondered the question.

"If you choose to follow along, I won't stop you," the angel finally answered much to Hunter's delight.

"I take you've brought your bow with you," Damiel then commented with a somewhat snide tone.

Hunter quickly fetched his weapon of choice that had been tossed a short ways onto the beach from the impact that first brought him and the angel to crash land onto the beach.

"Never leave home without it!" Hunter declared, as he held up the sling holding his bow before fastening it once more across his back.

Damiel could only roll his eyes with resignation, and without saying another word he unfurled his wings and flew off into the inky blackness covering the Dilmun Sea in the direction of the Gate residing outside the fog bank hovering upon the surface of the water just offshore like some phantom ghost.

And trailing close behind was Hunter.

CHAPTER FOURTEEN

BEAUTY AND THE BEAST

It was not an uncommon sight to see Ava Delacroux on any given day strolling the sidewalks that wound their way through the heart of Cain's Corner.

Mondays, it was a trip to Brighton's Food Mart whose owner, Harold Hoffman, would instantly stop without fail any task he was in the middle of doing and rush to greet his most loyal–if not particular–customer upon her arrival and escort her through the store to assist in collecting the list of needed grocery items for the week.

Tuesday afternoons, Ava had tea with Mrs. Alice Kirkegaard while Wednesday afternoons were reserved for yet another tea date with Mrs. Hilda Buford. It was a casual affair once enjoyed together by all three women. That is, until Mrs. Buford's rambunctious Corgi gave chase after Mr. Whiskers, Mrs. Kirkegaard's odd and creepy hairless cat, and in the midst of the pursuit reduced the two-thousand-piece puzzle Mrs. Kirkegaard had recently completed with painstaking care pridefully displayed on a nearby table into a jumbled and indecipherable pile upon the floor. Needless to say, the war between dog and cat instantly ignited hostilities between Mrs. Kirkegaard and Mrs. Buford, most notably when Hilda, offended when Alice inveighed against the beastly behavior of her precious Corgi, compared with snide frankness the wrinkly Mr. Whiskers to a piece of undercooked bacon with legs.

Thursdays proved to be a far more relaxing time, for that was when she visited the beauty salon for her usual touchup to her always impeccable coif. After all, she had to look her best when she played Bridge the following afternoon during the weekly gathering of her women's auxiliary group. Saturdays, on the other hand, were a more solemn affair; that was when she went to St. Michael's Cemetery where she spent a large portion of the day quietly sitting at the gravesite of her beloved daughter Elisabeth, who had passed away expectedly, yet no less tragically, a little more than a year earlier.

Then, or course, there was Sunday, when she went to St. John's Cathedral where she faithfully attended mass without fail.

No matter the business that directed her feet down various streets and neighborhoods through town, Ava's return home always followed the exact same route through a sprawling park full of shade trees and flowery shrubs surrounding a pond where she always stopped to feed the families of geese and mallard ducks leftover pieces of bread she carried in a plastic bag inside her purse. Once the ducks and geese, not to mention the one or two squirrels looking to take advantage of a free handout, were fed, Ava would continue on her way until she reached the end of the park where she then migrated to a walkway that ran alongside the tranquil, bubbling path of Stevens Creek which she followed the rest of the way to the serene, sleepy neighborhood where she lived.

It likely, then, would have been quite odd to any of Ava's neighbors familiar with her routine and who happened to be outside or gazing out of their window one particular Saturday afternoon to catch sight of the elderly woman rounding a corner on her return home; a corner that was not only located on the complete opposite and furthest end of the street where she lived and led not to St. Michael's Cemetery from where she would have been returning, but to the swath of forest which bordered the neighborhood.

Dressed in a light flower-print dress, Ava made her way along Tudor Drive where the clicking of her heels ticked off the pace of her steps that were a touch more brisk than the more unhurried stride she was known to demonstrate after a somber visit to the cemetery. Now and then, her gaze would furtively look to the rooftops of the houses she passed, as well as to the tops of trees. When finally she reached a yellow-with-gray-trim house appearing all the more picturesque with a wall of pink Bougainville covering a large trellis attached to the side of the home near the porch and a stately willow tree positioned just so in the center of a green lawn, she paused but a moment to glance at the black metal mailbox attached to a wooden post near the street curbing upon which was inscribed in white lettering "Parrish."

She then proceeded up the walkway to the steps of the porch where, again, she paused; this time to admire a rosebush in full bloom. Gently, she took hold of the stem of one of the blood-red roses, and as she leaned in to inhale the perfume emanating from the velvety soft pedals her eyes once more scoured the trees and rooftops of the nearby homes. Seeing nothing out of the ordinary, she made her way to the front door, yet refrained from knocking.

Instead, she directed herself to yet another walkway leading the way along the side of the house to a backyard beautifully landscaped with seemingly every imaginable flowering shrub known to sprout from the ground. Yet surrounded by exotic birds of paradise, sunset-colored hibiscus and purple Dahlias, not to mention vibrant arrangements of foxgloves, goldenrods, daylilies, hydrangeas, and even more roses, just to name a few, there was only one thing that captured fully and immediately the elderly woman's gaze. It was the sight of another women, wearing the exact same dress as she was, kneeling beside a vacant patch of flowerbed beneath the shade of a large ornamental Japanese maple tree growing nearby where she was busily using a hand shovel to prepare the soil for a couple of plants she was looking to add to the garden.

Quietly, and with noticeable intrigue, she watched the woman go about her task until, finally, she parted her lips and announced her presence with two cordial words: "Hello, Ava!"

~ ~ ~

Up until that precise moment, the woman focused on tilling the soil believed herself to be the only known Ava Delacroux to exist in the world; or, at the very least, the only one to possess the image of the face reflected back by any mirror into which she looked. So it was quite understandable when she looked up to see who it was who had addressed her that the blood instantly drained from the face that was no longer her's alone.

"What in the devil's name is this?" the real Ava managed to gasp, though with a very real fear heard in the tremble of her voice.

Even before the question left Ava's lips, her eyes instinctively shifted their focus to the ground where the visitor stood in an urgent search for the shadow her clone cast upon the grass where she fully expected to find a sinister shape whose movements were independent of the body to which it was connected.

Only she saw no such thing, much to her surprise.

"If it's Infectors you are looking for, you can rest assured there are none here to be found," the woman said to Ava.

Her ears then caught the unmistakable whiffle of wings, and when she spied a glimmer of relief pass across Ava's face, she turned her head not so much as an inch when an angel, striking in beauty as he was in strength, descended from the sky from out of nowhere to land behind the imposter with his eyes aflame, wings flared and sword poised to strike.

"May I ask what gave me away?" the fake Ava inquired.

"For starters, I observed Ms. Delacroux return from her weekly visit to the cemetery with my own eyes not an hour ago," the angel replied in a voice reminiscent of the deep rumbling resound that lingers following a loud clap of thunder.

"But if you wish to know the biggest tell of your ridiculous charade, I'll be more than happy to enlighten you," continued the angel. "The woman in whose shoes you are attempting to walk has a way of carrying herself with an elegance and grace that you, if I may be so frank, are noticeably deficient of."

The jibe didn't appear to affect the woman. In fact, it was quite difficult to make out much of any expression on the fake Ava's face as her countenance suddenly began to change and remold itself as if it were a living mound of clay being resculpted by an invisible pair of hands. Instantly, the likeness of Ava faded from view and emerging in her place was Lilith.

She turned to level her dark swallowing gaze on the angel looming behind her and the corner of her mouth, which was painted blood red, curled upward like a cat stretching after awakening from a long nap.

"Pity all those etiquette classes I enrolled myself in have proven to be such a waste of time, she replied with a smile that was at once menacing as it was beguiling.

The angels eyes threatened to incinerate her as they flared brightly with contempt, but Lilith quailed no one bit in the face of such an intimidating presence. Instead, she turned her back to the angel with a coquettish flip of her raven-colored hair and focused her attention on the lush beauty of the garden surrounding her.

"My, my, my, but you've certainly shown yourself to possess quite the green thumb to cultivate such a...heavenly retreat," Lilith remarked with a pleasantness that seemed strangely disjointed from the mouth from which it came.

She strolled about the yard, seemingly admiring the bouquet of colorful blossoms adorning the numerous bushes and shrubs, before stopping at a particularly resplendent rose bush.

"If one didn't know better, I'd say you were on your way to creating a miniaturized and, dare I say, pedestrian version of the Garden of Eden for yourself," Lilith commented while taking hold of one of the amber-colored buds in the beginning stages of unfolding its pedals and leaning in for a sniff.

"The green thumb responsible for all this belonged to my daughter, not me. It was her hobby for many years; I just do my best to maintain it the way she would've liked it to remain," Ava replied as cordially as she could manage.

Her dark gaze staring past the rose in her grasp, Lilith looked more like someone who had just inhaled the putrid stench of a rotten egg than the delightful perfume emanating from the bud and replied simply, "How...sweet."

"Unlike Eden, I most certainly am confident in declaring outright that any serpent charmed enough to slither its way into this garden will not be long for this world," the angel was quick to state with a credence few, if any, would challenge.

Ignoring the angel, Lilith turned her attention to Ava.

"If you would oblige me, I'd like to have a word with you," said Lilith, before adding in an unmistakably forthright manner, "In private!"

Again, the angel interjected before Ava could respond. "You're mad if you think I am going to allow her within reach of your deadly coils," he said.

"My dear doltish Yairel, you know as well as I if my intention in coming here was to do her harm, I most certainly would have achieved my aim before your knight-in-shining-armor-descent from the sky."

A gleam of malevolence pulsating deep within the inky wells of her eyes indicated most clearly she was as confident in her menacing remarks as the angel was with his own threats, if not more.

"It's quite important, I assure you," Lilith, turning once again to Ava, implored. "That is to say, I assume you still hold within you a dutiful concern with anything regarding the subject of your grandson, am I correct?"

The mention of Jacob caused an instant, if not brief, shadow of panic to surface in Ava's face; something that did not go unnoticed by Lilith.

"It's okay, Yairel," Ava said, before the angel could set free the words poised on the tip of his tongue as he parted his lips. "I'll speak with Lilith."

Then somewhat apprehensively, though not so much by fear, Ava looked to Lilith and said in as cordial and cool a manner as one could manage extending an invitation to a particularly large and hairy tarantula, "We can go in the house, if you wish."

Lilith gave the quaint, two-story residence a once-over with her dark gaze, replied with an agreeable nod and swept past Ava while flashing an oh-so-smug smile at Yairel who could do nothing more than stew where he stood as he watched with some weight of trepidation as the two women slipped inside the home.

~ ~ ~

Ava lead the way to the large sitting room where she usually spent her time knitting, enjoying a nice cup of hot tea in the afternoon, or curled up with a good book.

There she quietly took a seat on a plush, emerald green sofa and, with her hands folded just so upon her lap, followed with a watchful gaze as Lilith slowly made her way through the room with gliding footsteps while taking careful inventory of her surroundings, from the books filling a bookcase stretching the length of one wall, to the delicate Lladró figurines decorating the oak mantle above the fireplace.

An elegant brass clock housed within an exquisite crystal dome on a nearby table ticked off the passing seconds with the same staccato often associated with a time bomb right before it's set detonation.

"May I ask how you came to learn of my whereabouts here in Cain's Corner?" Ava asked, finally, when the silence—and worse, the ever-maddening tick-tock of the clock—became insufferable.

"You and your family's concealed existence in this humdrum hamlet has never been all that secret—at least, not to me," answered Lilith, much to Ava's surprise. "While there are others who would have paid handsomely to uncover the hidden X on the map showing the precise location of this house, I've never had any particular pressing need or desire to enlighten such bounty hunters, nor to pay you a social call until this moment."

As she spoke, her attention became suddenly focused on the covers of several record albums residing next to a vintage phonograph on a large shelf housed within the bookcase. One of the album covers, featuring an alluring portrait of Ava in her younger days as a renowned singer starring in Camille Saint-Saëns' epic opera "Samson et Dalila," was quick to catch Lilith's attention. Rapt with intrigue, she fell silent while carefully studying what was inarguably a still-life of beauty and poise reminiscent of a Baroque painting created by one of the Old Masters staring back at her. Suddenly, the tonearm of the record player moved of its own accord and positioned itself delicately on the grooves of the vinyl album that also, inexplicably, began to spin upon the turntable.

The majestic, euphonious sound of Ava's recorded voice singing "Mon coeur s'ouvre à ta voix," marred only by the occasional crackle or pop of the needle siphoning the melodious notes from the vinyl disc, suddenly filled the room, drowning out instantly both the tense silence and the beating of the brass clock's mechanical heart. Ava instantly grew uneasy in her seat, her folded hands now nervously fidgeting with one another, when for the first time the passionate beauty of her voice caused her immediate discomfort.

"I saw you perform this song once," Lilith remarked suddenly out of the blue.

"You...you saw me perform? On stage?" questioned Ava who wasn't certain her ears had heard Lilith correctly.

"I believe it was in the winter of 1952. The Royal Opera House in London," said Lilith as her eyes remained glued on the young Ava staring out from the album cover in her hand. "At the time, you were referred to as the Aphrodite of the opera world; a modern-day Helen of Troy whose striking beauty enslaved men's hearts but whose voice had the power to bring entire nations to their knees. It goes without saying you were quite handsome in your day, but let's not kid ourselves; reducing a mortal man to a slobbering lap dog with a simple purse of one's freshly painted lips is no great feat to crow about. The true test of one's reported allurement is the ability to bend the knees of more loftier and sophisticated beings. Angels, for instance. So naturally, as you can imagine, I was compelled to see with my own eyes the mortal woman who had managed to bring to his knees one such angel who before then had proven himself extraordinarily averse to matters of the heart."

She gave the album cover one last lingering look before setting it down where she found it, and turned around to focus her attention on the flesh-and-blood Ava seated on the sofa.

"As luck would have it, I was nearly deprived of seeing you perform that night," continued Lilith. "The singer who was to play opposite you in the role of Samson had suddenly taken ill."

"I remember," said Ava, when Lilith paused as if waiting for some response. "The performance was threatened to be cancelled. That is, until a last-minute replacement was announced."

"And what a replacement it was. One would have thought Heaven itself had intervened, only not quite. Who could have imagined the great and reticent Gothamel would reveal himself to be such an impresario of the stage," Lilith commented with a lilt of sarcasm before her demeanor grew once more serious. "It was the performance of a lifetime. The standing ovation you received from the enraptured audience remains the longest the opera house ever witnessed, and the curtain calls too many to count. The two of you inhabited the skins of Dalila and Samson better than the two souls to whom they originally belonged.

"It was on that night I saw first-hand that the rumors I had heard were true," Lilith continued as her stare remained fixed on some faraway point only her eyes were privy to see. "The mighty Gothamel had, indeed, fallen in more ways than one, and a surprising mortal woman with a voice like a trumpet named Ava Delacroux wielded the battle-ax that enabled such an unexpected feat."

The beguiling strain of Ava's voice came to an abrupt halt when the tonearm of the phonograph suddenly jolted back seemingly by its own volition, dragging the needle across the vinyl in a savage and cringing manner hostile to the ears.

With the phonograph stilled, and silence once again settling itself upon the room, Lilith proceeded to make her way to the large bay window overlooking the front of the house, her long flowing black gown dripping with organza trailing behind across the floor like a stretch of shadow. Ava, however, was quietly, if not cautiously, focused on far more discernible slinking movements coming from within Lilith's long black mane of hair. To Ava's eyes, it was as if the tresses themselves were alive. Or, worse yet, some unseen living thing had taken up residence within the jet-black tresses. And, at first, Ava silently pooh-poohed such outlandish thoughts. Then again, the urban legends surrounding Lilith contained whisperings far worse to be imagined.

The sight of Lilith closely perusing the numerous framed photographs arranged across the length of a long mahogany table positioned in front of the window instantly doused Ava's musings over what may or may not be concealed in her guest's hair, particularly when one of the photographs found its way into Lilith's hands. It was an aged black and white photo, showing her as a young woman standing beside an ever-youthful Gotham and a young fair-haired boy. Until recently, the photo had been hidden away in a cigar box at the bottom of a hope chest, along with a bundle of letters, a feather and a flower that never showed signs of withering no matter how many years passed; the testament to a secret Ava no longer saw a need, nor wished to keep concealed, despite the lingering sadness attached to it.

Watching Lilith as she stood staring at the photograph with a fixed intenseness that all but caused the silver frame in which it was housed to slowly begin melting, Ava suddenly lamented her move to bring her past out into the light.

"My son, David." she forced the words from her mouth, when the tense silence grew to be too much to stand for another second.

"So I guessed," Lilith replied quietly. "The Light Bearer whose radiance was extinguished almost as soon as it was set alight."

Whether it was the words themselves or the callous, off-the-cuff manner in which they were spoken, Ava found herself visited by a familiar pang deep within her chest.

"There was another," Lilith was suddenly heard to blurt out.

"I'm sorry...another?" Ava, looking somewhat puzzled, echoed.

"Child of course. A son fathered by Gothamel," Lilith, glancing back at Ava over her shoulder, a hint of smile on her lips, replied. "Surely, he told you about it."

Whatever unease Ava may have felt occupying the same space inhabited by Lilith's menacing presence suddenly dissipated, and her doughty spirit once more returned to straighten her back and wipe away the intimidation reflected in her eyes.

"He told me. He told me all about it: both about the child and the one who was his true love long before my name found his tongue. Her name was Damira, and she was not only a beautiful angel but your sister, as well."

Ava recognized clearly when the faint smile aimed her way disappeared completely at the mention of Damira's name that she had revealed something Lilith not only didn't anticipate her knowing, but was preparing to wound her with by disclosing it herself, and with relish. And it was in that realization that Ava pressed forward.

"The way I understand it–that is, the way Gotham shared the story with me–Damira so loved Gotham that she sacrificed her wings in exchange for mortal blood to run through her veins in order to give him a son," Ava continued. "Sadly, she and her precious baby who was days away from being delivered into this world met a tragic end, most ironically, in the River of Life at the hands of a pitiful and unimaginable soul driven by an inconsolable slight to the heart.

"Yes Gotham told me all about it. You fell in love with Gotham and, when your affections went unrequited, you murdered your own sister, not to mention an innocent child!" Ava declared in a withering tone to ensure there was no misunderstanding who the death-dealing culprit was in her blunt accounting.

~ ~ ~

Lilith remained deathly still for some time staring at Ava with eyes that gleamed like the points of two daggers.

"I'll try to refrain from taking offense by your obvious contempt for me. You do, after all, know a bit about losing a child."

She then turned her attention once more to the framed photograph which had sparked the ghoulish subject of conversation. "If you don't mind me saying, your threshold for forgiveness is commendable. I wouldn't expect to hear much if any timbre of sympathy lacing your tongue when speaking about Gothamel's loss, most notably his unborn child."

"What would you expect? For me to dance a jig?"

"He did kill your child, did he not? Murdered him in cold blood." A gleam of sadistic glee surfaced in the pools of Lilith's dark eyes before she added with noted cruelty, "And all over a sword."

There was fiendish coldness to Lilith that Ava found repugnant. It helped explain her unnaturally, almost deathly pallid skin. For the longer Ava was forced to bear being in the presence of this ghastly woman dressed in a diaphanous dress of black as though she were on her way to a glamorous wake, the more she was convinced not a single drop of blood existed in her body to lend color to her flesh. And that was solely due to the fact that Lilith somehow managed to exist without the aid of a working heart, Ava was convinced.

"Contrary to what many at first came to believe, David's death was a bit more complicated than the way you care to describe it," Ava noted cooly. "David, in fact, sacrificed his life in order that Gotham might regain his."

"Yes...so I've heard," Lilith remarked indifferently. "A most poignant and noble display of love for one's father, and yet I can't help to wonder how many fathers would be able to muster the will to bring the ax down upon the neck of their own child, no matter if he readily placed his own head upon the executioner's block."

Ava said nothing in return, nor did she need to. Lilith spied instantly from the sudden noticeable heaviness weighing down upon the old woman, despite her efforts to conceal it, that she was not the only one to ruminate over such things. And, again, the corners of her mouth curled with gleeful pleasure.

She turned her attention back to the table of framed memories, and Ava was relieved to see the one photograph she had containing the image of her son returned to its spot, only to feel her back rise up again when Lilith reached for another framed picture; this time it was of her deceased daughter Isabeth.

"Your daughter was a very beautiful woman," Lilith said, after staring for some time at the image of Isabeth looking healthy and radiant with her windswept hair blowing about her while at the beach.

"Yes, she was. Quite beautiful," Ava, wondering how it was Lilith had come to recognize her daughter from the numerous photographs, echoed.

"It must be, to say the least, difficult."

"Losing a child is never an easy thing. Somehow I've managed to survive the loss of both of mine." Ava replied, though not without feeling noticeably more uncomfortable speaking on such a sensitive topic with the woman in black.

"I don't mean about her unfortunate death," corrected Lilith. "I was referring to the difficulty of watching Gothamel become such a protective and, dare I say, paternal presence in her own child's life–a child that was conceived by Samael, his greatest foe–in the wake of having extinguished the life of your own son."

Always a woman of cool and collected poise, Ava felt the rare rise of ire begin to percolate inside her. In an instant, the sharpened daggers that were unsheathed in Lilith's dark stare suddenly found their way into Ava's. With a subtle wringing of her hands, she took a steadying breath and, in a calm, if not uncongenial voice that made it crystal clear she had reached her end with the pleasantries of chit chat, said, "You said you wished to speak with me about something in regards to Jacob. If you wouldn't mind telling me what exactly has brought you to Cain's Corner, as I'd like to get back to my garden."

Lilith replied with a polite smile and took a seat on the chair positioned directly across from the sofa where Ava sat.

"Alright, since you wish to cut to the chase, here it is: I wish to offer you the rare opportunity of a second chance to right a wrong," she said while nonchalantly smoothing out the voluminous sheer fabric of her dress that overflowed the constraints of the chair in which she was seated.

The vague proposal was intriguing, to say the least, if not niggling.

"And what wrong do you suggest I've committed, exactly, that I need to right?" inquired Ava.

"Don't misunderstand me, it's not anything you've done, per se," Lilith replied almost apologetically. Then, leaning forward, as if to share a juicy piece of gossip with a close girlfriend, she said in a whispery voice, "It's an extraordinary, dare I say divine thing to have a Nephilim born into one's family. You bore not only a Nephilim, but a Nephilim who would later be revealed to be the Light Bearer to boot. Unfortunately, Gothamel made sure such a light did not burn very long."

The subject of her deceased son was wearing thin on Ava.

"But then came the day your late daughter Isabeth gave birth to a son—a Nephilim son—and again he was revealed against all probability to be the Light Bearer reborn. How could you not feel anything but a deluge of blessings and favor raining down upon you from Heaven above?" cooed Lilith. "Which begs the question: How could you, in all good conscious, and after all you've suffered, send your grandson willingly into the embrace of Eden, and with Gothamel as his minder no less, at the risk of seeing fate repeat itself, as it is known to do."

"What would you have me do? Keep him imprisoned inside this house under lock and key? Have him fitted with a pair of leg irons that allows him to venture no further than the reach of Cain's Corner?" asked Ava.

"There are other means someone as dear to Jacob as you are to him can employ that are just as effective, if not more, in constraining a young Nephilim as leg irons," said Lilith. "You're not only his grandmother, you are at this moment the most important person left in his life. He would go to the ends of the earth if you requested it of him, and that is just what I am suggesting you do. Summon him back to Cain's Corner. Stress upon him the direness with which you need him home. More so, convince him in a way only you can impress upon him that the Nephilim life, not to mention one unfolded for a Light Bearer, is not for him. Persuade him to relinquish his Sword of Destiny."

"And why would I agree to do such a thing?" Ava, who appeared more amused by Lilith's requests than intrigued, asked.

"Because at the moment the well-being of your precious little grandson is in danger, and the only destiny awaiting him is darkness, if not death," Lilith replied bluntly.

Ava, uncertain whether or not the statement was meant to be a threat or warning, seemed unfazed either way and was quick to pose a retort with equal candor: "By you?"

"Me?" Lilith responded with a guileless gasp that was all too comical to witness.

"Come now, Lilith! We've been dancing around this touchy subject since you first arrived," said Ava. "It's no secret your relationship with Samael. And earlier, when you were looking at the photograph of my daughter Isabeth, I could see plainly in your eyes that neither is the sorted fact that Jacob was conceived by Samael. Do you expect me to believe you don't feel a certain way about such circumstances?"

Lilith sat quiet for a moment, her ice cold stare fixed intently on Ava, until a slight thaw allowed her lips to part.

"I'll admit, I was more than a little taken aback when Thaniel revealed to me one night in the Silent Forest the truth which had been hidden from me regarding the boy. Only the towering army of trees, with whom I once kept company and whose presence kept the revealing radiance of the moon at bay, could have prevented such truths from being made known to me. For it was right there, unconcealed and unmissable on his face. The eyes; he had his father's eyes. And when I realized what Thaniel had told me was true, I readily admit my first impulse was to destroy him."

There was an unnerving if not sinister purr in Lilith's voice as she spoke, and an even more menacing pulse alive in her far-off gaze as she recounted that revelatory night not so long ago in the Silent Forest. Then, just as quickly, the ominous shadow that had swept over and gathered about her dissipated when Lilith became conscious once again of Ava's presence.

"Clearer heads eventually prevailed," she then said in a way that was not entirely persuasive. "I came to see the forest from the trees, at least from the vantage point from where Samael was left a limited view of the world while bound and left to rot in the Infernal Desert, and I came to understand there existed only one manger that would not only guarantee the safety of his only son to be delivered into this world, but provide the boy with an invisible shield needed to protect him from the vengeful sword of his most zealous enemy. Once I learned your daughter was nothing more than a modern-day Trojan horse to transport his heir, whatever feelings I may have had about the sorted circumstances, as you so put it, were put to rest. And whatever recent thoughts I may have had concerning Jacob Parrish were passing at best.

"Yet trust me when I tell you, as I forewarned you earlier," Lilith quickly noted, "he finds himself this moment navigating straits most dangerous. Of that, I am certain."

~ ~ ~

"If not by you, then who?" questioned Ava.

"I would think the answer would be obvious," replied Lilith, "considering the case that's been brought before the Iudicium Tribunal involving your grandson."

"The Iudicium Tribunal?" Ava echoed with a light chuckle. "What danger does the Iudicium Tribunal pose to Jacob? As I understand it, the hearing is nothing more than a formality to settle once and for all the skepticism surrounding Jacob and the very high likelihood that he is the Light Bearer. The only one who has proven himself to be a fly in the ointment in that regard is Sandel, yet, as vindictive and ill-natured as I've heard he can be, I'd hardly deem him as dangerous—at least in regards to Jacob's well-being."

Lilith responded with a curious tilt of her head and an even more curiouser stare.

"You haven't a clue as to what has been going on these recent weeks, have you?"

The question only served to make Ava grow all the more anxious, much to Lilith's private delight.

"I'm not talking about the hearing to determine whether or not Jacob is the Light Bearer," said Lilith. "I'm talking about case brought quite unexpectedly before the Tribunal by Samael asking for custody of the boy."

The color instantly drained from Ava's face. "Custody?"

"That is what they call the legal redress for a father seeking sole guardianship of his child, is it not?"

Ava did her best to keep her composure, but Lilith could see in the anguish slowly rising like an incoming tide within the old woman that her words carried the same painful barbs as those revealing the solemn news of a loved one's untimely passing.

"I refuse to believe the Iudicium Tribunal would consider for a second, placing the care of a young boy into the hands of an unspeakable monster!" Ava, quickly gathering about her wits, declared defiantly.

"And for the sake of argument, I would be in complete agreement with you; if, in fact, this was a case being decided in your mortal world. But it is not," said Lilith. "The law concerning Nephilim children is altogether clear: guardianship is wholly placed in perpetuity in the hands of the father, monster or not. Thaniel proved himself to be most shrewd when he plucked that seed of ingenuity from his brilliant mind and handed it to Samael."

"Thaniel? Thaniel suggested this to Samael?" Ava, looking all the more stunned, asked.

"If I'm not mistaken, word has it the Tribunal is poised to render its decision tomorrow," Lilith said, ignoring Ava's question. "Of course, there's always the chance its members might unanimously decide to unite together in a brazen demonstration to ignore the law and rule against Samael, but I wouldn't get my hopes up; not with Sandel being the masterful influencer he is. He is dead set against your Jacob being named a Nephilim in the same breath as his own son, much less Light Bearer, no matter how many Graces the boy may be found to possess. What better way to be rid of the whole unpleasant matter than to willfully and happily have your hands bound by a divine edict from on high that would reunite father and son and send both back to the nether reaches of the Underneath?"

The images conjured by Lilith's words of Jacob being forced into Samael's unwanted embrace and escorted into the putrid realm where all shadows are banished were too terrible for Ava to even contemplate.

"I know what you are thinking: there is no way Gothamel would allow for such thing to take place, and you are quite right about that. And therein lies the danger I warned you about earlier," said Lilith.

"What do you mean?" asked Ava.

Lilith leaned forward in her seat, her cold dark eyes wide and fixed, much like an aroused cobra with its hood flared before it strikes.

"Gothamel's love for Jacob runs almost, if not as deep as his hatred for Samael. You know as well as I there is no written law nor governing body, nor force of nature, earthly or beyond, great enough that would ever compel him to abide by the custodial rights Samael is demanding to be restored to him," said Lilith.

"Death..." The word passed through Lilith's lips and struck Ava like a cudgel. "Death has proven itself to be the one equalizing force favored by Gothamel when it comes to his rivalry with Samael. You, more than anyone, have witnessed firsthand the limits Gothamel will go in defense of the celestial good. Would you have me believe the seed of such contemplations stemming from my lips has never come to sow itself in your thoughts?"

Ava sat deathly quiet for some time trying to stay afloat of the rising tide she felt engulfing her at an accelerated rate before stating with as much faith as she could muster, "Gotham wouldn't do that!"

"Wouldn't he, though?" Lilith answered without pause and a skeptical rise of her brow. "He killed your first born in cold blood in order to keep a sword from falling into Samael's hands. What do you think he would do to ensure the prophesy of the Light Bearer not come into the possession of the

Underneath and be perverted into a weapon of destruction by the dark forces, especially when the vessel of such a prophesy is none other than Samael's own son?"

Lilith's aloof pronouncements proved too much for Ava's ears to bear. She rose abruptly from the couch and moved across the room where a large, round ornate mirror hung on the wall in an attempt to hide both her tears and swelling fear which were impossible to conceal any longer.

"Why are you telling me all of this?" Ava asked, once she had managed to steady the tremble in her voice.

"I told you earlier: I'm here to help you right a wrong. This is a fight between Gothamel and Samael. Anyone who stands in the middle of such a clash has no hope of surviving, and right now that someone is Jacob. You've already lost your son to this battle; trust me when I tell you Jacob carries with him the same fate."

Lilith's voice had a mellifluous, spellbinding quality, much like a lightly plucked harp, even when the words it sounded were bleak, conjured and unspeakable hallucinations. Watching Ava in a way that resembled a raptor patiently eyeing a burrow from a high place for the opportune moment when a mole makes the fatal mistake to emerge from its safe spot underground, Lilith could see her sway was slowly working on the old woman, and again she used all her hypnotic prowess to reel her in.

"Even if I wanted to do as you suggest, Gotham would never allow it, and I highly doubt there is anything I could say that would change his mind," said Ava as she continued to stare deeply into the reflective glass of the mirror before her.

"There was once a time you brought the great and mighty Gothamel to his knees, and all without having to utter a single word."

The sound of Lilith's sedative voice, suddenly right at her ear spooked Ava, but not nearly as much as the unnerving sight of Lilith inexplicably standing directly behind her own reflected image from out of nowhere. Such willies, however, vanished in an instant when a most extraordinary thing began to happen.

Looking deeper into the mirror, Ava spied something peculiar happening to her reflective self, in particularly her hair. What had been meticulously coiffed to resemble a white cloud floating in the sky began to darken to a rich auburn color. As it did, the strands of hair grew magically in length, freeing themselves from the tacky hold of hairspray to fall in long, luxurious ringlets across Ava's shoulders and down her back.

The hair was only the beginning.

Just as quickly, the years that constituted Ava's long life and resided in her face in the form of wrinkles and sagging skin receded as well. Beneath the dress she wore, Ava could feel her aged body adjust itself to a more youthful posture as the aches and pains she had long grown accustomed to vanished. And when she glanced at her hands, she no longer saw the liver spots dotting her skin, or weathered fingers made crooked by the ravages of arthritis, but the beautiful blemish-free hands of her youth.

Certain she had slipped into the embrace of delirium if not utter derangement, Ava asked somewhat fearfully, "What is happening to me?"

"What does it look like? You've been given the gift of your youth, and without the aid of some fabled fountain," answered Lilith. "When Gothamel lays his eyes upon you, there is not a request you could make that he will refuse to fulfill for you."

The longer Ava stood staring at her newly reborn youthful self, the less trepidatious she felt until, finally, she couldn't help but beam forth her newfound fresh-faced smile.

"Can this actually be real?" she questioned while gracefully turning from side to side to take in all angels of the metamorphosis revealed within the mirror, and doing so without the hinderance of the achy stilted movements that had miraculously been cast from her limbs.

"A shame, really. I've always felt the breath of life given to mortal beings to be a cruel gift, for as soon as its received, it instantly falls victim to the ruin of time and, like a plucked rose under the glare of the sun, gradually withers away," Lilith remarked casually as her gaze slowly, almost enviously raked itself over the vision of loveliness before her. "You now have been given everything you need to reclaim the life you once knew: a voice amongst voices with the power to reduce the steeliest of men to tears, and the effortless ability to return you to your rightful place as the preeminent artist of the world's stage; and perhaps more importantly, the staggering beauty that once had the power to melt Gothamel's impassive heart and draw him like a lighthouse guiding a ship caught in a dense fog into the shores of your embrace, and most certainly will do so again.

"A life of happiness is at hand, and the cost for it but a pittance," Lilith was quick to add with the purr of her hypnotic voice. "All that is required of you is to persuade your precious grandson to leave Eden, and step away from the light of the star under which he was born. Only by convincing him to return to Cain's Corner and reject the moniker placed upon him as Light Bearer will you save him from a certain destructive fate. Have him relinquish into Samael's care, the sword that will lead him to a destiny with death, and you will finally know peace as a family, with Gothamel at your side."

As Ava listened, she suddenly found her reflection in the mirror was no longer standing alone, but joined much to her surprise by those of both Jacob and Gotham. The living portrait was a stark reminder of the framed photograph she had which captured herself and Gotham standing with their own son David, only Jacob now stood where David once had. In an instant, Ava was visited by a feeling of mourning, and yet she could not ignore the overwhelming sense of longing she felt for the image surrounding her. More than anything, she wanted a way to pass through the reflective glass of the mirror and embrace the flesh and blood reality of the mirage smiling back at her.

Her smile no longer alighting her youthful beauty, Ava shifted her penetrating gaze to Lilith's reflection, and in doing so sent the conjured likenesses of Jacob and Gotham to dissipate from sight like wisps of a dream. And in a voice that was neither icy nor hostile, she stated simply to the treacherous vision in black, "Behind every great sin, you will find a woman."

~ ~ ~

"I beg your pardon?" Lilith, clearly taken aback by the comment, muttered in reply.

"Something I suddenly recall Gotham saying to me once many years ago," said Ava. "I didn't take offense to it then as I likely should have, but only because at the time he spoke those words you were the topic of discussion. Now, at this very moment, I understand he was quite right in his declaration."

A gloom of offense swept across Lilith's cold expression like a slow-passing storm cloud, and an air of inhospitableness quickly gathered about her.

"Perhaps I'm equally as sinful, for I admit I came close to selling out to your demands, though it would have been for far more than a pittance as you presented, at least in my eyes," continued Ava, "I won't lie and say it doesn't nourish my self-indulgence to step once more into the skin of my youth, if for but a moment. But I have already lived those years and have no desire to retrace a path I've already tread, even to remedy some of the painful pitfalls along the way."

"You'll lose Gothamel. Forever!" declared Lilith.

"I remember the day Gotham delivered me near death and caked in filth from the depths of despair of a German concentration camp, where all beauty, including my own, had all but ceased to exist. Whatever bond Gotham and I came to share, it stemmed not from beauty, but the heart."

Ava's reply only served to further incite Lilith.

"And what of Jacob? Are you willing to risk the pain of sending yet another Nephilim born into your family to his grave?"

"Believe it or not, I love Jacob as much as my own departed son. I've come to know intimately the dangers that stalk young Nephilim boys, and not a day goes by where I don't ponder such fears. And while there is nothing I wouldn't do to keep him safe, I can't help but think turning him away from his destiny would be far more painful, and perhaps even dangerous, not just for him, but for the rest of us mortals, as well," said Ava. "Jacob was brought into this world to serve a singular purpose. And if that purpose involves ridding this world of the likes of you, Samael and the rest of the unholy dregs from the Underneath, then why would I mull, even for a moment, the idea of leading him away from the light of the star under which he was born, as you so eloquently phrased it?

"So you'll forgive me," Ava continued defiantly, "when I make clear to you that I, in the most strenuous of ways, decline your most desperate offer. You'll also understand me when I ask you to make leave of me and my home this instant."

Ava had no sooner voiced her demand than an unpleasant gust of wind blew past her. She immediately felt a change and, even before she glanced back into the mirror, she knew the youthful beauty of her younger days she was allowed to briefly revisit had vanished, and the aged woman with white hair had returned.

And as she looked down at her wrinkled hands and felt the uncomfortable stiffness in her slightly crooked fingers when she wriggled them, she couldn't help but mourn the loss. But only for a moment.

Lilith stood silent for some time and held the elderly Ava in a gaze most withering, and Ava braced herself for the coming of something far worse than being returned to her aged state; like being utterly obliterated from the face of the Earth, for starters. Instead, Lilith did something unexpected; she smiled, and in an uncharacteristically breezy manner she said, "As you wish."

As she prepared to part company with Ava, however, something caught her eye. She circled around the homey room to a round mahogany table upon which resided a large crystal vase holding a splendid bouquet of coral-colored roses Ava had recently picked from her garden.

"All good intentions aside, I knew before coming here that it would be difficult at best to convince you to go along with my stratagem, as it were," she said while openly admiring the colorful floral display. "If there is one thing I've come to learn, it's that mortals have never been known for being particularly percipient when it comes to making decisions that best serve their interests."

With her back turned to Ava, Lilith proceeded to do what anyone with a functioning nose would do, and allowed her nose to lean in closer to the roses. Only instead of breathing in the enticing perfume coming from the velvety blossoms, Lilith opened her mouth and exhaled a wisp of black vapor that swirled around the buds like a brief fog episode before disappearing into the folds of the fragrant petals.

Then turning around to face Ava, who was heedless of the ominous substance with which her flowers had been dusted, Lilith smiled and said in a most pleasant manner, "At the very least, this has allowed us the opportunity to become acquainted with one another at long last."

~ ~ ~

After assuring Ava she need not be seen out, Lilith bid the old woman goodbye and left the same way she arrived. Once outside in the sun-lit garden, her smile widened, and it was accompanied by a mischievous snigger.

"You look like a constrictor that's just satiated its appetite by swallowing down a whole litter of defenseless puppies."

Yairel's condemning voice caught Lilith by surprise, and when her gaze shifted like a bolt of lightning and found the commanding angel standing in the exact same spot she had earlier left him, Lilith's gleeful mood wilted somewhat.

"It must by truly humbling to be an angel of your once great but obviously dwindling stature to be cast down from Heaven's light into the mortal pit to serve as a minder for a geriatric not long for this world," Lilith remarked with a snide tone, and even more contemptuous look. "But let me put you at ease by assuring you not a hair on her head did I so much as touch."

"You'll understand my aversion to trusting a single word that passes by your lips as I am more than acquainted with the wretchedness that is your company, just as I am in knowing whatever patch of grass, or stretch of dirt your shadow passes over, an unseen plague is never far in its wake," the angel spat, as he watched the beautiful but deceitful Lilith slink her way through the garden as though she were taking a stroll through a park.

"My, my, my, Yairel, but you sound suspicious," Lilith replied coquettishly. "Pray tell, what dastardly deeds has that feverish little brain of yours convinced you I've been guilty of performing?"

Yairel grew quiet, simmering in his visceral contempt he held for the duplicitous woman.

"I do not need to put my hand to the fire to know it burns," he grumbled finally.

"Poor Yairel! Always wary a bogeyman is lurking around every corner and hiding beneath every bed," Lilith taunted. "Rest assured, the house is uninhabited by such monsters."

"And so it shall remain," Yairel declared. "This secluded pocket has, until this day, managed to stay hidden from your befouling influences. Should you or any of the cretinous infestations of the Underneath dare to step foot in Cain's Corner again, your welcome will be inscribed on the blade of my sword. And not even the good-natured old woman you left inside will be able to stop me from adding the hue of your blood to the colorful garden she has cultivated."

Lilith was astute enough to know when to mind the sass of her tongue in favor of keeping the blood referenced by Yairel flowing unimpeded through her veins.

"It is a beautiful garden, isn't it?" she noted instead, turning her attention to the spray of flowers surrounding her.

Lilith then sashayed her way to one of the numerous rose bushes where, much to the angel's growing annoyance, she proceeded to grab one of the blood-red buds and, unaffected by the thorn that pierced deeply her thumb, fill her nostrils with its fragrant scent.

"May I?" she then asked Yairel with a polite smile. "You're right about the Underneath; it is quite...unpleasant."

"You'd need to uproot every shrub and then some," the angel grumbled, though he did not deny her request to pluck the single flower.

Lilith's pleasant smile was quick to melt, much like an ice cube left in the sun, when Yairel made the unfortunate mistake of turning his back on her and began to make his way for the gate thinking she would be following right behind him. In that blind moment, Lilith turned her attention back to the roses and, just as she had to the bouquet of flowers inside Ava's sitting room, she breathed forth the odious black vapor from her mouth onto several buds.

Only when Yairel was heard calling for her with patience growing thinner with every passing minute did Lilith force forth her sinister smile.

"Coming!" she sang cheerily in return.

With her rose in hand, Lilith surrendered in the most courteous of manners to being escorted out of the yard, and then out of Cain's Corner by Yairel.

All the while, the dark vapor she had breathed forth to mingle with the roses migrated like a brume from shrub to shrub until it had covered the entire yard before vanishing like a passing phantom.

CHAPTER FIFTEEN

Max and Kairo found themselves standing in the middle of a sidewalk oblivious of the steady stream of people bustling past them on their way to work as they stared at a nondescript three story building nestled amongst other similar buildings lining the block on the opposite side of the street.

"This it?" Kairo asked, after the two had studied the brick-and-mortar facade for some time.

"Looks like," replied Max, while double-checking the address written on the piece of paper he clutched in his hand as well as the modest sign affixed above the entrance to the building, replied. "My guess is there probably aren't a whole lot of businesses named Morgan Antiquities to confuse people."

"So now what do we do?" asked Kairo.

"We go inside, naturally."

"And say what? 'Greetings! We're in the market for a walking stick, preferably one owned once by Moses. You wouldn't happen to have one in stock, would you?' "

Max shot his friend a quieting glare out of the corner of his eye.

"Don't be a drongo!" he said. "I'll think of something. Just keep your lip buttoned and let me do all the talking."

Following that instruction, Max led the way across the street to the building. Stepping inside, the two boys found themselves in a small reception area where the noticeable silence was punctured by a middle-aged woman sitting behind a tidy desk busily tapping away at a computer keyboard.

"May I help you?" she asked, without so much as glancing at the two boys, nor pausing her fingers.

"Yes," began Max with a clearing of his throat, "we're here to see a Cyprus Morgan."

"Who's here to see Mr. Morgan?" the receptionist asked in a tersely robotic tone.

"We are," Kairo, leaning forward a bit to aid the woman who was obviously hard of hearing, stressed naively.

The woman's fingers ceased their dancing and, when she shifted her gaze away from the computer screen and saw the visitors standing in front of her desk were mere teenage boys, she lowered her head in order to peer over the pair of glasses which were perched on the end of her nose.

"And just what matter of business would require you to see Mr. Morgan?" the receptionist inquired in a voice laced with an English accent that had a fantastic ability of making her innocuous question sound much more like an accusation.

"If it's all the same to you, it's a personal matter," Max answered as politely as he could.

It proved, however, not polite enough, as the woman's nose turned itself upward in offense of the reply.

"Mr. Morgan doesn't see anyone without an appointment," she declared, and immediately returned her fingers to the task of typing.

"Oh please! Couldn't you make an exception?" Kairo pleaded, despite Max's earlier instruction to keep quiet. "It's very important that we see him, and we've come such a long ways."

"I'm afraid it's out of the question," the receptionist noted brusquely. "Mr. Morgan is an extremely busy man; much too busy to be bothered by every Tom, Dick, and Harry who wanders in from off the street."

Kairo was about to offer another plea when Max grabbed him, directed his attention to a large door at the far end of the reception area with a nameplate reading "Cyprus Morgan" affixed to it, and proceeded to whisper into his ear.

"I'm not sure that's such a good idea," Kairo answered warily when Max had finished.

Max, however, didn't appear to be fazed by his friend's apprehension.

"We're sorry to have bothered you," he then said to the receptionist, without so much as a nod from the woman in return. "By the way, you may want to have Mr. Morgan think about adopting a cat for your office. It'll be a big help with your vermin problem."

"Vermin problem. What vermin problem?" the receptionist huffed with annoyance as she tried to stay focused on her task at hand.

"You know...mice."

The receptionist's fingers froze in mid-type. "Mi–did you say mice?"

It was hard to tell which held more fear: the woman's voice, or her unsettled expression.

"The-there's no mice in this building!" she voiced as forcefully as her trembling lips would allow her, though it seemed more in attempt to convince herself than anyone else.

"That's funny. Coulda sworn it was a mouse that ran across my shoe just a few seconds ago before scurrying underneath your desk," Max said before turning to Kairo. "Didn't it look like a mouse to you, Kairo?"

"It sure looked like a mouse to me as well," Kairo agreed, though he didn't share the same look of tickling amusement as his friend.

"Sure was a cute little bugger," said Max. "If you'd like, I could try and catch it for you."

The receptionist, wholly clutched with fear, nodded her head vigorously and managed to gasp a strenuous "Please!"

Knowing what was about to occur, Kairo couldn't help but feel sorry for the dowdy woman when Max slowly lowered himself down onto the floor and out of sight of the receptionist's unblinking gaze to peer under the desk where he was soon heard to declare, "Never mind, I was mistaken!"

There came a heavy sigh of relief from the woman. That is until Max was heard to say, "It's a rat!"

If the receptionist was frightened before, she was positively petrified at the news of an even larger reviled rodent loitering anywhere near her work space; so much so that Kairo felt moved to convince Max to think up a new, less traumatizing plan to get into Cyprus Morgan's office. But it was too late. When Kairo glanced back at the spot where Max was crouched down on the floor, his friend was nowhere to be seen. What he did see was the unmistakable long, hairless tail belonging to a rat disappear from sight underneath the desk.

Kairo braced himself for the inevitable scream about to make itself heard, but even he—or rather his eardrums—wasn't prepared for the magnitude of the high-pitched shriek that squeezed itself from the receptionist. With an agility she hadn't possessed even in her youth, the woman leaped onto her chair and desperately began attempting the impossible feat of scaling the air about her for higher ground by means of an invisible ladder. Kairo did his best to try and calm the woman, but it proved a futile task while the brown rat, circling the floor with its beady eyes and twitching nose, remained in her sights. Only when the rat raised up on its hind legs in what appeared to be an attempt to climb up onto the chair did the poor receptionist find the courage within herself to hurl herself across the desk in a maneuver similar to, but far less polished than, a gymnast clearing a pommel horse and run for dear life from the building in a quickly fading chorus of screams.

"You think the rat was a bit much?" Max asked, once he had transformed himself back from his rodent guise.

"Maybe a tad," Kairo, rolling his eyes, replied.

~ ~ ~

When finally the two boys discreetly opened the door to the office the receptionist had denied them entrance to and poked their heads inside, they found who they presumed to be Cyprus Morgan sitting behind a stately and pristinely organized desk seemingly unaware of, or perhaps indifferent to, the screeching ruckus that had transpired only moments earlier on the other side of the door.

Instead, he had his nose buried in a sizable ledger and appeared much more like that of a banker than an adventurous archeologist clad in khaki safari wear, with a sable fedora perched upon his head and armed with a Smith and Wesson revolver and, perhaps, even a leather bullwhip attached to the hip while scouring the hidden corners of the world for undiscovered antiquities. At least, that is how Max and Kairo imagined such a person rumored to have in his possession one of the greatest and most powerful artifacts of the Bible.

Cyprus Morgan, in contrast, looked to be a man who was more comfortable in a suit and tie rather than jungle attire, and his hand clutching a briefcase over a bullwhip. He was a reserved, if not distinguished man in his early sixties of average height and salt-and-pepper-colored hair, who early on in life came to carry the telltale indentations on the sides of his nose caused by the weight of his spectacles, not to mention the horizontal creases caused by a chronic case of disquietude lining his forehead. It was while he removed his glasses to give his eyes a much-needed rubbing from scanning the ledger that Max and Kairo made their presence known with a subtle clearing of the throat.

Mr. Morgan peered across the room through squinting eyes before remembering his glasses which he quickly returned to his face to better see the two blurry figures.

"Yes?" he asked looking somewhat caught off guard at the sight of two teenaged boys standing in his office.

When Max and Kairo introduced themselves to the man and requested a moment to speak with him, Mr. Morgan betrayed the source of the deep furrows marking his forehead, at least partly, when he grew noticeably impatient and called out for his secretary, Ms. Colderfield, through the open door.

"I have a feeling she may be a bit indisposed at the moment," said Max.

"What do you mean indisposed?" queried Mr. Morgan.

"I think he means she saw something that spooked her and, well...she took off running down the street screaming," answered Kairo.

"What did she see?" Mr. Morgan inquired, narrowing his eyes on the boy.

"A mouse."

"Rat," Max was quick to correct his friend.

Muttering to himself about the nonsense of such a thing, Mr. Morgan got up from behind his desk and, storming past the boys toward the entrance to his office, looked out in the reception area where, indeed, there was no sign of his secretary, nor of the troublesome rodent that had sent her in a mad dash to an early lunch break. He then turned abruptly on his heel and, on his return to his desk, extended to the boys in passing, a gruff "Thank you for your visit" that was more a curt dismissal than a cordial salutation.

When Max and Kairo attempted to impress upon the man the importance of needing to speak with him, Mr. Morgan in a very blasé, yet equally dismissive manner suggested the two boys should be sure to set up an appointment with Ms. Colderfield upon her return.

"Whenever that may be," he was then heard to grumble under his breath, somewhat peevishly.

"We haven't got time for that!" Kairo exclaimed, before Mr. Morgan's attention descended once more into his ledger. "Please, all we're interested in are some answers to a few simple questions about the staff of Moses."

At first, it looked as if Mr. Morgan had caught sight of the rat that had chased Ms. Colderfield from the office suddenly scurrying across his own desk beneath his very nose.

"The staff of–Did you say the staff of Moses?" he asked, before settling back in the oversized leather chair on which he was seated.

A faraway look surfaced in the pupils of his eyes as his fingers absentmindedly twirled about his pencil.

"I haven't heard about the staff since–"

His tongue caught itself as his gaze settled itself intently on Max and Kairo. "What possible interest would two young boys your age have in the staff of Moses?"

Seeing their opportunity and having no intention of losing it, Max and Kairo were quick to settle their behinds onto the cushions of the two chairs positioned in front of Mr. Morgan's desk.

"You see," Max, his brain shifting into overdrive, began, "the two of us are working on a research paper for school."

"A research paper?" Kairo echoed with notable puzzlement.

"Yes, a research paper," Max repeated in a tone that all but instructed his friend to zip his lips.

"And what school would this be?" Mr. Morgan inquired.

Max's mouth went instantly dry, and his eyes shifted to Kairo who looked as though the same fistful of cotton balls had found its way into his mouth as well.

"Um...Havenhid School for Boys," Kairo managed to reply, as if his very words were laced with nitroglycerin.

"Havenhid, Havenhid," Mr. Morgan pondered the name to himself, causing the lines on his forehead to deepen. "I'm afraid I'm not familiar with that institution."

"Not surprising. It's not fairly well-known," Max was quick to deflect. "The point is, we decided to do our paper on famous biblical relics. You know, the Ark of the Covenant, the Holy Grail...Spear of Destiny."

He paused purposefully upon mention of the spear and watched for any noticeable reaction from Mr. Morgan, but spied nothing.

"We heard on good authority that you were an expert on the walking stick used by Moses—you know, the one he supposedly used to part the Red Sea," Max continued. "And that you may even know where it's located."

The two boys then braced themselves as the stated purpose of their visit was allowed to sink its way into Mr. Morgan's ears. What would his reaction be, they hadn't a clue. Would he laugh in their face? Or, perhaps, take hold of each boy by an ear and personally exit them from his office?

"It would appear your source, whoever that might be, has confused me with another Cyprus Morgan," said Mr. Morgan finally.

Max and Kairo looked to one another with identical looks of puzzlement.

"And just how many Cyprus Morgans do you have working here?" Kairo inquired somewhat reluctantly.

"At the moment, just myself," Mr. Morgan replied. "Allow me to formally introduce myself to you: I am Cyprus Morgan the third. My father–also, Cyprus Morgan–was the one who was the so-called expert, as you put it, on the staff."

The two boys relaxed with relief. At least they were on the right track.

"And where might we find him?" inquired Max.

"The East Finchley Cemetery."

When, for a moment, it appeared as though the art of simple math had eluded the two boys, Mr. Morgan added, "He's been deceased three years now."

It was not the news Max and Kairo expected.

"Oh…we're sorry to hear that. We didn't know," said Kairo.

"I don't suppose there's anything about the staff he might have shared with you before he passed, is there?" Max asked with little hope in his voice.

Mr. Morgan sat silent for a moment or two, with a faraway look fixed in his gaze, as though quietly debating with himself how, or whether, to answer the question.

"Growing up, there was rarely a conversation I shared with my father that didn't involve that blasted staff in some way or other," he muttered to himself in a way that was more rueful than bitter.

"Don't get me wrong; I idolized him as much as a son can revere one's father," he then exclaimed when it seemed he suddenly became aware of the two teenaged guests he had momentarily forgotten seated in front of him, "Cyprus Morgan–the senior, that is–was at a time one of the most renowned and celebrated archeologists known the world over. Many of the priceless antiquities you can find on display today in some of the most esteemed museums are courtesy of his work: Treasure from the tomb of an Egyptian pharaoh; the wreckage of a barge belonging to a Roman emperor astonishingly preserved at the bottom of the Mediterranean; hundreds of ancient manuscripts dating back to the time of Jesus buried beneath the very path Christ walked on his way to Calvary.

"Historic as these discoveries were, however, they more often than not were the accidental unearthing stemming from an altogether different pursuit."

"What do you mean accidental?" asked Max.

"My father had no inclination in following in the footsteps of Howard

Carter," replied Mr. Morgan. "While the uncovering of the tomb of King Tutankhamun was one of the greatest discoveries the world had ever known, past and present, opening the sarcophagus of a dead boy king who once ruled over Egypt was not fantastical enough for Cyprus Morgan."

"I don't mean to offend you of anything, but your father sounds to be a bit of an alf," Max commented with his usual, blunt Australian tongue. "What could be more fantastical than discovering the burial chamber belonging to King Tut? I mean, they pulled a golden coffin, thrones and chariots out of that tomb; not to mention a solid gold death mask."

A slight smile formed in the corners of Mr. Morgan's thin-lipped mouth.

"You yourself touted the answer just a little while ago in your request to see me," he said. "You see, my father was a ghost hunter; a miner who spent his life knee-deep in creeks panning for fool's gold. It wasn't the discovery of the treasures of ancient kings or ruins of forgotten cities that drove him, but rather the hunt for Heaven's treasures–the mythical relics of power birthed from that book of tales called the Bible and presumably lost within the mortal world; Ark of the Covenant, Spear of Destiny, The Holy Grail, to quote your examples. The very artifacts whose lingering mysteries and secrets would come to infect countless archaeologists, treasure hunters and grave robbers with the same fever that would visit my father.

"There was one particular relic, however, which would end up taking him to all four corners of the earth in his farcical search of it: the staff of Moses," Mr. Morgan continued. "I'm not quite sure when his fixation with the staff started, or why, but a fixation it most definitely became. He was obsessed with it; consumed with finding it. Even when I tried to remind him of the faceless treasure hunters and grave robbers before him whose collective efforts in their quest gained them nothing more than a hole dug clean through the center of the Earth from one end to the other many times over, and a massive pile of dirt. In the end, it destroyed my father's marriage to my mother. As well, it caused the two of us to become estranged for many years."

Max and Kairo sat silently in their seats for a moment or two, not certain what exactly to say. It certainly wasn't their intention to uncover a wound that was obviously still festering.

"Just because the staff or the Ark haven't been found, doesn't mean they don't exist," Kairo said, finally, when the silence became a bit too loud.

The argument seemed to tickle Mr. Morgan.

"I remember once when my father attempted to persuade me in believing in the existence of Nephilim," he remarked with a waggish chuckle. "Would you care to make the argument to convince me that just because none of us in this room has ever seen a Nephilim doesn't mean they don't exist?"

Both boys squirmed uncomfortably in their chairs, doing their best to avoid eye contact with the other as their faces came to share identical tints usually found on beets.

When it became clear the younger Cyprus Morgan had nothing but skepticism seasoned with a dash of disdain to offer in their search of the staff, Max and Kairo thanked the man for his time. Just as they were about to disappear from his office, Mr. Morgan, perhaps taking note of the disappointment the two boys shared in leaving empty-handed which was made visible in the slump of their shoulders and slow shuffling of their feet, beckoned them back.

"In many ways I'm as much a relic as the antiquities with which I find myself surrounded. Surprising as it may sound, it's not often I come across members of the younger generation such as yourselves expressing an interest in history, and even less in the artifacts that helped shape it. I'd hate to be the one responsible for dousing such interest with cold water." He seemed to be quietly contemplating something swirling about in his head while mindlessly tapping his two main fingers upon the top of his desk, when suddenly he rose from his seat.

"Now, I'm not altogether sure if what I am about to show you will help you with your assignment, but...follow me!" Mr. Morgan instructed with a cloak of mystery.

Max and Kairo could only offer up a shrug to one another in reply and promptly followed after him.

~ ~ ~

Without any further explanation, Mr. Morgan led the two boys past the vacant reception area and down a short hallway leading the way to a door upon which was affixed a black sign with white lettering reading "Storage." With a flip of a nearby switch, a pale-yellow light flickered on to illuminate a stairwell just inside which quickly came alive with the *TAP-TAP-TAP*ing of feet as the trio descended the concrete steps. Three floors later, they came upon another door; this one unmarked. Mr. Morgan fumbled about in his pockets for a ring of keys and quickly found the one to unlock the door.

Following another flip of a light switch, Max and Kairo found themselves inside a large, dank and gray concrete box of a room lined with rows and rows of towering wooden shelves. It was the objects cramming the shelves, however, that instantly captivated the two boys: hundreds of priceless artifacts unearthed from the cavities of once-hidden tombs and the archeological sites of lost civilizations buried for untold ages beneath shrouds of sand. The skulls and sun-bleached bones from what could only have once formed the moving flesh-and-parts of several species of long-extinct dinosaurs occupied several shelves. Elsewhere, a collection of cuneiform tablets and seals shared space with a large inventory of ceramic, wooden and ivory busts and statuary. A number of silver and bronze Phoenician bowls decoratively inscribed with hunting, battle and biblical scenes were displayed on another shelf.

Several artifacts much too large to be housed on any shelf resided at far ends of the room, including three black granite statues depicting a strange entity composed of a human body with the head of a lion. They appeared to be standing guard over a nearby painted wooden coffin unearthed from the same forgotten tomb hidden deep beneath Egypt's sands as they had been. The coffin itself was remarkably preserved, with the colorfully detailed face and headdress imprinted on the outside of the sarcophagi looking just as bright and vibrant as the day they were painted. Beautiful as it was, Kairo couldn't help but feel a tad bit creeped out being in its presence as his thoughts began to ruminate over what might possibly reside inside the coffin, considering it came from the land known particularly for its mummies.

Astounding as the relics—large and small—were, there was one in particular that seized the attention of both boys. An Assyrian statue carved out of gypsum and looming alone in a far corner of the room was both a towering and terrifying sight. Far more schizophrenic in appearance than the three half human-half lion statues, this muscular figure boasted hooves for feet, two pairs of wings, and a solitary head which sprouted a different species of face on each of its four sides: an ox, an eagle, a lion, and a man. Max recognized instantly the intimidating creature carved in stone, as he had the undeniable misfortune of coming face to face with the flesh-and-blood version not so long ago when he and Jacob snuck off to the Tree of Life during a torrential rainstorm in search of the Sword of Destiny Jacob believed to be hidden in the burial crypt of Gotham's son David. In his attempt to retrieve the sword, however, Jacob sounded the alarm of the Immortalis when his mortal feet crossed the border formed by the delicate flowering plants, and the terrifying four-faced creature—known better as the Cherubim—soon appeared with a flaming sword in hand to answer the cries.

The encounter was one Max would have sooner preferred to purge from his memory banks, while Kairo, who learned of the creature through a second-hand retelling of the confrontation, found the stone version of the Cherub frightening enough to never want the bad luck of ever running into the real thing. It came as a relief, then, when the sound of Mr. Morgan's voice drew their attention away from the menacing statue.

"Mind you, I haven't taken much time to go through them, so I can't tell you one way or the other if you'll find anything noteworthy. But you're free to go through them if you'd like," Mr. Morgan said after setting a large dusty box he'd retrieved from a nearby pile of many more identical boxes onto a table.

"What's this?" Max, sharing the same blank expression as Kairo, asked.

"The personal research papers belonging to my father," replied Mr. Morgan. "It isn't much, but then again he was never big on record-keeping. Even when it came to the staff of Moses. If there is anything of record, it'll be in here."

~ ~ ~

Left alone to their fishing expedition, Kairo and Max began the task of wading through the number of ragtag items in the box which consisted mainly on crumpled papers, newspaper clippings, photographs from excavation sites, and a couple leather-bound journals detailing in part those excavations. It soon became apparent to both boys that the more papers and photos they riffled through, the less hope they held in finding a nugget of information to lead them to the staff.

"I don't know about you, Kairo, but I think we've headed straight into a billabong," Max announced with a dispirited sigh, after a while.

Kairo likely would have agreed with his friend's assessment, but he was too busy skimming his way through an old, tattered ledger he had earlier pulled from the bottom of the box. It contained what looked to be an inventory of relics obtained through the senior Cyprus Morgan's numerous archeological digs, as well as the museums and private collectors into whose hands the priceless artifacts were eventually passed. It was a tedious endeavor on Kairo's part to read through the pages of entries, to say the least, as Cyprus Morgan's handwriting proved to be as onerous a task to decipher as the Hieroglyphics found in the burial chamber of an Egyptian pharaoh. Yet it was while Max continued in his grumbling of coming so far on a wild goose chase that Kairo came upon something that made him suddenly straighten up and caused his concentrated frown to deepen.

"Hold up, I think I may have found something," he said, laying the ledger down on the table in order to give Max a look.

"Right there," Kairo, placing his finger on one of the penciled entries, said. "The notation references 'Moses' staff,' but I can't make out the entire listing, can you?"

Max leaned in for a closer look, his eyes squinting harder and harder the more he tried to make sense of the chicken scratch he was attempting to decode.

"This Cyprus Morgan certainly has the handwriting of a serial killer, eh?" Max remarked before giving up.

Kairo, however, wasn't ready just then to call it quits. He raced up the dimly lit stairway with Max in tow and back into Mr. Morgan's office where he dropped the ledger on top of the one the younger Cyprus had finally been allowed to return his attention. When Kairo requested his help in translating his father's writing, Mr. Morgan gave the entry a look and, at first, it appeared he, too, had been called upon to transcribe some alien language.

"My father may have been a great archeologist, but he had the handwriting of a doctor," Mr. Morgan joked before sliding open the top drawer of his desk to retrieve a magnifying glass which he promptly used to assist in the task.

"Ah, yes...this entry is in regards to the map," said Mr. Morgan after a brief moment of study.

"Map?" both Kairo and Max echoed.

"I can't believe I had forgotten about the map," Mr. Morgan muttered to himself, seemingly forgetting about the antsy teenagers hovering in front of him.

"What map?" both boys pressed impatiently, again in unison.

The urgency of the question seemed to shake Mr. Morgan from his momentary trance.

"When I told you my father was obsessed with the staff of Moses, I was not exaggerating," he said. "He spent hours upon hours of every single day researching the staff and documenting the staff's trek, not only when it was in Moses' possession during the exodus when he led the Israelites from their bondage in Egypt, through the parted waters of the Red Sea and to the Holy Land, but also hypothesizing its possible journey following Moses' passing. The result was a map he painstakingly put together in great detail that eventually included an 'X' at the location where he believed the staff came to rest, and where it resides to this day."

"I don't understand...he never found it?" asked Kairo.

"Trust me, if Cyprus Morgan had ever uncovered the staff of Moses, the entirety of the world would have known it," Mr. Morgan remarked with a smile.

"So then what's the entry in the book?" pressed Max.

"The ledger, like the one you seem persistent in keeping me from focusing my attention beneath it, is a standard log we've kept since Morgan Antiquities opened its doors recording the transfer of artifacts we've acquired."

"Transfer? You mean like sell?"

"We deal mostly in loans to museums. But, yes, sometimes sales to private collectors, depending on the piece," Mr. Morgan explained before his expression darkened. "The question is, who would have the slightest interest in, either to borrow or purchase, a worthless map pointing to a phantom relic?"

It was the same question both Kairo and Max were quietly asking themselves, and they waited with bated breath when Mr. Morgan peered once more through the magnifying glass in his hand and reexamined the puzzling entry in the ledger.

"It would appear he, in fact, did sell it on August 6, 1962."

A tense look suddenly came over Mr. Morgan.

"What is it?" asked Kairo.

"Nothing," Mr. Morgan replied dismissively, as a more mournful look settled its weight upon him. "It's just...that was shortly after he came to me and revealed he had finally solved the mystery of the staff's whereabouts. He was so excited about it, like he had outshone Howard Carter by discovering the tomb of Ramses the Second. By that time, I was so sick of hearing about that staff and having to witness my father's ridiculous obsession with it that, well, I'm ashamed to say I responded to his excitement somewhat cruelly."

Both Max and Kairo couldn't help but feel a tad sorry for the man, but the ticking of the clock was growing louder inside their heads with every passing minute.

"Does it say who it was who bought it?" Kairo couldn't help but ask.

Shaking off the momentary sullenness which had settled upon him, Mr. Morgan turned his attention back to the ledger.

"Hmmm...that's interesting!" he muttered with intrigue. "It offers just a single name."

Max and Kairo leaned forward on the balls of their feet in anticipation, though never in their wildest dreams would they have ever expected the name that finally emerged from Mr. Morgan's lips.

"It says the map was purchased by someone named Lilith."

Lilith?

CHAPTER SIXTEEN

"X" MARKS THE SPOT

"If that don't beat all! What are the chances we'd come all this way in search of the staff of Moses only to find out someone beat us to it nearly sixty years earlier; and by Lilith of all people?" Kairo grumbled, as he and Max sat on the bottom step of a nearby stoop outside the Morgan Antiquities building to lick their wounds. "Question is why, and what would she want with the staff in the first place?"

"I think it's pretty obvious; She's also aware of its power. So while we're out searching for it in order to use it to destroy the Scucca Urns, my guess is Samael already beat us to the punch by several decades to ensure that scenario never happens," answered Max, while chucking another small pebble from a handful of gravel he scooped up from a nearby flowerbed and attempting to score by making it into a trash bin on the opposite side of the street. "One thing is certain: we've officially not only run into a billabong, we've driven the boat full speed straight onto the beach."

The boys' sulking deepened all the more at the thought of the long journey back home ahead of them and, worse yet, the idea of returning to Havenhid with empty hands. Then, as Max attempted a couple more shots at the trash can, a light bulb illuminated above Kairo's head.

"Do you remember the date Mr. Morgan read from the ledger on when the map was sold?" he asked suddenly.

"August 6, 1962," Max replied. "Why?"

A cunning gleam glistened in Kairo's eyes to match an even craftier smile that slowly unfolded beneath his nose.

"Let's just say I'd hold off on declaring the S.S. Minnow a shipwreck just yet," he said.

"S.S. Minnow?" Max, looking to his friend as if he were a stubby short of a six pack, echoed.

Before he could question what Kairo meant by his cryptic, not to mention dated "Gilligan's Island" TV show reference, Kairo suddenly vanished before his very eyes. Likewise, Max disappeared from Kairo's sight, only in his case the people walking along the sidewalk, the cars and buses being driven along the streets, and even the clouds drifting across the blue sky abruptly changed course and began to move not only in reverse, but at an ever-increasing speed. It was the one thing Kairo had still not managed to get accustomed to whenever he utilized his Gaze of Drifting: the discombobulating speed with which one gifted with such a power was hurled into the warp of the past when attempting to maneuver the bearing of time. For Kairo, it was like riding the most terrifying rollercoaster moving at a speed that all but sucked the very life out of him as everything around him became a dizzying blur, until he was forced to shut his eyes for fear of his guts exiting his body through his mouth.

As he always did, Kairo breathed forth a debt of thanks when the ride came to as abrupt a halt as it did when it began and he opened his eyes to find himself, surprisingly, fully and completely intact. He was still seated in the exact same spot on the stoop where he had moments earlier been sitting next to Max, and the building behind him, while looking somewhat less weathered and aged in appearance, still donned the Morgan Antiquities sign. Kairo found the rest of his surroundings, however, had changed drastically. The modern BMWs and Audis common on London's streets had suddenly been replaced by the classic, long-retired Ford Cortinas and Hillman Imps. They were far from the only retro-looking changes Kairo noticed. The men and women—even kids his own age—seen walking by were all dressed in vintage clothes, and at first it looked as if they might be extras on the set of a movie retelling the assassination of John F. Kennedy.

Spying a newsstand across the street, Kairo made a mad dash through the crush of traffic sparking a chorus of honks from angry drivers and grabbed a copy of the newspaper. "Actress Marilyn Monroe found dead at 36; pills suspected" blared the headline across the top of the front page above a large black-and-white photograph of the blonde, sultry actress. Kairo, however, had no interest in the bombshell news that had passersby picking up copies of the paper left and right. He focused his attention, instead, on the small display of type noting the day's date just below the masthead.

August 6, 1962.

He'd hit his mark, but had he hit it too late? Again, he raced across the street and quickly darted inside the office building he had just left sixty two years in the future and found himself in the reception area that strangely hadn't changed all that much. Not surprisingly, Ms. Colderfield was nowhere to be seen, but in her place was an equally pinched secretary by the name of Ruth Quidmire, according to the nameplate Kairo spied on her desk. And instead of tapping away on a computer keyboard, her fingers were banging away across the keys of a bulky, old fashioned IBM Selectric typewriter.

"May I help you?" she asked without so much as a glance in Kairo's direction.

Having been on this merry-go-round before, Kairo sought to save himself some frustration.

"Yes, um, I wonder if you might have by chance seen my mouse...that is, er, rat."

As expected, the typing ceased instantly.

"You see, he got away from me and came running inside here," continued Kairo. "You can't miss him. He's brown, and quite large. He goes by the name, er...Max."

Ms. Quidmire was on her feet in a flash.

"Find him! And quickly!" she ordered calmly, even as her eyes, wide with fright, frantically scoured the floor in every direction at once.

While she didn't run screaming from the building like Ms. Colderfield, she did the next best thing and raced full speed to the door leading to the restroom on the opposite side of the room as though she had a bad case of the trots and locked herself inside. It was all Kairo needed to walk unhindered into Ms. Quidmire's boss's office which, much to his disappointment, he found empty. An anxious queasiness came over him when, suddenly, he remembered the storeroom downstairs. Faster than Ms. Quidmire was to the bathroom, Kairo bounded his way down the stairwell leading to the concrete room. Gone was the towering statue of the terrible Cherubim, along with the painted Egyptian coffin and the three lion-headed stone carvings holding watch over it. There was only half the number of shelves that Kairo remembered, and they were only half filled with recently discovered artifacts. It was the man dressed in a khaki safari shirt and matching khaki pants and boots seen seated at the nearby table with his back turned, however, that instantly grabbed Kairo's attention.

"E-excuse me," the boy asked after a nervous clearing of his throat. "You wouldn't by chance happen to be Cyprus Morgan, would you?"

There came no reply; only the continuing sound of furious scratching. When Kairo cautiously stepped closer, he saw the man was busily writing. In fact, it appeared he was noting an entry into the same ledger that directed Kairo to step backward in time to that very moment in which he now found himself standing.

"Cyprus Morgan?"

The name had barely left Kairo's mouth again when the man turned suddenly, as if startled out of a deep sleep. Kairo immediately spit from his mouth the cat that had taken hold of his tongue and introduced himself in a somewhat awkward fashion. Surprisingly, instead of jumping to his feet in alarm at finding a strange teenage boy in his storage room from out of the blue, the archeologist returned the introduction in a most relaxed and cordial manner. Kairo couldn't help but wonder if the man's placid demeanor was aided somewhat by the half-filled bottle of bourdon and empty glass resting a hand's-reach away on the table in front of him.

One thing was certain: the senior Cyprus Morgan was not exactly what Kairo had expected. He was quite young, for starters–approximately in his mid-thirties, Kairo guessed, which made sense seeing as he had traveled more than sixty years into the past. The man was also noticeably handsome and, eerily enough, bore a striking resemblance to the world's most famous archeologist created by Hollywood in a series of adventure movies Kairo had grown up watching, from the scruff of unshaven whiskers that darkened his face and deep tan baked into his skin from the collected hours he spent in the sun, to the glint of excitement for the unknown alive in his eyes.

Time being of the essence, though, Kairo denied himself a moment to scour the room in search of a brown fedora or a leather bullwhip lying about to complete the image seated before him and proceeded to state the reason for bursting into the storeroom unannounced before the effects of the bourdon faded, and Cyprus thought better of throwing him out onto the street on his keister, which he obviously looked more than capable of doing.

"What interest would a boy have in the staff of Moses?" Cyprus inquired in the same way his elder son had once Kairo had finished. "And what's more, how did you come to learn of my map?"

"Your son told us...me about it," said Kairo.

The mention of the junior Cyprus instantly darkened the man's demeanor.

"My son has made it more than clear to me his feelings about my supposed preoccupation with the staff," he remarked glumly. "I can't imagine what would cause him to bring it to your attention."

"Please...it's a long and involved story. But you see it's incredibly important that I find the staff, and I was hoping you might be willing to help me," said Kairo.

"You...are looking...to find the staff of Moses?" Cyprus replied slowly, as if his ears had somehow mistaken the boy's words. "May I ask why?"

Kairo opened his mouth to speak, then quickly thought better.

"I wish I could," he muttered meekly, "but like I said: it's long and involved."

"As you wish," Cyprus replied without a hint of offense. "Not that there's anything you could have said that would inspire me to share with you my map. It is, after all, the roadmap to what is undoubtedly one of the greatest lost relics noted in the Bible, not to mention ten years of my blood, sweat and tears in trying to find it. I haven't even confided in my own son where the location is; I'm sure you'll understand why I won't share it with you."

The unpleasant thought of Lilith shoved its way to the forefront of Kairo's thought, and he felt a sudden unpleasant heat bloom inside his core and quickly spread its way through his limbs as Cyprus returned his nose to his ledger. Kairo's ears carried the echo of an invisible clock ticking off the passing seconds at an ever-increasing speed which only made him all the more nervous. For all he knew, Lilith was on her way to the Morgan Antiquities building; perhaps even walking through the front door that very moment and being greeted by Ms. Quidmire who assumed the coast was clear of any rampant rodent and found the bravery to venture out of the restroom and return to her desk.

"I'm a Nephilim," Kairo suddenly found himself blurting out, though in a restrained quiet declaration.

"I'm sorry, what?" Cyprus, not paying much attention to the boy, replied.

"Nephilim. Your son mentioned you believed in their existence," said Kairo. "I'm one of them. I'm a Nephilim."

"That's quite like my son: only hearing every other word," Cyprus grumbled with sigh of frustration. "What I said was I was open to entertaining the notion of their existence, not at this current time in history but more like six thousand years ago. Besides, you're hardly look anything like the monstrous aberrations described in Genesis."

"Yeah, well, you're about to get a lesson in what is fiction and what is actually fact," said Kairo.

In an instant, Kairo felt he might in fact hurl his guts right in Cyprus Morgan's face. The rules governing Nephilim were clear: under no circumstances was a son of an angel ever to reveal his true self to the mortal world at large. And as he grabbed the hem of the t-shirt he was wearing and slowly began to lift it up over his torso, an overwhelming urge to reverse course and plead insanity took hold of him. The terrifying image of Lilith, however, proved far more persuasive, and when she once again flashed before his eyes it was all it took for Kairo to pull his shirt over his head in one quick motion.

The storeroom became as silent as a tomb as Cyprus Morgan sat with a stricken look frozen on his face in the sight of the large pair of gray-colored wings sprouting in the all their glory from Kairo's back and casting their speech-stealing shadow on both the stunned archeologist and the table at which he sat.

~ ~ ~

As quickly as he revealed them, Kairo folded his wings from sight and wriggled back into the concealment of his shirt.

"I hope now you understand how serious I am when I tell you it's important I find that staff," said Kairo.

"The what?" Cyprus, who remained clearly staggered, mumbled.

"Moses' staff," Kairo pressed. "You do know where it is, don't you? That is what your son led me to believe."

Cyprus sat with eyes fixed on the boy for another moment or two before he rose up zombielike out of his chair and crossed the room to an old beat-up desk. There he promptly began digging through a litter of books, folders and papers until he came upon a particularly tattered piece of paper twice folded. He then returned to where Kairo remained standing and, with his hand visibly shaking, dropped it on the table.

"What's this?" Kairo asked.

Cyprus instructed Kairo to take a look while his eyes remained transfixed on the boy's back. Carefully, Kairo unfolded the worn document which revealed itself to be a crudely drawn map marked by at least a dozen barely decipherable notes scribbled along the periphery which could only have come from Cyprus' hand.

"This is it? This is where you think the staff is?" Kairo asked with growing eagerness.

"I'm fairly certain," Cyprus replied, though his quiet tone made it difficult to gauge his confidence.

Kairo leaned in for a closer look and immediately pointed out three large triangles drawn in pencil near the center of the map. "What are these?"

"Pyramids," answered Cyprus. "Specifically, the pyramids of Khafre and Menkaure, and the Great Pyramid of Khufu."

Kairo's gaze shifted to Cyprus.

"You think the staff is in Egypt?" he inquired incredulously. "But how could the staff have ended up in Egypt? I mean, the whole point in Moses leading the Israelites to the Promised Land was to get as far away from Egypt as possible."

Cyprus agreed with the boy, but he soon made it clear his years-long trek to uncover the fate of Moses' walking stick had led him down more than a few unexpected twists and turns.

"The Bible states Moses died in the land of Moab and it was there that God buried him in a place which remains secret to this day. Early Christians, however, determined Moses was buried on Mount Nebo, in what is today Jordan. A church was built around a makeshift tomb believed to be the resting place of Moses, and continues to be visited by Christian pilgrims today," said Cyprus. "What sparked my hunt was not to uncover where Moses was buried, but what became of the staff given to him by God, which has never been found in any tomb, nor the body of Moses, for that matter."

In a fleeting moment, it appeared the jaw-dropping revelation revealed by Kairo had been momentarily forgotten by Cyprus.

"The Midrash believes the staff was handed down through the generations and was in the hands of the Judean kings before the First Temple was destroyed. Some contend it was placed inside the Ark of the Covenant and hidden forever from the world by Jeremiah. Still others have fervently claimed it currently resides inside a historical museum in Istanbul. Ten years ago, however, I made a discovery that disputes all those theories."

Cyprus then proceeded to retrieve one of the artifacts residing on one of the nearby shelves displaying numerous other relics and showed it

Kairo. It was a fragment belonging to a much larger clay tablet inscribed with cuneiform text.

"The text on this tablet asserts the staff fell into the hands of an evil entity and, for reasons unknown, secreted it away here," Cyrus said, while his finger took aim and came to rest upon a large "X" etched upon a strange drawing on the map.

"You think the staff is buried somewhere in a pyramid?" asked Kairo.

"Not a pyramid," corrected Cyprus. "The Sphinx."

~ ~ ~

For someone who had witnessed more than his fair share of incredulous things in his short, young life, Kairo found the idea to be more than a little preposterous. Still, he had come too far to dismiss the notion outright.

"If you know where the staff is, then why is it still only an 'X' on your map?" he asked the man.

"Finding where the staff is buried has been a task in itself. Retrieving it is an altogether different one," answered Cyprus. "The Sphinx is one of the greatest enigmas to ever exist. In the Ancient Greek myth of Oedipus, it guarded the city of Thebes. Anyone wishing to enter the city had to first answer a riddle in order to pass through the gates of the city. If they answered wrong, the Sphinx would devour them. In reality, it would appear the Sphinx has been entrusted to guard the staff, and the answer to its riddle is the sole key to the door behind which it is locked. Trust me, I know firsthand. I've made two attempts already and, well...let's just say I'm in no hurry to press my luck with a third try."

"What's the riddle?" asked Kairo.

"Unfortunately, it's different for everyone who attempts to gain entrance to whatever hidden chamber resides with the Sphinx," said Cyprus. "And before you ask, I have searched high and low all around the perimeter of that stone beast, and short of using several sticks of dynamite to blow it clean off its foundation, there exists no other way inside."

Kairo stood quiet for some time pondering what the archeologist had disclosed to him. If there was one thing that had the potential of being more terrifying, or at the very least equally as terrifying as Lilith, it was a giant limestone carving of a Sphinx who instantly gobbles down those unfortunate souls who failed to correctly answer its riddles.

Lilith...

The name made itself heard inside his head like a gust of wind and promptly reminded Kairo of the expeditious nature of his visit to Cyprus Morgan.

"I hate to tell you this, but there is someone desiring to get their hands on this map even more than me," Kairo said with an underlying urgency. "And, unfortunately, she is on her way here this very minute."

"She?" Cyprus inquired looking suddenly confused.

"Do you know a woman by the name of Lilith?" Cyprus shook his head.

"Well, she knows you. That is, she knows you have discovered where Moses' staff is. More importantly, she knows you have drawn up a map leading to it, and she is coming here to collect it," Kairo did his best to explain.

"What do you mean coming here to collect it? She can't have it, whoever she is!" Cyprus barked defiantly in return.

"And we're going to make sure of that because you're going to give it to me?" said Kairo.

"You?" Cyprus, not appearing to like the alternative choice any better, replied. "Why would I hand over my map to you?"

"The tablet fragment you showed me earlier explained how an evil entity is responsible for securing the staff somewhere within the Sphinx. Believe me when I tell you this woman Lilith is beyond any evil entity you can imagine," said Kairo. "I can't explain to you how I know, but trust me; if you don't give the map to me, you will be making an entry in your ledger there on the table of its sale to her before the day is through."

Cyprus couldn't have looked any more disoriented than he did at that very moment if Kairo had taken a sledgehammer and taken aim at the side of his head. Kairo, in return, couldn't help but feel somewhat rueful for being the cause of leaving him spinning upon the floor like a top.

"I know you don't know me from Adam. But remember what I shared with you just a little while ago?" Kairo asked while motioning over his shoulder to his back with his thumb. "I wish I could explain things more clearly, but I can't. All I can do is ask that you trust me like I did you by revealing my secret."

The appeal seemed to break slightly through the shroud of fog Cyprus found himself engulfed within, and he quietly folded up the map on the table and handed it to the boy who returned the gesture with a smile of gratitude.

"By the way," Kairo, pausing one last time before bolting from the storeroom, said, "your son is going to follow in your footsteps. He's quite proud of you."

The departing remark brought a visible light to the archeologist's face, and as he watched Kairo race through the door and disappear up the stairwell he offered a soft, "Good luck!"

Luck was the one vital charm of which Kairo quickly discovered himself to be most in need of; that and an unerring mastery of his Grace to transport himself back to where he had started. For just as he exited the Morgan Antiquities building and began scoping out both ends of the sidewalk as he took his place on the stoop outside waiting for the coast to be clear of witnesses to perform his disappearing act, he was met with a most unnerving sight.

Making her way down from the far end of the street leading to Morgan Antiquities was Lilith. Dressed in an all-leopard print ensemble, she resembled a feral feline from the jungle slinking its way along the sidewalk in search of lunch. Almost immediately, her dark eyes focused themselves on Kairo, and Kairo, in return, froze in fright. Please, he silently hoped to himself, let her dismiss me as some irrelevant British kid loitering outside. His wish, however, was quickly dashed when her eyes narrowed on him like two lasers, and a glint of recognition stemming back to the night in the Silent Forest when the Sword of Destiny was denied her ignited within her pupils.

Her steps quickened, as did Kairo's heart, especially when he noticed Lilith take notice of the folded map clutched in his hand.

Faster she moved toward him, anger enflaming her beautifully painted face. Somewhere within, Kairo found the courage to flash the tigress swiftly descending upon him, a bold and toothy smile, even as she thrust forth her arms and unleashed from her claw-shaped hands a blackness aimed directly at him. Whatever is was, whatever hidden horrors it contained, Kairo would never know. At least, not that day.

He had disappeared.

~ ~ ~

The day had only a couple more hours of sunlight left, when Max and

Kairo found themselves standing between the two mammoth paws of the Sphinx.

"I don't know if this is the right time to bring it up," Max said to Kairo while the two marveled at the colossal human-headed lion stone figure in repose before them, "but have you taken a moment to consider just how deep a hole we've managed to dig for ourselves since we started this excursion? And I'm not just talking about the fact that we are technically AWOL from Havenhid."

"What hole are you talking about?" asked Kairo.

"A hole so deep I'm surprised the two of us aren't sharing an order of Kung Pao chicken at this very moment. For starters, that disappearing stunt you pulled back in London to go fetch that map. Or have you forgotten the cardinal rule where Graces are concerned that specifically states we're forbidden to do anything that affects the history of mankind?" said Max. "And speaking on that point, what do you think Anahel's reaction is going to be when he finds out you revealed your Nephilim status to an archeologist sixty years in the past?"

"If we're going to get technical about it, I didn't break any rules when I went back in time to get the map. I simply made an edit that prevented Lilith from getting her hands on it, and since Lilith isn't a human by any measure, I don't think I could be found guilty of affecting the history of mankind," argued Kairo. "As for revealing my wings to Cyprus, well...the way I see it, his son already told us he believed in their existence. I merely provided him proof.

"Besides," Kairo was quick to add, "No one, most of all Anahel, needs to find out about any of this as long as the two of us keep our mouths shut."

A most discomforting look came over Max as he tilted his head back to look once more into the face of the Sphinx which, despite being battered by centuries of weathering and vandalism, remained intimidating, and the teen couldn't help but debate whether a pact of silence regarding the latest exploit the two boys faced would even be necessary.

"Well...we might as well get this over with. Personally, I'm tired of standing here feeling like a plate of barbecued snags that's about to get feasted on. Besides, we're due to meet up with Eksel in a few hours, and frankly I'm ready to get home...if we're so lucky," Max mumbled.

As the sun continued its slow bow into the West, a welcoming breeze began to rise up to help sweep away the harshness of the day's heat. Kairo surveyed the nearby walkways usually filled with tourists visiting the Sphinx and found them to be nearly completely empty.

"So, what do we do?" Max asked with hint of impatience.

"I'm not sure. Cyprus didn't say," said Kairo. "My guess is we introduce ourselves to the Sphinx and let it know why we're here."

Max shot his friend a look as if he had bats flying out of his cake hole.

"Is that right?" Max walked up to the Sphinx and placed his hand on the humungous paw as though shaking its hand and, in a manner dripping with mockery, proceeded to make the introductions. "My name is Max, here with my good mate Kairo. And while we are most honored to meet your acquaintance, I'd love if we could skip the formalities and you could just show us whatever secret entrance you have hidden so we can grab the staff of Moses and call it a day; and hopefully without you eating me. But if you do, I hope you choke!"

At first there was nothing, except for the whistling of the wind as it blew its way through crevices around the monolith.

"There, you see? Nothing!" Max contended with a dismissive shrug.

Then, despite Max's display of contempt, there came a sound from a large stone tablet erected between the Sphinx's paws near the chest of the statue. The hieroglyphics etched upon the face of the tablet receded into the stone and, just as mysteriously, a riddle surfaced in its place.

> *Lives upon the ground, one color, but not one size;*
> *Kept under heel, yet easily flies.*
> *From light comes its birth, night its death;*
> *A gathering of storm clouds can steal its breath.*
> *Big as an elephant and weighing not a pound;*
> *It rarely gets lost, and never needs to be found.*
> *No matter how fast your feet take flight;*
> *You'll never outrun it, try if you like.*

For some time, the two boys stood staring at the puzzling rhyme with dumbstruck looks fixed upon their faces.

"One question," said Max, finally. "If we get it wrong, does the Sphinx eat just the person who offers up the answer? Or do we both count as one entree?"

The wheels inside Kairo's head, however, were already spinning in search for the one and only answer that mattered at that moment. Some time passed with both boys pacing separate paths in front of the waiting Sphinx, each mumbling certain phrases of the riddle over and over again to themselves and looking more and more frustrated as the key they desperately sought remained elusive. Every now and then, one of the boys would light up in thinking he had cracked the code and, careful to keep their voice from being overheard by the Sphinx, would whisper their guess into the other's ear only to be greeted with a disappointing shaking of the head.

Finally, as Kairo stood before the tablet reading the riddle for the gazillionth time with a weary look of hopelessness in his eyes, his gaze happened to drift off to the right where the Sphinx's paw rested upon the ground, and he noticed his shadow cast upon the smooth stone.

"That's it," he muttered at first to himself. "That's the answer to the riddle."

He then turned to Max who looked as though he was about to resort to pulling out large clumps of hair from his scalp at any moment.

"I know the answer to the riddle!" Kairo exclaimed before yelling out his guess with gusto: "It's a shadow!"

A look of horror came over Max not only from the declaration of the word "shadow" that reverberated in an echo off the Sphinx, but also due to his failure to tackle his friend in a timely manner and plant his hand firmly over his loud, blabbering gob. Max instinctively turned his gaze upward and braced himself for the expected sight of the sphinx craning its neck in his direction while opening its hungry stone mouth.

However, nothing happened. The Sphinx remained motionless, the wind continued to blow and, for a moment, both Max and Kairo wondered if the Sphinx had even heard the answer. Or what's more, was the legend about the riddle of the Sphinx just that: a legend?

But only for a moment.

Kairo noticed the riddle upon the tablet recede from sight back into the stone and the original hieroglyphics that had earlier disappeared reappear. Then, suddenly, there came a rumbling from deep within the earth. The seismic disturbance was accompanied by the crackling of rock and fragments of stone falling loose or breaking apart. Max and Kairo quickly scurried out of the way when, to their astonishment, the Sphinx's right paw slowly began to slide its way outward across the ground.

When the Sphinx finally stopped moving, and the ground ceased to shake, the two boys saw a narrow opening had been exposed beneath where the paw had originally rested. With cautious steps, they approached it and saw what appeared to be an entrance of sorts revealing the beginning of a flight of stone steps descending their way into a dark unknown.

"Well," Max muttered, as the two wondered what waited for them below, "all I can say is thank you, mate, for saving me from becoming Max on the barbie today."

~ ~ ~

Max led the way down the stone steps, pausing only when the darkness they entered became too thick to see through, even with penetrating Nephilim eyes. He was about to bring forth light with the aid of his Grace that gifted him the ability to summon such earthly elements when several torches unexpectedly ignited on their own simultaneously. Both Kairo and Max froze instantly when the flickering firelight revealed not some narrow underground tunnel they believed they had entered, but a massive chamber that extended for untold fathoms into a pit of black beneath them.

Far more unnerving to the boys were the stone steps upon which they stood. They formed a steep staircase which turned direction several times in its descent into the chamber. The steps themselves, however, were extremely narrow and, coupled with the absence of any sort of railing to grab hold of if needed, proved to be to anyone who set foot upon them, wings or no wings, to be as disconcerting an experience as maneuvering a tightrope across the Grand Canyon.

It was likely due to the confidence that comes from being in the possession of wings that spurred Max and Kairo to continue forth on in their descent down the steps a little faster than someone without their gifts. Eventually they came to a plateau where another mysterious entry led the way inside to yet another cavern. It, too, became illuminated by nearby torches that magically ignited with a burst of flame when the boys entered.

Immediately, Max and Kairo spied the treasure guarded by the Sphinx: Moses' legendary staff. It was standing upright, imbedded in a mound of rock much like a flag marking a plot of land. The mound of rock itself was surrounded completely by a large body of water whose surface was as smooth as a sheet of glass.

"So what now?" Kairo asked the obvious question.

"We go grab it, natch," Max replied before stripping off his t-shirt and unfolding his wings.

Kairo appeared less eager than his friend to hurry and collect their prize.

"I'm not sure about this," he said. "Doesn't this seem just a little too easy?"

"Easy? You're yanking me, aren't you? We just faced being eaten alive by a massive hunk of rock over a riddle, and you think this has been too easy?" Max protested.

The bad feeling that settled itself inside Kairo's gut like a heavy lunch since entering the cavern continued to stay with him. Making his way to the very edge of the pool, he peered down with a suspicious gaze into the water which was as black as obsidian, and was greeted by his reflection floating upon the mirror-like surface.

"There's something about this place," Kairo remarked quietly. "Something eerily familiar."

Before he could figure out what that something was, there came a flapping of wings, and when he looked up he found Max already touching down on the mound of rock rising up from the center of the pool. Max found the staff to be much as he imagined it: a nondescript walking stick used by shepherds thousands of years ago, though it was slightly taller up close than it appeared from a distance, exceeding his six-foot frame by a good couple inches. Also, surprisingly enough, there was found near the top of the staff a live shoot sprouting from the ancient rod of wood, and attached to the shoot were what looked to be a dozen or so pink-and-white almond blossoms.

After sizing up both the staff and the rock upon which it was planted, Max took a hold of it. Then, feeling very much like Lancelot pulling the sword Excalibur free from a stone, Max uprooted the staff from the mound of rock with little resistance.

"You see?" he cried out to Kairo with a victorious smile while holding up the staff. "Nothing to it!"

His smile quickly vanished when he heard a splash of movement in the water near where his feet were perched upon the rock. Yet when he looked at what had caused the splash, he saw nothing; not even so much as a ripple upon the water's unusually smooth surface. Not one to be easily spooked, Max inched his way to the edge of the mound and peered down into the black water and, seeing nothing but strongly sensing something, he used the edge of the staff to cautiously probe the water. Then, convinced his ears had played a trick on him after stirring the water for a moment or two and seeing nothing out of the ordinary, Max pulled the staff from the water. As he did, something with uncommonly sharp claws suddenly reached out from beneath the black surface and attempted to grab hold of the walking stick.

Max, with his lightning reflexes, managed to deliver a glancing blow to the devilish hand and send it back into the unseen depths.

"What was it?" Kairo asked with a tinge of panic in his voice when Max landed beside him.

"Hades if I know," Max, his vigilant eyes continuing to scour the water, replied. "Something reached out of the water and tried to grab the staff, and judging by the looks of it, it wasn't human."

It was then Kairo remembered why the cavern—and in particular the pool of water—looked so familiar to him as a barrage of images flashed before his eyes. They detailed the frightful moments Thaniel was pushed into the deceptive-looking Through inside the Silent Forest and was overcome by a swarm of ravenous creatures called Feeders who dragged him down into the Underneath as Lilith looked on with menacing glee.

"Lilith..."

"What about her?" asked Max.

"Cyprus Morgan showed me a tablet he discovered which revealed the staff was placed here by an evil entity." Kairo waited for a response from Max who continued to look at him as though waiting for the punchline of a joke that so far wasn't the slightest bit funny. "Don't you see? That evil entity was Lilith, or maybe even Samael. They knew the staff was the only thing that could destroy the Scucca Urns and the Scourges contained inside them, so they hid it here where it would likely never be found. Lilith wasn't coming for the map because she happened to be on the hunt for the staff like we were; she was trying to prevent Cyprus from exposing where the staff was."

There was suddenly heard another splash and, as both boys slowly turned their attention back to the pool, their eyes widened like saucers at the sight of some godawful creature climbing its way out of the water and onto the mound of rock where the staff previously resided. If one squinted his eyes, it looked, at first glance, to be a species of monkey, from the shape of its body and long tail, to the way it walked on all fours on its knuckles. With eyes fully open and focused, it was immediately clear the creature was a subhuman aberration far removed from any known species or life form known to exist. Its hairless, wrinkled body was grayish in color and slimy, its back hunched and its slender tail sprouted numerous needlelike quills. The face of the creature, however, was where the true horror bloomed. With its dead but fierce eyes clouded in gray and a mouth that unfolded itself like a flower to display a nightmare of razor-sharp teeth, the creature resembled something of an evolutionary lab experiment gone horribly wrong.

"We've got to get out of here!" Kairo declared urgently. "Don't you see, this is a Through leading to the Underneath...exactly like the one we saw in the Silent Forest."

"Relax, mate!" Max, looking guarded, yet relaxed at the same time, replied calmly. "If this is anything like the Silent Forest, then we're okay; as long as we steer clear from the water. Remember, they're locked in. As long as we don't come in contact with them, and they with us, we've got nothing to worry about."

No sooner had he uttered those words, however, than the creature opened its hideous mouth and, like a trumpet, blew forth a bone-chilling screech of a cry. The only thing that could have shifted Max and Kairo's shared looks of terror from the ghastly Feeder was the rippled movements suddenly spied coming from the water.

Worse, still, was the sight of the head of a second Feeder rising up from the black depths, followed by another, and then many. And despite Max's confident deduction that the assumed Through came equipped with an impregnable wall through which the inhabitants of the Underneath could not pass, much like the now-destroyed Through in the Silent Forest, the boys' jaws dropped in unison when the Feeders proved otherwise by crossing the boundary of the pool and settling their knuckles upon the dry ground.

"Suddenly, the idea of being scarfed down by the Sphinx doesn't top my list of things I hoped to avoid today," Max was heard to utter.

In as calm a manner as they could, both Max and Kairo slowly began to back their way out of the cavern, and with every step they took, the army of Feeders that had assembled on the outskirts of the pool slowly advanced toward them. The Feeder who remained standing on the rock in the center of the pool let loose another high-pitched wail. Then, with a mighty lunge, it cleared the wide stretch of water to the dry land with a single jump and, locking its savage eyes on its prey, it immediately sparked a furious charge toward the two Nephilim.

Without a moment's pause, Max and Kairo turned on their heels and raced for their lives with lightning speed. Upon exiting the cavern, they shirked the path of stairs and, instead, unleashed their wings as they dove into the open abyss of the cavern in a desperate attempt to escape the gnashing teeth of the Feeders hot on their trail. Upward they soared, their wings furiously rowing them swiftly toward the breach of sunlight above. Behind them, a swarm of Feeders spilled into the main chamber like ants from a disturbed anthill; hundreds of them, and then thousands, clamoring just as speedily up the narrow staircase and, like a scurry of insects, along the walls of the cavern.

It was with the faintest sense of relief that Max and Kairo exited the hidden chamber, and they prepared to continue forth in their escape in the direction of the Gate leading back into the safety of Eden where Eksel was expected to be waiting for them when, suddenly, a familiar rumbling made them pause. They saw the temblor was being caused by the Sphinx whose paw was slowly moving back to its original position upon the ground, and in the process concealing from view the entrance to the secret chamber beneath it.

Both boys breathed a sigh of relief, but it was short-lived when, to their horror, one of the pursing Feeders managed to scramble through the ever-shrinking aperture in the ground. It was followed by another, and then another. A good dozen of the repellant creatures managed to climb their way to their surface until those who followed after were gruesomely stilled in their attempts by the crushing weight of the Sphinx's paw as it finally erased all evidence of the chamber's existence.

~ ~ ~

The Feeders quickly surrounded the two boys, and the first thought to come to both Max and Kairo was to simply flee from the wingless demons and make their escape straight up into the sky. They also were cognizant enough in their fear to recognize how much deeper the hole of trouble they had already dug for themselves would grow if they left behind such monsters they technically were responsible for releasing from their cage into the world at large.

"I don't expect this is going to be quite as enjoyable as a good 'ol toss the thong competition," Max was heard to utter under his breath in reference to a popular game involving rubber flip-flops played in his native country on Australia Day while unsheathing his sword from inside his wing.

Both boys took a battle stance against the snarling Feeders, and Max was quick to discover his words to be an understatement, if ever there was one, when the demons came at them full force. In an instant, two of the Feeder were deprived their heads when they lunged at Max and Kairo and the swords that swung in their direction. Yet as skilled as the two boys were in the fighting abilities they had honed at Lions Bite, they were quickly overwhelmed by the onslaught of gnashing teeth, slashing claws and stinging tails. Max, especially, found his hands full, literally, while trying to battle against the fiendishly rabid Feeders with a sword in one hand and guard the staff he and Kairo had gone through great lengths to find in the other.

During a particular ferocious face-off against three of the Feeders, one of the creatures managed to deliver a deep and painful wound to Max's torso with its lacerating claws causing Max to lose hold of both sword and staff. Seeing his defenseless state, the Feeders were quick to descend upon him, and Max, recognizing the peril he was in, instinctively rolled away from the staff to regain his sword in order to slay one of the Feeders that most certainly would have ended him had he not. In doing so, he was greeted by what was possibly the only other thing capable of diverting his focus from the attacking Feeders: the sight of Creed Maggert emerging from the shadow of the Sphinx.

At first, Max was certain he was hallucinating, or that, possibly, the changing light from the now setting sun was playing tricks on his eyes. But as he watched the image of Creed walk over to where the staff resided unguarded on the ground and took hold of it, the more certain Max was that it was no mirage; especially when the image spoke to him.

"Looks like you and your friend have gotten yourself into quite a pickle," Creed said with a mocking sneer while observing Kairo in the distance oblivious to his presence as he continued in his own desperate skirmish against the Feeders.

The two other Feeders Max had yet to kill suddenly turned their murderous sights on Creed and lunged at him. Creed not so much as flinched at the sight of the demons coming at him and instead greeted them with his sword already in hand, and with two precise swings of his blade ended them in an instant.

"Despicable things, Feeders are. The Underneath's version of feral swine, but man can they ever deliver a nasty bite," Creed remarked as he proudly regarded his kill bleeding out at his feet.

"Wh-what are you doing here?" Max managed to ask.

"I guess, like you, I'm just out on a typical treasure hunt," answered Creed as he looked over the staff now in his possession. "Amazing, isn't it? You'd think after all this time, these lands would have been picked clean of valuable relics such as this?"

Max's demeanor instantly darkened, and he no longer gave two hoots how or why Creed was suddenly there. All he cared about was ripping the staff out of Creed's clutches, but as he moved to do so Creed motioned to three more snarling Feeders slowly creeping up on Max with their dripping fangs exposed and ready to rip through anything that got in their way.

"Thanks again," Creed said with a smile most punchable, as he again gleefully examined the staff in his hand.

"Oh, and one more thing," he quickly added in parting, "good luck to you...mate!"

With the Feeders stalking their way closer to him, Max readied his sword and, with an indescribable anger rising up from the deepest pit of his stomach, he leveled his rage-filled eyes at the sight of Creed flying away with the staff of Moses in hand, and he opened his mouth and set forth a cry to follow after him:

"CREEEEEED!"

CHAPTER SEVENTEEN

The election of the new pope was at hand.

A melodious drone of a Gregorian chant filled the Vatican as the one hundred and fifteen cardinal electors, singing the hymn "Veni Creator Spiritus," walked in procession from the Pauline Chapel, following morning mass, through Regia Hall to the Sistine Chapel, where the Conclave to choose the next leader of the Catholic Church was set to begin.

Waiting to greet the procession outside the entrance to the chapel was Cardinal Octaviel Dolus. Unlike the cardinal electors who were wearing their blood-red and white-laced vestments, Cardinal Dolus was dressed in a black cassock with scarlet piping, matching fascia and a large golden crucifix around his neck. It was far from the only thing to set him apart from his fellow clergy. He was also noticeably younger than the other graying (and balding) cardinals, not to mention markedly handsome, aside from a particularly unsightly scar just above his left temple that he managed to keep mostly hidden under the cover of a shock of his thick, dark hair.

Cardinal Dolus offered a cordial bow of his head to the singing cardinal electors, as they entered the chapel made famous world-wide by Michelangelo's exquisite Renaissance frescoes adorning the vaulted ceilings. Once the procession had finally filed its way inside and into the sights of Jesus peering down from "The Last Judgment" where the cardinal electors would swear an oath to absolute secrecy, a voice announced to anyone who was not part of the Conclave and firmly ordered, "Extra omnes!" ("Everybody out!").

Cardinal Dolus looked on in silence, watching intently as the doors to the chapel were shut, and then locked. Only when he observed that the Conclave had been secured from any outside influence, and the solitary key to open the doors to the chapel had been placed into his hand to safeguard, did he turn on his heel to contend with other matters of the day.

As he made his way through the stately halls of the Vatican, he was trailed close behind by a young, sandy-haired deacon named Wesley Latimer whose angelic face betrayed his twenty six years of age.

"How long do you think it will be before we know?" the young deacon inquired eagerly.

"As long as it takes," Cardinal Dolus replied dryly. "That said, I wouldn't be all that surprised if white smoke is seen rising into the sky from the Vatican roof before the setting of the sun."

"And you're confident they will make the right choice?" The deacon pressed with an unapologetic anxiousness as they came to the foot of a massive spiral staircase which could only be described as magnificent with its herringbone-paved steps and granite columns lining the spirals.

Pausing his ascent up the stairs, the cardinal settled his darkly intense gaze upon the deacon. "As the Camerlengo of the Holy Roman Church, one of the duties entrusted to me is to perform a Vatican-sanctioned ritual to verify the death of a pope, which I have so done," he said. "It is also encumbered upon me to oversee the Conclave that will determine who the next leader of the Church will be. And while I may not be casting a ballot, you can rest assure, when all is said and done, the faithful who are gathering outside the walls of this storied institution at this very moment will be presented with a new pope most deserving to them."

There, suddenly, was heard a stampede of feet descending the spiral staircase from above, and when the cardinal and deacon looked to see who was the cause of the commotion they were greeted by the sight of several soldiers of the Swiss Guard coming swiftly toward them.

"We have a breach!" one of the guards alerted the two men as they stormed by them.

Cardinal Dolus and the deacon looked on with visible disconcertion as the group of guards slipped from sight as they charged their way down a nearby corridor where, almost immediately, another ruckus sounded. In a flash, one, two and finally three of the guards were sent hurling backwards through the air, as if the corridor itself had tasted their presence and spit them free of its mouth in revulsion.

For a brief moment, all became uncomfortably quiet.

Befuddled by the sight of the three burly guards sprawled unconscious upon the marble floor before them, the deacon turned a cautious eye to the sound of unhurried footsteps coming from within the corridor from which the men had been violently expelled. Cardinal Dolus, however, appeared to grow more intrigued by the same footsteps the longer his ears honed in on them and, when Damiel finally emerged into sight with Hunter at his side, he looked no more surprised by the angel's appearance than he did the procession of cardinal electors he greeted earlier at the Sistine Chapel.

"Well...this is, indeed, a rather unexpected surprise," Cardinal Dolus said placidly. "Am I to presume you to be serving as herald for a message from Saint Peter himself on what can only be deemed a momentous day?"

"If I were, the vile, if not appropriate words to form said message would have caused such a missive to erupt in flames the moment I stepped foot on such hallowed ground," Damiel replied with a low growl of disgust.

Unlike the cardinal, Damiel slowly approached the staircase visibly staggered at the offensive and unforgivable image of his Fallen brother standing before him in clerics clothes.

"It's been no secret the sanctity of this Church has been infiltrated by the foul vermin of the Underneath for some time. Sadly, I've been unenlightened by the extent of the infestation until this very moment," Damiel, his eyes alight with outrage and burning their way into the cardinal's, said.

"I'm sorry if my presence here offends you. But, lest ye forget, it was your own liege's son who declared everyone is welcome at his table. Even the most wretched," Cardinal Dolus said with a withering smugness. "Naturally, one would assume someone proven to be so...righteous...would extend his embrace to include his house as well."

"It's a long time coming, but it would appear you and I finally agree on something," said Damiel. "You are most wretched, Octaviel."

It was then that Deacon Latimer, looking equally offended at the angel, stepped forward after listening to the back and forth, and addressed Damiel forthrightly, "You will understand when I insist that under this roof you respectfully address the Camerlengo of the Holy Roman Church as Cardinal Dolus."

Damiel, who until then was not even aware of the deacon's presence, stared at the young man as though he had just been struck upon the face. It was not the first time the two had met, and while he recognized him immediately, the angel chose to first address other matters.

"Cardinal Dolus? Cardinal Dolus. Dolus..." Damiel pondered the name aloud, before looking to Octaviel with a somewhat amused look on his face when the Latin translation of the word "dolus" unfolded itself to him. "You most certainly adopted the perfect name to go with your deceitful ruse."

Then, as if an unheard voice suddenly whispered into his ear, Damiel's gaze focused itself suddenly on the cardinal's left breast.

"It would appear as Camerlengo you have fallen lax in duties," Damiel declared.

"I'm sure I don't know of what you are speaking," Octaviel replied.

"The ring concealed in your breast pocket—the Fisherman's Ring," Damiel, his eyes still fixed on the visible yet discreet bulge in the hidden pocket of the cardinal's frock. "One of the first duties of the Camerlengo, after declaring the Pope dead, is to ensure his Holiness' signet ring is destroyed by cutting it in half with a pair of shears."

"Why would it be destroyed?" asked Hunter who had remained a quiet observer.

"To signify the end of the deceased pope's authority," explained Damiel whose eyes remained firmly locked on the cardinal's. "And more importantly, to prevent its use in the forging of documents. No ring, no power!"

As Hunter listened, he glanced over to the deacon who was staring back intently at him, and to his surprise he spied an undeniable flash of gold erupt from deep within his eyes. It was the same kind of glimmer one might spy in the pupils of angels, and Nephilim, and Hunter knew instantly Wesley Latimer was no ordinary deacon.

Damiel's attention, meanwhile, seared its way into Octaviel's very being. "You are sadly mistaken, brother, if you think I'm going to sit back and allow you to usher in Miseriel's plan to further defile my father's house by installing one of his mortal marionettes as the mouthpiece for the Eternal, as well as dictate the faith and morality of the world at large," he hissed while his intimidating presence loomed ever closer, forcing Octaviel to back his way up several steps of the spiral staircase behind him.

"I'm downhearted to learn of your less-than-favorable opinion of Cardinal Menard," Octaviel replied, though hardly bothered. "Unfortunately, for you, the Conclave is already in progress, and by my estimate the first round of votes are currently being cast."

"I will disinfect these once-sacred halls you've sullied before the first wisp of white smoke escapes the chapel's stack," Damiel threatened, before narrowing his blazing eyes on Octaviel. "Starting with you."

In an instant, Damiel's sword was in hand, its blade brilliant with white light, and he descended upon Octaviel.

"I would be heedful, Damiel, and not allow your self-righteousness to get the better of you, or you may quickly find yourself suffering the same, if not worse sting by the same blade you wield," Octaviel was quick to warn while seizing up when he suddenly felt the cold steel of Damiel's sword pressed uncomfortably against his throat. "Need I remind you of the standing oath which binds our father's hands when it comes to meddling in mortal matters? Drawing forth my blood will undoubtedly douse the ember of disdain I see burning so brilliantly in your eyes, but I ask you, is the outcome of the Conclave worth the permanent scarring of that beautiful countenance of yours?"

The two remained locked in their hatred for one another, each reliving at that very moment the shared memory, suddenly resurrected, of their last face-to-face encounter during the Great War in Heaven, when Damiel proved himself the greater angel in a bloody combat that sent Octaviel plummeting from Heaven and into the abyss of fire and damnation.

Octaviel's words, however, supercilious as they were, managed to pierce the fog of contempt which had fully enveloped Damiel. Gradually, a sense of relief (along with a sadistic grin) came to Octaviel when he felt the pressure of the blade against his flesh ease.

"Speaking of blood, where is Miseriel?" Damiel inquired with as calm a voice as his smoldering anger would allow.

"Miseriel?" Octaviel replied with a chuckle. "What possible business would Miseriel have here of all places?"

"Don't patronize me Fallen. I can smell his unmistakable stink as I stand here. I also know about his abhorrent hand in the kidnapping of innocent Nephilim, and you're going to tell me where I can find them."

An expression most serious suddenly came over Octaviel. "Kidnapping. Nephilim? That is quite the imagination you have there, Damiel," the angel, forcing forth a weak smile that faded as quickly as it appeared, muttered. "Now, then, you'll understand if I cut this thorny reunion short. After all, we'll soon be welcoming a new pope into our midst,"

Then, looking to the deacon, Octaviel sternly instructed, "Show them out!"

~ ~ ~

"Follow me!" Deacon Latimer barked at Damiel and Hunter.

Damiel shot Octaviel a last withering look before complying with the order. Octaviel's penetrating gaze followed the angel and his young traveling companion, Hunter, as the deacon led the way out of sight down the same corridor the two had made their grand spectacle of an entrance. When any further disturbances failed to make itself heard, the cardinal proceeded to continue with his day and began his climb up the spiral staircase.

"I don't know what I find to be more repugnant," Damiel grumbled with disdain as he strode down the empty corridor, "a Fallen parading through the halls of the Vatican in a cardinal's frock, and in the role as Camerlengo no less, or a former student of mine who has betrayed his oath of the Nephilim brotherhood to join forces with the Underneath."

The bitter statement instantly pricked Hunter's ears.

"You were a student at Havenhid?" he inquired with noted surprise.

The deacon responded abruptly, like someone on the receiving end of a particularly barbed insult, and was quick to hush them. Then, with eyes scouting one end of the corridor followed by the other to ensure they were not in eyesight of anyone, he swiftly ushered them into a nearby room before securing the door behind him.

"You would be smart to mind your tongues," the deacon advised in a low and cautious voice. "What you stated to Octaviel concerning the sanctity of the Church having been infiltrated by the Underneath is not an understatement. There are eyes and ears everywhere."

"Who's Octaviel?" Hunter, looking more and more confused with every word traded, asked.

"He was amongst the third of Heaven's angels who revolted against our father and chose the sweltering perdition of the Underneath over the Light," answered Damiel.

"And despite however it may appear, I have not betrayed my oath. In fact, I'm more than a little offended you would think I could ever be in cahoots with Octaviel or any other Fallen. I would have thought Zophiel would have explained as much to you," said the deacon.

"Zophiel?" echoed Damiel who was suddenly wearing the same confused look upon his face as Hunter. "What does Zophiel have to do with finding you masquerading as a deacon?"

Mindful to keep his voice no louder than a whisper, the deacon explained how he, as well as other Nephilim around the world, had been recruited by Zophiel to join the small army of moles he had discreetly been assembling to help impede the encroaching ambitions of Miseriel and his dark forces.

"Whatever institutions the Underneath have managed to infiltrate–and there are many–you will find one or more of us there keeping close watch to learn whatever insidious plan they are conjuring. And in many instances to derail those plans," said the deacon, who then turned to Hunter and formally introduced himself. "I'm Wesley. Wesley Latimer."

"Hunter Wylde," Hunter replied with an equally cordial handshake. "So, are you the only undercover Nephilim here, or are there others?"

"There's a few of us here. We've found the Vatican to be a particularly active hotspot for malignant forces, especially recently," said Wesley. "So far we've been pretty lucky keeping our true identities under wraps. But Octaviel is quite shrewd, and I'm beginning to wonder if he is starting to suspect something awry. After today, no doubt he will know."

"What do you mean?" asked Damiel.

"It was I who learned of the scheme to abduct several Nephilim. I overheard Miseriel telling his plan to Octaviel and a couple other sketchy characters who I'd never before laid eyes upon but who had the scar of the Fallen clearly marked on their foreheads. You know the Vatican; you know how immense it is. There are so many rooms—private rooms—where such a conversation could, and should have taken place. Yet Miseriel chose to do so in a room outside of closed doors."

"You think they wanted you to hear of this plan?" asked Damiel.

"Not me per say. But I think they wanted the plan heard, and to test if these walls have ears," answered Wesley. "I warned Zophiel as much, just as I warned him that I was certain this scheme of Miseriel's was nothing more than a trap for you."

"Trap or not, I can't leave those Nephilim in his hands." There was an unwavering look in Damiel's eyes both Wesley and Hunter knew could, and would not be softened by any argument either put forth.

"Now tell me," the angel then asked, "where are they?"

"That, I'm not sure," said Wesley. "Miseriel asked the same question to one of the Fallen with him—a menacing-looking Fallen with shaggy blond hair—but the answer was kind of...well, for lack of a better word, vague."

"What did he say?"

"The one place where all good Christians earn their rightful applause," Wesley replied.

~ ~ ~

Damiel had only to ponder the words Wesley shared with him but a moment or two before he and Hunter found themselves standing in the shadow of what was undoubtedly Rome's most renowned landmark outside of the Vatican: The Colosseum.

"You actually think Miseriel brought a bunch of abducted Nephilim here? To one of Italy's biggest tourist attractions?" Hunter asked incredulously, as he tilted back his head to take in the imposing arched walls of the colossal ancient structure.

Damiel said nothing in response and proceeded, instead, through an iron gate, and then an arched entryway leading inside the Colosseum. Hunter followed close behind, mesmerized by the towering stone pillars and walls which, like Swiss cheese, were pocked with numerous holes; many of which served as nesting pods for swallows. Damiel led the way down a long noticeably modern walkway which led to a large half-moon-shaped platform where the floor of the arena once stood, and Hunter's jaw immediately dropped at the view suddenly unfolded before him.

The first thing Hunter found himself confronted with was the sheer size of The Colosseum. It was far bigger than any photo he had seen of it; at least as big as some of the modern-day stadiums crammed by football fans to watch the Super Bowl.

Looking down towards his feet, as he stood at the railing of the platform, Hunter was given a bird's-eye view of the crumbled catacombs once hidden beneath the long-vanished arena floor, and he couldn't help but imagine the countless slaves and animals who once occupied the network of underground tunnels anxiously waiting their turn to take part in the blood sports above them. Hunter then turned his sights to the towering walls encircling him where rows of seats were once crammed with tens of thousands of frenzied Roman spectators crying out for the spilling of blood for their entertainment.

"You can almost still feel them here, can't you?" he asked aloud to no one in particular.

"Who?" asked Damiel.

"The gladiators who once fought in this arena."

Damiel shared no interest in the ghosts of fallen warriors still lingering amongst the stone ruins.

"I'm more concerned at this point about those whose presence are strangely absent," he said, closely surveying the congregations of tourists moving like streams of ants through the ruins.

"What'd I tell you? They're not here! Bringing them here would be like showing up in Grand Central Station," said Hunter.

Damiel shot the young man a mulish look and declared defiantly, "They're here!"

With that, Damiel turned on his heel and began to retrace his steps back to the entrance of The Colosseum, leaving Hunter scrambling to keep up with the angel as he maneuvered his way through the throng of incoming tourists. When Hunter finally managed to exit his way outside, he found Damiel already rounding the far perimeter of the elliptically shaped arena and darted off after him.

"They're definitely here!" Damiel repeated emphatically when Hunter finally caught up to him. "It's just a matter of entering through the right door in order to find them."

The right door?

"I'm pretty sure the only way in or out is back where we just came from," Hunter argued.

Damiel ignored the lad, carefully examined each of the large arched openings he passed as he continued to circle the outside of the stadium when his feet abruptly came to a standstill.

"This is it!" he declared, standing before one of the numerous, uniform arched openings.

When Hunter pointed out the obvious obstacle standing in their way–bars of steel sealing off any entry through the archway–Damiel calmly replied "Not here," and directed the young man's attention upward to an identical archway making up the second level of the structure.

"There!"

Before Hunter could respond, there came a loud rustling of wings as Damiel disappeared from his side and swiftly ascended to the second-floor opening. A sigh of exasperation left Hunter as he carefully scoped out the immediate vicinity around him for any unsuspecting passersby and stripped off his t-shirt to unfold his own set of wings. In a flash, he was standing on the ledge of the archway beside Damiel.

"Seems like a long and unnecessary way around to land in the same spot we just left two seconds ago," Hunter muttered as he slipped back into his shirt.

Damiel replied with a smug curl of his lip and gave Hunter a deriding pat on his head saying, "How preciously unworldly of you."

It wasn't until he followed Damiel inside that Hunter quickly discovered the veracity of the angel's taunting remark. For when he crossed the shadow of the archway cast down by the sun hanging in the sky overhead, Hunter was greeted with a fleeting disorientation of the senses, as if he had stepped through an invisible film that bleared his eyes. When clarity returned, Hunter was instantly gobsmacked to find himself surrounded not by the ragged and crumbled ruins The Colosseum had become, but the shining monument it once was long ago.

The familiar towering walls of the outer structure that the cruelties of time—and a violent earthquake in the fourteenth century—had caused to fracture and, in places, collapse altogether were now wholly intact. Massive decorative Doric and Corinthian pillars used throughout were now pristine and blemish-free. The marble used to form the tiered seating throughout the arena gleamed brightly in the sunlight.

"How is this possible?" Hunter, his eyes wide and unblinking while gazing at the splendor stretched out all about him, wondered aloud.

He glanced back at the archway, then past the opening to the outside beyond for some glimpse of the time warp he had obviously stepped through and, when he saw clearly the modern world still in existence within his sights, he asked again, though more urgently, "How is this possible?"

His desire for such an explanation, however, quickly dissipated when he turned his eyes downward in the direction of the arena floor. For starters, it was fully intact, and the crumbling remains of the catacombs were no longer visible to the outside world. But it was that which was erected in the center of the sand-covered platform that caused Hunter's breath to instantly catch itself in his chest. Standing upon marble pedestals positioned at various points around the arena floor were fourteen teenaged boys. They were tightly bound at the wrists and ankles, gagged and visibly frightened; they also appeared to be soaked from head to toe with some kind of oily substance that glistened in the sun.

Hunter turned to alert Damiel, but the angel's gaze had already come upon the unsettling discovery, and the flame of his anger was impossible to ignore.

Their descent to the ground level was swift, and when they finally set foot upon the sand of the arena floor they were greeted by a commanding voice that penetrated its way to every corner of the coliseum: "Come, we've been expecting you!"

~ ~ ~

While Damiel had gone into The Colosseum expecting to find Miseriel and, with any luck, the Nephilim boys he had somehow snatched from their fathers' protective watch, he was not at all taken aback to find, instead, Arrestel who was, not surprisingly, found relaxed upon an elaborate throne-like seat in the premiere section of the arena once reserved for the emperors of Rome.

The sight brought an instant look of contempt to Damiel.

"It would seem, more often than not these days, that wherever I happen to find myself to be, there you are, just outside the periphery of my shadow," he said.

The observation brought a smile better suited for an executioner to Arrestel who replied, "Like a tiger hunting his prey."

"More like a nettlesome rat combing the floor for the wayward crumb to fall from the banquet table," Damiel retorted.

Arrestel's perpetual glower made it difficult, if not impossible, to tell whether the snide comment proved offensive to him.

"The view from here is really quite...enticing, I must say," said Arrestel. "I can see why the great Caesars of Rome built these playgrounds of death, and how they brought the men, women and even children who filled its seats by the tens of thousands to a state of religious euphoria. Ah, the spectacles they were privileged to experience: Man pitted against beast; against one another; witnessing firsthand and up close what a Christian carcass could be reduced to when thrown to a lion. I can still see it now: the mangled bodies, the severed limbs; the enviable job of the one tasked with ensuring the defeated gladiators were truly dead by staving their skulls with a heavy, merciless mace; the scarlet death which would carpet the entire arena floor making it appear like a glorious sea of blood."

As he spoke, staring off into the distance with a faraway look, a disturbingly rapturous expression swept over Arrestel, as though he were imagining the revulsive scenes he described and found untold bliss in such gory musings.

"It's not often I find myself looking upon mortals with any semblance of value or esteem, yet I must admit they won me over but a smidge with the creation of this most indulging of sanctuaries."

Such remarks only further solidified the weight of disgust Damiel held for his Fallen brother, and made no effort to conceal it.

"You better than anyone should know that which feeds on the blood of innocents is not long for this world, be it an imperious empire as Rome...or a disagreeable Fallen whose tether to the Underneath is in obvious need of tightening," Damiel remarked casually, yet pointedly. "I'm surprised to find you here and not Miseriel. That is the whole point to this little charade, isn't it: to goad me to step foot on your turf for a confrontation? Now, here I am, and yet Miseriel is nowhere in sight. Where is he?"

"Busy." Arrestel answered, after pausing to feign a mulling of his thoughts. "Today's a big day, after all, with the announcement of a new pope just a puff of smoke away."

Damiel did all he could to resist Arrestel's obvious needling and keep his expression an empty void, even while the proceedings of the Conclave taking place at the Vatican remained present in the back of his mind. As grave a situation as the Church found itself to be in, nothing was more important at that very moment than to free the bound-and-gagged Nephilim placed on display on the marble pedestals around him from their captives.

"You foolishly wade into shark-infested waters when you come between an angel and his son," said Damiel.

"Perhaps," Arrestel replied cooly. "Strangely, I've found once you've spilled the blood of one of your good-for-nothing halflings–much less the eradication of an entire brood as it happened at Akdamar Island–it can be quite...habit-forming."

The mention of Akdamar Island caused a flare of golden ire to ignite in Damiel's eyes and, try as the angel did to conceal it, Arrestel spied it, and he smiled an unsavory smile.

"Dear me, where's my sensitivity?" Arrestel said suddenly with mock chagrin. "I tend to forget your own son was amongst the pile of dead bodies found in the church on Akdamar Island. How crass you must find me to bring up such a painful memory, and with such rapture."

Never had Damiel found his ability to restrain himself to be a near impossible exercise except, perhaps, when he found himself face-to-face with Miseriel at a masquerade ball in Venice. Hunter, who was also at the ball and witnessed the long-coming confrontation, recognized instantly the pent-up rage which was about to erupt like an underground hot spring.

"You and I both know what he's doing," Hunter said to Damiel. "He's baiting you. Don't take it."

Damiel looked to him, his eyes ablaze like twin cauldrons bubbling with molten gold, and offered a reluctant nod in reply.

"I see you've brought one such halfling along with you," Arrestel, taking notice of Hunter for the first time, said. "Pity. Had I known, I would have arranged a place for him amongst the others."

"Lay a finger on me, and your entire hand will be the latest detached limb to be left in this arena!" Hunter spat.

The threat appeared to bring a perverse pleasure to Arrestel who narrowed his gaze of intrigue all the more on the young man.

"You're Zophiel's son, aren't you?" he asked. "You've acquired a reputation for being more than a little meddlesome in your short life. In fact, there's several Pethens who have been fervently overturning every rock on God's green earth in search of you. And, of course, you know why."

"Haven't the foggiest!" Hunter replied with smug impudence.

"Said the ungrateful brat of a Nephilim who not only broke his father's heart by his self-righteous betrayal, but brought about the senseless and, sadly, painful death of his own mother when he chose to break one small commandment: Thou shalt not steal."

Now, it was Damiel who stood witness to the slow boiling of anger rising up in Hunter and stepped in to stem the inevitable eruption. Once he had managed to still Hunter, Damiel, eager to make leave of The Colosseum, walked over to the pedestal closest to him and gave the bound Nephilim standing upon it a nod of reassurance that everything would be okay. He then drew his sword and, with the pedestal being as tall as he, he moved to reach upward with his blade to cut through the rope binding the boy's ankles. Before he did, however, his intrigue about the shiny tar substance covering the bound boys got the best of him, and he ran the fingers of his free hand across the viscous gel and brought them to his nose for a sniff.

"It's pitch oil," he said with a burst of alarm.

He then looked to Arrestel, and the sneer of glee returned his way proved more than unsettling.

~ ~ ~

"Do either of you know where the term 'Roman candle' comes from?" Arrestel asked, and immediately Damiel swallowed knowingly.

"Once upon a time, Rome was under the rule of a particular diabolical emperor named Nero," Arrestel continued in a soothing voice, as though he were reading a bedtime story for all in attendance inside the arena. "Now, Nero had a particular revolution to a segment of the population called Christians—and, in his defense, how can you blame him—and he devised all sorts of various tortures especially for them. One of these tortures became known as the Roman candle. Simply put, the accused were bound, covered in pitch oil and set aflame. Not all at once, mind you. In order to prolong the suffering of the condemned, the fires were started at the feet, and being as pitch oil was slow-burning the torment was, to put it mildly, lengthy.

"But what a dazzling display of light they proved to be; that is, once you acclimated yourself to the screams and wailing coming from those being burned alive," Arrestel continued with ghoulish mirth. "Nero reportedly used these human candles to illuminate his formal parties as well as supply amusement for his dinner guests. I can only imagine the display they would provide in this very arena."

Naturally, Damiel knew exactly to what Arrestel was inferring.

"I've always known you to be in possession of warped faculties, Arrestel, but this is truly deranged, even for you." Damiel then motioned to Hunter and instructed, "Help me to cut these boys free, and be quick about it."

Seemingly unbothered, Arrestel watched from his assumed throne in the emperors box as Hunter rushed off to a neighboring pedestal.

"Of course, if such things are disagreeable to you, we can always resort to the more tried-and-true pedestrian methods," Arrestel remarked casually before either Damiel or Hunter could sever the bonds of the boys they were poised to free.

There was something about the manner in which Arrestel spoke that caused Damiel to go motionless and turn a suspicious gaze on the menacing figure lounging on his throne. Hunter froze as well, but his attention turned not to Arrestel, but the creaking sound of a large trap door hidden beneath the sand covering the arena floor suddenly opening.

"Uh...Damiel?" Hunter uttered softly while staring at the large black void just a hop, skip and jump away from where he stood.

Slowly, Damiel turned his head, not at the beckoning of Hunter's voice, but to an unnerving growl that was heard to come from some unseen thing lurking somewhere in the depths of the black pit. Everything grew eerily still, and Damiel, looking noticeably more uneasy in the face of such quiet than when the ominous growl met his ears, motioned Hunter closer to his side.

"Prepare yourself," he whispered to Hunter who was equally anxious. "We are not alone."

No sooner had he uttered the ominous words than a lion sprang forth from the darkness of the pit. It was not, by any means, any ordinary lion; this lion, like the extraordinary coliseum surrounding it, was an imposing and spine-chilling creation. Its size was that of five lions merged into one; its jaw, lined with razor-sharp teeth, looked capable of swallowing a grown man (and angel) whole, possibly at the same time; and when it came charging out into the daylight, its fearsome yellow eyes were the first to reveal its ravenous lust for blood when they instantly fixed themselves on the prey of fresh meat it came upon in the arena.

It was a loud and terrifying sound the lion made when it opened its mouth to roar, and Hunter instinctively readied his bow in one hand and an arrow in the other. The fight, when it finally came, was swift and ferocious. Like a squall, the lion pounced violently, and Hunter, focusing on the big cat's paws and, specifically, the cutting claws attached to them, was caught off guard when Damiel gave him an abrupt shove that sent him flying several yards and out of the reach of receiving a painful and deadly slashing.

With Hunter out of the way, Damiel and the lion slowly circled one another. The Lion struck first, coming at the angel with its claws poised to shred flesh. Damiel proved himself faster, spinning out of the way of the big cat's swiping paw, then immediately swinging his sword to deliver a stinging gash to the lion's side. The enraged lion roared with pain, and in an equally swift movement that caught even the angel off-guard, the savage creature made an unexpected lunge at Damiel. This time the incoming paw connected with its target with a powerful, bone-crushing blow which not only knocked the brawny angel clean off his feet, but managed the impossible feat of dislodging his trusty sword from his unyielding grip.

Never one to betray fear, Damiel, nevertheless, couldn't conceal the sweat which began streaking his face once he realized he was weaponless when the lion positioned itself knowingly between the angel and his only chance for leaving the arena in one piece: his sword.

The lion, its tail whipping the air about it with languid flicks, growled in anticipation as it advanced with an assured demeanor of victory. As the big cat slowly crouched closer to the ground in preparation to pounce, Damiel, left to the devices of his fists and wings, braced himself for a feral and bloody fight in which he was about to find himself entangled, and he was ready for it. Suddenly, the lion let loose a roar of attack and sprang into action. The strength in Damiel's arms and chest tensed and bunched itself into an impregnable skin of armor at the unnerving sight of the lion launching into the air toward him, mouth agape and fangs gleaming in the sunlight. Then, at the moment Damiel prepared to meet the fury, three incoming arrows, one right after the other, intercepted the lion's attack and struck the feline dead-center between the eyes. A final roar echoed through the air before the lion fell heavy upon the ground in a dead, motionless heap.

Dumbfounded, Damiel turned and looked to the second tier seating behind him where the arrows had come. There, looking quite pleased–proud, even–stood Hunter who, recognizing the direness of Damiel's situation, had managed to scramble from the arena floor one level up and fire off three arrows aimed at the lion while in a full sprint along the pedestrian walkway.

"I had it handled," Damiel, not accustomed to having anyone coming to his rescue, much less a Nephilim, grumbled.

"I'll go ahead and take that as your churlish way of saying thank you," Hunter replied with an even wider smile that only made Damiel all the more surly.

In the instant that followed, however, Hunter's look of amusement dissipated and a look of immense suffering was suddenly upon him when the end of a sword punched its way through the center of his chest as cleanly as a knife slicing through an apple.

~ ~ ~

Damiel looked on in horror as the stricken Hunter's seized body slowly went lax and toppled forward onto the marble seats beneath his feet, and when he saw Miseriel standing there stone-faced with his blood-stained sword in hand he sent forth an indescribable wail that shook the whole of the coliseum.

"NOOOOOOO!"

Swiftly, the angel scrambled over a stone barrier and across the tiered seats to where Hunter lay splayed and immediately placed his hands upon the bleeding gash the visibly stunned boy had suffered to the chest.

"WHAT HAVE YOU DONE?" Damiel screamed half with rage, the other half despair.

"I would think it apparent," Miseriel answered coldly. "I've put down an intolerable halfling, and a thief at that. You see, we too, mete out just punishments for crimes we deem unforgivable...just like our merciful father."

Damiel's eyes left Hunter but for a moment to peer down at the arena floor behind him where his sword lay abandoned and useless upon the sand.

"I know what you're thinking, Damiel. Better yet, I know exactly what you're feeling, and what a conundrum it is," he heard Miseriel's voice coo in his ear. "That overwhelming sense to kill me where I stand is almost too much for you to endure. Ah, but what to do about it? If you release your hold on the boy's wound and go for your sword, he will most certainly die. And if you don't, you will be left with a grievance that is sure to eat you alive and, still, the boy will most certainly die. I sympathize with your dilemma, truly I do."

The radiant suns that were Damiel's eyes were ablaze with wrath as he desperately tried to keep his focus on reversing the flow of red seeping from the sticky, pulsating wound beneath his hands, even as maddening images of Miseriel's taunting sneer flooded the interior of his head.

"Not to worry," Miseriel was then heard to say. "It would seem Arrestel is about to lend you comfort in the form of prayer by lighting a candle."

Lighting a candle?

Damiel spun his head around to look once again toward the arena, and his eyes widened in horror at the sight of Arrestel stepping down from the emperor's platform with a lit torch in hand. The angel screamed in protest as Arrestel made his way to one of the pedestals and the terrified boy perched upon it.

Miseriel sniggered with amusement, and Damiel began to look with frantic desperation all about him. His searching gaze fell upon Hunter's bow resting just beyond the boy's motionless fingers, and he instinctively grabbed for it, along with a couple arrows scattered about beside it. With blurred haste, Damiel nocked the bow, spun around and let fly the arrow like a bolt of lightning. It stuck Arrestel dead center in the wrist like a nail used in a crucifixion, causing him to drop the lit torch while screaming out in pain, and firmly impaled his arm to the pedestal.

Then, without so much as a moment's pause, Damiel turned back around and, with the second arrow he had in hand, took aim at Miseriel. The sight of the arrow coming at him with great speed caught the usually astute Miseriel off guard. But just as the point of the arrow was about to pierce the center of his chest, Miseriel vanished in a burst of furiously cawing black ravens which circled about Damiel and the rest of the arena in an angry frenzy of beating wings and sharp talons before flying off to an unknown refuge.

Damiel quickly put Miseriel out of his mind and, tossing aside the bow, turned his attention back to Hunter whose face had begun to take on a deathly pallor.

"I hate to admit it, but apparently you were right...those who fail to live by sword risk perishing by the sword," Hunter managed to speak, painful though it was.

"You will not perish. Not if I have anything to say about it!" Damiel grumbled defiantly with his hands once more pressed against the young man's chest in order to deliver from them the divine grace of healing.

"Can't say you didn't try to warm me. Intrepidness...it has an unwelcome habit of piercing daring young lads such as myself right about here," Hunter muttered through strained gasps and heaves.

Damiel looked to Hunter's hand that he managed to place upon his own just above his mortal wound, and he was instantly reminded of what he believed to be words of wisdom he attempted to impart on the young man the day of their wager at Lions Bite.

A halting and unpleasant gurgling was soon heard to rise up in Hunter's throat, and he began to gasp and struggle for breath. Damiel became more desperate. He began cursing the wound, and then his own hands as he felt the fatal gash slowly repair itself beneath his touch, yet not quickly enough. Then, just as suddenly, Hunter slowly fell limp as his body released one final lingering breath.

"Don't you do this to me!" Damiel seethed quietly to himself with an anger that was quickly being overcome by anguish before raising his voice so that its demand reached the heights of Heaven itself. "DON'T YOU DARE DO THIS TO ME!"

Tears, rare as they were, spilled from the mighty angel's eyes, watering his hands and coalescing with the crimson red oozing between his fingers. Finally, for the first time in his existence, Damiel conceded to defeat. Everything became unnaturally quiet, and Damiel was left to his grief in the company of that silence. Such silence, however, was short-lived when Hunter, quite unexpectedly, opened his mouth suddenly and took a deep breath of air into his lungs.

The tears that filled Damiel's eyes instantly evaporated and a joyous smile descended upon him when he examined Hunter's chest and saw the laceration caused by Miseriel's sword was nearly healed.

"Seeing as you're an angel, it's a bit disconcerting to know one way or other, but...am I dead?" Hunter, still a bit dazed and weak from his ordeal, asked.

Damiel's smile widened all the more.

"No, you're not dead. You're most certainly not dead!" Damiel answered with a joy-filled chuckle.

All was not completely well; at least it wasn't in Arrestel's case. The Fallen angel's wrist, run through by the arrow shot by Damiel, remained pinned to the pedestal, and any attempt Arrestel made to free himself of the arrow firmly embedded into the marble caused excruciating pain. The unfortunate predicament soon drew the focus of Damiel's attention. With Hunter's condition improving with every passing minute, Damiel excused himself and made his way down to the arena floor where his sword lay on the sand.

"Like I told you earlier, Arrestel: that which feeds on the blood of innocents is not long for this world," Damiel remarked with a calmness Arrestel found deeply unsettling.

The groveling pleas that came from the despicable Fallen fell on deaf ears and, more importantly, proved to be a fitting testament to mark his last moments when Damiel made his way toward him, sword in hand.

~ ~ ~

Needless to say, the captive Nephilim were more than relieved when finally the gags were removed from their mouths and tethers cut free from their limbs, and even happier still when they were reunited with their grateful fathers. After a flurry of thanks, and the last of the boys were homeward bound, Daniel and Hunter themselves were looking forward to returning to Eden. Damiel, however, could see Hunter was still in need of recuperation and not quite ready for such a long journey.

Instead, they found themselves a bench in a secluded corner outside the walls of the Vatican offering a view of the faithful who had begun to gather in a rapidly growing congregation inside St. Peter's Square. They were huddled beneath a canopy of umbrellas to shield themselves from the cold drizzle of rain that was falling, as they continued their prayerful vigil that news of a new pope would be forthcoming.

"And you're honestly telling me you've never shot an arrow before," Hunter pressed Damiel while reclining on the bench.

"For the thousandth time that you have asked, no I have shot not an arrow before this day," Damiel replied.

"Well, if that's the truth, I have to admit it was pretty impressive...hitting two targets like that one after the other, that is," Hunter admitted somewhat begrudgingly.

"I managed to hit one target," Damiel corrected sourly. "The other escaped like Houdini in a flight of birds."

"But if he hadn't, you would have nailed him dead-center. I was watching, and that arrow was aimed straight at Miseriel's heart." Then, more contritely, Hunter said, "I want you to know, when we get back to Lions Bite, I'll make more of an effort to learn the ways of the sword."

Though he was sure to keep it hidden, Damiel smiled slightly when he heard those words, knowing Hunter likely would have rather suffered another sword impaling its way through his chest rather than to make such a concession.

"You know, in a lot of ways you remind me a lot of my son Theron," said Damiel. "He, too, was a rather headstrong lad–intrepid, dare I say. I remember trying for the longest time to force him to fight with his sword in his right hand, but he insisted on using his left. Oh, how it angered me; and yet I knew, despite his obstinance, when the time came for him to finally step foot in Lions Bite, not a single Nephilim with whom he would cross swords with in competition would ever beat him.

"You keep your bow; for with your bow you are untouchable," Damiel then said with a sincere voice, and an even more sincere look in his eyes, much to Hunter's surprise. "Just promise me from here on out you'll work on being more mindful to your blind spots."

The two shared a heartfelt chuckle before Hunter suggested it might be time to start back for Eden. Damiel looked into the young man's eyes and argued otherwise.

"I think we'd better hold off just a little while longer," Damiel advised. "It's not a quick fix when someone has been run through with a blade. The scar on the outside may have faded, but it's a little bit slower going when it comes to the insides. Besides, the last thing I need is for you to fall out of the sky halfway home."

Just then, an elderly woman dressed all in black, carrying an umbrella in one hand and a brown wicker basket filled with rosaries in the other, passed by and offered Damiel one of the trinkets. Damiel politely declined, at first, but then, upon the woman's insistence, took two of the strands of beads, one of which he handed to Hunter.

"Thank you," said Hunter.

"Don't thank me, thank the lady," Damiel replied.

"I don't mean for the rosary; I meant for saving my life," said Hunter. "If it weren't for you, I wouldn't be sitting here right now."

The acknowledgement caught Damiel off guard.

"Well, truth be told, if it weren't for you plugging that lion with several of your arrows, I'm not all that certain I'd be sitting here myself," Damiel said with a heart-felt smile. "So I thank you, for saving my life."

There suddenly came a growing commotion from the crowd, and Damiel instantly rose to his feet and followed the people's rapt attention suddenly fixed on the slender, rust-colored chimney sprouting from the roof of the Sistine Chapel and, more importantly, the puffs of white smoke seen billowing from it.

"What does it mean?" Hunter, suddenly on his feet beside Damiel, asked.

"It means the Church has itself a new pope," answered Damiel.

Yet while the hordes of faithful erupted in boisterous cheers and the joyful singing of praises for the good news for which they had been patiently awaiting, a somber look far darker than the dank skies above settled itself over Damiel.

CHAPTER EIGHTEEN

THE WAGER

Max burst into Creed's room without so much as a courtesy knock, pausing but a moment to search the room for the target of his visible anger. When he spied Creed sitting casually in a chair in the center of the room as though he were expecting the ill-mannered intrusion, and holding the stolen staff in his hand like a king with a scepter to boot, Max's eyes narrowed with loathing.

"You dirty tosser! I'll be making a mitt out of that face of yours in two shakes of a lamb's tail!" Max declared with gusto.

It was by Heaven's grace that Kairo, Ethan, Leos and Jacob, unsuccessful in slowing their friend's heated charge through Havenhid in search of Creed the moment he set foot back in Eden, managed to prevent Max from making good on his promise, though it took every ounce of strength all four boys could muster to restrain Max and keep him from putting his balled-up fist into Creed's very punchable face.

At the same time, Creed, without so much as a glance at either one of them, motioned to his lapdogs—two fellow Nephilim named Ivan and Vance whose brawn was certainly more impressive than their brains—to stay put where they were when they stepped forward to assist with the incoming threat.

"You seem a bit testier than usual. Bad day?" Creed remarked with a smile that only managed to rile up Max all the more.

"You might say he's a bit angry. We both are!" said Kairo. "You stole that from us: Moses's staff!"

"What? This old thing?" Creed, looking over the walking stick he held with feigned confusion, said. "That's a pretty serious, not to mention, inflammatory charge you're leveling. I hope for your case you have proof to support such a claim."

Every word that came from Creed's mouth only seemed to further agitate Max.

"Please, I beg you, let me just put my fist in his face," he pleaded with his friends, while struggling to free himself from the four sets of arms straining to hold him back.

"I would think twice about striking the son of an Archangel," warned Creed. "You might just find yourself in the unenviable position of being the first person since Adam and Eve to be sent packing from Eden. No doubt, that would prove to be quite a proud feather in your father's cap."

Loathe as he was to consider any words of advice coming from Creed, especially on matters of protocol, Max couldn't argue the fact that, while it would bring undeniable and immediate pleasure to him, cleaning Creed's clock, no matter how deserving it might be, would result in prompt and very unenjoyable consequences. And so, with a good amount of disgruntlement, he relaxed his fists which, in turn, allowed his well-intentioned friends to relax their hold on him.

"It was you, wasn't it?" Jacob turned and asked Creed once it was clear Max had cooled his heels. "It wasn't Thaniel who sent me that mysterious note pointing us in the direction of where we might find the staff. You sent it!"

Creed reacted to the deduction with a smirk of amusement.

"Guilty as charged," he admitted with a snigger. "In my defense, though, you are mostly to blame for my tactics."

"Us? This ought to be good," Ethan quipped.

"It so happened I was in the common room the other day minding my own business and doing my reading assignment for Study when I innocently overheard the bunch of you going on about a walking stick once belonging to Moses," said Creed.

"So in other words you were eavesdropping," Leos chimed in.

"Call it what you like," Creed snapped in return, before turning a contemplative gaze to the staff in his hand. "So often these days it seems the only thing we hear about is the awe-inspiring power of the Sword of Destiny. I must say, it was kind of refreshing to learn there was another relic in existence that was equally, if not more powerful."

"Nothing is more powerful than the Sword of Destiny," Kairo was quick to object.

"And yet only one of the two has the ability to destroy a Scucca Urn," Creed argued in return.

Much to the dismay of the other boys, it became evident Creed had more than a gist of the situation at hand.

"And how is it you knew where to find it, when neither Vessel or even

Thaniel knew?" asked Jacob.

The anger-inducing smug grin once more surfaced on Creed's face. "There are quite a few advantages that come with being Sandel's son which, it goes without saying, is something none of you will ever be accustomed to experiencing. One of those advantages is information," he said. "I don't want to divulge exactly where, or from who I learned what I did regarding the staff's whereabouts; the main point is I did.

"The only real hurdle standing in my way was getting my hands on it. As the two of you came to learn, discovering where the staff resided was one thing; retrieving it, however, involved an entirely different set of skills," Creed, looking specifically at Max and Kairo, continued.

"So you decided to use us to do your dirty work, knowing how dangerous it was, while you watched from a distance," charged Kairo.

"And nearly got us killed by a bunch of savage Feeders without raising a finger to help us," Max spit with renewed anger.

"Oh, please, spare me! Feeders are nothing more than overgrown piranha with legs. A Nephilim unable to defend himself against a few Feeders shouldn't be allowed the right to call himself a Nephilim," argued Creed. "Besides, I killed two of them for you without so much as breaking a sweat."

"If you don't mind me asking," Ethan interrupted, once Max managed to calm himself again, "why do you even want the staff in the first place?"

"Oh, but I don't want it. I mean, what use do I have with an old man's walking stick?" answered Creed, before resting his gaze on Jacob. "But it's valuable to you; so, therefore, it's equally as valuable to me."

Jacob didn't betray any reaction of surprise; he figured as much from the moment Max, looking like he'd been in a pretty nasty brawl and seething with retribution, returned to Havenhid and explained what had happened before stomping off to begin his hunt for Creed.

"What do you want in exchange for it?" Jacob asked.

"What makes you think I'd ever consider parting with such a priceless artifact?" said Creed.

"You just said you had no use for it," Ethan quickly reminded him.

"I guess I did, at that."

"What do you want in exchange?" repeated Jacob. The inquiry brought a conniving gleam to Creed.

"Well, now, I guess there would be no harm in haggling for the fun of it," Creed muttered aloud, while giving the staff a thoughtful once over. "Of course, this is just off the top of my head, but it would seem to me that someone interested in an item as powerful and valuable as Moses's staff should be prepared to trade for it with something of equal power and value."

"What do you have in mind?" Leos asked suspiciously, knowing all too well Creed already had a certain something already in mind.

And he was quick to reveal it, when he looked to Jacob and said, "Your sword."

~ ~ ~

The room became quiet, as no one at first seemed to believe what their ears just heard.

"You're really out of your tree, you know that, muppet?" Max finally declared with a snigger of disbelief. "The Sword of Destiny belongs to one, and only one person: that would be the Light Bearer. And in case you need reminding, which apparently you do, that would be Jacob, here."

"Your blind allegiance to your mate was precious in the beginning, really it was," said Creed. "But if you really think the Iudicium Tribunal is going to formally declare the son of Samael—a dirty Weed—as any kind of divine anointed one then you are even more pathetic than I originally pegged you to be."

"That remains to be seen, doesn't it?" Leos shot back.

"Besides," said Kairo, "either way, what makes you think Jacob would even consider your offer to trade, even for that old staff?"

"Oh, I didn't—at least, not at first. You see, I know exactly how important that sword Gotham lovingly bequeathed to Jacob is to him. I know attempting to get him to give it up willingly would be like trying to wrangle the last existing bottle of booze from the hands of a desperate drunk," said Creed. "But tomorrow the tribunal is going to render its verdict on whether to uphold Samael's petition that his parental rights over his own child be returned to him, and, well, I think we all know how that's going to turn out, whether you want to admit it or not. So now, suddenly, this relic of the Bible—the staff of Moses—is your last ditch effort to hopefully smash your way through enough Scucca Urns to render Samael powerless enough to free yourself from his grasp—or at the very least, use as a bargaining chip to force him to relinquish custody."

Leaning forward, Creed looked to Jacob and, with an ear-to-ear grin spread across his face, inquired, "That was your brilliant plan, wasn't it?"

Jacob stood quiet, refraining from saying anything as Creed ran his mouth in his uniquely smug, gleeful way, though the glowering look he fixed upon his arch nemesis said more than his tongue ever could.

"Surprisingly, even now, I don't think you would loosen your fingers to trade your sword for this staff," Creed, luxuriating in Jacob's obvious hatred and scorn of him, then said. "That's why, to show you I'm not the louse you think I am, I'm willing to settle this matter with a friendly but competitive wager."

Anyone who knew Creed Maggert—and, indeed, everyone present in the room was more than acquainted with the boy's acute slithering talents, including his two lap dogs—was immediately suspicious of any effort to draw a veil over the very thing in which he himself took great pride: being a first-class louse.

"What kind of wager?" Ethan questioned with a suspicious squinting of his eyes.

"If Jacob here accepts my challenge, I'll put up the staff of Moses against his Sword of Destiny; winner takes all," said Creed. "That means if I lose, you win the staff and, even better yet, save yourself from your new, and I'm guessing unairconditioned digs in the Underneath. However, if you lose, you graciously surrender your sword to me, and pack your bags."

"Hold up there, Speedy Gonzalez," said Leos. "What exactly is the challenge?"

"Going head to head," answered Creed, "inside The Crucible."

It was clear by the trade of glances that followed, none of the boys were prepared for such a gauntlet to be dropped at their feet.

"That's a pretty one-sided challenge, if you ask me, Chief!" said Max. "You know all of Jacob's time since he's gotten back has been spent before the Tribunal. He hasn't had a chance yet to go to Deep Thorn, much less run the Crucible."

"I think that's the point," Ethan grumbled under his breath.

"If you're interested in a fair contest, how 'bout you compete against me, instead?" challenged Max.

"My only interest is in becoming the new and more suitable owner of the Sword of Destiny," Creed replied snidely before leveling his gaze on Jacob. "It's either my way, or Samael's way."

One could almost hear a pin drop in the moment or two that followed as all eyes turned to Jacob. When Max recognized his friend was actually entertaining the idea of taking the bait dangling before him, he immediately stepped in to take matters into his own hands.

"There is another way," he said. "I could just end this right here and now and take back what was mine in the first place by wrenching that staff out of your wormy hands."

He began to make a beeline straight for Creed before he even finished voicing his threat, and Creed, well aware of Max's scrappy nature, appeared momentarily timid. He responded in a flash by tossing the staff he clutched in his hand onto the floor at his feet. The staff, instantly upon hitting the floor, transformed itself from a walking stick into an extremely large and terrifying cobra. Max froze dead in his tracks and his eyes widened like saucers at the sight of the coiled, hooded serpent blocking his attack and hissing venomously.

"If you cared anything about your continued health, I'd take three giant steps backward," Creed, looking once more relaxed now that he was no longer at risk of Max's fists, advised.

When Max proved resistant to submitting to the demand, despite the threatening obstacle in his path, Jacob grabbed hold of his friend by the shirt and yanked him back out of harm's way.

"I'll do it," he then said to Creed. "I'll run against you in The Crucible."

Satisfied, Creed reached down and grabbed the spitting cobra by its tail, and the snake instantly straightened itself in his hand and transformed back into its original shape of a wooden staff.

"If anyone had any doubts whether or not this staff was the real deal, I guess now we know," Creed, looking quite pleased with himself, remarked.

~ ~ ~

They agreed—or rather Creed made the unilateral decision to which no one argued—to meet at Deep Thorn at dawn the next morning, well before the hour the Tribunal was scheduled to reconvene.

"Well? Where is it?" Creed bellowed at once upon his arrival at Jacob and his crew who had already been waiting for a good ten minutes.

"Where's what?" asked Jacob.

"The Sword of Destiny, titmouse, what do you think?"

In the matter of seconds since Creed's arrival, Jacob was filled with an overwhelming desire to level what he saw as a blond-haired, walking, talking hemorrhoid standing before him.

"I don't have the Sword of Destiny," Jacob replied matter-of-factly.

"If you'll remember, it was your father who forced Jacob to hand his sword over to Gotham until the end of the Tribunal hearing," Max jumped in to remind Creed.

The explanation only served to irk Creed all the more.

"How do I know you're not going to welch out on our wager after I smoke you?" Creed whined while holding his ante in hand.

"Because, unlike you, we keep our word," said Ethan who quailed somewhat when Creed turned an unpleasant scowl his way.

"I don't welch on my bets," Jacob asserted dourly, before motioning to Ivan and Vance who were standing like two mindless but obedient shadows behind Creed. "Besides, you have Frick and Frack there as witnesses to our agreement. Not to mention my friends; they're not going to lie no matter what the outcome."

Creed made no retort on whether or not he accepted Jacob's word except for a grimace. The two camps then separated and retired to individual makeshift corners to prepare the two opponents for the competition which consisted primarily of stripping Jacob and Creed out of their t-shirts so their wings could be bound in accordance with the rules of stepping foot in The Crucible.

"If any of you have any words of advice, I wouldn't mind hearing it," Jacob proceeded to ask his four closest companions who were busy securing his wings with a hearty length of vine.

"I've been racking my brains trying to think of something that might give you an edge," said Max who sounded none too optimistic. "Truth is, The Crucible is always changing and is never the same for anyone entering."

It wasn't exactly what Jacob hoped to hear; neither was it without some comfort. After all, if The Crucible was ever-changing like Max said, then Creed would be at the same disadvantage as he was, despite having had the advantage of previously running The Crucible.

"There's still time to call this off," Max was heard to whisper. "I mean, think about it: is it really worth the risk of losing the Sword of Destiny? Especially to that weasel?"

"What's riskier? Losing in The Crucible, or when I appear before the Tribunal in just a little while from now for their verdict? Either way I lose the sword," Jacob noted glumly. "No way am I going to be sent off with Samael like some twisted modern-day version of 'The Addams Family.' And this is the only option left to prevent that from happening."

With his mind seemingly made up, and his wings securely bound, Jacob made his way back with his posse of friends to the entrance of The Crucible where Creed, flanked by Ivan and Vance, was waiting with growing impatience.

"So...what do we do?" Jacob asked.

"We walk inside," Creed replied with a devious grin when he spied an unmistakable veil of nervousness in his opponent's gaze as it darted to the ominous hedge beside which they stood. "And then it's every Nephilim for himself."

"As long as you remember wings and Graces are off limits," Ethan was quick to remind all present, particularly one certain individual who turned a scorching look his way in return.

"We're all familiar with the ground rules, pipsqueak," barked Creed.

With that, Jacob and Creed positioned themselves at the threshold of this mysterious and forbidding pocket of Eden which until that moment had belonged firmly and exclusively to the Silent Forest. In an attempt to calm what felt to be a swarm of butterflies suddenly let loose inside the cavern of his chest, Jacob took several deep breaths as inconspicuously as he could so as to keep his jittery state from reaching Creed's ears.

When the word was finally given, the two boys entered The Crucible through an opening in the hedgerow which appeared as magically as it disappeared once they had stepped through it. Immediately, Jacob's heart began to race when he found himself surrounded by a murky darkness.

"I've got just seven words for you Parrish: Your sword is as good as mine!" Creed's voice pierced the silence accompanying the gloom.

Then, as though answering a starting pistol only he himself could hear, Creed took off in a flash, racing off toward the sunlight in the near distance and the beauty of the forest bathing in its light. Shoving aside all lingering hesitation, Jacob followed suit and took off after his rival like a blind man without a cane in hand to help guide his way through whatever strangeness lay in wait for him. For a good mile or two Jacob ran, cautiously probing every bit of his surroundings while remaining fast on Creed's tail, but there wasn't anything his penetrating Nephilim eyes managed to spy which seemed out of the ordinary. In fact, the deeper into the walled-off patch of forest he ran, the more Jacob found it to be unlike any other stretch of forest scattered across

Eden.

Just when a sense of ease had returned to Jacob, however, the kaleidoscope of butterflies inside him were set aflutter when the ordinariness displayed by the forest soon demonstrated itself to be anything but. Trees began to move. Noticeably. In fact, the whole of the forest appeared before Jacob's very eyes to come alive and move about of its own volition. Suddenly, what had until then been reminiscent of the punishing obstacle courses Damiel had his young students run repeatedly at the start of their training through the forest surrounding Lions Bite became a cake walk when the hurdles greeting Jacob's nimble and fleet-footed steps grew all the more challenging. Futile, even.

Mountains, where there shouldn't have been mountains, appeared at one turn of the path, while gorges, where there shouldn't have been gorges, paved another turn. Trees made swipes at the two boys racing through their ranks with gnarled claw-shaped branches while vines attempted to seize limbs or necks with their snaking snares. There were even too-close-for-comfort instances when several giant flesh-eating plants, similar to a Venus flytrap, though far more terrifying, attempted to make a meal of Jacob in passing.

Where the surrounding forest failed in its efforts to stymie the efforts of both Jacob and Creed from succeeding in navigating its cursed terrain, the creatures who resided inside it attempted to succeed. These were not the familiar animals which roamed the lands of Eden, where even the ferocious-looking lion was as docile as a cuddly kitten. There was nothing familiar about the creatures which lived inside this closed-off Eden within Eden, nor was anything docile about them either. They were both of the winged and four-legged variety, but it was immediately obvious to anyone who had the misfortune of laying eyes on them, their existence was, and had always been, confined to this secluded neck of woods. And while they were far from the horrendous demonic beasts spawned by the Underneath, they exhibited a less-than-friendly disposition to those who intruded on their otherwise peaceful seclusion–particularly Nephilim.

It was while Jacob was desperately trying to outmaneuver three especially nasty and vicious breed of bird that he found himself wondering if they, and the rest of the inhospitable creatures he crossed paths with, were a product of the unfortunate sin which came to foul this swath of forest by Eden's first inhabitants, or were they the lingering outcome of God's wrath which took hold of the land in an unforgiving grasp soon after?

Whatever the answer, of which he never fully came to a conclusion, Jacob proved to be able-bodied and adroit enough to meet head-on the ever-growing number of obstacles–the trees, the flesh-eating plants, the unpleasant creatures–and emerge from them unscathed with just the right amount of skill and speed until he found himself, impressively, no longer trailing Creed, but in a neck-and-neck race beside him. For some distance they mirrored one another, racing vigorously against the other along the ever-changing path before them like a pair of playable characters competing in a video game. Only when an incoming snag in the shape of a forest creature or a sudden and abrupt change in the landscape attempted to take the air out of their sails did they break ranks to clear the impediment with a choreography of fancy foot work and brute strength.

Just when Jacob was about to finally pull ahead of Creed and put his rival on the receiving end of his dust, he caught sight of something quite out of the ordinary, not to mention unexpected, out of the corner of his eye which managed to snag him by the heel in a way none of the other obstacles had so far managed. It was a blond-haired boy about his age, standing amid a cluster of flowering shrubs seemingly observing the foot race as though he were the sole spectator in an empty stadium.

Strange as it would be to come upon anyone in the middle of the forest–not to mention this particular forest–it was familiarity of the boy himself which caused Jacob to bring his feet to a reluctant halt and cede his imminent lead to Creed.

"It can't be," Jacob muttered to himself while narrowing his eyes on the blond boy who suddenly turned and disappeared down a barely visible path leading deeper into the forest.

Throwing all caution to the wind, Jacob was quick to follow after the boy. Nearly running down the skinny path, Jacob raced to catch up to the boy, but the boy was nowhere to be seen.

Then, when Jacob was convinced his eyes had played a costly trick on him, he came upon a small clearing where he found the boy, standing and facing his direction as though he were waiting.

"It can't be," Jacob muttered again to himself while slowly looking the strange boy up and down with a stricken expression.

"Your name by chance isn't David, is it?" Jacob asked finally with a note of apprehension while the image of a near identical boy frozen in a familiar black and white photograph shared with him by his grandmother blazed inside the confines of his memory. "The David who was Gotham's son?"

"Don't be nervous," the boy replied.

"Nervous? What's there to be nervous about happening upon the ghost of someone who's been dead for some time?" Jacob said more to himself than the apparition standing before him.

"I figured this was the safest place to make myself known to you with the least amount of freak out," said David.

"Who's freaking out. I'm not freaking out!" Jacob declared with a high-pitched gusto that suggested otherwise. "For all I know, you're just another trick–a hallucination–conjured up by this weird forest to try to keep me from making it to the end."

"You're going to have to make a decision pretty quickly on whether you think I'm a hallucination or not. We haven't a lot of time," the boy noted calmly.

"Time for what? What's this about?"

"The missing pages to my journal. You need to find them," said David.

The directive hit Jacob sideways.

"We did find them...that is, Anahel found them," he replied.

"Not all of them. There was more."

"I-I-I don't know what to say. Anahel said the pages he found in some book in the Library–the ones in which you explained the real motive behind your death–was all that was there," Jacob explained, yet his intrigue was suddenly raised. "What's so important about the rest of the pages. What did they say?"

"There's no time to explain...not now," David, sounding at once edgy, said. "All I can say is, there's an invisible barrier before you of which you've yet to see, which neither the Sword of Destiny or Moses' staff can clear out of your way."

"Barrier? What do you mean? What kind of barrier?" asked Jacob.

"If you have any hopes of fulfilling your fidelity as Light Bearer, you must find those pages," David replied, befuddling Jacob all the more.

"I don't un–"

Understand, Jacob was about to say about the so-called barrier, and what it had to do with him being the Light Bearer and, most importantly, how he came to find himself standing in the middle of the forest having a conversation with his uncle who was the exact same age as himself. But before he could finish voicing his confusion, a billow of fog swept in from out of nowhere, encircling Jacob and obliterating David, as well as the surrounding forest, instantly from his sights.

Everything grew eerily quiet, as most things do within the chokehold of a dense brume, and it was within such blaring silence Jacob become aware of a presence outside of his own moving about him. It was the first time since entering The Crucible, even in the face of the unfriendly critters which called it home, that he wished he had his sword within reach. And never more so did Jacob's desire for his sword visit him than when a massive mask of a face—Samael's face—emerged before him from the vaporous mist and looked upon him.

"My son...Son of Samael," the familiar voice from Jacob's nightmares, and more recently his hearing before the Iudicium Tribunal, hissed forth from the fog-sculpted bust. "There is only one fate for which you are destined, and it is not as the Bringer of Light."

"David?" Jacob called out to the ghostly apparition which had led him to this nightmare shaped by the cold, dank fog. "Are you there? I can't see you!"

There came no reply, except the one spoken by the disembodied head of his father: "By now, you have lost the Sword of Destiny," it said. "Come to me, before you lose something far more precious to you."

"This isn't real. This isn't real," Jacob began repeating to himself under his breath in the hopes such a recitation would cause whatever sparked the figment of his imagination to take shape before him to disappear.

Only it didn't.

"Your place is with me, my boy," Samael's voice continued to wheel about Jacob in an almost hypnotic way. "Stop resisting me, Jacob; accept who I am, and, more importantly, embrace who you know yourself to be deep down inside yourself."

"NEVER!" Jacob, his rising angst finally reaching its boiling point, screamed in return.

It was to his great relief, then, that he suddenly heard David's voice pierce its way through the thick gray soup.

"Where are you?" Jacob called out desperately to the voice.

"Run, Jacob, while you still have a chance to beat Creed," the reply came.

Feeling nearly defeated, Jacob answered, "What's the point? Creed has to be celebrating his win by now."

"Never mind Creed; he's dealing with his own setbacks, but not for much longer," said David. "Just set your sights to your left and keep your feet headed in a straight line."

Jacob did what the voice instructed and turned to his left, but he soon hesitated where he stood when the only thing he could see before him was the choking gray mist and not a single other thing, until David's voice once again met his ear and issued a demanding "GO!"

In a flash, Jacob took off in a full run to flee the reach of the shroud of fog that had momentarily imprisoned him and, more so, the lingering echoes of Samael's voice trailing after him.

"YOU'LL NEVER ESCAPE ME!"

Before long, the mist of fog grew thin before dissipating entirely and, much to Jacob's immense relief, he found himself once again in the sunny, cloudless presence of the forest, even if the trees and animals and everything else of which the forest was made resumed their attacks on him.

His feet carried him faster than they ever had before in an urgent drive to make up for the time he lost and close whatever gap now separated him from Creed. The only source of hope he held in his chances to still beat his rival, dim as it was, resided in the news David had shared revealing Creed was dealing with his own setbacks—whatever that meant. It wasn't long, however, that Jacob soon felt a presence closing in on him on his right side and, peering over his shoulder, he was neither thrilled or disappointed to find it was none other than Creed himself. The expression on Creed's face revealed he felt exactly the same way when coming upon Jacob, for both boys realized at that moment they each had the chance for victory in their grasp.

Their battle to overtake the other for the lead became brutal, and oftentimes unsporting. When they weren't navigating their way through treacherous and ever-changing obstacles or evading the living things of the forest by the skin of their teeth, they attempted to do to the other where The Crucible had failed to succeed through far more brutish and pedestrian tactics involving mainly their fists.

It was while both were engaged in a ferocious trading of elbows aimed at the other's face while sprinting full speed toward the glorious sight spotted off in the distance of a hedge marking the entrance to The Crucible where they had started their contest that the path upon which they raced suddenly gave way and collapsed from beneath their feet. Before he knew it, Jacob found himself dangling over what appeared to be a bottomless gorge the size of a football field, clinging desperately to a tree root protruding from the side of the cavern he managed to grab hold of to keep from falling to his death.

Glancing about him, he felt a slight panic move through him when he failed to see any sign of Creed, when clumps of dirt began to pelt the top of his head. Looking up, Jacob saw the cause of dirt spilling down on him was caused by a pair of sneakers standing at the edge of where the path had broken away, and looking further upward he quickly realized the feet filling the sneakers belonged to Creed who had somehow or other managed to escape the fall.

"That's quite a predicament you've managed to get yourself into," Creed commented as he peered down at his hapless rival while wearing a grin of smug amusement.

"Thanks for pointing out the obvious. Now, if it's not too much trouble, would you mind giving me a hand up," Jacob grumbled.

Surprisingly, or perhaps not, Creed made no move to stretch his arm down into the gorge and help Jacob climb up out of the hole. Instead, he turned his gaze toward the entrance of The Crucible residing just on the other side of the chasm.

"Actually...come to think of it, it would be too much trouble," Creed muttered matter-of-factly.

"You're not going to just leave me here hanging like this, are you?" Jacob asked incredulously. "Even you can't be that big of a horse's ass."

"Oh, don't worry! You just hold on tight and I'll make sure the first thing I do is send someone in to fish you out of that old hole," Creed vowed through his smirk. "That is, after I collect the prize waiting for me for beating you in The Crucible."

A collective of flowering adjectives began to assemble themselves inside Jacob's head in one long profane string, but instead he inquired. "And how exactly are you going to do that. No way can you clear the jump you'd need to make to reach the finish line. And I don't see any other way around."

Jacob's declaration only seemed to water Creed's devious smile, and much to Jacob's shock he watched as Creed's wings slowly unfolded themselves into view.

"You dirty, rotten cheater! You broke the rules. Your wings were never bound," Jacob groused.

"I would think you'd have educated yourself by now, chump: I never wager a bet I know I can't win," Creed noted with an air of conceit. "Now if you'll excuse me, there's a sword I've been eagerly anticipating to hold in my hands waiting for me."

Before Jacob could tell Creed what he could do with the sword he so coveted, Creed fluttered his wings loudly before flying off over the chasm toward the waiting entrance–and in this case, the exit–to The Crucible. He'd only managed to glide halfway across the gorge when, much to Jacob's surprise, it looked as if suddenly some unseen thing took hold of the clearly startled Creed who barely managed a shriek of terror when, in an instant, he vanished into thin air as though impossibly pulled through some invisible keyhole.

It took several attempts for Jacob to pull himself up out of the hole. The far more daunting prospect was figuring out a way across the chasm without having to resort to using his own wings, an option not really available to him anyway seeing as how his wings were properly bound and the vine used to bind them out of his reach to loosen. The only recourse left to him was making a miraculous leap over the maw keeping him from exiting The Crucible. And even though he surmised correctly Creed's inability to successfully vault over such a great distance, Jacob held faith that his feet would deliver for him a different outcome.

It took Jacob a moment or two to psyche himself out enough to make a try for it, and even then, he found himself aborting several tries at the final moment when he was about to launch himself blindly into the air. Eventually, frustration gave way to anger–anger stoked by the thought of Creed holding possession of his sword through duplicitous means–and it was that anger which drove him headfirst at the challenge laid literally at his feet.

When finally he emerged from the opening formed for him by the hedge, a boisterous welcoming of cheers from his friends greeted him. Max promptly grabbed the staff of Moses from Ivan, who along with Vance looked on at the celebration with glum expressions, and placed it in Jacob's rightful hand. The only one who appeared even more miserable (and noticeably discombobulated) was Creed who was sitting on the ground looking as though he had been, as Max most poetically put it, dragged through a hedge backwards.

~ ~ ~

Shortly after dawn the following morning, just as the awakening sun swept away the last remnants of night and dressed Eden in a brilliant shade of goldenrod, Jacob made his way to Lions Bite.

There, as expected, he found Gotham greeting the new day as he usually did: shirtless and with his sword in hand, facing off against some unseen foe. At first, Jacob refrained from announcing his presence, knowing the angel retreated to such solitary moments at Lions Bite whenever he needed to work through private interior battles taking place within him. More likely, the cause for his silence stemmed from the fact the two had not spoken one word to one another since the great sword caper debacle. Since then, Jacob had kicked himself more times than he could count for pulling such a stunt on Gotham. And while his intention was never to hurt the angel, Jacob had been left haunted by the expression of raw disappointment etched on Gotham's face the night he learned of the ruse.

The memory of that shameful moment nearly caused Jacob to slink away and quietly return to Havenhid. Instead, he quickly found himself mesmerized by the performance taking place before him in a repertoire of movements demonstrating the nimble skills of the most learned of martial artists as well as the graceful and precise motions of a dancer.

Gotham, however, took notice of the boy almost immediately, lurking in the shadows of the massive slanted slabs of rock which formed Lions Bite, though he did not acknowledge the boy's presence.

"Uh...hey there!" Jacob finally forced himself to call out meekly while he was able to manage some semblance of courage.

"I don't mean to disturb you," he then said. "I was just hoping I might be able to have a moment to talk to you."

"So talk," Gotham replied tersely, again without looking in the boy's direction as he continued on with his routine.

He most definitely is not going to make this easy, Jacob thought to himself as he humbly stepped out into the brilliance of the sunlight flooding the grassy arena.

"It's just...we haven't spoken since, well, for a while," Jacob began, "and I really don't care too much for it. In fact, I hate it quite a bit."

"Maybe you should recruit your puppet master in crime and, with any luck, he can succeed again in worming his way into my head to maneuver the levers controlling my mouth," Gotham remarked while concentrating on his invisible opponent he continued to battle.

"I guess I deserve that," Jacob conceded, though with a growing bit of annoyance, as Gotham remained more focused on his workout rather than the sincere apology he was attempting to give.

"Look, what I came out here to say is that I am really sorry for what Leos and I did to get you to give me back the Sword of Destiny," Jacob finally blurted out brusquely. "Even though our intention wasn't malicious or meant to demean you any way, it was still a dirty ploy on our part, and I've been sick about it ever since. Leos feels just as badly and, well, if it wasn't for the fact he's terrified you might incinerate him if he ever comes within your eyesight, he'd likely be here, too, to apologize. And I know my saying sorry may never make things right between us again, but I thought it was important to say it to your face."

The moment Jacob uttered the word "sorry," Gotham ceased his regimen and finally turned his gaze upon the boy. And when Jacob had finished his apology and, with head hung low, turned to leave the angel to his training, Gotham said to him, "Apology accepted."

Jacob paused his feet and glanced back at Gotham as though he wasn't sure if his ears were playing tricks on him.

"Really? Just like that?"

"Sure, why not?" Gotham replied while casually looking over his sword which gleamed brightly in the sunlight. "You expressed your remorse in a manner I believed to be sincere. It's only right that I release any ill will on my part and accept it in the same spirit with which it was given."

The angel's words, and the amiable manner in which they were spoken, instantly lightened Jacob's mood and placed a smile on his face.

"That's great to hear!" he exclaimed with glee-filled relief. "I was prepared for you to never forgive me. Or at least make me grovel for a bit."

"I'll admit the thought crossed my mind. After all, having someone close to your heart deceive you in such a manner is very hurtful," said Gotham. "Then again, I don't believe your purpose was malicious when you pulled your stunt, as you so noted in your apology. In your mind your intentions were good and focused on a moral outcome, no matter how misguided you actions ultimately became."

"Exactly!" Jacob agreed vigorously. "I could never deliberately deceive you. Unfortunately, it became an unavoidable means to an end in order to try and throw a wrench in Samael's plan to gain custody of me."

"You might say, in the same way Damiel acted without malice when you became a similar means to an end in a ploy he came to view as equally righteous," Gotham noted without missing a beat.

The correlation and the sly manner in which it was aimed his way caught Jacob with all the subtlety of a cuff on the head and left him momentarily sputtering for a response.

"Is that your artful way of suggesting I make amends with Daniel?" Jacob huffed contemptuously at such a thought.

"I'm not suggesting you do anything," answered Gotham. "I'm merely reminded of a verse in the Bible which states: 'Do not judge, and you will not be judged. Do not condemn and you will not be condemned. Forgive, and you will be forgiven.' "

Knowing he couldn't argue or protest the angel's well-aimed observation despite his overwhelming desire to do just that, Jacob kept his lips sealed tight and quietly stewed in his umbrage for a moment or two.

"I'm not making promises," he finally stated petulantly.

Truth be told, the ongoing squabble he had with Damiel was the last thing of worry on Jacob's mind. Even his more recent falling-out with Gotham, though he was more than happy to finally have the matter mended and put to rest, wasn't at the top of Jacob's list of concerns—not while the hour of judgment before the Iudicium Tribunal ticked its way ever closer.

"It's not looking too good, is it?" Jacob quickly steered the conversation to the other elephant keeping company with them.

"What makes you say that?" Gotham, trying to conceal his own doubts concerning the forthcoming verdict which had been weighing heavily on him, asked.

"I spoke to Etirsa when she visited here. I just got a sense things weren't going in my favor."

The reply appeared to irk Gotham. "You'd do well for yourself not to put too much stock in other people's predictions, especially when they concern you. Just remember it ain't over till it's over."

The testy retort managed to bring the first semblance of a smile to Jacob's face.

"Never thought I'd hear an angel quote Yogi Berra," he said.

"Yeah, well, when the quote fits...speak it," the angel quipped awkwardly.

"I just can't believe there is actually a distinct possibility I could find myself being handed over to Samael like some dog in the pound and forced to leave Havenhid." As Jacob spoke, he began chucking small rocks he picked off the ground one at a time, each one sailing further in distance than the previous one as his anger slowly began to bubble. "If only my mom was still alive and could go before the Tribunal. She'd set things straight."

Then with a mighty heave he tossed the remaining rocks in his hand and told Gotham he'd see him later when it was time to leave for Halcyon.

"What did you just say?" Gotham, suddenly looking at the boy as though he had sprouted a third arm, asked.

"I'll see you later. I'm heading back to Havenhid to rest–before we have to–."

"No...before that. About your mother."

There was a wild gleam in Gotham's eye; as though Jacob had somehow come to reveal the unknown mystery of life known only to God above them.

"I just meant if she were still around she'd let the Iudicium Tribunal know in no uncertain terms how she wouldn't have touched Samael with a ten-foot-pole had she known what he really was," explained Jacob.

Somehow Gotham's smile grew even wider and, grabbing the boy by the head as though it were a ripe cantaloupe, he planted a giant kiss square on Jacob's forehead.

"What's that for?" Jacob bellowed at the sudden, and most unexpected, show of affection.

"Like I said," declared Gotham in a jubilant whisper, "it ain't over till it's over!"

Before Jacob could ask Gotham what he meant, the angel vanished in a fluttering flash of wings that carried him into the sky and onward toward Havenhid.

CHAPTER NINETEEN

As slyly as they could without being seen, Max and Kairo hurriedly, yet quietly, tiptoed their way to a pair of vacant seats behind the other spectators in the back of the great, opulent room inside Halcyon where the Iudicium Tribunal was soon set to preside. They carried with them, as inconspicuously as they could manage, the staff of Moses concealed in a large gray wool blanket which they hid out of sight beneath their chairs, along with a sack carrying the three Scucca Urns they retrieved earlier in the morning from the Greffiers' watchful guard.

Peering over his shoulder in anticipation of their arrival, Jacob breathed an anxious sigh of relief when he spied his friends settling into their seats without drawing any unwanted attention upon themselves. Or so he thought.

"What are they doing here?" Jacob heard Anahel's stern voice in his ear just as he traded a thumbs up gesture with Max and Kairo. "I thought I made my feelings clear that everyone was to attend their classes as scheduled with no exceptions."

"Please don't hold it against them," pleaded Jacob. "They know today could significantly alter the course of my life forever, as well as theirs. I think they just really wanted to be here to lend their support, and, frankly, I could really use it."

Instead of marching over and taking the two truant boys by their ears and directing them back to Havenhid, Anahel turned forward in his seat with a disgruntled grunt.

"Very well," he muttered. "However, you can make it known to them they will most assuredly make up for the time missed in their studies."

Shortly, thereafter, the members of the Tribunal entered the room in a single-file procession. Jacob carefully studied the face of each angel, but seeing as how they had shown themselves to be a notably somber group during the course of the hearing, it was difficult for him to gauge their mood. One thing was certain: the ominous feeling which sat like an anvil in the pit of his stomach was only growing stronger.

As the members of the Tribunal took their seats, a blur of movement swept past Jacob and Anahel in a gust of wind and settled itself in the form of Gotham in the empty chair next to them.

"Where have you been? The hearing's just about to start!" Anahel, who had been growing visibly more uneasy with every passing minute of the angel's tardiness, said crossly.

"There was something I needed from your room and, since you had already departed, it took me more than a minute to locate it," said Gotham.

Before Anahel could inquire what, exactly, Gotham might have required from his room, Arafiel's voice called for the attention of everyone present. After brusquely calling the hearing to order, Arafiel proceeded to make public several last-minute procedural adjustments, the most notable of which concerned the glaring absence of the very person whose charge had all but derailed the original purpose of the Tribunal's hearing: Samael.

"After great consideration, as well as counsel from my fellow members of this most esteemed body, I have granted a motion put before this court that access to these proceedings by the petitioner in this case—that of course being Samael—be limited to remote means," said Arafiel.

Jacob realized the instant he glanced over to where Sandel was seated and spied the self-satisfied smirk on the pallid angel's face, which of the members had voiced the motion. And while he wasn't certain at first what "remote means" entailed, he soon found out when Arafiel gave a subtle nod to a member of the Tribunal seated near him who proceeded to take in hand a large silver pitcher from the table and walk over to the noticeably vacant spot where Samael would have appeared before the court. There, he raised the pitcher to roughly his own height and slowly poured out the water inside in a straight line. The water moved like a slow molasses, flowing downward in much the same way a velvet curtain in a theater descends across the front of a stage at the close of a play. Immediately, Jacob was reminded of the night he risked his life going unaccompanied through The Gate in his desperate bid to find Gotham and warn him of Thaniel's plot to kill him. It was then, beneath the fire-lit dome of the church on Akdamar Island, that Johiel had performed the same identical ritual to bind his memory of having ventured outside Eden's border.

Sitting transfixed in his chair wondering who amongst them was about to have their memory bound, Jacob watched as the water finally reached the floor forming what could have easily been mistaken to be a tall rectangular-shaped mirror. It wasn't until flashes of color began to erupt within the smooth sheet of water and congregate with one another to form shapes which at first were indecipherable that Jacob realized the purpose of the "mirror" was not to bind anyone's memory.

"This is outrageous!" Samael blurted angrily when his reflection surfaced within the window of water.

The clarity of Samael's presence was extraordinary. Anyone entering the room blindly that very moment would have mistaken the mirage as flesh and bone. In fact, Jacob noticed almost immediately that Samael, ironically, was being broadcast into Eden from the confines of the church at Akdamar Island. Nor was he alone, as Johiel could be seen receded in the background keeping a watchful eye on the proceedings, while Thaniel stood at Samael's side.

"You have no right to deny me my due process before this court; and a mock court at that!" Samael bellowed.

"No one is denying you a thing, Samael," Sandel responded in a most lackadaisical manner. "You more than anyone should realize the sacred ground that is Eden, and it's certainly withstood its share of having the muck of the Underneath soiling it. While we allowed accommodations regarding your own offensive trespass when you unceremoniously brought your petition to this court, I'm sure you'll appreciate the decision by the members of this body to avoid suffering a similar affront."

"Heaven forbid," Samael muttered under his breath with unbridled disdain.

"As for your denigratory remark aimed at the legitimacy of this court," continued Sandel, "there exists no scales of justice more balanced, or impartial, whether you wish to acknowledge such truth or not. The decisions handed forth by this body are based on one thing, and one thing alone: the law. And, in the end, it is the weight of the evidence, not the character of the plaintiff or defendant standing before us, that govern such rulings—no matter how ignoble."

Samael, glowering at Sandel, replied simply, "That remains to be seen."

~ ~ ~

Looking to move past the initial unpleasantness, Arafiel's voice once more took command of the room and announced the Tribunal had reached a decision in the matter Samael had brought before the court concerning the custody of Jacob. A rumble of growing anticipation arose from the spectators seated in the room which caused Jacob to squirm all the more uncomfortably

351

in his chair while Gotham rose in swift manner from his.

"That said," Arafiel promptly continued, as his gaze settled itself on the angel who looked quite anxious to address the court, "I received a short time ago a message from Gothamel who made it known to me the existence of an important piece of evidence he wished to enter into the record before any final judgment be rendered."

The news caught Sandel off guard and caused him to instantly straighten himself in his seat like a tabby cat who had just caught sight of a mouse scurrying across the kitchen floor.

"Evidence?" he spat discourteously. "You had ample time to present all the evidence you could scrounge up before the court recessed to begin deliberations."

"In all fairness, this case was dumped before this court without any warning or allowance to Jacob and his counsel for the preparation to gather such evidence," Gotham replied in as cool and amiable manner as he could. "This new evidence was not available to us before your deliberations and, I would strenuously argue, may very well change how you may choose to ultimately rule."

Visibly miffed by the unexpected development, Sandel turned to Arafiel and demanded, "Why wasn't this brought to my attention earlier?"

While Sandel's demeanor, icy as his snow-white hair and hypothermia-inducing glare, was prone to make even the fiercest of angels come to heel, Arafiel was not counted amongst them.

"Despite your misplaced illusions, Sandel, I never have been, nor will I ever be, under the weight of your thumb," Arafiel noted matter-of-factly. "My duty to this court is to relay such developments in the timely manner in which I receive them, and I have thusly done so."

Etirsa, looking radiantly demure, attempted to redirect the daggers each angel had leveled on the other.

"If Gothamel has evidence pertinent to this case, I see no reason why we shouldn't make an allowance to hear it," she said, and immediately found herself on the receiving end of Sandel's contempt-filled stare. "You yourself boasted but a moment ago how the legitimacy of this court was built upon the rulings based on the thoughtful weight of evidence in relation to the law. I may just be an interim member of this Tribunal, but as such I can say, I'm not all that comfortable rendering any decision in this matter while knowing material evidence has been withheld."

Her strongly voiced argument drew a murmuring of support that gradually grew louder from the other members of the Tribunal, much to dismay of Sandel who slumped back in his seat with a scowl of defeat when Arafiel gave Gotham the okay to proceed. Gotham, in turn, looked to Etirsa and, as though coming to the realization of how distant and aloof he had been behaving toward her, he offered a meek smile and nod of genuine thanks for her support before turning to Anahel.

"What is going on? What is this new evidence of which you are speaking?" Anahel asked in earnest and about which Jacob was equally desperate in knowing the answer.

Gotham's answer came in the simple gesture of reaching inside his shirt and retrieving from its confines the instantly recognizable decorative blue feather belonging to the Illume and, thusly, answering the question of what Gotham had gone in search of in Anahel's room.

"I don't understand," Anahel, looking most perplexed, recalled.

Gotham said nothing in return, but instead looked deep into Anahel's eyes and, in the intimate way angels (and Nephilim) were gifted in communicating with one another without parting their lips, a look of clarity quickly washed its way over Anahel.

"Oh course. And quite brilliant!" Anahel muttered as he took the feather from Gotham with a cunning gleam in his eyes.

Trying, and failing, not to be the only remaining one of the three with no clue of what was going on, Jacob sat back in his seat with a huff of frustration as Anahel approached the Tribunal.

"You all of course are familiar with this," Anahel, holding up the vibrant and luminous blue feather for all to see, said. "Each year, the highly anticipated Illumination celebration culminates with the hunt for the elusive Illume, a deceptively beautiful bird, and a one-of-a-kind of its species, who emerges from its life of seclusion once a year in search, sadly, for a non-existent mate. It's the rare Illumination when the Nephilim competing in the hunt succeed in capturing the evasive Illume. This feather is a keepsake from the most recent hunt in which Jacob and his friend Max emerged as victors.

"Not to worry–the Illume is prone to regrow its lost quills quite quickly," Anahel was quick to note. "Those like this one, however, are more precious than the pearls found in oysters, or sparkling diamonds secreted away inside a lump of coal; for they carry within them a power similar to the Grace of Gazing. And, through that power, the Nephilim lucky enough to be included in an Illumination where the Illume is part of the ceremonies are given an invaluable glimpse into the true purpose of why they have been brought to Eden by illuminating the truth of the world as it exists. And so it will do so here at Halcyon."

With those words, Anahel turned and approached Jacob who suddenly felt himself grow nervous when he was asked to hold out his hand. Having experienced a sigil visible only under the light of the moon branded on the inside of his wrist by the same feather, Jacob thought nothing of it when Anahel brought the tip of the feather to his main finger. Only, instead of an expectant cool, tingly sensation, he yelped with pain when the sharp point of the quill pierced his skin and drew a drop of blood which Anahel carefully collected on the tip of the feather.

"You could have warned me it was going to sting," Jacob complained.

"Sorry, about that," Anahel apologized to the boy. "It's going sting."

Then turning once again to face the Tribunal, Anahel held the feather up for all to see.

"With this, we will be allowed to gaze into the very moment Mr. Parrish here came into existence," said the angel.

"And what exactly, if I may be so bold to ask, is the purpose of this exercise other than serve as a spectacle of an ill-suited peep show?" Sandel grumbled.

"That, as the saying goes," replied Anahel, "remains to be seen."

Then, just as Jacob, Max and Kairo had witnessed on the night of Illumination, Anahel took aim with the feather and launched it like an arrow. All eyes watched in eager anticipation as the blood-tainted tip embedded itself like a dart to a cork scoreboard into the marble floor at the exact center of space created by the Tribunal's U-shaped table where witnesses were called to offer up their testimony. At once, a dark luminous pool began to spread from the point where the feather had planted itself across the floor like a spill of oil and, much like the window of water from which Samael and Thaniel watched the goings-on, myriad colors slowly giving shape to images began to percolate from deep within the spreading dark mass.

Soon the members of the Tribunal, including Sandel, leaned forward in their chairs to gain a closer look of the vision of a night-drenched room that unfolded itself for all to see. At the heart of the vision was a young and beautiful woman fast asleep in bed, and Jacob, with a twinge in his heart, instantly recognized the woman to be his mother, Isabeth. Any longing he may have felt for her in that moment dissipated suddenly when another presence–an ominous, wraithlike figure–made itself known. It entered the room in the form of a shadow, seemingly cast from the billowing folds of the sheer curtains being blown about by the wind coming in through the open window. The specter floated about the room with the ease of an autumn leaf caught in a breeze, dancing along the ceiling and walls, then disappearing beneath the blankets covering Isabeth at one end of the bed before emerging again at the other. When the strange phantom finally came to rest at the foot of the bed, one could plainly see the ghostly being possessed two great dark wings. It was also clear, despite its transparent nature, that the unearthly figure was none other than Samael himself.

The hearing became silent as a tomb as those in attendance watched with intrigue as Samael, hovering over Isabeth like a winged phantom of death on the hunt for a soul, retrieved something within his clothing near his heart. What it was, no one could see due to the crush of the night surrounding him.

Suddenly, he was upon her, nuzzling her neck and kissing her cheek in a manner which proved exceedingly creepy for all who watched as Isabeth continued to sleep unaware of the sinister figure beside her.

"You don't know it yet, but you, dear Isabeth, are about to join a particularly elite company noted in the annals of history," Samael was then heard to say as he gently, though no less creepily, brushed the sleeping woman's temple. "In the same way my divine father chose a handmaid named Mary to bear him a child, so I choose you."

Samael then rose to his feet and, standing upon the bed over Isabeth, his attention quickly returned to that which he held in his hand–a small black vial, as a glint of moonlight managed to finally reveal. Carefully, he opened the top, and when he did a bright luminance spilled out into the night from within the vial. Samael was then seen to pour the contents of the vial out over the sleeping figure beneath him, and as he did Jacob noticed Gotham and Anahel trade similar looks of an uneasy nature with one another. For what was released from the vial was a small orb of light, about the size of a pea and gleaming brilliantly. It floated for a moment or two in the air like a miniature star before it began a slow and graceful descent toward the vicinity of Isabeth's stomach where it vanished from sight.

~ ~ ~

For some time, Sandel sat with a blank look fixed on Gotham when the image that had unfolded upon the floor, soon after also vanished.

"Well? Is that it?" Sandel asked finally with notable irritation. "You interrupt the proceedings of this court with an appeal to present what you deem to be dire evidence on behalf of the boy. Where is it? Or did I somehow inadvertently miss the reveal of acquittal in that brume of memory we just witnessed?"

"That you would pose the question informs me justice is indeed blind in more ways than one. But permit me to serve as your white cane," Gotham replied pointedly to Sandel as he made his way to the center of the room to pluck the Illume's feather from the floor before addressing the rest of the Tribunal.

"I'm sure like me, those of you in this room likely reacted to the revelation that Samael had come to sire a son with, to put it subtly, shock," said Gotham. "I had, after all, for all intents and purposes, sentenced Samael to his end days by confining him to a state of perpetual rot nearly forty years before he managed to taint the dutiful role of fatherhood. Nonetheless, as we all are aware, even a cage fixed with a lock to which I held the only key, cannot fully hinder someone like Samael from roaming."

As someone who benefitted from one of the six Graces inherited by the sons of angels allowing them to move with ease through the corridors of time from one place to another, Jacob knew exactly to what Gotham was referring.

"Now, I have spent every minute of every day since Samael brought his petition to you in a desperate search to uncover a means—some possible loophole—to annul his parental claims of custody over Jacob. Admittedly, I acknowledge in failing in my search. That is, until early this very morning when I was gifted with words of wisdom, accidental as they may have been, coming from the mouth of a particularly astute babe," Gotham continued while shooting Jacob a knowing wink before returning his attention once more to the Tribunal. "I came to the stark realization that desperately missing from these proceedings was testimony from the boy's mother. For she would convey to you as she fervently did me, shortly before her death, her desperate bid to ensure the wardship of her beloved son be placed in the hands of his grandmother and then, when he had come of age to make the journey to Havenhid, into my guardianship. She made clear, in no uncertain terms, Samael was never to have anything to do with Jacob."

"Such a shame she's dead and can't illuminate these tedious proceedings with her testimony. But even if she could, you and I both know her maternal desires in this matter aren't worth a hill of beans," Samael said with a grin curled at the edges by arrogance.

"Hill of beans?"

"I believe that which Samael is referring is what was touched upon when he first made his claim," Thaniel who had been standing somewhat submissively beside Samael spoke up. "All matters regarding Nephilim children, including guardianship, fall under the sole purview of the father, not the mother."

"I can't recall a time I've ever come to challenge your superior intellect, Thaniel. This, however, would be one," said Gotham. "In fact, the parental rights guaranteed those of us who have or will choose to bring forth into a world a son is not absolute."

"Would you care to elaborate?" pressed Arafiel. Gotham, however, hardly needed prompting.

"Samael long ago earned every blackened etch of the mark of the Fallen that came to be seared upon his temple. He did not, however, in being branded by that mark escape the laws which govern all angels, sitting and Fallen," said Gotham. "When he consciously chose to sire a child, his means of doing so were limited. Profoundly. Naturally, he could roam by physically transporting himself outside the boundaries of the Infernal Desert, but it would do him little good seeing as I had bound him with the Herrinsu vine whose tether he could not escape and would remain shackled to his limbs. Unless, of course, he chose to roam on a more transcendent plane where he was free to leave both his body and the vine which tightly bound it. That, too, though, is fraught with limitations which, I dare say, would make conceiving a child with a mortal woman a near impossibility. And yet, leave it to Samael to discover a way to do the impossible. Except in doing so, as everyone who witnessed it just a moment ago, he relinquished all rights to the child over which he now seeks to assert custody."

The room grew noticeably quiet, and even Samael appeared momentarily thunderstruck.

"What sort of riddle are you attempting to spin?" he balked at Gotham.

"No riddle whatsoever. In fact, it's all written here in plain Celestial," Gotham replied, as he reached once again into the hidden folds of his shirt to retrieve an aged parchment containing the script used by angels.

"And what might that be?" inquired Sandel who had been patiently listening.

"What we commonly refer to as the Commandments of angels," said

Gotham. "Something that, frankly, has been sadly overlooked during these proceedings."

Gotham didn't look all that surprised when both Sandel and Samael failed to comprehend his reply, and so he proceeded to enlighten them.

"Samael, inarguably, conceived a child on the night in question; of that, there is no doubt. He did so, however, through deceptive means," Gotham began to explain. "The Commandments governing angels clearly spell out that while we are allowed to pursue relations with mortals, it must be both mutual and consenting to all parties involved and, more importantly, it must stem from a seed of genuine love. I think I don't speak out of turn when I say it was more than apparent to everyone present in this hearing who witnessed it that Isabeth Parrish was in no way, shape or form a willing or consenting participant the night she came to conceive Jacob.

"Therefore," the angel continued adamantly as he approached the table where the Tribunal was seated and slid the document sealing Samael's fate toward Sandel, "based on the very word of law you yourself heralded as this court's divining rod which states, an angel's rights concerning his child are to be nullified should he be found in violation of said rules, I see no other course of action left you than to dismiss this nothing-less-than-laughable petition Samael has brought before you."

Sandel remained silent for some time when Gotham had finished, and it became evident, at least from where Jacob sat, the white angel was far from pleased to have such a damning bit of evidence brought to light before the court, especially when the withering expression fixed on his face somehow managed to harden even more so when his gaze strayed away from the document cited by Gotham, and settled itself on the boy in a most uncomfortable way.

"I protest this character assassination!" Samael, who wasn't about to take something as revolting as the truth lying down, exclaimed. "Unless you can bring that dead woman into this room and substantiate your claim to the Tribunal, you have no way to prove Isabeth Parrish did not consent to bearing my child, nor that his conception was absent the deepest expression of love on her part."

Despite hearing such nausea-inducing tripe, Gotham calmly responded by turning to the Tribunal and saying, "Quite surprisingly, I was summoned by Isabeth shortly after she discovered she was with child. She told me all about the mysterious and charming stranger who had been invading her dreams and attempted to seduce her. He revealed himself to be an angel–the unFallen variety, that is—but her instincts told her better. I can assure you her feelings for Samael included neither love nor allurement; in fact, quite the opposite. And while the great abundance of love she did come to have for the son she chose to bear, she was beyond devastated by the deceptive and criminal manner in which he was brought to her.

"Of course, none of you are obligated to take my word for what I've told you," he then told those listening intently to his claim. "I'm more than happy to offer my hand to anyone interested in seeing and hearing Isabeth's version of events for themselves as I did."

Of course, Jacob knew Gotham was speaking of the gifted means angels had of instantly sharing the memories they carried inside their heads with others through the simple and unobtrusive touch of their hands.

"I know I speak for myself when I say I don't think that will be necessary," Etirsa was the first to respond. "I had refrained from solidifying my decision on this matter until you were given a final opportunity to address this court. Now, after hearing about this compelling and, I must say, disturbing development, I have no choice but to reconsider my initial verdict and vote against Samael's claim."

Gotham traded twinkles of hope with Jacob and Anahel as Etirsa's declaration soon sparked a spectacular turning of the tide. In quick order, the other members followed suit and, like a falling of dominoes one by one, what was expected to be a traumatic verdict against Jacob became a unanimous indictment against Samael. Even Sandel, much as it aggrieved him to do so, was forced to concede to the law he held in such high regard and hand Gotham the victory he so handily deserved. Samael, meanwhile, bellowed and screamed in revolt at what he deemed to be an outrageous though expectant miscarriage of justice, leaving many in the room thankful a sheet of water kept them safe from the reach of his ire.

"This marks the third time you have brought unwelcome upheaval into my life: first by stripping me of my birthright, followed by imprisoning me in a hellish desert for a crime you yourself committed; and now this," Samael spoke directly to Gotham once Thaniel had managed to quiet somewhat the still simmering rage. The focus of his wrath remained pointedly fixed, however, on Sandel.

"Don't think for one second, White One, the judgment rendered here today is the final say in this matter," Samael growled at Sandel. "You and your blasted law are an insufferable combination, and the days of your righteous pronouncements are fast coming to a head, I assure you that."

"You? Daring to deem me insufferable? Has a statement dripping with such rich irony ever before been uttered?" Sandel replied before surrendering to raucous laughter.

Then, when the chuckles ended as abruptly as they began, Sandel coldly stated, "Do yourself a favor, Samael, and mind to whom it is you're speaking, and don't issue threats your sword is incapable of cashing. Or next time you just may find yourself at the bottom of a very deep and cold ocean instead of that desert paradise Gothamel left you."

"I believe it is you, dear brother, who has naively come to underestimate the wiles of my nature," Sandel retorted. "But you will come to discover much sooner than not that it will take more than an impenetrable gate to protect yourself from the wrath of my indignation."

It wasn't in Sandel's way to shrink in the presence of such a threat. Nonetheless, there was something about the way Samael lobbed his warning that gave him pause, if but for a passing moment. He turned to shoot Samael a glare of spite in response but as he did the window of water suddenly collapsed into a puddle upon the marble floor, and Samael and Thaniel vanished from sight.

Filled with elation that the prospect of being forced to live with Samael had passed by him, Jacob thanked Anahel and, especially, Gotham with the biggest bear hugs he could deliver. Even Max and Kairo looked relieved they wouldn't be forced to resort to pulling out the staff of Moses they had concealed underneath their chairs and start shattering the Scucca Urns they snuck into the hearing if the decision by the Tribunal had managed to go the other way, as they feared.

It was while Etirsa made her way over to where Jacob was basking in the merriment of the news with his two friends to extend her own felicitations to both him and Gotham that there suddenly was felt a marked shuddering from the floor beneath their feet.

CHAPTER TWENTY

"What could that have been?" Etirsa wondered aloud.

Before anyone could venture a guess, there came another jolt, followed by another, each stronger than the one before it. Suddenly, it became as if Halcyon had fallen victim to a powerful earthquake. The ground began to shake and roll violently. Several large cracks fractured a section of the floor in the center of the room, causing Etirsa to lose her balance.

Gotham, with his lightning-quick reflexes, managed to grab hold of her and keep her from stumbling, but not before large chunks of the marble floor buckled upward suddenly in their path and caused the two of them to freeze where they stood when, to their unfathomable disbelief, they were brought face to face with the terrifying cause of the destructive temblor as it slowly emerged from the giant hole it had finished punching its way through.

As gently as he could manage, Gotham shoved Etirsa out of immediate harm's way and drew his sword. Anahel and the other angels who formed the Tribunal unsheathed their swords as well while looking on with dread at the monstrous creature in whose company they suddenly found themselves. The first thought made immediately certain to all present: the thing—whatever it was—did not belong to the family of beasts birthed by Eden and roaming its lands, even amongst the most unusual of them. One would even be inclined to argue (adamantly, even) against the classification of such a creation as an affront to beasts when it far more resembled that of a...monster.

In clearer terms, it appeared to be a reptile of sorts; much like the giant, dragon-like monitors found on tropical Indonesian islands, only ten times larger in size. Its eyes were red as blood, and its mouth lined with twin rows of nasty, sharp teeth. More unusual was its scaled hide, which looked to be more armor than flesh.

"What is it?" someone was heard to cry out.

There came no reply, but it was instantly clear who was responsible for unleashing it as the echoes of his pointed threat was recalled by all struggling for an answer: Samael.

Gotham was the first to jump into action and immediately rushed the creature, sword swinging. Taking aim, he attempted to end the creature then and there by burying his blade into the creature's side and discovered, instead, he would have better success trying to run his sword through a wall of rock. The monitor-like monster screeched in anger at the attempted assault and sent the angel flying with an effortless swipe of his clawed foot. Then, with another shriek, it revealed just how formidable it was against the sword by displaying a pleated frill that flared up around its neck and head revealing not only the same hard, armor-like scales covering the rest of its body, but the addition of nearly a dozen threatening spikes.

After witnessing the mighty Gotham getting batted aside like some pesky fly, the entirety of the other angels in the room descended in force upon the creature. Jacob watched in disbelief as the angels unleashed a fury of attacks at different target points and, when he saw them meeting the same futile result as Gotham had while desperately trying to evade the claws and teeth that swiped and snapped back in retaliation, he instinctively grabbed for his own sword. To his horror, he found the sheath hidden within his wing empty and felt a twinge of dread run through his veins remembering he had been forced to give up his tried and true weapon to Gotham for the duration of the proceedings before the Tribunal.

Before he had a chance to contemplate an alternative, Jacob heard a scream ring out from the other end of the room. He searched the calamity strewn about in front of him and soon saw it had come from Sandel. Having met the unfortunate blow by one of the clawed feet that left him stunned and sprawled out on his back like an unfortunate upturned turtle, Sandel attempted to slink away in retreat from the approaching monster. The other angels, led by Gotham and Anahel, swung into action to create a diversion but, as Jacob was quick to notice, the creature paid them and their useless weapons no mind and, instead, appeared to focus the entirety of its attention solely on the cowering Sandel.

While he despised Sandel as much as Sandel did him, Jacob couldn't bring himself to stand idly by and watch the creature have at the angel in a manner which, oddly enough, mirrored several of his recent daydreams. Forgetting the fact he was without sword, and ignoring the calls following after him from both Gotham as well as Max and Kairo, who had both drawn their weapons the moment the creature crawled out from the ground, Jacob raced through the rubble toward Sandel. In a flash, he maneuvered his way undetected past the frightful sight of the curled claws slowly tapping their way across the marble floor and, not a moment too soon, dove like a baseball player sliding into home plate the last ten or so feet to where the visibly panicked angel laid, jumped to his feet and launched two fireballs hastily conjured from his fingertips directly at the advancing lizard.

The monster let loose a roar of outrage, though Jacob wasn't sure if it was in response to the fiery projectiles that hit the beast's chest and promptly extinguished themselves, or the fact he had brazenly dared to come between the creature and its dinner.

"Bet you wish right about now you wouldn't have been so gung-ho on taking my sword away from me," Jacob couldn't help but quip over his shoulder to Sandel who looked none too amused.

Again, the monster roared, only this time much louder, and much closer, as it leaned in to give Jacob an up-close-and-personal-glimpse of its flesh-ripping teeth (not to mention a most unpleasant whiff of its rank breath that made death smell like a bouquet of roses). What Jacob took immediate notice of, however, was that in place of a long, slithering forked tongue one would expect to find on a lizard-like replicant such as the one looming before him, there was instead a rather lengthy tentacle.

Seven of them, to be precise.

And before he could make sense of what exactly he was seeing, one of the squid-like tentacles shot forward, wrapped itself tightly around his middle and snatched him off the ground. The sight of the boy being seized sparked a new round of desperate assaults from Gotham and the other angels. Even Max, whose feet were growing hotter with every second he stood on the sidelines, was ready to charge into the fray. But before he did, Kairo took hold of him by the shoulder and said, "I've got a better idea."

The "better idea," Kairo revealed, resided beneath the chairs where the two had earlier been sitting in the form of a biblical walking stick and three Scucca Urns concealed in a blanket and sack.

"You think it'll work?" Max, looking none too confident, inquired.

"Do you have any other options we haven't considered?" answered Kairo. "This thing is obviously Samael's doing to get back at Sandel and the rest of the Tribunal, just as he threatened. If it's true destroying these urns steals away his power, then maybe it can help stop this thing."

Without another word of argument, Max quickly set about to unwrap the staff while Kairo rifled through the sack for one of the urns. Yet just as Max was about to take a swing at one of the urn with the staff he grasped like a baseball bat, the creature suddenly swung its head around and leveled its angry red eyes on the two mischief-making Nephilim. At Kairo's frantic urging, Max finally swung the staff, and as he did, the monster followed suit with its massive tail, knocking Max clean off his feet in one direction and sending the walking stick sailing in another.

"Leave them be!" Jacob, still in the clutches of the slimy tentacle, hollered when the creature momentarily forgot about Sandel and turned on his two friends.

The creature ignored Jacob, along with the swarm of angels buzzing about with their swords, desperate to find a way to stop it. It advanced aggressively, first toward Kairo who managed to grab the Scucca Urn and scurry out of the way, and then Max who was oblivious to the approaching incubus as he frantically searched all about him for the staff. Watching with growing urgency while confined to the python-like coils of the tentacle squeezing him, Jacob managed to reach his way around his side to pluck free from one of his wings, a feather whose plumes, by design, were deceptively razor-sharp and extremely lethal.

Wielding the feather like a dagger, Jacob began slashing his way through the constricting tentacle. The creature seized up and screamed with pain while Jacob met his own throbbing discomfort when he finally hacked himself free and came to a hard landing upon the floor. After quickly wriggling his way free from the limp grasp of the amputated tentacle, he found himself, much to his displeasure, staring into the face of the monster whose moment of pain had transformed itself into a mask of pure and radiant rage. The creature opened wide its teeth-lined mouth and unleashed an ear-deafening shriek while displaying the remaining six tentacles that were its tongue, though not a one dared to take hold of the boy again.

Jacob attempted to calmly swallow down the bubble of distress that made its way up from the pit of his stomach as he prepared for his inevitable end. Much to his surprise, however, the creature turned away from him and, once again, set its inflamed sights on Max. It was then Jacob felt an almost intolerable feeling of impotence swell within him as he witnessed with utter helplessness Gotham and the other angels repeated failings to keep the giant lizard from creeping its way toward his friend. Just as suddenly, the paralysis gripping him gave way to a familiar incoming tide of uncontrollable rage. It flooded its way through every muscle and tissue in his body, revealing itself in brilliant, pulsating flashes of gold deep-set in the ire roiling the pools of his eyes.

He set off like a gazelle, vaulting and bounding his way along the same path of the creature while skillfully avoiding its large crushing, clawed feet. Then, with swift and nimble movements, Jacob scaled the behemoth reptile and landed on the bridge of the creature's nose which he promptly straddled. What he planned to do at that point he hadn't the faintest notion.

His only goal was to focus the creature's attention off his friends. Now he found himself staring into the massive red orbs of the surprised creature's eyes which narrowed themselves on him in a most unsettling way. Instantly, the lizard screeched and began to buck and sway in an effort to shake the boy off him. Jacob, struggling to keep from being thrown, tried to dig his fingers into the beast's hide which only caused the monster to thrash all the more violently. And the more Jacob's body was subjected to the painful jerking movements, the greater the rage welling its way through him became. He found himself wishing for bigger hands to crush the skull in his grasp as his desire to drain every bit of life from the creature became almost all-consuming.

It was then Jacob noticed something familiar, and yet entirely different at the same time. The veins leading from his hands to his arms began to reveal themselves through his skin like dark ribbons. It was the same sort of manifestation he had become used to whenever he employed the use of the one Grace which made him solely unique amongst Nephilim: the Grace of life. Only this time there was something very unusual happening: the blackness coloring his veins, he noticed, looked to be flowing outward instead of inward and seeping from his fingertips before spreading its stain slowly across the armor-like skin of the giant monitor.

In an instant, the creature began to pitch and flail much more vigorously than before, as the blackness gradually spread across its body like a dark shroud. The last thing to darken was the monsters eyes and, when they finally went cold, the flesh and blood nightmare grew strangely still before ultimately toppling over into a lifeless heap upon the floor.

~ ~ ~

"What did you do to it?" Kairo asked Jacob after a quiet moment, as he stood along with everyone else staring at the now-dead creature.

"Nothing...that is...I don't know," answered Jacob whose attention, unlike the others, was fixed intently on his hands which he slowly rotated before his rapt eyes. "I was desperate to find a way to stop it from attacking you. I wanted it dead. Then suddenly, my hands...it was like what happened the day after Azrael visited Eden and I was able to bring The River back to life again...

"Only different," he added quietly, almost fearfully.

Anahel traded an uneasy look with Gotham and went in to take a closer look at the creature.

"What the heck was that thing anyway?" Max asked no one in particular.

"My guess would be a Hybrid," answered Anahel.

"A what?" said Jacob.

"A Hybrid," echoed Gotham. "You've encountered one before the night I discovered you in the Silent Forest when you severed one of Lilith's arms. Do you remember?"

How could I forget? Jacob thought to himself. "The arm...it turned into some kind of monstrous snake or something and tried to attack me."

"That's what's known as a Hybrid," said Gotham. "It's an unusual ability unique to those who make up the Darkness that allows them to manifest themselves into separate creations–almost always monstrous–using snippets of their physical beings as simple as a strand of hair, clipping of a nail or, as in Lilith's case, an arm."

"Knowing Samael," Anahel interjected, even as he continued to appear wholly absorbed in examining the dead carcass laid out before him, "I would speculate he wilily left a part of himself behind during that initial visit he made to Halcyon to initiate his custodial claim with the Tribunal–perhaps something as discreet as a drop or two of blood to hedge his bets on the probability of never being allowed to set foot in Eden again."

"We're all quite lucky, especially you, Sandel," Arafiel remarked to the white angel who remained worse for wear since the attack. "No doubt you owe young Jacob Parrish a word of gratitude. After all, if it hadn't been for his commendable display of bravery, Samael most assuredly would have succeeded in making good on his threat."

A look closely resembling that of horror-filled swept over Sandel at Arafiel's suggestion. But as all eyes shifted to the battered angel looking significantly less intimidating as he stood in his disheveled state quietly nursing his wounds, Sandel realized he had been boxed into a most unfortunate corner.

"Thank you," he managed to mumble in a voice barely audible. "I'm...indebted."

It was as if the angel had been forced to bite into a particularly sour lemon in uttering two simple words, and Jacob couldn't help but savor the enjoyment of witnessing what was certainly the most intolerable moment in Sandel's long and esteemed existence.

"I would argue Samael is entitled to a helping of thanks himself, especially from the members of this Tribunal," Anahel, finally turning his intensely focused attention away from the fallen creature, added.

"Samael? You must be joking!" balked Arafiel.

"To the contrary. By unleashing this terror on Halcyon, Samael has done all of us present here the favor of solving once and for all the contested notion of whether or not Jacob Parrish is, indeed, the Light Bearer. And he has done so in a way that was witnessed in the presence of the Iudicium Tribunal," explained Anahel.

"Light Bearer?" The mere mention of the name–particularly in connection with the boy–brought a pulse of life from the subdued Sandel. "In what way do you mean to suggest the issue has been solved?"

"Much has been quarreled about in this very room in regards to the evidence pointing to Mr. Parrish as being the Light Bearer foretold in the Apocryphal prophesies. The crux of that evidence has hinged itself on a single contention: does the boy, in fact, possess the singular, indubitable faculty imperative to authenticate such a claim which, as we all know, is the one power reserved to angels and angels alone; the power to heal. However, I submit to you now, new evidence, perhaps even more compelling, that I've no doubt will finally lay the matter to rest," Anahel said confidently.

Seeing he had everyone's undivided attention, Anahel continued: "The power to heal is indeed an extraordinary thing. It is not just a gift relegated to the mending of broken bones or curing illnesses, but rather a staggering, and dare I say, schizophrenic ability to hold the bloom of life itself in the palm of one's own hand. For let us not forget, as it is quite easy to do, that with the power to direct life with the touch of a hand we also hold the ability to navigate something of arguably equal weight with the other: Death."

The word "death" brought a stark look to the faces of all who were listening to the angel, including Gotham who himself was oblivious to where Anahel was leading with his argument.

"Azrael is a perfect example of what I speak. He carries out his duties, morbid and unpleasant as they may be, armed with the same power as the rest of us. Though because he operates on the dark side of the moon as opposed to the rest of us in the light, we sometimes mistakenly infer he possesses some insidious power. In fact, he works his healing Grace no differently than the rest of us, but with the opposite hand so to speak. But make no mistake, by guiding souls from their mortal coil into the afterlife he, like the rest of us, is mending the same broken bones and curing the same illnesses," said Anahel.

"Do you not finally see? The answer lies in the monstrous heap right before your very eyes," he then stressed to those who were listening raptly to his every word. "When Mr. Parrish here sent this creature to its eternal sleep, just as he did when he awakened The River from death's grasp, he removed all doubt regarding who he is. You yourself, Sandel, quoted the Apocrypha in question at the start of this inquest: 'He will draw into his very veins every affliction; his right hand will carry the lantern radiating the flame of Life, and his left the scythe of Death.' What more, I ask you, do you need to convince you the Light Bearer stands in your very presence?"

"And what proof, exactly, do you have the boy is responsible for bringing down this beast?" Sandel was quick to argue. "I certainly didn't witness it!"

"Perhaps your view of events was somewhat obscured while you were cowering on the floor," Gotham suggested dryly.

"Then I ask you: who is responsible for the creature's demise?" Anahel argued while pacing about his fellow angels. "Did one of you unbeknownst the rest of us prove victorious in discovering a soft spot in the armored hull of the beast with your sword? For I all but shattered my own blade attempting with all the strength I possessed, to hack what proved to be unhackable.

"Or perhaps," he continued in a more subdued yet equally firm tone as he came to stand beside Max and Kairo, "the beast's death was the result of two crafty Nephilim armed with a walking stick and certain restricted accoutrements of which will most certainly be addressed at a later time."

Both boys, realizing their ploy had been observed by Anahel in the midst of the chaos, smiled nervously in reply.

"What I can say for certain is that which I observed with my own eyes: Mr. Parrish bravely astride the creature's snout and slowly draining it of its ferocious and malignant life until the fire in its eyes went out," continued Anahel. "Is it not possible for the rest of you to cast free from your minds whatever perceptions or prejudices you may find yourself continuing to hold about the boy due to the simple unfortunate fact of his parentage?"

Anahel saw his words were being carefully considered, but it still wasn't enough for him. "Or perhaps, yet," he was quick to suggest for added incentive, "you would like Mr. Parrish to demonstrate yet another test of his abilities by bringing this Hybrid back to life."

Sandel moved to speak, but Arafiel abruptly silenced him before he was able to utter a single word in retort with a simple gesture of his hand.

"I don't think that will be necessary, Anahel."

The head of the Tribunal then looked to Jacob who couldn't tell one way or the other through the expression fixed on him whether Anahel had managed to finally prove his case.

"I believe we have heard all there is to say on this matter."

CHAPTER TWENTY-ONE

HARMONY

It felt to Jacob like déjà vu when, later that same evening, he was greeted with a celebratory roar from all the other Nephilim boys who had gathered together in the Hall of Light in a show of cheer for the surprising news which had obviously beat his return to Havenhid.

And yet, unlike the festivities marking his original Blessing months earlier, the impromptu celebration was a notably more low-key affair, though just as cheerful, perhaps even more so. For this time around, with the Iudicium Tribunal finally making the official declaration that Jacob Parrish had, indeed, proven himself without question to be the Light Bearer foretold, there was no chance of a repeat occurrence of Sandel storming the party and deflating the merriment as he so memorably did during Jacob's Blessing.

Much as he was delighted not only in having the contested matter of whether he was or was not the Light Bearer finally laid to rest, as well as experience for the first time the freeing feeling that he was no longer some imposter everyone around him couldn't help but glance at sideways every now and then, the real celebration, at least for Jacob, was knowing he would wake up in the morning at Havenhid surrounded by his friends and the Guides he considered to be his family. Not a family dictated by blood, like Samael, but one designed by love.

And as he stood in the center of the great Hall basking in the warmth of the good spirits filling the room, he retreated inwardly momentarily for the first time since the Tribunal delivered him from Samael's grasp and, looking upward to where the vaulted ceiling remained folded back to reveal a twilight sky colored in brilliant streaks of golds and reds by the setting sun, he thought of his mother and uttered a quiet and simple, "Thank you!"

~ ~ ~

"If I may have everyone's attention."

The familiar tenor of Anahel's voice was suddenly heard to fill the vast expanse of the Hall, bringing with it a hushed silence as all eyes focused themselves in his direction.

"It would seem good news has a way making the rounds in quick order through these hallowed halls," said Anahel who like Jacob and Gotham was surprised by the reception that greeted them upon their return from Halcyon. "And what good news it is. Only a few months ago we found ourselves gathered together under similar circumstances to celebrate the Blessing of young Mr. Parrish. But, as most of you will experience in one form or another in your lives, sometimes credence requires quite literally the assistance of a leviathan to crawl out from the depths to sway the most hardened of believers, even those of us who reside in divine light. How proud I am, then, to be able to stand here before you and say unequivocally that from this moment forward all speculation and reservation surrounding your classmate is no more. For I would at this time like to make formal the announcement of which you undoubtedly are already aware, and that is the Iudicium Tribunal has made it known in its ruling that Jacob Parrish has, in fact, proved himself to be without a shadow of doubt the Light Bearer."

Jacob couldn't help but beam when the declaration ignited a roar of boosterish cheers from his fellow classmates; all, that is, except for Creed and his cohorts Ivan and Vance who Jacob spied through the sea of hands giving his hair a friendly tousling standing off to the side away from the gathering with arms folded looking like a trio of Gloomy Guses.

"And just for the record, I would like to make mention that I never for a moment doubted that you had been chosen to serve in such a noble and most important role," Anahel added with a reassuring smile.

"Likewise, I believe the record reflects clearly the fact I doubted you plenty, as you well know," Eksel who was standing nearby chimed in while giving Jacob a playful poke. "I was certain you were a bad seed planted in this garden by the hand of the Underneath itself. It just goes to show you how ignorant even an angel can sometimes be."

"It's okay, Eksel. There were more times than not I'm sure I had more doubts about myself than everyone here put together," said Jacob.

"No doubt, the past few weeks proved themselves to be difficult, but the manner in which you have managed to navigate these recent choppy waters has been commendable," said Anahel. "And dare I say an exemplar of someone so anointed as yourself."

Not accustomed to being on the receiving end of such complimentary words, especially after being the mark of several character attacks during the course of the hearing, Jacob felt his face flush slightly when a familiar voice spoke up suddenly.

"If you are through with all of your fawning, there is something I'd like to say to the Light Bearer, if you wouldn't mind."

Jacob and the rest of room turned to find Gotham, who had inconspicuously ducked out of the festivities earlier, patiently standing with his hands casually folded behind his back.

"To start, there is something I have been eager to rid myself of since the day it returned to my life and has since served as a nuisance I find myself regularly tripping over in my chamber," said Gotham, before bringing into view the majestic sight of the Sword of Destiny he had concealed behind him. "I believe this belongs to you, and I would very much like to return it to the hands in which it belongs."

Then, pausing a moment, his gaze shifted from the boy to settle themselves on Leos standing just off to the side who instantly felt his blood run cold. "And I'd most certainly like to do it of my own sound and sober mind, if there be no objections," Gotham noted cooly, before shooting an impish wink at Leos who, since taking part in the Great Sword Caper had avoided the angel (and his wrath) at all costs, smiled with relief that absolution appeared to finally be at hand.

In the past, whenever Jacob took the fabled sword into his hand, it carried with it a weight of power that was more onerous than confidence-building; as though he were being wielded by the weapon rather than the other way around. Now, strangely, the Sword of Destiny felt noticeably different in his grip. No longer did it feel like a power struggle between flesh and steel, but a sort of mutual shaking of hands.

"There's one other thing," a noticeable enough apprehensive timbre sounded in Gotham's voice to shift Jacob's attention from his sword. "It's no secret that when your grandmother managed to persuade me, in that way of hers, to take you under my wing, both figuratively and literally, and bring you to Havenhid, I was less than pleased, to put it nicely. In that time, you've proven yourself to be exacerbating, obstinate, willful and an all-around pain in the...halo."

For a moment, it seemed to Jacob the good vibrations of his party was about to pop like a burst balloon.

"That said, if there's one thing these past couple weeks have clearly proven is how much you've come to mean to everyone gathered in this Hall. And more importantly, how much you've come to mean to me," Gotham, who was by no means a disciple of sentimentality, noted with a glistening of emotion in his eyes. "I don't know what I would have done had the Tribunal ruled differently today and placed you into the charge of Samael. I do know I never want to face such a trying ordeal again. And it's why I stayed behind after you and Anahel departed Halcyon with Max and Kairo, to speak with Arafiel and, well...here."

In an awkward fumbling about, Gotham retrieved an envelope from a fold in his shirt and handed it to Jacob. The first thing Jacob noticed was the seal on the envelope–the seal of the Iudicium Tribunal–which was identical to the summons delivered to his bedroom window by a Gyrfalcon months earlier in Cain's Corner. Refraining from asking the obvious question, Jacob proceeded somewhat nervously to unseal the envelope and open the document enclosed inside which, not surprisingly, was written in Celestial. He had only read the first few lines when his expression collapsed, and he looked to Gotham once more as though a phantom had reached out from the confines of the document and delivered a stinging slap across his face.

"Is this true?" he finally asked.

"Crikey Moses! Enough with the cloak-and-dagger stuff. What's it say already?" Max, not waiting for an answer, pressed impatiently.

When Jacob remained frozen where he stood like a deer in headlights, Gotham gave the boy an encouraging nod.

"Whereas, a unanimous decision was declared by this court to deny a petition brought before this court by Samael to assert his God-given parental authority over his son, Jacob Samson Parrish; and whereas, this court recognizes the vital importance of a father's role in the shaping of a child into manhood, least of all a Nephilim child," Jacob began reading in a soft voice, "it is hereby ordered, adjudged and decreed by the authority appointed to the Iudicium Tribunal that, after submitting his own heartfelt appeal to the effect of Jacob Parrish's future well-being, Gothamel shall be granted sole and permanent custodianship of said minor."

The room grew noticeably hushed, and for the first time those present in the Hall, including both Anahel and Eksel, were greeted by something far more rare than witnessing all nine planets in the universe aligning themselves in a perfect line: Gotham betraying a hint of trepidation.

"I don't know what to say," Jacob, visibly overtaken by what was certainly an unexpected declaration, uttered quietly.

"You can say no," Gotham replied. "That is, the Tribunal issued the decision with the stipulation that it meets with your approval."

Jacob finally lifted his teary eyes from the document to look at Gotham, and the angel, certain the boy was about to exercise the escape clause granted him, steadied himself for the incoming arrow.

"I hate to be the bearer of bad news," said Jacob, "but there's no way I'm going to let you get out of it that easy–especially after that obstinate crack!"

It took a moment for Gotham to register the toothy grin aimed his way to realize his legal gesture had not only been accepted, but enthusiastically embraced. And for all who looked on, it was difficult to determine who was more elated by the news: the boy or the angel.

~ ~ ~

Few things would have proven capable of stealing Jacob's smile during such a joyous moment; one being the sudden appearance of Damiel entering the Hall through its grand doors with Hunter at his side, both looking just slightly better than death warmed over.

"Where in blazes have the two of you been?" Anahel inquired gruffly. "I was this close to assembling a search party to uncover your whereabouts."

"It's a rather involved story I'd sooner discuss at a later time, if it's all the same to you," Damiel replied with a weary sigh. "It appears we've arrived in the middle of a celebration of sorts. Anyone care to enlighten me on the occasion?"

"I'm not a hundred percent sure, but I think Gotham just adopted Jacob," said Ethan.

Damiel immediately looked to Gotham for clarity.

"To make a long story short, the Tribunal decided today to finally recognize Jacob as Light Bearer," explained Gotham.

"Well...we knew eventually they would come to their senses. After all, the truth is undeniable when it makes itself visible to all who wish to see it," said Damiel.

"Better still, the custodial matter concerning Samael and Jacob has been settled," said Gotham. "The Iudicium Tribunal decided against Samael's petition."

Gotham knew the effect hearing such words would have on Damiel. Sure enough, it took all the strength Damiel had within him to keep concealed the onslaught of emotion that seized hold of him in that instant, as the anvil of intense guilt he had carried since learning of Samael's action tore itself free of his soul and gave way to an overpowering flood of solace.

"That is good news, indeed," Damiel remarked hoarsely while focusing his gaze firmly on Jacob as he struggled to stifle as best he could the visible quivering of his bottom lip. "I can't begin to consider how I might possibly continue to go on had the decision gone the other way. To think I was responsible for having placed you in such a precarious situation–intentions be damned–is something I'm not sure I'll ever resolve within my soul. I just hope, if I may dare say, that you can one day forgive me for my misdeed. Even if I am unable to forgive myself."

Never before had Jacob witnessed Damiel–the epitome of strength, both inner and outer, and fortitude–to be so chastened. It stirred the boy all the more to know such self-condemnation was so thoroughly watered by the angel's undeniable love for him, even if the anger he had been adamant to hold onto made him appear mulish.

"Well, then..." Damiel, looking suddenly uncomfortable, muttered, "I will leave you to your well-deserved celebration."

As the angel turned to leave the Hall and retire to the seclusion of his chamber, Jacob, unable to sequester himself any further in the bubble of his intransigency, called out to him.

"I was hoping you might stick around and join the party," Jacob said with an awkwardness only a lingering case of petulance could cause.

The invitation caught Damiel off guard.

"Did I hear you right? You want me stay?" asked the angel.

"That, and I was hoping, maybe, with the hearing over and all, you might be willing to take me on as a student again at Lions Bite...seeing as I'm officially the Light Bearer and all," Jacob suggested somewhat meekly.

For the first time in a long while, the makings of a smile made itself visible on Damiel's face.

"I've been known to take on the stray charity case now and then, if you twist my arm just right," the angel replied.

When finally the two made official their suspension of hostilities and the mending of their once tight bond with a surrendering hug, Jacob couldn't help but shoot a smug little grin to Gotham and make his voice heard inside the angel's head saying, *"I think this proves just how obstinate I am not."*

Just then, as if the gathering inside the Hall of Light couldn't become even more merriment-filled, Zuriel, who had been noticeably absent from the festivities, suddenly appeared, and he was not alone. To the surprise of everyone, most notably Hunter, Predmore was awake and walking around, albeit in a garishly colored set of pajamas, for the first time since he lapsed into unconsciousness after taking a bullet in the shape of a poisonous spore aimed at Hunter by a deadly flower inside The Crucible. No one was more elated than Hunter, who had spent untold hours at Predmore's bedside since the accident, to see the boy finally up and around. He made a mad dash for Predmore, with the rest of Nephilim following at his heels, and snatching the boy up in his arms he spun him around surrounded by a chorus of gleeful cheers.

As Jacob stood watching, joining in the laughter, he couldn't imagine the possibility of another day filled with so much happiness. And he found himself quietly wishing that there existed a Grace which would allow him to preserve that day where he could live for all eternity. It was while he was enraptured in such a wonderful daydream that he turned to look at Gotham standing some ways away from him. The angel was beaming with good spirits just as much as he was; so much so that Jacob couldn't help but take notice of the stark contrast between the blithe Gotham now standing before him and the grim, humorless Gotham who first introduced himself to the boy one afternoon inside a high school gymnasium.

Then, as if the angel had honed in on the boy's silent contemplation of his transfiguration, the smile upon his face faded from sight. Even more so, it was obliterated. As if he had been struck by some unseen phantom of pain, Gotham became, in an instant, a reflection of great distress and even greater sorrow. He wavered for a moment on his feet, like a fighter who had just taken a blinding blow to the head, before, finally, and with great reluctance, he turned his gaze to Jacob which burned with an undisclosed doom.

Jacob opened his mouth to inquire what was wrong, but before he could voice a single syllable a sharp but very familiar pain exploded in his side. It stole his breath and left him staggering upon his feet. He had come to know well this pain; rather, the pain had made itself intimately known to him. He likened it to the ringing of a bell or the herald of a trumpet blast that made itself heard whenever danger or a darkness was about to make itself known in his life. Only this time the pain was much sharper, and much, much more intense; so much so that it brought him down to a knee on the floor.

Desperately, he grappled for the one and only thing with the power to reveal the source of his suffering: the Sword of Destiny.

Sure enough, the blade of his sword was alive with visions, and a draw of blood emerged from the tip and spilled its way slowly across the gleaming steel. He struggled to focus his eyes on the images within the blade, and to his horror he saw they were of his grandmother. She was lying on the floor inside her home with a bouquet of flowers scattered all around her.

Jacob looked to Gotham with panic in his eyes, and he realized by the expression staring back at him that the angel had come to see the same vision.

And it was then the celebration came to an abrupt end.

CHAPTER TWENTY-TWO

THE FINAL BOW

It wasn't long after that Jacob and Gotham touched down in Cain's Corner like two overgrown hawks in the full light of what was otherwise a beautiful, sun-filled afternoon (and surprisingly avoiding detection from the Harris' seventeen-year-old son two doors down who was in the driveway washing his car, as well as Mr. Talpert from across the street who was out mowing his lawn). Without so much as a pause for breath following the labored trek at record speed across half the world's skies, Jacob raced inside the house through the front door and bolted up the stairs where he happened to run straight into Dr. William Graham, his grandmother's longtime physician, who was on his way down the staircase at that precise moment.

"Careful, young man, or I'll be needing a doctor myself," the gray-haired but spry doctor said with a good-natured chuckle when, upon a closer look, he came to recognize the boy as Jacob. "Well, this is a surprise! Your grandmother had informed me you were away at school."

"Yes, sir. I rushed home as soon as I heard she wasn't well," said Jacob. And before the good doctor could start drilling him on whatever phony school his grandmother had conjured up during their gab session, Jacob quickly asked, "How is she?"

The doctor's expression grew suddenly serious, lending little if any comfort to the boy.

"Not too good, I'm afraid," Dr. Graham noted soberly while removing from his nose a pair of old-fashion-looking spectacles which he proceeded to clean. "She doesn't appear to be in any pain, but it is as though life is slowly draining from her body. Thankfully, Ms. Buford came by for a visit when she did and discovered your grandmother on the floor in the sitting room. Apparently, she had just up and fainted while in the middle of creating a floral arrangement with some roses and other flowers she had earlier picked in her garden."

"What's wrong with her?" asked Gotham, who by then had caught up to Jacob on the stairs, drawing a suspicious look from the doctor.

"And you are?" Dr. Graham inquired.

Gotham paused a moment to consider his answer before replying, "A friend of the family."

Dr. Graham's curious gaze narrowed itself on the tall, long-haired stranger with golden eyes.

"Didn't I see you...?" the doctor began as he was reminded of an old black-and-white photograph he had once spied displayed in the downstairs sitting room of Ava Delacroux some seventy years earlier standing beside a young, fair-haired child, and a man remarkably similar in looks to the stranger before him. But looking all the harder at Gotham, the doctor quickly shook such thoughts of nonsense from out of his head with a dismissive, "Never mind...it's impossible!"

Then returning his focus to the question at hand, he said, "If you want my professional diagnosis, I would say what is ailing your grandmother is, simply put, the unavoidable cycle of life. I know it's a difficult thing some find to face, but the undeniable truth of the matter is Ava Delacroux is a woman of–"

He was quick to catch his tongue, knowing Ava would be none too happy to discover her age being batted around in such conversation.

"Well, let's just say she is a woman of a certain age," he offered more diplomatically, "and that age, at some point, catches up to a person, even someone as vibrant as your grandmother. After giving her a thorough examination, I haven't been able to find anything else that could be playing to her condition."

It wasn't exactly the answer Jacob was hoping for.

"The best thing you can do for her, at this point, is make sure she gets plenty of rest. See to it she remains in bed which, as both you and I know, will be a task in and of itself," Dr. Graham said, while giving the boy a reassuring squeeze of his shoulder. "Ms. Buford is up with her now in her room looking after her. I was just on my way to have a prescription filled for her. I'll be back a little bit later to look in on her and see how she's doing."

The doctor, understandably, was left to see himself out as Jacob tore up the remainder of the staircase and down the hall where he nearly had himself another collision, this time with Ms. Buford who was quietly exiting Ava's bedroom, and made a desperate gesture to Jacob and Gotham to maintain the silence. After offering Jacob a pleasant if not abbreviated greeting, Ms. Buford relented to Jacob poking his head inside and having a short visit with his grandmother (as if she had the slightest chance of stopping him) as long as he was quiet.

"If you need me, I'll be downstairs in the kitchen preparing her some tea and persimmon cookies she asked for," she said before giving Gotham the same curious look Dr. Graham had earlier as she slowly made her way to the stairs as Jacob and his large, familiar-looking, golden-eyed friend tip-toed into the room.

~ ~ ~

Despite the afternoon hour, the inside of the bedroom was dark, with only a couple shafts of daylight slipping past the drawn drapes. Ava, who was peacefully at rest in her bed, immediately opened her eyes at the sound of footsteps, and while she was surprised to see Jacob in her sights, she was even more so to discover Gotham shadowing behind the boy.

"What in the dickens are you doing here?" she asked as she struggled to sit up.

Jacob rushed to her and sat on the bed beside her to make sure she remained where she was.

"We heard you weren't well," said Jacob. "I was worried. I wanted to make sure you were alright."

It was abundantly clear, however, that Ava wasn't alright; not by a long shot. She looked drawn and her complexion sallow. Her usually impeccably coifed hair was limp and lifeless. More noticeable, still, was how weak she looked. And while Ava's small, petite stature which made her appear somewhat frail to the eye had always before been bulked up by an indisputable inner strength which radiated outward from somewhere within her core, the familiar glow of spirit was but a flicker.

"Phooey!" Ava spat defiantly. "It's just some seasonal virus I picked up. I'll be back to new and on my feet before you know it."

Jacob didn't hold nearly as much confidence in his grandmother's self-diagnosis. In fact, as he sat on the bed staring into her eyes, he felt as if somehow by accident he had inadvertently used one of his Graces to step back into a particularly dreadful moment in time he would fight with his dying breath to avoid ever revisiting. For it wasn't all that long ago he sat on the edge of another bed, in another room in the same house, staring into another pair of sickly eyes: his mother's.

Then, he had naively chosen to believe his mother's assurances of a recovery that never came, even as her beauty had been replaced with a mask of death. And when he awoke one morning to discover he had been conned into believing in the arrival of a miracle, he was then denied the opportunity to take matters literally into his own life-giving hands, something he had never found within himself to forgive. And it was the bitter recollection of that horrible, unforgettable day that stirred Jacob to place his hands upon his grandmother not just to save her from whatever ailed her, but to save himself from the unavoidable heartbreak that would surely accompany the shade of Azrael's approaching shadow.

Ava, recognizing the gesture, lifted Jacob's hands which were already revealing their healing veins off her and stated in a firm unequivocal voice, "No!"

"What do you mean no?" Jacob, looking confused, balked. "I can save you."

"It's not for you to come between me and the destiny God has set in place for me," argued Ava.

"Not up to me to... What, you're okay with just dying?"

"Who, may I ask, has already fitted me for a coffin?" asked Ava. "And even if it were, as they say, my time, you and I both know the day would eventually visit us."

"I can't believe how casual you are about this," Jacob, looking at his grandmother as if she had sprouted a third eyeball, said. "You're all I have left. You can't leave me. You just can't!"

Ave paused her tongue as a softness of understanding came over her.

"My dear Jacob, I have been here to help nurture and raise you in this very house since the day you first pushed your way out into the world," she said in the quiet, comforting way only a grandmother could speak. "I was there when you took your first step. I watched you build your first tree fort. I sat in the first row beside your mother when you performed as Elvis Presley in the fourth grade talent show."

"Ugh...please, don't remind me," Jacob groaned while wincing at the memory.

"What I am trying to say is I have helped guide you as far as I can along the path that has been your life so far," said Ava.

"But I still need you," argued Jacob, to which Ava replied with a sympathetic yet firm shake of her head.

"You needed me to help keep you safe and shape you into the young man sitting in front of me now, and I have done so," she said. "What you need now is for someone equipped with the tools I most certainly lack to mold you into the Nephilim you are just discovering yourself to be; someone like Gotham."

Until the mention of his name, Jacob had momentarily forgotten about the angel who he looked to find quietly standing in the center of the bedroom staring at the ceiling with a hint of revulsion caused by a noxious scent undetectable to normal noses fixed on his face. The revulsion slowly graduated to a burn of anger as his penetrating gaze shifted to a nearby dresser and, more specifically, the bouquet of flowers arranged in a crystal vase atop it.

"If that's how you feel, you'll be pleased to know the Iudicium Tribunal decided, just today in fact, to deny Samael's attempt to take custody of me," said Jacob. "Even better, they made Gotham my permanent guardian."

The news brought a quiver to Ava's lip. Yes, I know," she replied.

"You did? But how?" questioned Jacob.

"I was recently visited by an adorable finch who told me all the details. As well, it also conveyed to me Gotham's intentions concerning you and sought forth my approval," said Ava. She then looked to Gotham who now stood in front of the dresser staring intently at the arrangement of flowers in front of him and added, "Which I most happily gave."

~ ~ ~

"Would you mind leaving us and going downstairs to lend Ms. Buford a hand with the tea?" Gotham suddenly asked Jacob.

There was a quiet yet unmistakably ominous tone in Gotham's request that caught Jacob's ear.

"Yeah...sure," the boy replied to the angel whose back was turned to him, preventing him from better gauging what felt to be an abrupt–tangible, even–change in mood. Getting up from the bed, he made his way to the door where he paused to ask, "Is anything the matter?"

"I would just like a private moment to speak with your grandmother," Gotham answered, only this time with a growing impatience.

Jacob knew better than to argue the point and quietly slunk out of the room, closing the door behind him.

"That was a bit curt," Ava chastised Gotham once they were alone. "What is it that's bothering you?"

She had no sooner asked the question when the drawn curtains suddenly parted of their own accord. Likewise, at the precise same moment, the window flung itself open. Gotham grabbed the vase from off the dresser and spun around. His eyes, ablaze in radiant gold, fixed themselves on the colorful spray which proceeded to wither into a dry and dead bouquet before instantly bursting into flames, causing Ava to yelp with fright.

"Shield your eyes!" Gotham barked.

Ava was about to comply with Gotham's order when she happened to take notice of a translucent auroral haze of green suddenly illuminated by the abrupt intrusion of sunlight floating overhead. Gotham raised the vase of flaming flowers to the mysterious light as though he were brandishing a lit torch to ward off an encroaching bear, causing the mysterious green haze to glow all the more prominently in the presence of the fire. With her eyes wide with fright, Ava once more let out a shriek when a large blinding fireball, similar to a lit match coming in contact with a plume of propane, suddenly and unexpectedly erupted across the ceiling, and the green haze was no more.

"When was she here?" Gotham asked once he disposed of the vase and its burning contents by hurling it through the open window before turning his fiery gaze onto Ava who remained in bed looking appropriately terrified at what she just witnessed.

"Of whom are you speaking?" she asked while her eyes remained fixed on the ceiling.

"Does her name honestly demand mention after what just happened?" Gotham replied testily. "I'm speaking of Lilith."

The utterance of the name managed to pull Ava's gaze downward.

"She showed up not even a week ago," Ava admitted, "while I was outside working in the garden."

Gotham, growing even more agitated, wrestled with himself to keep his anger contained.

"And where, may I ask, was Yairel in all of this?" the angel asked, before immediately stomping over Ava's attempt to answer him. "Here I task him as sentry to watch over you, and unbelievably, he allows the Mistress of Death, of all people, to walk up on you unhindered. I will have his head for this!"

Ava, who had long-ago become familiar with Gotham's occasional bouts with pique, remained unflustered in light of his latest tantrum.

"Before you go lopping off heads, you should know the facts. Fact one is Yairel positioned himself between Lilith and her shadow before either of us were aware of his presence. Fact two is he was more than prepared to consecrate a plot of my garden to serve as her final resting place," explained Ava before adding with a tad bit more caution, "And fact three, if you must know, is that it was I who ordered Yairel to stand down and allowed Lilith to come inside for the private conversation she wished to have with me."

Gotham was visibly taken aback by the revelation.

"You...invited her into this house?" he asked with disbelief.

Before Gotham could erupt into a renewed tirade which, by the conflagration reigniting within the eyes leveled upon her, looked imminent, Ava confessed it was the pull of intrigue which led her to open the door to her home to the woman with whom she long had an undeclared rivalry and often wondered about, and she believed Lilith's unannounced visit was guided, at least in part, by the same curiosity. And while Ava was open in recounting the conversation the two women had while sitting across from each other in the sitting room separated by a phantom sheet of glacial ice, she was mindful to omit certain broached topics the angel would likely find barbed–most notably the mention of the deaths of Damira and Gotham's first son.

"She wanted me to talk Jacob into coming home to Cain's Corner. Permanently," Ava suddenly blurted out for fear Gotham would spy her suppressed thoughts regarding Damira and her son. "She wanted me to talk him into giving up the Sword of Destiny."

Gotham's response was not exactly what Ava expected: he let out a laugh.

"What in God's green earth would ever make her think you'd agree to such a thing?" He asked.

Ava was hesitant at first to answer. "She tried to convince me it was in my best interest, and Jacob's. She said anyone who stood in the middle of the fight between you and Samael would have no hope of surviving," she said finally. "Mind you, this was during the hearing when Samael was trying to gain custody of Jacob. She said you'd never relinquish someone–especially one with the power of the Light Bearer–to Samael. She told me you'd end them if it ever came down to such a matter, and she cited David as her proof."

Again, Ava braced herself for an outburst she was certain would come. Instead, the room became silent as a crypt, and Gotham grew colder than any corpse housed in marble.

"And did you believe her?" he asked in a voice barely audible.

"The fact Jacob is still in your care–in more ways than one I might add– should provide a sufficient answer to your question."

Ava couldn't help but take pity on the angel, even as she scolded him. As she heard her own response to him, however, her attention suddenly turned upward once more to the ceiling.

"That's what that little spectacle was all about, wasn't it? Punishment for not going along," Ava said before her disposition darkened. "And I take it I was more than a little presumptuous to think the last few days of feeling under the weather was the result of some passing virus, huh?"

Gotham remained stoney-faced and said nothing in reply. Not that he needed to say a word; a faint glistening of tears had all but doused completely the golden glint of ire smoldering in the cauldrons that were his irises. And for one passing moment, Ava was loathed to appreciate the angel's unwavering penchant for candor.

"My...I must look a fright," she said suddenly, wishing to change the subject to something far more brighter and avoid Gotham's gaze all at the same time. "I wish you would have warned me you were coming so I could have at least tried to make myself somewhat more presentable."

While Ava attempted to busy herself by fiddling with her hair, Gotham came and sat on the edge of the bed beside her.

"You know you exist only as a vision of beauty in my eyes," Gotham remarked as he looked upon her lovingly.

Ava couldn't keep from blushing, though not from flattery.

"How gauche you must find me," she noted with disdain, "an old woman concerned about her own vanity at a time like this."

Gotham, though, knew vanity was the one thing furthest from Ava's mind.

"Let me fix this, Ava," Gotham implored softly, then promptly placed a finger on the old woman's lips when it looked as if she were to reject his proposal. "I understood the reason you gave the boy when he pleaded with you to allow him to make you well, and I commend the reverence you hold to the one who made you. But this isn't the destiny into which you were born; it's one that's been tainted by a benevolent force."

Ava sat quietly, and for a moment Gotham wondered if she was even listening to him.

"When Lilith was here, she brought to light a pivotal moment in my life that, strangely enough, I had not given much thought to since it occurred," Ava said when finally she spoke. "Lilith said she was present in the audience the night I first performed in 'Samson et Dalila.' Do you remember the performance?"

The mention of the opera brought the curl of a smile to Gotham.

"How can I forget? It was winter, 1952, The Royal Opera House in London," he said. "Somehow you managed to cajole a once-great angel onto a stage to perform like an organ grinder's monkey before a bunch of elite mortals."

"A monkey with a voice only Heaven could have created," said Ava with a playful smile. "I was sure you'd win the audience over, but you proved me wrong. You captivated them."

"You give me far more credit than I am due," Gotham noted humbly. "You forget I was not alone on that stage."

"No, I haven't forgotten," Ava remarked softly. "I've lost count of the number of times I've performed as Delilah. That performance, though, remains the one I remember in crystal-clear detail, and the one I hold dearest to my heart. Especially when I sang 'Mon coeur s'ouvre à ta voix'— 'My heart opens up to your voice.' Of all the Samsons I've played opposite, never before, or after, have I performed the song with such conviction."

As she spoke, Ava appeared to slowly retreat from herself and drift off into the protected confines of the long-ago memory which had unfolded itself like the pedals of a flower in bloom.

"I fell in love with you instantly that night," she said.

Gotham found himself swept into the looking glass of his own memories of the same night and, when Ava's heartfelt declaration met his ears, his heart was instantly engulfed by both blissful happiness as well as pangs of sadness.

"My life should have ended with a whimper in the Treblinka death camp," Ava continued, her momentary trance broken and her refocused attention coming to settle itself intently upon Gotham. "I was prepared then as a young girl to die, but other forces at work had different plans for me."

Gotham was caught off guard when Ava reached over and placed her hand upon his.

"I don't believe I ever properly thanked you for revealing your true self the day you appeared and delivered me from that hell-hole. Because of you, I went on to have a life; and what a helluva life it's been, hasn't it?" she noted with a strained and hoarse chuckle. "I've been gifted with a great many joyful years. I've also lived through my fair share of grief, and just between you and me, I wouldn't change anything if you allowed me to start over and do it all again. But I think you'll agree with me when I say there comes a time when a life, especially one as long as mine, has to graciously excuse itself from the banquet table for fear of being considered a glutton."

Gotham sat quietly and watched as Ava reached over to the nightstand beside her bed for a folded square of paper, and his heart tightened in his chest when he saw they were the once-missing pages torn from their son's David's journal which Jacob had given to her.

"The last time you were here, you politely endured the choleric rantings of a mother who thought she had made peace with the loss of her child; that is, until the revelation contained in these once-lost journal pages made itself known to me." As Ava spoke, she was overtaken by a swelling of emotion which revealed itself in a sudden welling of tears. "Oh, how I prayed the past few days that I might be given the chance before my time on earth expired in order to express the immense remorse for the cruel things I said to you that day."

"You've done nothing to seek forgiveness from me," Gotham said as he attempted to commiserate with Ava.

"Please, let me say what it is I need to, for my sake," she pleaded through tears suddenly beginning to trickle down her cheeks. "When I read our son's thoughts and what he was wrestling with in these pages, it was as if I was learning about his death again for the very first time. I could never fully embrace the depths of a son's love for his father which would allow him to give up his own precious life in order to restore yours while, in turn, steal it away from my own without so much as a thought in such a cruel and thoughtless manner. I came to blame you for that painful sacrifice in which our son robbed from me in order to give to you."

It arrived in that moment, despite the decades that had passed since the horrific loss the two would come to know, when Gotham finally came to understand the pain festering inside her had mutated itself into a harboring of resentment toward him.

"Oh, Ava..." he cooed with sympathy.

"Please know, I never held your unwavering love for our child in doubt," Ava continued before he could say anything more that might cause her to lose her ability of speech altogether. "You gifted me with a blessed child, and you proved yourself to be a loving and dedicated father, both of which I am eternally grateful for. How thoughtless and unfair I was to allow the injury I felt when I read these journal pages to sully your uprightness. Thankfully, the finch you sent to deliver your message seeking my consent for you to petition the Iudicium Tribunal for custody of Jacob helped me realize the error of my thinking."

The statement caused Gotham's head to tilt with curiosity. "What did my petition to the Tribunal concerning Jacob have to do with David?" he asked.

"Have you ever really taken notice of Jacob when he's in your presence? He absolutely adores you," said Ava, and try as he might, Gotham couldn't conceal the visible flattery that swept over him upon hearing such a compliment. "It's the exact same look David used to have whenever the two of you were together. And like David, I don't think Jacob would hesitate a single second to lay down his life for you if it came to it. Such is the nature of unconditional love; it is both rose and thorn. How could I ever fault you for the lengths either would go to demonstrate their unyielding love to you?"

Gotham, naturally, found any utterance of words difficult in that moment.

"You must know in your heart that I never would have accepted even the passing musings of the scheme David concocted in those pages. Nor can you begin to imagine the unendurable guilt I have carried since learning the truth of that horrific day. Better I should be a monster who slaughtered his boy than to live knowing the one thing I cherished most in life gave up his in the hope his blood would wash clean the scar of disgrace which once marked me," Gotham said woefully, "I'd have sooner walked into the bowels of the Underneath of my own accord like a sacrificial lamb than allow what came to transpire. And if there was a way my blood could have been spilt upon the Northern Lands instead of David's, it would have be done so ten times over."

Deep in her heart, Ava always knew what Gotham stated to be true, even when her anger, spurned by the pain of losing her boy, blinded her. Still, it offered a warmth of comfort to hear it be said out loud. And in that warmth, she felt the pain and resentment that had long resided in the depths of her soul take leave of her, and she breathed forth through the flow of her tears a sigh of relief.

"I am a blessed woman. I have a beautiful grandson who I adore, not to mention a vision of heaven seated in front of me who has held my heart captive in his hand since the first day he entered it. You don't know how good it makes an old woman feel knowing the two people she loves most in the world have the power to keep her in their lives, and desperately wish to do so," she said. "But now I hope you will understand when I say that perhaps, Lilith has, strangely enough, done me a great service. A day hasn't gone by where I've not missed David, or my beautiful daughter, Isabeth. How I long to see their faces and hold them in my arms again, not to mention my family who weren't as lucky as I was at Treblinka. To be reunited with all of them again is what warms my heart these days."

"Of course I understand...in more ways than you know, Ava," Gotham said in a soothing voice of comfort.

Gotham wiped away a wayward tear spilling down Ava's cheek with his thumb as he gently cradled the side of her face in the soothing confines of his hand. And as he did Ava, suddenly embarrassed over her sniveling state, especially in light of Gotham's collected demeanor, said, "How I wish I possessed at this moment your enviable ability to impersonate the Mona Lisa as impeccably as you do."

"I'm sorry?" Gotham replied with a blank stare.

"I'm just admiring the arid state of your eyes while I'm sitting here blubbering like a baby," said Ava. "Here we've just come to the sobering realization that Lilith has managed to fatally poison me, and by my own roses to boot. Call me old-fashioned, but I would think such a revelation would be enough to squeeze from you at least a single tear."

Following a contemplative moment, Gotham offered a subtle nod of understanding.

"The murderous ploy levied against you has incited within me an emotion I have not felt for some time," he said, "and the perpetrator of this heinous deed will unfortunately soon be introduced to it, of that I whole-heartedly promise you."

Behind the cool and measured manner in which Gotham spoke resided a hornets nest of animus whose buzzing did not escape Ava's ears, but before she could express her growing worry about the glint of vengeance she spied in his eyes keeping company with her own reflection, Gotham continued:

"You can be certain, if I were seated before you bearing the shameful mark of the Fallen, I would be devastated to find you in this state. My sadness would be inconsolable—so much so that I would pay no heed to your desire to accept this twist in your fate in a desperate bid to quell my own despondency. For any attachments a Fallen may form as an exile is confined to the fleeting moment of a mortal life where the eventual arrival of Death serves a reminder of their imprisonment. Trust me when I tell you as someone who has walked in the shoes of the accursed, there is no greater suffering than being separated from those you love most by a single door which has been closed to you for all eternity."

While he may have been successful in cloaking the angst of which he spoke from revealing itself in the mask he wore, he was less effective in concealing its somber presence from his tongue. It was then, Ava came to realize how exquisite Gotham's pain was compared to her own when it came to loss.

"I suddenly have a humbling appreciation for your recent redemption," Ava noted softly.

"Now, perhaps, you'll understand the absence of tears in my eyes," Gotham said with a comforting smile. "For a long time, Death existed as an enemy to me. Now, it's returned to being the beautiful gift it's long served as being. For its days of loitering in the periphery of darkness like some haunting phantom, reminding me of a time too soon to come, when I would be forced to look upon the one I have come to love most, one last time before saying goodbye for all eternity have ended."

~ ~ ~

Gotham suddenly rose from the bed and, standing in the center of the room, stretched out his arm to Ava and said, "Come!"

"What do you mean? Come where?" asked Ava.

"Whilst it's true I need not ever say goodbye to you," said the angel, "I most certainly never tire of saying hello."

What kind of crazy shenanigans is he attempting to get me to partake in? Ava wondered to herself while appearing visibly confused. And when Gotham, again, motioned her to him, she reluctantly pulled back the covers despite, much to her chagrin, being dressed in what she considered to be an unflattering "little old lady nightie."

Her weakened state was noticeable in the shaky, unsure steps she made away from the bed toward him. Just when she thought she might lose her balance and stumble forward, her hand found its way into his, and in that instant, Ava witnessed the walls of her bedroom dissolve into nothingness. In place of her bed and the rest of her furnishings, along with the floor and ceiling which also disappeared, a grandly decorated stage suddenly surrounded her.

Ava recognized instantly the stage and, more importantly, the opulent theater to which it belonged—the Royal Opera House of London. Yet, before she could determine whether what she saw was actually there or a delusion played upon her by her own eyes, there came the sound of applause from behind. She quickly spun around and her eyes widened all the more at the sight of an elite and impeccably dressed audience enthusiastically clapping for her from their seats inside the magnificent theater adorned in rich red velvet and beautifully gilded in gold. Her bewilderment-filled gaze slowly rose to the second and third balconies of the horseshoe-shaped auditorium she inexplicably found herself standing front and center of where she found even more theater-goers wildly applauding from the elaborate box seats.

A look of horror suddenly swept over her when she was reminded of the less-than-flattering state of her appearance—namely, the little old lady nightie she was wearing. When she looked down in an attempt to somehow shield the source of her mortification, however, she discovered much to her astonishment she was no longer wearing her unsightly nightie but a stunning, diaphanous gown of emerald green. And when she reached up to smooth her bed-mangled hair into something more presentable, she felt not the familiar cotton-candy texture of her gray coif but rather the thick, luxuriant tresses of the auburn mane of her youth elegantly styled into delicate curls falling about her bare shoulders.

Her hand...

She took notice of it, suddenly, as she ran her fingers through her youthful hair, and found it somehow lost all signs of age, as did her face when she instinctively reached up and felt her now smooth and taut skin.

"What's happening?" she was about to ask herself when she then became conscious of her other hand and, more importantly, the feeling of a warm firm hand clasping it. Even though there was no sign of her hand being held by another, she knew the invisible embrace belonged to Gotham, and she knew immediately how the impossible was suddenly possible. And she smiled.

The applause finally died down, and the notes to a familiar melody rose up from the orchestra pit at the foot of the stage to greet her. Her lips betrayed a timid quiver as they parted, causing her pause. Gotham had given her the wondrous gift to retreat into her past and step in the beauty of her youth that had long left her. But had he, she couldn't help but wonder, returned the jewel that was her voice once more into her throat as well? There was only one way to find out, and so, with the coils of fear tightening its squeeze on her, she opened her mouth to set free the beginning words to "Mon coeur s'ouvre à ta voix' and quickly came to realize the answer.

Ava needed only to sing a verse of the seductive mezzo-soprano aria to seize command of the stage upon which she stood and remind the transfixed audience why she had rightly been christened the Aphrodite of the Opera World. Her voice, at once both primal and delicate, swept through the theater with the force equal to that of a tsunami. Like a disembodied spirit, it slunk about serving to intoxicate the members of the audience in whose captivated eyes Ava had transformed herself into the living and breathing biblical seductress Delilah.

Delilah...

As she sang, she realized she was not alone on the stage and turned to find the object of her pleading aria standing just off to right, and her heart skipped a beat. It was Gotham, costumed as Samson, the legendary warrior known for his great strength, and the mane of hair from which it came, and Delilah's paramour. And what a Samson Gotham made; Ava had told the angel as much just a short time earlier. So mesmerizing was Gotham as the biblical figure come to life in all his imagined thewy brawn and might that Ava doubted the real life Samson could rise to the challenge of portraying himself as effectively as the angel. It was not Samson, however, to whom Ava sang of her heart's longing, but to Gotham; nor was her plea to convince him of her love in order to discover his secret and betray him false, as was Delilah's aim.

And so it came to be that Ava Delacroux delivered what would become her greatest rendition of the song which made her famous world-wide—even more so than the phenomenal performance she gave on the very same night, at the exact same moment, in the very same theater in 1952. Her voice all but razed the famed theater to its foundation as it rose to a crescendo, roiling about the couple in growing swells of untrammeled yearning. And as she sang she spied quite accidentally a familiar, if not unwelcome face in the audience. It was Lilith, peering down at her from behind a pair of bejeweled opera glasses from one of the box seats on the second-floor balcony. Seeing the evil minx who had purposefully poisoned her watching the performance did not come as a surprise, oddly enough. After all, Lilith had confessed she had attended the show during her fiendish visit. Nor did it throw Ava from her stellar performance. If anything, it provided the perfect inspiration to bring the show to its stunning conclusion.

As the aria neared its climax, Ava and Gotham embraced one another tightly in their arms and stared deeply into one another's eyes with unbridled longing. "Respond to my tenderness," Ava sang in French to her Samson, and in return Gotham answered in kind to his Delilah, "With kisses, I'll dry your eyes."

Gotham's resonant, powerful tenor voice was nothing short of Heaven sent. It was as halting as a trumpet signaling the end times, yet its rich, velvety timbre was delicate in caressing the senses, all at once. Never before, however, had a voice raised the rafters of the theater with such a force of dominance and passion as when Gotham sang the final bars of the aria: "Delilah...Delilah, I love you!"

When the song ended, the audience was instantly upon its feet and responded to the sight of Gotham and Ava locked in a passionate kiss with frenzied applause. The only one in attendance not clapping or cheering was Lilith, who all but crushed the opera glasses in her hands at the sight of the embrace.

What had proven to be a triumphant, if not touching moment ended as abruptly as it began when Gotham felt Ava go limp in his arms. In an instant, the applauding audience vanished, along with the stage and the rest of the theater, and in its place the familiar walls that formed Ava's bedroom rose reassembled themselves. Gone were Samson and Delilah, and standing in their place in the center of the bedroom was Gotham holding in his arms a now-elderly Ava. Gazing into her face, he became crestfallen.

She was gone.

CHAPTER TWENTY-THREE

ENTER THE DRAGON

As Jacob sat with his gloom-filled gaze fixed on the bronze coffin adorned with a magnificent spray of yellow roses, he couldn't help but take notice of how beautiful the morning was. The last thing his grandmother would have wanted was for her funeral to be a dreary, rainy affair. She would have much preferred–insisted, really–to have the sun shining brightly and the chirping of birds to serve as the musical entertainment, as they were readily providing at that moment in the otherwise serene surroundings of St. Michael's Cemetery.

Gotham sat beside him, quiet and stony-faced, his doleful eyes also leveled on the flower-draped casket, but clearly focused on something miles away from the cemetery. Oh, the anger Jacob demonstrated at the angel when he returned to his grandmother's room from the kitchen with her tea to find she had passed, and that Gotham had allowed her to, when he–or himself, for that matter–could have kept her from leaving their lives.

It was only when Gotham managed to calm him enough in order to convey the last wishes of his grandmother in the exact way she had explained them to him that Jacob finally surrendered to the angel's consoling embrace. And even though he would continue to miss her, Jacob, strangely enough, found the death of his grandmother did not add another thorn to his heart the way his mother's had.

Despite the fact Ava Delacroux was a well-known star of the opera stage, the graveside service was a small and unpretentious affair per Ava's implicit instructions. Jacob recognized several of the faces of those in attendance, most notably Ava's afternoon tea companions, Alice Kirkegaard and Hilda Buford, who had mended their falling-out, at least long enough to lend one another comfort as they huddled together and wept into their clutched handkerchiefs over the loss of their friend. Then there was Mr. Hoffman, the owner of Brighton's Food Mart who offered Jacob a sympathetic nod, along with Dr. Graham and several members of the church Ava attended on Sundays. There were also several people in attendance who Jacob had never seen before, but judging from the air of sophistication they seemed to carry about with them, he laid bets with himself they were relics from Ava's days on the stage paying their last respects to the once great "Aphrodite of the Opera World," especially when Gotham stood up to give the eulogy and their expressions became that of someone who had seen, quite literally, a ghost.

When the service finally ended, Jacob stood up and approached the casket with a box he held in his hands. It was not any ordinary box, but the aged cigar box Ava kept secreted away at the bottom of a cedar chest which she revealed to him more than a year earlier, along with the unbelievable secret it held inside: the secret of who he truly was. The box concealed several other things. Chief among them was a bundle of letters, along with a large gray feather from the wing of an angel, tied together by a delicate ribbon which Jacob ensured were placed before the funeral inside the coffin with the one to whom Gotham had written them. What remained was a flower which Jacob removed from inside the box as he stood beside the casket and brought out into the sunlight.

It was a uniquely beautiful flower; one he'd never before laid eyes on until he set foot in Eden. One would have an impossible time trying to describe its color, as it was constantly ever-changing. Not only did the hue of the dainty petals gradually bleed with every color of the rainbow, there was an iridescent quality to the remarkable flower that made it appear as if it had been spangled with numerous shimmering diamonds, making it all the more dazzling to behold, especially in the sunlight. Stranger still, the plucked flower Jacob held between his thumb and forefinger appeared as fresh and alive as it did the first time he viewed it so many months earlier and, more so, when Ava was given the treasure by Gotham decades earlier.

Gently, Jacob placed the colorful memento at the center of the rose bouquet draped across the top of the casket. Then, after silently bidding his grandmother a final goodbye, he redirected his gaze across the cemetery and took notice of something most odd that instantly stifled the brewing of tears he was attempting to quell. Beside several large tombstones, he spied a familiar-looking, fair-haired boy about his age standing next to a woman who looked remarkably like his...mother. They appeared to be observing the service and, try as he might, Jacob couldn't focus his eyes to get a better look at the boy or, more importantly, the woman due to the glare of the morning sun, even with his acute Nephilim eyes.

It was then Wray and Ty, who were amongst those in attendance to pay their final respects, approached the casket to console their dear friend. At first, Jacob paid them no mind as his attention was firmly fixated on the woman and boy across the way who began a slow retreat once their presence had been spotted. Only when they passed behind a particularly large tombstone and seemingly vanished into thin air before his very eyes did Jacob finally take notice of his friends.

Ty was the first to assail Jacob with a smothering embrace of a hug. Jacob, for his part, couldn't help but take note of the spit-and-shine job his best friend had put forth for the occasion. After all, it wasn't every day one was given the delightful opportunity to see Ty Wrenwood, whose attire consisted entirely of jeans and t-shirts three hundred and sixty five days out of the year, sporting a painfully stiff suit-and-tie look complete with dress shoes. In fact, the only other time Jacob was given such a treat was at the high school homecoming dance right before he left for Eden. And while Jacob was appreciative Ty had opted for a more somber color palette appropriate for the occasion instead of the garish orange sport coat he chose to wear at the dance, his eyes couldn't avert the sight of his friend's thick, and usually tousled mop of hair that had been gelled within an inch of its life and slicked down into a hard shell reminiscent of a gleaming bowling ball.

"I see we're still trying to perfect the Michael Corleone look," Jacob commented with a teasing grin.

"Give me a break. It was either that or Elvis 'The G.I. Blues' years," Ty replied glumly.

Before Jacob could move onto Ty's tie whose pattern, strangely, consisted of a collage of penguins, Wray pushed her way between the two boys to offer up her own condolences. Not surprisingly, Jacob found Wray's embrace to be much more soothing, and surrendered himself completely to it as he would a comfy pillow for his head after an especially taxing day.

"Thank you for coming," Jacob said as the two hugged.

"Of course!" Wray replied as if there existed any possibility of her not coming to the funeral. "I adored her. In many ways I thought of her as my own grandmother."

"She liked you a great deal as well. I know she enjoyed the times you would stop by and look in on her while I was away. I know I appreciated it," said Jacob.

Wray stood looking at Jacob with the little crinkle that would form between her eyebrows whenever she was feeling angst, and Jacob recognized immediately something far more troubling than the death of his grandmother resided behind the tears in her eyes.

"What is it? What's the matter?" he asked her.

"Duh, I'm at a funeral," she replied with a forced smile.

Jacob searched more deeply her gaze with his own. "There's something else. Tell me."

"Now's not the time. Can we just discuss it later?"

"No," Jacob said adamantly. "Something's obviously bothering you and I want to know about it."

Wray threw her arms once more around Jacob catching him slightly off guard; but nothing quite as much as what she came to whisper in his ear.

"Your father paid me a visit."

~ ~ ~

With the service over, Father Carey led the procession of mourners to the Parrish home where a small wake was been planned. There the guests were left to continue celebrating the life of Ava Delacroux as they nibbled over a buffet of finger sandwiches, deviled eggs and cakes while a greatest hits of Ava's operatic performances played on a phonograph in the background, allowing Jacob to sneak away upstairs with Gotham, Wray and Ty and hole themselves up in his bedroom for a most urgent discussion.

"What do you mean my father–that is, Samael–paid you a visit?" Jacob bellowed when the appropriate moment finally presented itself to him to respond to the bombshell Wray had dropped on him at the cemetery.

"Just as I said: I came home one day and there he suddenly was," said Wray.

Gotham, who knew something critical had transpired to herd them upstairs and behind closed doors away from any prying ears, straightened instantly at the mention of Samael's name.

"Samael made himself known to you here, in Cain's Corner? When?" he inquired.

Wray looked to the ceiling for a moment or two in thought. "Four, maybe five days ago."

"You serious? Samael? Here?" Ty, looking legitimately spooked, asked. "Why didn't you tell me?"

"Please! If I told you, it would have ended up on the front page of The Cain's Corner Chronicle," Wray retorted with a dismissive chortle.

"Would not!" Ty spat with offense at such an allegation.

"You couldn't help yourself from blabbing the 'Game of Thrones' series finale to me before I even had a chance to watch it."

"Uh, okay Miss Sensitive, how about exercising a little perspective between apples and oranges. You're talking about a TV show; this is real life," said Ty. "Besides, I saved you from suffering through what was easily one of the most disappointing endings to a TV series ever."

After a slow roll of his eyes to seemingly push back the oncoming of a headache, Gotham abruptly put an end to the trivial bickering between the two by calmly asking, "Can we please try to focus, children?"

Wray couldn't help but shoot Ty a last frigid look of contempt before resuming her account of meeting Samael, hopefully, without any further interruptions. Her story began when she returned home one afternoon from school. After grabbing herself a cool drink from the fridge to help cool her from the unseasonably warm day whose sweltering presence, strangely enough, was markedly more noticeable inside the air-conditioned house. Leaving the kitchen, Wray was about to head to her bedroom where the first order of the day was to call Jenny Pickler to get the latest gossip surrounding Erin Jenkins and her rumored nose job, when the sight of a strange man sitting casually on one of the overstuffed chairs in the family room with his hands positioned prayer-like in front of him as though awaiting her arrival, stopped her dead in her tracks.

"Allow me to introduce myself: I'm Samael," the man said with a subtle smile that was more sinister than friendly. Then, as if to end his announcement with a punctuation mark, he added, "Jacob's father."

Much to her surprise, Wray didn't feel her blood run instantly cold being in the presence of the Fallen angel who until then had always existed inside her head as someone with horns on top of his head or, at the very least, sporting a devilish goatee of sorts.

"How did you know where to find me?" she asked, trying not to sound nervous.

"Your favorite flower is the gardenia, your happiest memory is a kiss you shared with my son at a high school dance, your greatest fear is loneliness, and your biggest secret is—well, we'll just keep that between the two of us, for now. Trust me, I'm not reliant on Google Maps when there is someone in the world I am interested in seeking out," came the reply.

Wray crossed her arms in front of her, as an uncomfortable feeling swept over her. It was as if she had suddenly been stripped naked even though all her clothes remained in place. Only it was a different kind of nakedness—a jarring vulnerability of having your innermost self exposed for the entire world to see, especially when it involved her own private secret which she was begrudgingly grateful to Samael for not speaking aloud.

"Something the matter?" Samael asked, after a tense moment of silence.

"Not a thing," Wray lied. "It's just...I'd always heard how much Jacob looked like you. I guess I'm just surprised to see first-hand exactly how much."

The comment made Samael sit up straighter in his seat as his mouth stretched itself wide with pride. "You don't say. A real chip off the ole block, huh?"

Admittedly, Wray found Samael to be strikingly handsome, aside from the unappealing scar marring his forehead just above his left temple. Yet in spite of Samael's pleasing features, she was quick to clarify her observation was not intended to be a compliment.

"I'm not all that confident Jacob would agree with you," she said. "In fact, to be blunt with you, it's only recently that I managed to talk him out of having his face, uh...rearranged."

"You mean surgically altered?" Samael, looking none-too-pleased such discussion had taken place, asked.

"I think he was partial to more invasive means...like diving face-first into an electric sander," said Wray.

Samael cocked his head and eyed Wray more closely while pondering whether or not she was serious or, far worse, toying with him.

"Well," he said half smiling, "it remains flattering to me to know the young woman my son is sweet on appreciates the countenance with which he was born."

There came suddenly a *THUD!* that caused both Samael and Wray to direct their gazes to the vicinity of the ceiling above them. Samael's eyes rolled slowly inside their sockets from side to side as he listened intently to the faint pitter-patter of a half dozen footsteps that would have had many a child wondering if Santa had moved up the date of his annual gift-giving pilgrimage.

"My guess is that would be your guardian angel Darrel, predictably returning to his nest after making certain you've made it home from school unmolested and yet, ironically, leaving the door to your sanctuary unguarded for me to enter through with ease during his absence," Samael remarked of the angel Gotham had dispersed, along with Yairel, to watch over Ava and Wray. "Of course, you are more than free to scream for him as you are considering doing now and turn what has so far been a cordial exchange into something far more...unpleasant."

It was becoming more clear to Wray the unique ability her unexpected visitor had in peering inside her skull and reading her thoughts. And while the first cause of action she had contemplated was to, in fact, alert Darrel to the intruder in their midst with a well-pitched scream, Wray also wasn't too keen on learning what "unpleasant" turn of events awaited her for doing so and decided, instead, to keep her lips sealed.

Besides, Wray couldn't deny the fact she was becoming more intrigued with the enigmatic figure she had come to hear so much about, even if those things had painted inside her mind a portrait of a Fallen angel too insidious and malefic to be believed.

~ ~ ~

"What is it you want from me?" Wray asked finally.

The girl's cooperative demeanor brought a grin of glee to Samael.

"This isn't about what you can do for me, but what you can do for yourself," Samael said in a voice that all but dribbled honey from the corners of his mouth. "You've made quite an impression on my son. One might even conclude he's become a smitten kitten from all the uplifting things he's had to say about you."

'Smitten kitten' wasn't exactly the sort of vernacular Wray expected to come from the one who held court in the hellish realm known as the Underneath.

"Not to sound rude, but how would you know what kind of an impression I've made on Jacob, good or bad? Last I heard the two of you have never spoken before, and I for one know Jacob has no desire to break bread with you anytime soon," she said.

Samael couldn't deny the girl was bold in the way she spoke in the face of someone of his known caliber. Whether such boldness stemmed from fearlessness or stupidity, he had yet to determine.

"You're quite right about that," Samael admitted with an awkward smirk. "It's an odd circumstance, I confess, being estranged from one's own child. Do you know I have not laid eyes on Jacob–in the flesh, at least–since the day he was conceived? Not until the hearing before the Iudicium Tribunal, that is."

Wray's ears perked up at the mention of the Tribunal.

"You were present at the hearing to determine whether Jacob was the Light Bearer?" she asked.

"No," Samael replied. "I was present at the hearing arguing my parental rights as his father to secure sole and irrevocable custody of him."

Custody? Wray felt her face drain itself of color.

"You share the same look as Jacob did when I submitted my petition to the Court," Samael, his dark gaze boring itself ever-deeper into Wray, said. "You're quite right: I found on our first meeting that he does, indeed, carry a strong if not uncanny resemblance to me, if I do say so myself. Unfortunately, the occasion didn't really lend itself to the two of us having a proper father-and-son reunion. I was, however, able to momentarily sift my way through his innermost private thoughts and I stand by my earlier assertion of the impression you've made on him."

The furthest thing Wray was interested in, however, at least at that precise moment, was how smitten a kitten Jacob was where she was concerned.

"Why would you do such a thing? Why would you try and take him away from his family and friends, especially when you know he wants nothing to do with you?" asked Wray.

"Because he's my flesh and blood," Samael answered matter-of-factly. "And because he has a better chance to stay alive if he were to reject the threatening embrace of Havenhid for the safe cover of my wing."

"Threatening? Havenhid? That's ridiculous!" Wray said incredulously. "Gotham, Damiel, his friends...they would never do anything to harm him."

"You're quite correct in your assumption," Samael agreed. "It's the very real danger he faces from the forces of the Underneath from which I seek to deliver him."

Ah, mortals! Samael muttered with disdain to himself inside his head when his attempt to clarify his point failed to erase the confounded expression on the girl's face. And so he slowly rose to his feet and stretched out his hand toward Wray saying, "Perhaps it would help if I were to show you what I mean."

Wray remained frozen where she stood, not moving an inch to accept his hand.

"I assure you, if I came here with the intention to do you harm, the crime would have already been committed," Samael said, trying his best to ease the girl's apprehension.

When Wray finally brushed away the inner voices advising her otherwise and stepped forward to gingerly take Samael's hand, she immediately regretted the decision when something so jarring and frightful in its unveiling that could only rightfully be assumed to be death itself descended upon her in a flash. The walls, ceiling and floor–her entire home–incinerated before her very eyes, and to her instant horror Wray found herself standing on a formation of clouds amid a vast expanse of sky alight with fire and angry with flashes of lightning. Rage could be heard everywhere in a chorus of screams and curses; then those who were the source of the caterwauling suddenly filled the sky all around for as far as the eye could see.

Angels.

A multitudes of angels.

They were raining down from the heavens in every direction, in a fury of wings and wrath. Teeth gnashing, they spewed vile and obscene insults at the far larger army of angels who were driving them down toward the fiery pit that was opening up like the blossom of some hellish flower upon the earth. And as Wray stood standing in the middle of the bedlam terrified to her very core, an angel swept past her at great speed who she was shocked to recognize as being Damiel. He was mercilessly casting down one angel after another in a flurry of swings of his sword whose blade was ablaze with the same righteous fire emanating like twin beacons from his eyes. Then, in the distance, another familiar face fast emerged: this one belonging to Gotham. He was astride a phantom steed, leading a small army of angels also on horseback across the clouds in a ferocious charge to drive yet more angels with faces grossly contorted by rage and hatred from the higher plains toward the lake of fire below. And as more angels fell, Heaven made visible its rebuke in strikes of lightning which reached out like skeletal fingers and struck each angel squarely on the temple to permanently brand them with their offense.

Guilty!

Guilty!

GUILTY!

The thunderous condemnation by several stentorian voices caused Wray to spin around quickly, and the calamitous fate of the Fallen gave way to the damning judgment which would come to befall Samael before the Iudicium Tribunal. As Wray watched the compelling scene unfold itself with undivided intrigue, she was suddenly taken aback when yet-to-be-Fallen Samael, who she found to be a commanding vision in that moment, slowly gazed back over his shoulder to offer her a devious grin. Then, as Gotham issued the final verdict that would seal Samael's fate, horror once more pounced upon Wray at the sight of a combative and hostile Samael screaming with unbridled rage his vow of vengeance while his magnificent unfurled wings beat furiously to escape his inevitable ruination that revealed itself in the familiar lake of fire beneath his suspended feet.

"MY KINGDOM WILL COME!"

Before she knew what had happened, Wray found herself back in the safe, perdition-free confines of her home, with her feet firmly on the floor. There she struggled for several moments to catch a much-needed breath as Samael's screams of reprisal faded into the distance as all echoes eventually do.

"More than a third of my brothers, myself included, were swept that day from Heaven like so many stars whose light was suddenly snuffed out." The sound of Samael's voice startled Wray, causing her to spin around to find the Fallen angel, scar and all, standing behind her. And before she could ask the obvious question of what had transpired just moments ago, he continued, "As you just witnessed, we were cast into the fiery realm called the Underneath or, if you prefer, Hell, as it's better known by you and your kind. And it is there we have been left to endure the intolerable flames of an unjust punishment for all these eons."

"At the risk of pointing out the obvious," Wray began cautiously, "but didn't you like, start a war in Heaven? It wasn't like God just decided one day to banish you."

The remark set off a detonation deep within Samael.

"YOU'RE DAMN RIGHT WE STARTED A WAR!" he bellowed, before taking a steadying breath that managed to bring the boil of his ire to a simmer, and while doing so he emitted what sounded like the snarling growl of some wild beast that caused goosebumps to rise up on Wray's arms. "How else do you propose my brothers and I were to break ourselves free of the shackles of an insufferable servitude we were forced to don? Well, now those shackles are gone, but our want for reparations remain. We are soon nearing the time when we, the Fallen, will rise up again—and in much greater numbers this time—against our oppressors to retrieve such payment, and we will not be appeased by an insulting recompense consisting of four measly acres and a mule.

"No, our demand is the entire plantation, you can be sure. Only there is an inconvenient hurdle we suddenly find ourselves confronted with called a

Light Bearer, and he holds in his possession a weapon that not only threatens our chance for triumph and supremacy, but can fashion itself into the one key which could imprison us in a new, stronger set of shackles for all eternity. Surely, you can understand after having the situation explained to you the imperativeness on my part of having such an obstacle...removed."

The casual and aloof manner in which Samael spoke left Wray cold.

"The way you're speaking, it almost sounds as if you are plotting to do away with Jacob," she said.

"I've always been a proponent of free will," said Samael. "It's when one's free will goes against the grain of my own that problems arise."

Wray couldn't believe her ears. "But he's your own son!"

"You seem to be under the illusion I bore a child in order to qualify for some annual father-son Pinewood Derby competition," Samael replied amusingly. "In fact, the siring of my son lent itself to no more than producing a strong and able heir apparent to help me secure what was meant to be an interim reign over the Underneath into a permanent throne. So you can see why this little inconvenient, if not farcical sleight of hand my father has craftily played on me by delivering to me my supposed vanquisher in the form of the Light Bearer has put me a tricky position."

"If that's the case, then why would you be trying to gain custody of him?" asked Wray.

Samael returned a look of equal bafflement Wray had trained on him.

"Because, as you are soon to find out if you haven't already, I am quite designing when need be. And the moment for seizing the aforementioned throne is at hand, which means I am still in need of a loyal co-conspirator–and if said co-conspirator comes armed with a particularly powerful sword, so much the better," said Samael, though his explanation did little to erase the deep-set judgment from Wray's face. "Don't get me wrong, it is not my intention to kill Jacob. Far from it, in fact. He is of my blood, after all. But I have already suffered one devastating blow beneath Heaven's heel; you can be sure I will not withstand another, and especially one delivered by my own son. Of that, you can be certain."

As he spoke, a noticeable darkness settled itself upon Samael betraying the fact something far more troubling was eating away at him.

"If I were to be completely honest, I might admit to a far more selfish reason on my part–vindictive, even–for petitioning the Iudicium Tribunal for custody over Jacob," Samael noted in a blasé manner, though Wray couldn't imagine anything more selfish than using one's own child in a coup. Yet when she inquired what the reason might be, Samael blurted a one-word response dripping with disdain: "Gothamel."

"I noticed almost immediately the day I presented my petition to the Tribunal that he has become quite enamored with Jacob. Even worse, Jacob has become equally enamored, if not more, with Gothamel," Samael recalled as he stared off into his thoughts. "If my righteous brother thinks he will replace the son he cut down in cold blood with my own, he will do so at his own peril. Perhaps, even, for the benefit of my own perverse pleasure. For you see, his doting affection for Jacob has revealed a chink in his once impregnable armor; a chink I spied clearly in all of its shining glory the moment I wielded my rights as the father of Jacob before him. And you can be assured I am going to find a way to forge that endearing affection he has for my son into a sword which I then intend to drive straight into his beating heart."

The vengeful-filled, faraway look in Samael's eyes left Wray feeling as though he wasn't so much speaking to her than talking himself through the vitriol and displeasure he harbored toward Gotham.

"Earlier you...you said the reason for your visit wasn't about what I could do for you, but what I could do for myself," Wray timidly attempted to change the subject in the awkward silence that followed. "What did you mean?"

Her voice appeared to break Samael out of whatever dark trance into which he momentarily slipped.

"Isn't it obvious?" he asked.

Wray replied with an awkward shrug and said, "Not really."

"No doubt you have been introduced to my beloved yet depraved Lilith in a roundabout way," Samael began, to which Wray offered a polite yet unenthused smile at hearing the name of the deceptively beautiful devilish nymph with a main of dark hair which served as a nest for poisonous serpents which she had read so much about in Jacob's journal. "She believed there was something to the sentimental old adage that says in part 'home is where the heart is' when it came to mortals, and thought our best leverage when it came to Jacob resided in his dear sweet old grandmother."

Wray instantly felt her heart quicken.

"And while I agreed with her in theory, it's no secret to the both of us that Jacob long ago placed his heart into your hands," said Samael with a devious grin. "And when a young boy places his heart into the hands of pretty young thing such as yourself, he may as well have just signed over the pink slip to his soul."

"You're saying you want me to try and persuade Jacob to turn his back on everything he knows and embrace the one person he loathes most in this world?" Wray said in a voice whose tone became more incredulous with every word she spoke. "Obviously, you can't believe for a minute I could convince him to do such a thing."

"To the contrary, I believe you could convince him his dear daddy has managed to ingratiate myself back into Heaven's good graces, and snared the title of saint, as well, to boot."

Wray stood silent for a moment thinking when her naturally obdurate nature rushed to the forefront.

"And if I refuse?" she sneered at Samael who didn't seem ruffled all that much by such mulishness.

"Well, then if efforts to remove the hurdle before me fail, I suppose I will have no alternative than to be forced to clear it," Samael replied calmly. "And, then, I fear it will be your heart that is fated to be broken; into pieces too numerous to count, I'm afraid."

The pointed threat was not lost on Wray, especially the last sentence which Samael hissed menacingly into her ear. Still, she thought of Jacob and in doing so managed to keep her stubborn wits about her.

"Like you said: Jacob has in his possession the one weapon that threatens any chance of you succeeding in your warped plan, and he knows how to use it. I think the odds are in his favor that he can handle anything you come at him with, so if it's all the same you I, along with my heart, will go ahead and take the risk," said Wray.

It was not the response Samael was expecting, though he managed to retain his calm demeanor. Then, without so much as an argument in return, he returned to the overstuffed chair where Wray first discovered him sitting.

"I am suddenly reminded of an old movie cliché that goes something like 'Ve haf vays of making you talk!'" he said with an uncomfortably sinister smile that perfectly complimented his equally menacing German accent. "I guess now would be the appropriate time to inform you that I have a most effective way in making you do exactly as I wish."

Not surprisingly, an ice-cold shiver made its way along Wray's spine, but before she could muster the courage to ask what he meant by such an ominous statement she felt a sudden and very unfriendly presence rise up behind her. And no matter how much bravery she fought to wrangle within herself, nothing could keep the terror from escaping Wray in a loud, glass-shattering scream when finally she managed the strength to turn around.

CHAPTER TWENTY-FOUR

"Well?" Jacob pressed urgently when Wray paused her story to collect herself. "What was it?"

"An Infector," Wray replied softly, as though even saying the name out loud might conjure one of the vicious demons from thin air.

Jacob and Gotham's gazes instinctively shifted downward in unison to Wray's feet in search of any telltale signs only shadows could betray that she had become a victim of what Infectors are known to do so very well. Thankfully, neither spied any such signs.

"Hold up a minute and put on the parking brake!" Ty blurted with a look of alarm. "You're not talking Infectors like the kind we had the unfortunate pleasure of seeing first hand in Venice, are you?"

"One and the same," answered Wray, as if the question needed to be asked. One doesn't mistake the vicious, body-stealing, smoke-like wraiths they first witnessed circling the gilded ceiling of the magnificent Doge's Palace during the masquerade ball with any other creatures born from the Underneath, no matter how horrifying.

Jacob, who had more than his fair share of run-ins with the ghastly creatures and knew the evil they were capable of carrying out, was reticent to ask the obvious question, though he finally forced himself.

"What happened?"

Wray, who seemed equally hesitant to answer, finally succumbed to the three sets of eyes boring their way into her with each passing second. What neither the angel or the two boys were prepared to hear was the three-word answer Wray provided in return: "I killed it."

"At least, I think I did," Wray was quick to add under her breath when the room went eerily quiet.

"What do you mean you killed it?" Gotham, who had a long and sorted history of separating the heads from the bodies of countless nasty Infectors, asked after digesting the surprising response.

Wray proceeded to recount the bone-chilling moment when the Infector advanced upon her in all of its monstrous darkness while Samael looked on with a twisted delight. She slowly backed away until she found herself pressed up against a wall with nowhere else to escape. Trembling with fear, she reached behind her as inconspicuously as she could and, just when the gnarled hands were about to take hold of her, she brandished a dagger concealed in the waistband of her pants and, with a grimace of revulsion and doggedness, Wray plunged the blade of the weapon straight into the mantle-covered face descending on her.

When she had finished describing the ear-splitting screams that erupted from the enraged smoky phantom as it struggled to pull the dagger from its skull before being reduced to a cloud of ash, the room became deathly quiet.

"This dagger...may I see it?" Gotham finally asked with notable calm.

Wray nervously, if not somewhat bashfully, lifted the hem of the attractive but modest black dress she was wearing to just above the knee revealing, to the surprise of everyone looking on, a glimpse of a leather sheath strapped to her thigh. And it was from that sheath Wray retrieved the weapon in question before she rearranged her dress back to the way it had been in the most ladylike of ways. Both Jacob and Ty's eyes grew large and wide at the sight of the dagger as it was handed over to Gotham, for it was clear that, while it may not have been a sword, it most certainly was capable of inflicting the utmost damage in the right hands. Even Wray's.

Gotham studied closely the uniquely designed silver dagger with all of its distinctive flourishes before turning an even more critical eye on its surprising owner and asking, "This is Caelestian."

"Caele-who?" Wray replied with notable confusion.

"Caelestian," Jacob repeated. "It's a word used to describe something derived from Heaven, like the language of angels. Question is how did you come about getting your hands on something like this?"

"Darrel gave it to me," answered Wray.

"Get out! And how exactly did you manage to finagle something like this from Darrel?" Ty jumped in before Jacob could inquire who, exactly, this Darrel person was.

"You know him?" Jacob, visibly surprised, asked Ty.

"Of course I do," Ty replied matter-of-factly.

"Well? Would somebody mind filling me in on who this mystery person is?" Jacob asked impatiently, as he grew increasingly annoyed over the fact he was not privy to the secret shared by his two best friends.

"Darrel is an angel I sent down to watch over these two like I said I would when they departed home from Venice," answered Gotham. "The question is why would he give you this dagger?"

"Frankly, as someone who's feeling a little cheated at this moment due to the fact that I was not given any such dagger, I wouldn't mind knowing the answer to that question myself," Ty, clearly miffed, mumbled.

With all eyes fixed on her once again, Wray recalled how learning of the existence of Nephilim, angels and, yes, even Infectors and Furies caused her to start focusing her attention more on the places in the world surrounding her that she before was prone to ignore, particularly the high places like trees and rooftops and, in general, the sky itself. And so it happened shortly after returning to Cain's Corner from what had been an eye-opening and, at times, frightening adventure in the seedy depths of Las Vegas and the romantic watery channels of Venice that she one day took notice of a surprising and mysterious figure perched on the rooftop of a house as she was driving home from school one day. A short while later, she noticed the figure on another roof and then another until she realized it was moving from house to house as it followed her. Once she reached home, she raced upstairs to her room and covertly snuck a peek outside through the slats of the blinds covering the window and, as she scoured the rooftops of the neighboring houses and caught no sign of the strange man, she heard a sudden thump coming from above as though a very large bird had just landed on the roof directly above her head.

She knew Gotham had promised to send a couple of angels to keep watch over her, Ty and Jacob's grandmother, and she was certain as could be that this was one of them. Intrigued, she was determined to meet this winged guardian, only the angel was equally determined to prove himself to be nothing but a figment of her imagination.

One day she arrived home from school as she normally did, only instead of going inside through the front door she went around to the side gate leading to the backyard. There she let loose a scream and, in a flash which proved surprising even to her, the elusive angel was suddenly there with his sword in hand ready to strike down whatever danger was waiting. When he saw, however, that no danger existed, his anger was immediate.

"Is this your idea of a joke?" the angel seethed with eyes blazing like two vats of molten gold.

At first Wray couldn't find her voice. It wasn't sparked by the fright of suddenly finding herself in the presence of such an intimidating being, but rather due to the fact the angel was the most beautiful thing she had ever laid eyes upon. His hair was like spun gold that fell to his shoulders in waves and framed a face so strikingly handsome it didn't seem possible creation could paint such an appealing portrait. Yet, as beautiful as the angel was, there was an unmistakable air of danger just as striking in scope of which one could not fail to take notice. It made itself visible in the magnificent pair of wings sprouting from the angel's back, to the sculpture of strength which shaped his impressive arms and torso that even the loose, billowy shirt he wore could not camouflage, and even more markedly in the blazing gaze which had settled itself firmly on Wray.

"N-n-no joke!" Wray managed to croak when the cat finally released its hold of her tongue. "It's just...I knew Gotham was sending someone to kind of guard me and my friend Ty and Jacob's grandmother, and I just thought it would be a neighborly thing if we introduced ourselves to each other. I'm Wray."

At first, the angel didn't react one way or the other to the gesture, even when Wray offered him a friendly smile.

"Darrel," he finally grunted. "Now, we've been introduced."

And with that he took to the sky with a sweep of his wings and disappeared over the roof of the house.

~ ~ ~

"So when you say this Darrel is handsome...just exactly how handsome is he?" Jacob suddenly asked while trying his best not to sound like some envious boyfriend.

"Dude, just...if you have any regard for your self-esteem, trust me when I say that is a question that can only be hazardous to your health," Ty suggested before Wray could answer.

"What's that supposed to mean?" Jacob grumbled.

"It means—and I say this with all due affection—on a scale from one to ten, Darrel ranks around 10,634 while you, if I were to choose to be particularly generous in my judging, fall at right about an eight. You do the math," Ty replied while giving his friend a supportive pat on the back which only served to annoy Jacob all the more.

"Are you interested in hearing the rest or not?" Wray, sounding like a mother stepping in between her sparring children, asked. When both boys answered by zipping their lips, she continued, "Anyway, despite our awkward introduction, Darrel remained one hard nut to crack. I would wave to him whenever I spotted him on some nearby perch high above, but he would do his best to ignore me, almost hostilely. Then one day I got a begrudging nod, and the nod soon became a hesitant wave, and before long he slowly warmed up to the niceties of conversation, brief as they may have been. Well, to make a long story short, Darrel eventually started showing me different ways I could protect myself if I ever found myself in a precarious situation."

"You're kidding us, right? Are you trying to tell us he's been training you how to fight?" Jacob asked while doing everything he could to suppress the chuckle fighting to escape from inside him which caused Wray's gaze to narrow itself on him like two aimed torpedoes.

"Find that amusing, do you?" she asked cooly. "Perhaps you'd care for a demonstration of what I've learned."

The offer instantly wiped away any sign of a smirk from Jacob's face, especially when he was suddenly confronted with an unpleasant flash of memory of being on the receiving end of a particularly painful punch delivered by Wray as he stood in the middle of Rabble-Rousers dripping with the remnants of chocolate milkshake that had been poured over his head.

"Trust me, I don't find the idea of your fists of fury in motion the least bit funny, especially when I now know they've managed to take out an Infector," he quickly kowtowed. "It's just the idea of you learning such things from an angel is, well...it's just a little weird."

"And that's how you came to have this dagger?" Gotham inquired impatiently, while Wray kept Jacob in her crosshairs.

"Darrel gave it to me a few days ago," she said. "After Lilith was brazen enough to show up at Ava's house, he didn't want to take any chances where I might be left unprotected."

"Oh, that's just perfect! Correct me if I'm wrong, but wasn't he supposed to be *both* our bodyguards?" Ty balked suddenly in protest. "I mean, what did he expect me to fight off the Liliths of the world with, my kazoo?"

"Maybe he thought your absurd, harebrained theories regarding Spock and the Vulcan mind meld was enough of a repellant to drive away any resident of the Underneath who might make the mistake of coming for you," said Wray.

"Do I even want to ask?" Jacob, who could never help but be somewhat titillated by his friend's mind wanderings and yet always regretted inquiring about them, asked.

"No," Gotham was quick to answer, "you don't. Besides, you have guests downstairs who have come to pay their respects to your grandmother. I think it would be impolite to not look in on them, don't you think?"

Despite not being much of a fan of wakes, Jacob agreed. But just as the group prepared to head downstairs Ty whispered to Wray, "Don't you think you should fill them in on the rest?"

Naturally, Jacob's keen Nephilim hearing heard the question as clearly as if Ty had shouted it at the top of his lungs, as did Gotham, causing both to pause in their steps.

"Fill us in on what?" Jacob asked.

Wray turned the crosshairs that were earlier trained on Jacob and aimed them directly at Ty who immediately regretted opening his mouth.

"I was going to wait for a more appropriate time to tell them, thank you very much," she grumbled under her breath.

"Tell us what? What is it with all the secrecy?"

"Trust me, it can wait until later," Wray attempted to brush away the subject, only Jacob who didn't like the existence of secrets he wasn't privy to wasn't having it.

"No way. I wanna know now, so spill it!" he pushed.

"Fine, have it your way," Wray acquiesced with a huff. "Only...I think it would be better if I showed you rather than try and explain it."

~ ~ ~

After taking some time to circulate amongst the friends and acquaintances gathered together downstairs reliving memories of his grandmother and making sure they were all doing well, Jacob casually disappeared into the kitchen and out of the back door where Wray and Ty were patiently waiting with Gotham.

The four piled into Wray's Jeep and took a short, five-minute drive to where the reach of houses and sidewalks ended and the surrounding woods began where they pulled over and parked. Without offering any clue of where they were going, Wray pointed to a faint path leading through the thicket of trees and brush.

For some time, they walked in silence. That is, Wray, Jacob and Gotham walked in silence; Ty was an entirely different manner. He chose to use the time as an opportunity to try and cajole Gotham into gifting him a weapon similar to the one Darrel had given Wray. Gotham, in a worthy testament to the Grace of patience and restraint instilled in him, appeared to be silently praying for such a weapon at that very moment in order to slice off his own ears, or cut out Ty's rambling tongue, though by the look in his pained eyes it was clear he was leaning toward the latter of his options with every step he took.

Jacob was actually thankful to have the angel's attention momentarily occupied, as it gave him the chance to have a moment alone with Wray.

"I want you to know I appreciate everything you've done today...you know, helping to make the funeral arrangements and basically handling all the details for the wake. I don't really know all that much about that kind of stuff, although you'd think I would by now," he said.

The acknowledgment brought a smile to Wray. "You don't need to thank me. I was more than happy to do it, especially when I think how the people gathered at your house right now would likely be feasting on a buffet of franks and beans and maybe a platter of Hot Pockets if things had been left in your hands," she said with a giggle and, in turn, bringing a smile to Jacob.

"Is it really true what my father said about me?" Jacob suddenly asked out of the blue and without a hint of the smile he wore moments earlier.

The question caught Wray by surprise.

"Refresh my memory."

"You know...that the only reason he had me was solely as a means to seize control of the Underneath?"

There was a glint of hurt Wray spied in his eyes despite Jacob's obvious efforts to conceal it.

"Would it bother you if I told you he did?" asked Wray.

"*Phhttt*...of course not. Why should I care one way or the other what comes out of his mouth?" Jacob spat dismissively.

"Look, I know your feelings regarding your—regarding Samael," Wray said while treading carefully in mining her words. "I know you hate him—"

"You're darn right I hate him. I hate him with every fiber of my being!" Jacob declared as the filaments of anger began to illuminate the inner depths of his irises.

"What I was going to say is that a lot of times hate is often mistaken for hurt. No matter what your feelings are toward Samael, I'm sure it couldn't have felt all that good to hear your birth was tied to such premeditated motives," said Wray. "After all, no child wants to learn they were brought into the world by any other means besides love."

Jacob plodded along, glowering at the path ahead of him, and said nothing in return, though Wray could almost hear the buzzing of his thoughts.

"It's alright to admit you're hurt," she offered softly, and immediately regretted opening her mouth when Jacob turned on her suddenly.

"Why do you keep saying that? Why do you keep implying I'm hurt or bothered when I'm not?"

There was a fire of anger alight in his face that Wray had never before witnessed. And while it caused her to pause, it did not make her shrink in its presence.

"Maybe it's because in all the times you've spoken about Samael and declared your unmitigated hatred for him you've never before referred to him as 'father,' " she explained calmly. "That is, until just a few moments ago."

If Jacob recalled using such a vile term in reference to Samael, he didn't reveal it one way or the other. If anything, Wray's bringing it to his attention only seemed to inflame him all the more.

"Just...drop it!" he spat venomously before stomping on ahead and away from the reach of Wray's company.

~ ~ ~

The group continued along until they reached the edge of a clearing where Gotham managed, finally, to escape Ty's exasperating voice when he came to stand beside Jacob to whom he muttered softly, "How I miss the days of the Civil War when cannon fire all but blew out of the insides of my ears."

As Jacob stood looking out over the field of tall grass gently swaying in the breeze from which the random chirps of frogs made themselves heard, he couldn't help but recall the last time he stood there the morning he woke to discover his mother had died and stormed off in anger into the pouring rain where he ripped off the rosary hanging around his neck, threw it at the sky and declared his hatred for God in that very spot.

Now, however, the memory only served to fill him with remorse, even as he absentmindedly fiddled with the mended rosary that had been returned to his neck.

"So where to, now?" he asked.

"Just around the bend of trees on the other side of the meadow," answered Wray.

"But there's nothing there, except the Harrison's old deserted barn," said

416

Jacob.

"You got it!" Wray replied with a cryptic grin before leading the way across the field of knee-high grass.

They soon came upon the derelict barn that once served as an oversized fort where Jacob and Ty would spend their summer afternoons and have the occasional campout when they were much younger. Just when Jacob was about to wonder aloud what purpose could they possibly have making a trip out to the rickety, old, deserted place, there was heard very plainly the ruckus of activity coming from inside. Intrigued, Jacob moved in closer to investigate, with the rest of the group following, to a large sliding door to the barn which he cracked open and poked his head inside for a curious peek.

Much to his surprise, Jacob was greeted by the sight of several dozen kids his own age lined up in rows of seven or eight. They were demonstrating various moves used in fighting; not just any old combat moves, but techniques he instantly found very familiar. In fact, for a minute, he thought he was back in Eden observing a training session at Lions Bite. Only the kids in the barn weren't just boys, but girls as well. Stranger still, upon closer look, they looked a lot like the kids he used to go to school with at Harpus High.

Certain he was suffering from some kind of delusion, Jacob gave his eyes a good rubbing and took another look. Sure enough, his eyes weren't playing any tricks on him. There was Hank Highwater, Alex Donovan, Travis Gill, and even Sharyn Krug who, the last time he saw her, managed to get a doctor's note to excuse her from P.E. so as to not risk ruining her precious manicure, and was now giving her nails not a second thought as she delivered blow after blow to whatever phantom attacker she was imagining in front of her.

"What the heck is going on here?" Jacob turned to ask Wray with unmasked confusion.

"Come on, and I'll show you," Wray replied with a smile.

As they made their way inside, their arrival didn't go unnoticed as someone was heard alerting the others with a tone of excitement, "Hey, look, it's Jacob!" Feeling all the more bewildered, Jacob quickly found himself surrounded by his old classmates who greeted him with a feverish excitement he never once came close to experiencing while he was attending Harpus High; in fact, quite the opposite. Despite all the clamor, however, his attention became focused on a tall and strapping figure with a mane of golden hair walking towards him whose presence could be described as nothing short of a Herculean warrior who had stepped out of the pages of a history book turned to Ancient Rome or Greece while, somehow, at the same time, looking like someone who had just traveled back in time from the distant future.

"You must be the one recently declared Light Bearer. I have eagerly been awaiting the moment I might finally meet your acquaintance," the golden-haired behemoth said. "My name is Darrel."

Jacob had already guessed as much the moment he looked into the aesthetically gifted face which had the uncanny and depreciatory ability to downgrade his ranking on the handsome scale from the respectable eight Ty had earlier given him to a humiliating three. In fact, as Darrel then proceeded to introduce him to the darker haired, yet equally handsome angel named Yairel standing quietly beside him who had served as bodyguard for his grandmother, Jacob came to the unsettling realization it was impossible to stand in the presence of an angel–any angel–and not feel like a complete bowser. Not to mention weakling.

"So what is all this?" Jacob asked once the familiarizations were over.

"Frankly, I'm more than a little interested in knowing the answer to that question myself," Gotham remarked, while eyeing both.

"It was actually all my idea," Wray spoke up to answer.

"What, exactly, was all your idea?" Gotham pressed.

Wray did her best not to become flustered under the intensity of the angel's stare that had come to settle itself upon her.

"When Ty and I returned home from Venice, I found myself unable to think about much of anything else except for everything we gone through on that trip: the Infected dogs and birds that came after us in Las Vegas, that Miseriel person and the weird, giant Pethen with him who almost killed Hunter, what happened in the church on that island cemetery," she began. "The moments when I could push it out of my head, I would begin reading Jacob's journal like he asked me to, and I found myself glad he shared it with me, because it's helped me to understand a bit more this brand new world he has suddenly found himself in, and I guess by extension, invited those of us who care about him into as well. But every time I came to the last entry he made in his journal, another would mysteriously appear; and then another, and another. Each one was about his trial before the Iudicium Tribunal, only I knew all of it was happening after he gave me his journal."

"I can explain that," Jacob interrupted. "Remember as we were saying goodbye in Venice when you were reluctant to take my journal because how else would I continue to write down my experiences, and I told you it was too complicated to explain, but I would manage to find a way? Well, I found a way to pop into your room at night when you were asleep and add to my journal."

"A real Peter Pan, this one is," Ty was heard to mumble under his breath.

"Can we expect an answer to surface soon during this journey down memory lane?" Gotham grumbled impatiently."

"The answer is I was struck by one entry early in your journal describing a church on some island in Turkey. Akad...Akdamin..."

"Akdamar," Jacob jumped in to set Wray's tongue straight.

"That's it...Akdamar. You describe a piece of a mural inside the church that illustrated the coming of the Light Bearer. The man, or rather angel who lived there—Johiel, I believe his name was—said it came from a little-known Apocryphal text, and part of that text states the Light Bearer would bring angels and mortals together to fight as one to help bring about the downfall of the Darkness," continued Wray.

"That's right," said Jacob, though still completely oblivious to how his journal led him to a gathering of his old classmates inside an old ramshackle barn.

"Well, then I was reminded of the cemetery we visited in Venice in the dead of night. Six angels appeared there; Zophiel called them Exiles. They called themselves your army and got down on one knee to pledge their undying service to you. And one day, when Darrel was showing me ways to protect myself, it suddenly came me," said Wray.

Despite Wray's visible excitement, Jacob still felt like he was mired in a dense fog.

"What came to you?"

"Don't you see? We are going to do as the Exiles did and form our own army. We're joining the cause!" Wray announced beaming. "Naturally, I thought it might be a long shot. After all, trying to convince our fellow classmates about the existence of angels, Light Bearers and whatnot and not end up in a psych ward is no easy task. But here we are, and it's where we've been the past several weeks training hard."

Jacob stood stunned for a good moment with his mouth agape.

"You can't be serious!" he finally exclaimed.

"Never mind serious. This isn't even on a trajectory to ludicrous!" argued Gotham.

"What's ludicrous about it?" Wray pushed back. "You say so yourself in your journal the prophesy specifically states the Light Bearer is going to be tasked with bringing angels and mortals together to take part in this battle. What is so ludicrous about the idea of your friends being part of that mortal camp that fights on your behalf?"

"I've heard it all now," Gotham bemoaned. "Humans thinking they're equipped to do battle against the Underneath–and they're children to boot.

"And you two," the angel barked suddenly at Darrel and Yairel, "what possessed you to entertain such foolishness?"

"To be honest, I didn't think Wray was serious; that is, until she showed up with nearly fifty younglings in tow," Darrel replied somewhat apologetically. "That said, she is right about the Apocrypha and, well...you might find yourself pretty impressed by what she and her friends have picked up in the short time we've been training them."

Before Gotham's brooding nature could darken even more by such assurances, Darrel looked to two of the teens standing nearby–a gangly ruddy boy named Jackson and a petite girl who looked to be no stronger than a flea named Jessica–and instructed them to the center of the barn with a nod of his head. All eyes then moved to Yairel who made his way to an assortment of old tools and contraptions left abandoned in the corner of the barn and grabbed up half a dozen large, rusted steel spikes in his hand which he then proceeded to throw one by one at Jessica. The girl immediately launched herself into a flurry of backflips and impressively dodged the onslaught of the five projectiles which blasted past her like bullets fired from a gun with each flip. Then, with an eye-opening double backward somersault, she masterfully evaded the sixth final spike before coming to a gold medal-worthy landing.

Immediately after, Yairel raised up three large bales of dry hay from the opposite end of the barn with just a subtle directive of his hand and sent them flying swiftly through the air in Jackson's direction. The boy revealed a moment of nervousness at the sight, but it quickly passed when he positioned himself into a fighting stance and, with two well executed kicks, disabled the assault in twin explosions of dry alfalfa. The third bale, however, he grabbed hold of midair and without a moment's pause spun around to meet the incoming sword Yairel hurled in his direction which imbedded itself in the bale Jackson had skillfully used as a shield in front of his vulnerable face.

The impressive demonstration brought a well-deserved round of applause from all; all that is except Gotham who simply disengaged himself from any further discussions on the matter and quietly walked away. Jacob was ready to follow after the angel and see what exactly was eating at him when he suddenly spied a familiar, and most certainly unexpected, face he had failed to recognize earlier, emerge from the sea of his classmates, which stopped him cold in his tracks.

It was Yul Dane, his long-time archenemy, and more notably Wray's ex-boyfriend (though she'd be immovable to the fact they had just been friends who went on a couple dates).

"Yul!" Jacob was so surprised at the sight of the blond muscled jock, he had forgotten the cardinal rule when it came to Yul's first name: don't use it. He was even more surprised when Yul didn't bat eye to its being used. "What are you doing here?"

"I thought it was all some big lame joke when Wray tried to convince me you were half angel; a Nephilim. But then she forced me to come out and meet Darrel and Yairel, and well...," Yul began as he slowly–cautiously, even–approached Jacob while carefully eyeing him up and down as though he were a rod of plutonium, "somethings you just have to see with your own eyes in order to fully believe."

Skeptical as Yul sounded, Jacob didn't sense any outward measure of hostility or invidiousness coming from the boy who had regularly used him as verbal punching bag. It wasn't, however, until he took notice of the same shared look of intrigue being reflected from the faces of his other classmates that he, with a certain degree of reluctance, not to mention self-consciousness, proceeded to strip off his t-shirt. As Jacob slowly–apprehensively, even–brought into view the pair of wings folded against his back for all to see, the looks of intrigued gave way to wonderment, as well as a collected gasp of awe. Yul was the only one amongst them who dared to reach out and touch one of the wings, though timidly. And, when he felt the feathers beneath his fingers were indeed real and not a figment of his imagination, a smile gradually came to him.

"Here the whole time I thought you just some annoying freak with two humps on your back. Turns out you were just an angel," Yul said with the chuckle of someone still nervously unsure about the reality in which he suddenly found himself.

"Half angel," corrected Jacob to which Yul nodded his understanding.

"Have to say I'm a bit relieved. Can't tell you how many nights I laid awake in bed trying to figure out the insane move you pulled on me during wrestling tryouts that put me flat on my back," Yul said light-heartedly before growing suddenly serious. "Think you could manage to overlook what a douche I've been to you in the past if I told you I was sorry and allow me to

421

remain a part of this army Wray's started? Cuz I'd sure like to put my bullying talents to better use."

Jacob stood silent for a moment, and while he hadn't the foggiest idea of what to make of the so-called army gathered around him or what it's future entailed, if it had any future at all, he recognized and appreciated the apology given to him by Yul as genuine, and he finally reached out and clasped the hand being offered to him.

~ ~ ~

Once everyone had sufficient time to get reacquainted, Darrel called for his group of students to return to their places in the center of the barn. As Jacob watched from the sidelines and growing more impressed, especially with Wray and Ty who had joined in with their friends as they usually did, he noticed Gotham standing a short distance away observing the training while brooding, and made his way over to him.

"You have to admit, they have managed to pick up some pretty first-rate skills," Jacob observed aloud, after looking on quietly with Gotham for a few moments.

"Please, don't tell me you are actually entertaining this foolishness," Gotham grumbled.

"Is it? Foolish, that is?" Jacob asked, drawing a withering look from the angel. "What I mean is, is it such a bad thing they're learning things that at worse can only serve to help protect themselves? We did, after all, just lay my grandmother to rest today."

"You know I don't begrudge anyone the means to defend themselves. Your young girlfriend, however, kicked off the recruitment of teenagers to raise up an army–her words–to fight on your behalf," Gotham said over the strained grunts coming from the newfound soldiery.

"It's hard to argue her logic. I mean, the Apocrypha does state the Light Bearer will bring angel and mortals together to band against the Dark Forces," argued Jacob. "It might seem a little far-fetched right now, but how do you know things aren't playing out as they're supposed to. It wasn't too long ago the idea that I, son of Samael, being recognized as the Light Bearer would have been considered just short of blasphemous."

"I know you can't possibly be that obtuse. We're talking about younglings picking up arms and going to battle against forces of unimaginable power," said Gotham. "You as a Nephilim know that even with all your special gifts and skills you are at a disadvantage against such power. Yet you're standing here meditating on the idea high schools all around the world should incorporate Advanced Demon Defense into their physical education curricular."

"Fair enough," Jacob conceded. "But then help me understand one thing: If it's not these younglings, as you call them, who then are the mortals who are fated to fight alongside the rest of us when it finally hits the fan like the Apocrypha states?"

It was more than the rare occasion when Jacob managed to stump Gotham, yet it was the one time he was genuinely hoping the angel had an answer to lob back his way. Instead, Gotham stood in silence with a blank stare. Whatever words Gotham had to offer when finally he opened his mouth to speak, Jacob was denied hearing them when someone suddenly yelled out, "What in the name of Tom, Dick and Aunt Gertrude is this? Has Lions Bite opened a franchise?"

Jacob recognized instantly the familiar voice dripping with the unmistakable Australian accent. Sure enough, he turned around and found Max at the entrance to the barn. Nor was he alone. Standing with him were Kairo, Leos and Ethan and bringing up the rear was Hunter and Damiel. Jacob rushed over to them, but Wray and Ty beat him to the welcoming exchange of hugs and handshakes.

"What are you doing here?" Jacob asked when he finally was given an opening to get his fist bumps in.

"What can I tell ya, we were in the neighborhood and thought we'd drop in," Max replied with his usual sarcasm.

"Truth is, we were worried about you," said Kairo.

"For reals," Ethan chimed in. "When someone goes through something life-changing like losing his grandmother, it's important they have their friends around him. At least, I know I would want them."

"We asked Damiel if he would mind serving as chaperone," added Leos, to which Damiel promptly noted, "I didn't need much cajoling."

It was clear Jacob was touched by the gesture. Max, however, remained engrossed by the training session happening in front of him.

"Seriously, what's going on here? Is this some secret assembly line for churning out Ne-fake-ilim knockoffs, or are you holding auditions to replace Damiel?"

His half-joking inquiry failed to amuse the angel in charge of defense training at Lions Bite.

"It's a long story," said Jacob.

"Well, could we go somewhere for a feed first? I'm so hungry I could eat the bum of a low-flying duck."

The colorful metaphor brought a giggle from Jacob. "Lucky for you, I have a buffet of good food set up at my house this very minute which you can gorge on all night."

Jacob was about to escort Damiel and his friends to his house when Wray stopped him.

"Did you forget? You were going to spend the night over at Ty's and then the three of us had plans to go up to Penuel Point tomorrow," she attempted to remind Jacob as indiscreetly as she could.

"That's right! With my friends showing up out of the blue, it completely slipped my mind. Well...would it be okay with you if I took a raincheck and rescheduled?" Jacob said, trying his best not to look like he brushing off his best friend and girl, and failing miserably.

Ty felt the uncomfortable burn envelope his face as it reddened with embarrassment and answered as unaffectedly as possibly with a simple "Sure."

"Why don't you come along with us? You're a part of this group, after all; minus the wings, that is," Max was quick to offer in his good-natured way. "Besides, last time we were together you never finished telling me your theory about how Jack's inability to pull himself onto the floating door with Rose after Titanic sank was really an act of suicide."

"Yeah, why don't you? Hang out tonight with us, that is," said Jacob. "Although, you don't have to feel obligated to wile us with your colorful 'Titanic' hypothesis."

Had the courteous invite first come from Jacob, Ty most likely would have happily accepted. But nothing screamed pity invite more than having the friend of his best friend be the one to try and extend what should have been a no-brainer courtesy.

And so Ty politely declined, feigning being tired and a need to get to bed early.

"Besides, I'm going to have my hands full tonight trying to get all this junk out of my hair," he added meekly while gesturing to his shellacked dome which looked in desperate need of the services of the hazardous chemicals unit of the EPA.

Even Wray, who was rarely the first to come to the defense of Ty, could barely hold back from the strong desire to kick Jacob squarely in the kneecaps when he refrained from pressing his friend to come along, which left Ty feeling even more dejected.

It wasn't that Ty begrudged Jacob his newfound friendships. He himself had come to forge an unexpected camaraderie with Max, Leos, Kairo, Ethan and Hunter over the course of their bizarre adventure in Las Vegas and Venice. In fact, his five new friends had shown themselves to be, in some ways, more accommodating and tolerant than Jacob when it came to his offbeat ways. And yet, no matter how much they tried to make him feel like one of the gang, Ty knew he wasn't, and no matter what he did or tried to change himself he understood clearly he never would be.

And so, as Ty watched Jacob throw his arm across the shoulders of Max in an affectionate embrace as he left the barn surrounded by his newly established brotherhood, it was impossible for him to suppress the green bile that slowly rose up from a fount of envy buried deep within him which suddenly came rumbling too life like a broken sewer main.

CHAPTER TWENTY-FIVE

Try as he might to ignore it, Ty never grew accustomed to the blaring silence that nearly always greeted him when he walked through the front door of the simple, two-story house where he resided, in a lived-in neighborhood not quite as picturesque as the one where Jacob lived. It was a silence which served as a constant reminder of the glaring void left by his mother when she decided one day to pack her things and disappear into the world when he was only five years old.

Life without a mother was something Ty never fully recovered from, and it only seemed to become more difficult to deal with as he grew older. In elementary school, he was teased mercilessly by a group of classmates led by an especially dreadful freckle-faced girl with pigtails and two missing front teeth who would stalk him around the playground during recess while singing a particularly cruel chant, "Your mother doesn't even like you! Your mother doesn't even like you!" Worse yet, was staring out into the school auditorium whenever he took part in the yearly talent show or Christmas play, and finding not a single familiar face looking back, not even one belonging to his dad, whose role as a sole parent quickly evolved to absentee parent.

It was also the time Ty developed his unique talent for shaping narratives when he began telling tall tales to the kids he went to school with, as well as teachers, to explain his mother's absence: she was a medical researcher working at an undisclosed location on a top secret formula to cure all the diseases in the world; she was away training to be the first female civilian to man an upcoming shuttle launch to the space station; or a particular favorite of his which went along the lines of the president of the United States negotiating for the release of his mother who was being held abroad in a hostile country while traveling.

One can only weave so many fabrications, however, before the hands of time eventually revealed them to be just that: fabrications. Nor were his classmates or teachers the only ones he sought to delude with such stories. Soon he was conjuring up outlandish theories to himself in order to explain away his mother's disappearance. After all, trying to make sense of how one's own mother could deliberately, and willingly, turn her back on her own child was far harder for Ty to confront than even the worst of the taunting he had to endure at school.

Eventually, as Ty grew older, the casing he had fitted around his heart became harder and more impregnable, and one day he came to discover he no longer cared about why his mother had deserted him, or pretty much anything having to do with his mother at all. His penchant for weaving elaborate and oftentimes inconceivable, head-scratching yarns had only just begun; only instead of his mother, Ty turned his focus on uncovering the deep and mostly specious underpinnings of subtext surrounding a wide variety of fictional pop culture characters as though he were a modern-day Hedda Hopper.

The first, and largely only subscriber to his verbal gossip rag (even if it wasn't of his own accord) was Jacob. The two became fast friends when Ty one day invited Jacob to learn how to Bungee jump off the Steven's Creek Bridge and, while there, regaled his with a mind-jumbling premise of what the "S" on Superman's uniform really stood for. Jacob, for the most part, found the ridiculous theories entertaining–thought-provoking, even. And the times they bordered on being exhaustive, which often was the case, he did his best to amuse his friend, knowing such zany, head-twisting concoctions were ignited by a spark that resided in a dark and hurt-filled place. And while Jacob would eventually down the line, be given a taste of the pain that settles deep in one's soul over the loss of a mother, he held no illusions, even with tears still dribbling from his eyes, his grief came close to matching Ty's. He at least had his mother's love and affection for the first fifteen years of his life, and his mother did not desert him. She was taken against her will.

It was that kind of understanding which fashioned an unbreakable bond between the two boys. And until that very day, Ty had never been given a reason to doubt for one minute the strength of such a friendship. Neither had he ever questioned whether the loyalty he offered unconditionally to Jacob was of equal weight to the loyalty he believed he had been given in return. Now, out of the blue, he found his thoughts were being skewed by doubts. Suddenly, he was gripped by a very real fear that terrified him; the fear he might one day wake up to find his best friend had abandoned him in as cruel a fashion as his mother had.

~ ~ ~

Ty retired to his bedroom where the deafening silence gripping the house was a little more tolerable. There he stood for some time in front of the window looking out to the neighborhood where two young boys could be seen engaged in a friendly game of basketball a couple of houses down the street. Ty's attention, however, was fixed on a framed photo he had taken notice of and picked up from his nearby desk. It was a selfie of him and Jacob standing with their arms draped over the other's shoulder atop Penuel Point.

The photo, and the memory attached to it, brought a slow smile to Ty's otherwise miserable demeanor. But it was quick to fade when the photo was replaced by the image that remained floating inside Ty's head of Jacob embracing Max in a similar manner earlier at the Harrison barn as they headed out with their other friends. Ty couldn't help but feel the trough of resentment that resided somewhere in his gut; so much so that its overflow filled him with an overwhelming need to hurl the cherished photo in his hand against the wall on the far side of the room and smash it into a million pieces. And he would have, too, had not the sound of a voice suddenly broke through the silence keeping him company and advised, "I don't think I would do that if I were you."

Startled, Ty looked to his left where the shock of discovering a strange man casually sitting in a nearby chair he knew without question, was vacant when he entered his room, sent him leaping (nearly out of skin) across his bed, and then as far away as the wall pressed up against his back would allow him to retreat. Hardly the reaction he had hoped to give if such a situation ever presented itself after all the time spent training with angels inside a barn.

"Don't get me wrong," the stranger continued with a friendly and pleasant voice as Ty remained stiff as a corpse staring back with abject fear, "there's nothing I enjoy better than a spirited display of acrimony. It's the red meat that feeds the beast known as rage, and helps it to grow healthy and strong. But it would serve me better at this moment if that ripe rancor of yours continues to percolate in your veins."

The man then proceeded to study Ty, seemingly with great amusement, before he leaned forward in the chair upon which he was seated and, with eyes dark as coal that were both forbidding and, strangely enough, beguiling, he remarked with a wily purr, "I assume from the look on your face there's no need for introductions."

Ty did the best he could to steady his quivering lips so as to keep from divulging how terror-stricken he was at the exact moment by the chattering of his teeth when he opened his mouth to answer.

"My guess is you're Jacob's father," Ty eventually managed to say. "Wray told me you've already paid her a visit."

"Then undoubtedly you already know the reason why I am here," came the reply, which did nothing to help calm Ty. In fact, quite the opposite.

"It's rare I make a misstep, or in this particular case, a miscalculation," Samael then said. "I was certain the path to regaining my son was through that curious girl while failing to see the many more preferable avenues of treachery a boy like yourself could provide to someone like me."

Ty felt his heart immediately begin to pound inside his chest as though someone was beating it like a tom-tom. So loud was the pounding Ty was certain Samael could hear it. And, indeed, he did.

"Believe it or not, I know exactly how you're feeling," Samael continued, as he rose to his feet and began to wander about the room while taking note of the various posters, books and various other teenage paraphernalia he came upon, only he wasn't referring to the cause of Ty's quickening pulse. "As a father, it's not easy being rejected by your only son; it's even worse to witness said son looking to another angel as a replacement. I can only imagine how hurtful it's been for you."

"Jacob hasn't rejected or replaced me," Ty managed to mumble.

"Maybe not officially, but you and I both know the pink slip is coming," said Samael. "You had already been relegated to third-wheel status the moment he and Wray started making googly eyes at one another. But let's be honest here, the moment Max and the rest of that Nephilim brood came into the picture, your position as Jacob's ride-or-die was reassigned to just...die."

"It's not true," Ty whispered in reply.

"One day Jacob learned he was a winged wonder known as a Nephilim, and a brand new world was opened up to him. And in that world he met other boys who were the same as him, and in that sameness, unbreakable bonds were formed," Samael continued. "Unfortunately for you, it's a world in which you don't belong and, frankly, are unwanted. You felt it yourself the first time you tried to immerse yourself in it in Las Vegas. And you witnessed the growing closeness between Jacob and his new friends, especially the one they call Max, just a little while ago. You can go ahead and deny it all you want, even as you stand here alone in your bedroom while Jacob draws closer into his life the company of his Nephilim brotherhood. But a day is fast approaching when he will one day choose this new world and the friends he made in it in the same cold manner your mother turned her back on you in exchange for what resided on the other side of the front door."

The mention of his mother was like a shank being driven into Ty's side, especially in the same breath as his friend Jacob.

"IT'S NOT TRUE!" Ty yelled out forcibly as tears began to spill from his sorrow-filled eyes.

The tears. They appeared to bring Samael pleasure.

"Would you care to hear a little theory I have regarding your long-lasting friendship with Jacob?" Samael suddenly asked Ty.

"Theory?" The question seemed to momentarily stump Ty as he was the only one he knew who carried an arsenal of such conversational monologues for nearly every topic under the sun, and then some.

"I was recently in a hospital to ensure a certain dying soul in arrears to me for a particularly hefty sum did not attempt to cheat me of the payment due me by a sudden deathbed conversion, and, as I patiently waited for him to take his last breath, I was entertained by a movie playing on the TV about a run-of-the-mill teenaged boy named Charley Brewster who discovers one night that he lives next door to a vampire," said Samael.

Ty's ears immediately perked up. "That would be 'Fright Night.' It's one of my and Jacob's favorite movies. We used to watch it all the time," he said.

Samael smiled. "Then you know Charley had a best friend named Edward who was better known as 'Evil.' He was an odd and intolerable boy with a grating personality; some might say the epitome of everyone who, for one reason or another, fails to fit in with the rest of the herd."

"If you're theory involves insinuating that I am 'Evil' to Jacob's Charley then you're a day late and a buck short," Ty argued, though with a semblance of caution. "Jacob tried long ago to make that a thing, and pin the 'Evil' nickname on me for laughs but it didn't stick."

"You still don't see it do you? Even now. You're not 'Evil,' you're Edward."

The comment caused something to click inside Ty, and an insufferable feeling of vulnerability swept over him and revealed itself in his gaze which Samael was quick to capture and keep locked by his own probing stare.

"Edward discovered sanctuary from all the pain he accumulated from his misfit life resided in his deep friendship with Charley, or so he believed. Only the true release of pain, he found, came when he became 'Evil' and realized there were other sanctuaries open to him.

"Your vampiric friendship with Jacob is no different," Samael continued as he slowly stepped closer to Ty. "You feed from it voraciously as though it were some life-saving elixir, and in many ways it is. Only it's not his blood that nourishes you, but his light, his essence. It keeps the pain at bay. It brings you into the fold of humanity; tolerance; understanding; compassion. Without it, you'd find yourself abandoned yet again and cast permanently into this well of loneliness."

For Ty, hearing the words coming from Samael's mouth was like having a hand punch its way through his center and rummage around the inside of his soul. And, despite his best efforts, he slowly began to melt from the excruciating pain.

"Now, however, Jacob is slowly beginning to turn the spigot off, and the walls are starting to close in," Samael continued as he stood before Ty, with only a sliver of light between them, staring into the boy's weeping face. "Suddenly, here you are, alone in a dark, fog-filled alley at night, just like 'Evil,' yet to realize the deliverance from all your hurt resides in the unexpected charity extended by a vampire."

The mention of the word "vampire" brought a glimmer of terror to Ty. Somehow, he managed to swallow down enough of his fear to inquire, "Am I to assume the 'vampire' in this little analogy of yours is...you?"

"All you have to do is take my hand," Samael replied in exactly the same manner the cinematic vampire of which he was referencing did to 'Evil.'

Ty slowly rolled his gaze downward to where he found Samael's extended hand looking exactly like the vampire's hand from the scene he remembered watching on the TV screen, long nails and all, and more tears spilled from his eyes.

"That's it, release your tears. Allow them to marinate your anger," Samael coaxed the boy.

Ty's eyes darted about the room, desperate to escape the "vampire" who had his back pinned against a wall and trying to seduce him to advance someplace his feet resisted stepping.

"I know what it's like to be cast aside by those who once embraced you." As the voice continued to purr in his ear, Ty's gaze happened upon the photo he was looking at earlier of himself and Jacob which he had dropped on his bed. And as he took account of the long-standing friendship perfectly demonstrated within the confines of the simple wood frame, Ty suddenly felt a burning resistance ignite inside him that instantly stemmed the flow of his tears as he firmly took hold of it as though it were a life preserver tossed his way.

"I don't want your hand. In fact, I refuse it," he exclaimed softly.

The expression of Samael's face hardened to the point that it appeared it might shatter into a million enraged pieces. In a flash, he retreated from where he stood before Ty, and back into the chair he earlier was found sitting in a blink of an eye. Ty instantly felt a semblance of relief to have his personal space no longer smothered by Samael's murky, dark energy. It also lent him a surge of mettle from having rejected such an oppressive force and finding himself unscathed.

"And if that's not clear enough, then listen up," Ty, who had the unfortunate knack of never knowing when to keep his tongue pinned between his teeth for the betterment of his health, then said. "I have at this very moment an angel of insane power watching over me to keep me safe from the likes of you. And if that weren't enough, Gotham and Damiel are also just a holler away. So if you know what's good for you, I would suggest you make your way back downstairs and out of this house."

The demonstration of chutzpah by the kid brought a dampening to Samael's demeanor.

"I had expected your friend Wray to be uncooperative. But you...," said Samael, stopping short of finishing his thought as he stared at the boy, before quietly muttering, "Pity!"

"And another thing," Ty was quick to add, now that he had summoned enough courage, "I might be all new to this alternative universe of angels and demons, but I've done some research and I know God won't allow you to force me to do anything against my will."

The assertion returned to Samael the wily smile he had momentarily lost.

"Well, you most certainly have got me on that account, I must say," the Fallen angel noted with a surrendering chortle. "And I'll admit freely to you it's the one restraint tying my hand that sometimes proves to be a real thorn in my side."

As Samael spoke, Ty's attention was drawn to the carpeted floor beneath his visitor's feet where a dark puddle of shadow began to stir and move about. Ty's eyes then began to slowly grow wider at the sight of the shadow rising up from the floor and gradually taking on a monstrous and, unfortunately, familiar shape.

"Fortunately for me and my needs, the same cursed constraints do not apply to Infectors," Samael said, as Ty found himself suddenly in the terrifying position of being face to face with one of the Underneath's most frightening and malevolent residents.

In an instant, any residue of bravery residing within Ty instantly disintegrated and, to his utter horror, he discovered the wall behind him prevented him from retreating any further from the black, smoky wraith coming toward him.

"Fear not! It will all be over before you know it," Samael cooed blissfully as he settled back in his chair as if to enjoy a movie. "Unfortunately, this is going to hurt you a lot more than it does me."

It was then a bawl of high-pitched screams unlike any ever heard before erupted from the house and echoed throughout the neighborhood until finally...silence.

Thank you for reading
The Quietus Hour (Book IV)
*Please add a review and share
your thoughts with others.*

Book reviews are extremely helpful for authors, and I
want to thank you for taking the time to support me and
my latest book. If you enjoyed this episode, please share
your review and encourage others to read and follow my
other books in this series

Tales of the Nephilim Brotherhood

The Crossing Point (Book I)

The Seventh Grace (Book II)

The Beloved Exiles (Book III)

The Quietus Hour (Book IV)

AND - COMING SOON

Book V
The Seventh Scourge